Mosaic

ALSO BY CARAGH BELL

Indecision

Regrets

Promises

Echoes of Grace

Gabriella

Published by Poolbeg

Mosaic

CARAGH BELL

POOLBEG

This book is a work of fiction. References to real people, events, establishments, organisations, or locales are intended only to provide a sense of authenticity, and are used fictitiously. All other characters, and all incidents and dialogue, are drawn from the author's imagination and are not to be construed as real.

Published 2021 by Poolbeg Press Ltd
123 Grange Hill, Baldoyle
Dublin 13, Ireland
E-mail: poolbeg@poolbeg.com
www.poolbeg.com

A catalogue record for this book is available from the British Library.

ISBN 978-1-78199-712-3

Typeset by Poolbeg Press Ltd

www.poolbeg.com

ABOUT THE AUTHOR

Caragh Bell lives in West Cork with her husband and five children. She enjoys writing popular romantic fiction as it offers escapism in a world saturated with bad news – her books are light, funny and addictive. Her trilogy – *Indecision*, *Regrets* and *Promises* – is set in Ireland. *Echoes of Grace* is set in the wilds of Cornwall, and her fifth book, *Gabriella*, is based in New York.

Caragh has a French and English degree from University College Cork. She teaches at Sacred Heart Secondary School in Clonakilty.

Caragh's books are available online and in good bookshops.

ACKNOWLEDGEMENTS

Thanks to my family for putting up with me. To my daughter, Fódhla, for proofreading the manuscript. To Aoibhe, Lughan, Oscar and Feidhlim, my other gorgeous children. To Sheelagh, Louise and Freyja for taking the time to read the story and offer their feedback. To my lovely parents-in-law, Kathleen and Eugene. To Romeo Cedric Fitzwilliam Daly, my puppy, for no other reason than for being so adorable.

I suppose I'd better not leave out my brother, Ian.

This book would never have been written without the existence of The Ludgate Hub in Skibbereen. It's the only place where I can truly get in the zone. Thanks to Elma Connolly and Gráinne O'Keeffe for facilitating my crazy hours.

When I was researching this book, I contacted lots of people regarding adoption in Ireland. Thank you to Eileen Harte and Sheila Whittle McCarthy for speaking so candidly about their own experiences. It really helped and I'm truly grateful.

To Dr Judy Lovett of The Adoption Authority of Ireland. Thanks for taking the time to help me out.

To Daniel O'Driscoll for his support and encouragement.

To all my friends at school. You're the best.

To Richard O'Flynn at The Yellow Door in Baltimore. You're officially the greatest salesman ever!

To Sylvia and Mike for all their support.

To Jackie McCarthy, Kevin Collins, Ruth Field and Adam Walsh at Fields of Skibbereen for being so helpful with book launches and sales.

To Paula and all at Poolbeg Press. This is our sixth book together!

To my editor, Gaye, for shaping this book and making it better.

To Jilly for all her loveliness. Her beloved dog, Bluebell, is forever immortalised in this book.

To my husband, John. My lobster.

Finally, to my wonderful parents. I discovered I was pregnant in my final year of university. Without your fierce love and incredible support, I could have been Mary. I was so lucky and I'll never forget it.

DEDICATION

For John

Chapter One

1995

The sun beat down from the cloudless sky. Mary shielded her eyes from its glare as she crossed the street. Cork City was busy. It always was on a Saturday. Teenagers loitered around shop fronts, women scurried past with large bags full of shopping and designer handbags, and buskers played Beatles songs, nodding and winking when someone threw a coin into the open guitar case on the pavement.

Her long blonde hair swung from side to side, tied up in a ponytail with a black bobble. Tall and slim, she was dressed in her favourite Levi 501s and her black Doc Marten boots. Her T-shirt had a large tongue printed on the front, the Rolling Stones logo, and her blue eyes were accentuated by black eyeliner. Her earphones were nestled in her ears, playing music she had recorded from the radio the night before. The DJ had talked over the intro of her favourite song, but she had managed to get most of it, her finger poised over the record button of her tape recorder. She really wanted a CD player, but her dad could barely afford the rent, let alone a luxury like that. Humming a Nirvana song, she crossed Saint Patrick's Bridge and headed up towards MacCurtain Street, where she had arranged to meet her best friend.

Mary Kennedy was an only child. Her mother had died of breast cancer when she was seven years old, so all she had was her dad Noel. He was a builder by trade but had given up work when he hurt his back three years before. The weekly benefit he received was barely enough to make ends meet so Mary had been waitressing since she was thirteen to earn some extra cash. They lived in a small terraced house near the famous Shandon Bells church just north of the River Lee.

Mary tried her best with the housekeeping. She had taught herself to cook from her mam's cookbooks. She kept an eye on special offers at the supermarket and bought the cheapest cuts of meat to keep costs down. Minced beef was their staple diet – she would mix it with gravy and peas one day and make a Shepherd's Pie the next. On a Sunday she would roast a small chicken, just like her mam used to do when she was a little girl.

Despite money being tight, Noel liked to have a punt on the horses now and then. Mary only heard about it when he won. "Go and buy some new clothes," an elated Noel would say, handing her twenty pounds. "You deserve it, love."

Mary would nod, but instead of going down to Patrick Street and blowing the lot, she would stash the money in a shoebox under her bed. She always kept as much as possible as a rainy-day fund. Sometimes the electricity bill was overdue or all they had to eat was Cornflakes. She understood that, of the two of them, she had better sense when it came to money. Her dad didn't mean to be so flighty; it was just his way. He had the kindest heart and she adored him. She understood how hard it was to raise a daughter all by himself. Because of this, she tried to cause as little trouble as possible. It wasn't his fault that his back troubled him and that he spent a fair share of their money in the local pub. He loved her and that was all that mattered.

On a Friday, sometimes she'd join him when he'd go for a pint. When she was a child he would buy her a Cidona – a fizzy apple drink – and a packet of Tayto crisps. Now, as she was seventeen, he would wink at the barman and get her a glass of beer. A blind eye was turned and she would sit on the old barstool, sipping a Heineken and listening to her father talk about hurling. On Friday nights there would be a crowd and sometimes a trio of musicians who would play traditional music. Mary had a beautiful voice and after a couple of drinks her father would plead with her to sing. Standing up straight and squaring her shoulders, she would start with songs like "The Fields of Athenry" and "The Black Velvet Band". However, her favourite song was "Willie MacBride", a song about an ill-fated soldier in the First World War. With her eyes closed, she would sing the sad song, putting her heart and soul into the words. Noel, proud as punch, would clap the loudest when she finished. "*That's my Mary!*" he'd yell. "*My little girl!*"

Her best friend Viola was sitting by the bay window of the small café when she arrived.

"Hey, girl," said Viola, smiling broadly.

Mary smiled and sat down. "Hey to you, too. How was your holiday in Kerry?"

"Desperate." Viola rolled her eyes. "It rained for the first half so we were trapped inside the mobile home playing *The Game of Life* and *Scrabble* with pieces missing.

I nearly went mental." She picked up the menu. "Will we get some cake? I've been dreaming of carrot cake for weeks. The food was basic in the campsite. Lots of beans on toast and stuff. Mum goes on strike when we go away."

Mary nodded. "I could eat cake."

"One between two though, okay? I need to look good for the club on Saturday."

Mary's eyes lit up. "I can't believe we'll finally get to go to Sir Henry's! Paddy is so amazing to get those IDs."

"My darling brother owes me for covering for him last weekend."

"Oh?"

"He arrived home, hammered, completely langers, and proceeded to dance on the sofa. I grabbed him and dragged him upstairs before Mam woke up."

"You saved his bacon sure enough."

A waitress appeared with a pen and a small notepad. "Can I help you, girls?" she asked in her strong sing-song Cork accent.

"A large slice of carrot cake," said Viola, smiling. "Two forks."

"Grand, girl. Cream?"

Viola shook her head. "No, not today. There's no point doing the complete dog on it."

Mary smiled at the waitress. "I'd like a coffee, please."

Viola nodded. "Me too."

The waitress scurried away.

"So, no news from Kerry then," Mary asked with a frown. "Janey, I thought you'd at least have some scandal."

Viola shook her head dolefully. "Nothing. There were no hot guys. Just noisy kids playing football and screaming."

"That sounds awful."

"It was. What's worse is our stupid video player broke and didn't record *Home and Away* or *Fresh Prince* so now I'm behind."

"I can tell you what happened."

"It's not the same."

The waitress arrived back with two cups of steaming coffee. "Cake's on the way, love," she said pleasantly.

Mary smiled at her and added some milk to her coffee.

"At least you get to go on holiday," she said. "I've been working non-stop in the shop."

"Well, now you've something to look forward to. Paddy's a legend alright for getting those fake IDs."

"How does he do it?"

"He's got contacts." Viola frowned. "I hope you got Saturday off. I mean, we need at least three hours to get ready, plus we have to down some vodka before we go out."

"Yes, yes. I asked for it off. Calm down."

The waitress arrived back again with a white plate. Sitting on top was a slice of carrot cake topped with cream-cheese icing and a sugar carrot on top.

"Jesus, that looks yummy!" Viola grabbed her fork with enthusiasm.

"So, how are things going with Martin?"

Viola swallowed a mouthful of cake and paused. "Good, I suppose. I mean, the last time we met was at the disco before I left for Kerry."

"Any major action?"

"Nope. I let him touch my boob behind the chipper, but that's as far as we got. His mam arrived to pick him up."

"Oh, Vi!" Mary giggled.

"Don't talk to me! I'll die a virgin at this stage. I mean, it's getting serious, Mary. We're the only ones left in our class. It's embarrassing."

"I don't think we're the only ones ..."

"Dymphna O'Sullivan lost it the night she got her Junior Cert results. That's two years ago. And she's got braces and everything."

"What's the hurry?"

"It's the nineties. We've got to be modern women. We can buy condoms legally now and all. It's our duty to go out and have fun."

When Mary arrived home, the house was quiet. Placing her bag on the floor, she walked into the sitting room. A framed picture of her mother stood on the mantelpiece and a picture of the Sacred Heart was on the wall by the window. A small television with rabbit's ears stood in the corner and she switched it on. The Angelus bells filled the room, signalling that it was six o'clock. Her father's mug of tea from that morning stood on the coffee table, the milk discoloured at the bottom. She brushed the toast crumbs off the counter and sighed. Was it that hard to use a plate?

Trudging upstairs, she pushed open her bedroom door.

"Hi, George!" she said to a poster of George Clooney on the wall. He was taking the world by storm in a show called *ER* and she had a soft spot for him. Anyone with brown eyes in Ireland was exotic as the general population had blue. George, with his Italian looks, was just dreamy.

She pressed play on her stereo and Oasis came on. Oasis were officially her favourite band in the world. She played their album *Definitely Maybe* over and over again, memorising the words. Humming along, she opened her wardrobe and riffled through the different tops and dresses. She needed to look older and sophisticated for Saturday. Having a fake ID was one thing, but you had to pull it off. She looked in the small mirror that sat on top of her dressing table and tried to pout.

"*Ugh*, you look stupid!" she said aloud.

Pulling down her hair from its ponytail, she shook the tresses free. Standing up straight, she tried her best to look worldly. Viola had promised to do her make-up – she was a whiz with eyeliner, so that would help.

The front door banged downstairs and she heard her dad's deep voice calling her name. Winding her hair into a bun, she twisted the hair bobble around it and yelled, "*Coming!*" She pressed pause on her stereo and hurried downstairs.

"How's my best girl?"

"Great." She leaned up and kissed his cheek. "Are you hungry? There's leftover stew from yesterday."

"Lovely." He headed for the fridge and got a can of beer. "Where are the rest? I thought we had a few cans left. This is the last one."

"Don't look at me!" she protested hotly. "There were a fair few empties on the coffee table this morning. You must have drunk them without noticing."

Noel shrugged. "I'd better savour this so. I won't have money until Thursday." He walked into the sitting room and took a seat on his favourite armchair. "What did you do today?"

"I met Viola for coffee." She paused. "She asked me over for a sleepover on Saturday night. We're going to watch a film that she taped off the telly and eat pizza."

"Grand."

"I'll be home early on Sunday for Mass."

"No bother." Noel closed his eyes and rested his head against the back of the chair. "You deserve to have some fun."

Mary felt guilty. She hated lying to her dad but she knew he wouldn't approve of her going to a nightclub. Being a lone parent, he was protective and, apart from the odd glass of beer he allowed her to have in the pub when he was there, she was not permitted to drink with her friends.

Chapter Two

On Saturday afternoon, Mary arrived at Viola's with a small bag packed with her toothbrush, a pyjamas and her outfit for Sir Henry's nightclub. They went up to Viola's room immediately and started to get ready.

"Sit down in front of the mirror," Viola ordered.

Her dressing table was covered in bottles and tubes of all shapes and descriptions. There were photos, ticket-stubs, beermats and cut-out pictures of Brad Pitt stuck to the discoloured mirror. Old editions of *Just Seventeen* were scattered around the floor. The Cranberries were playing on the stereo, Dolores O'Riordan's haunting voice singing about dreams.

Viola got to work on Mary's hair with the curling iron.

"When will Paddy be here with the IDs? I'm worried our plan will fall through."

"Oh, any minute now. He's getting them off Greasy Joe."

"Who?"

"You know, Joe Murphy. He did his Leaving Cert two years ago."

Mary shook her head.

"Has greasy hair, hence the name? Well, to be fair, it's because he's slippery too when it comes to bending the law."

"Nope. No clue."

Viola shrugged. "Anyway, Joe is our man. He has created a very successful business with the ID trade. Paddy said he saw him driving around in a new Fiesta with huge exhausts that deafen the nation when he passes. He's always playing 2Unlimited at top volume too. There should be a ban on techno in public places."

Mary giggled. "A new Fiesta? He must be the envy of all the boy racers in Cork."

Viola rolled her eyes. "You couldn't pay me to shift him. I mean, he puts at least two tubs of Brylcreem in his hair every day. He's a holy show. You'd be destroyed if you went near him."

"Martin might be jealous anyway."

"He would, yeah!" said Viola sarcastically. "I'm starting to think there's only one woman in his life – his mammy."

"I can't wait to see the inside of Sir Henry's. Everyone says it's the best nightclub in Ireland."

"It's all ahead of us, Mary. Soon we'll be in college and able to do what we want with real IDs, not dodgy ones."

Viola pushed the curled part of Mary's hair to one side and started on the straight side.

"Paddy was at the REM concert in Slane a few weeks ago."

"Really?" Mary sighed. "Oasis were supporting them. God, I would've loved to have been there."

"Oh, he said it was a great laugh. Someone threw a

stone at Liam Gallagher when he was singing and he lost the plot, shouting and roaring at the crowd."

"'Live Forever' is officially my favourite song."

"You don't say!" Viola grinned. "How many times have I heard you sing that bloody thing? One million."

"It's just so good. I can't decide if I prefer Noel or Liam. I mean, Noel is the genius behind the music but Liam is so sexy."

"Noel is out anyway. Shur, your dad's name is Noel. It would be mad confusing."

"So Liam it is. Mary Gallagher. It sounds so cool."

Viola busied herself curling the remainder of Mary's hair, humming along to the music. Ten minutes later, she unplugged the curling iron. "There, done!"

"Will you put on my eyeliner?" Mary asked pleadingly. "I always make a mess of it."

"Right so." Viola picked up a black eye-pencil on the table. "Tilt your head upwards so I can get under the lashes."

Mary obeyed and stayed still as Viola drew lines under her eyes.

"Do you want some on the eyelid too?"

Mary shook her head. "The bottom is fine."

"Now, close your eyes and I'll put on some eyeshadow." Viola opened a palette and set to work.

"This silver stuff is gorgeous," she said, carefully brushing it onto Mary's eyelids. "It's all sparkly."

"What would I do without you?" Mary squeezed her arm. "You're a wizard."

"Right, I'm finished." Viola stepped back and surveyed her work. "You look like a film star."

Mary gazed at herself in the mirror. Her blonde hair was

uncharacteristically loose and it framed her face. The slight curls at the ends gave it bounce and her blue eyes stood out thanks to the eye make-up Viola had artfully applied.

"Now, some lipstick and you're all set." Viola handed her a stick of Dior. "This is some fancy French stuff that I stole it off Mam. Quick, put on a layer, blot with this tissue and then put on one more coat. I need to put it back in her room."

Mary did as instructed. They stared at each other.

"We look amazing," said Viola seriously. "At least nineteen or twenty."

"Amazing," echoed Mary. "I love your body top."

"I love your Docs."

They hugged each other. There was a knock on the door.

"Vi? It's Pad. Come into my room there when you get a chance."

Viola's eyes sparkled. "Fair play to Greasy Joe, the legend. Our golden tickets have arrived."

Sir Henry's was one of Cork's most famous clubs. It was situated on South Main Street, near the Beamish Brewery. The characteristic smell of malt permeated the balmy summer night, emanating from the old black-and-white building where the stout was produced, as Viola and Mary hurried along the street, laughing loudly. The small bottle of vodka they had consumed in Viola's bedroom prior to leaving had taken effect and they were in tearing spirits.

There was a queue forming outside the club so they took their place behind a group of guys.

"Is my make-up okay?" whispered Mary.

Viola peered closely at her face. "Perfect, girl."

Within seconds, ten more people had joined the line and soon it was trailing down the street. Mary straightened her top and stood up straight. The fake ID burned in her pocket and she prayed silently that they would get through security. Her poor father thought that she was watching telly at Viola's in her pyjamas. She pushed away the guilty feeling and focused on the group standing in front of them – three young men. Two were clearly Irish as she recognised Dublin accents. The third was tall with long brown hair that fell just below his ears. He had dark-brown eyes and sallow skin and was taller than most of the people around him. He reminded her of an exotic Jim Morrison. Then he spoke and she inhaled sharply. He had broken English with a French accent. His voice was deep and as he spoke he ran his fingers through his hair and gesticulated.

Mary nudged Viola. "Check him out," she said quietly. "Wow or what?"

Viola shrugged. "A bit tall for my taste. Martin is a pygmy in comparison."

"I think he's gorgeous."

"Far too old ... I'd say at least twenty-two."

"*Hmmm.*"

The queue moved slowly.

Soon they were at the ticket booth.

The tall Frenchman stood back and let his friends get the tickets. His eyes met Mary's and he smiled.

Next it was their turn. Viola rose up to her full height. "Two, please," she said haughtily.

The woman behind the glass didn't even look up.

Viola slipped money through the opening and the tickets appeared straight away. The deep bassline of the music made the ground shake and soon they were in the dark central room. The main dancefloor was half full of dancing bodies. Many had neon necklaces and were nodding their heads in time to the beat.

"Come on!" said Viola. "Let's get a drink."

They walked up to the bar and waited for someone to notice them. Eventually a barmaid asked them what they wanted.

"Two vodkas and one Coke," said Mary. "We'll share the Coke," she added to Viola. "The price of it, like!"

Viola nodded. "Good thinking."

An hour later the club was full to capacity. The heat was stifling as people danced in unison to the same repetitive beat. Viola was chatting to a man with a beard who was studying psychology in the university.

Mary tapped her on the shoulder.

"I'm just going to get another drink," she said in her ear.

"Grand. See you in a sec."

Mary pushed her way through the crowd, avoiding puddles of spilt beer and trying not to rub against sweaty bodies. There was a big queue for the bar so she took her place. It moved slowly and the girl in front of her kept blowing cigarette smoke into her face. She coughed pointedly.

Suddenly someone took her arm. She started and turned to see the French guy who was in the queue earlier smiling down at her.

"I can help you if you want," he said in perfect English. "I am taller than you."

"Help me?" she repeated, flustered.

"You want to buy a drink, *non*?"

She nodded.

"Then tell me and I will get it."

"Two vodkas and one Coke."

He waved his arm and got the attention of the barmaid immediately. "Two vodkas and one Coke, please."

She nodded and grabbed two glasses from the side of the bar counter. Reaching over, he accepted the glasses from her outstretched hand and handed her a twenty-pound note.

"Oh no! I have money here!" protested Mary in alarm. "You don't have to pay."

"It's nothing," he said, handing her the glasses. "Now for the Coke." He waited for the bottle to be handed over.

"Thanks a million," Mary said, blushing. "There was no need ..."

"No problem."

"*Um*, I should get back to my friend ..." Mary placed the glasses on a small table and poured the Coke evenly into both. "I must give her this drink."

"Come back," he said suddenly. "If you want."

"Back here?"

"Yes."

She bit her lip. "Okay. I suppose I could. Wait here for a minute."

She set off through the crowd, her heart racing. Never in her wildest dreams did she think a gorgeous guy like him would even talk to her, let alone buy her a drink. She had to play it cool.

"Vi!"

"Yeah?"

Mary handed her the glass. "I'm just talking to a guy over there. Wish me luck!"

"A guy? Who?"

"Tell you later."

He was standing in the exact same place when she got back.

"I have something for you." He handed her a flyer with *Freak Scene* printed on it. "Look at the back," he murmured.

She turned it over and gasped. He had drawn a miniature sketch of her.

"Gosh, that's really good," she said in delight. "When did you ...?"

"Just before I talked to you. It's not the best I've ever done."

"It's perfect." She gazed at it in wonder. He had captured her expression perfectly. She folded it carefully and put it in her back pocket.

His dark eyes met hers. "Would you like to come outside? I want to smoke a cigarette."

"A cigarette?" Her heart began to thump.

"Yes."

"Gosh, I don't know." Suddenly she felt unsure.

"Just for a quick cigarette. The music is too loud to have a conversation. We can stay right next to the club so everyone will see. I'm not going to run away with you."

She blushed. "I didn't think that ..."

"*Ah, bon*?" He laughed.

"It's just, I don't even know your name."

"Ah, now I see the problem." He stood up straight. "My name is Raphael," he said, shaking her hand formally.

"I'm Mary," she answered with a smile.

"Come, Mary. Let's go."

Together they walked down the stairs and out into the

warm air. The sounds of the city filled the silence between them. There were pockets of people scattered around the street. He took out a Gauloise, lit it with a Zippo and then inhaled sharply. "You want one?" he asked, holding out the pack.

She shook her head. "I don't smoke."

He brushed a lock of dark-brown hair away from his face. "Mary. That's a pretty name."

"Thanks."

"What do you do in life, Mary?"

She reddened. She couldn't say that she was a schoolgirl.

"I go to college."

"*Ah*, where? In Cork?"

She nodded.

"What do you study?"

She paused for a moment. "Music."

"What instrument do you play?"

"I don't. I sing."

He blew a perfect smoke ring. "*Ah, bon!* Will you sing me a song?"

"Here? Now?" She laughed nervously. "No way."

"Please. I would like it very much."

She shook her head fervently. "Not a hope."

The air was balmy and a soft breeze blew, lifting her hair from her shoulders. Nervously, she flicked it out of her face. "So, why are you in Ireland? Do you go to college here?"

He shook his head. "*Non*, I don't. I study in Paris."

"Oh? What?"

"Photography. Moving film. My great-grandfather was a photographer. Louis Baptiste? Have you heard of him?"

She shrugged. "I don't think so."

"There is an exhibition of his work in the Crawford Art Gallery here in Cork. I'm just here to officially open it. In fact, that's where I was tonight. I go back to France tomorrow."

"Oh." She tried to mask her disappointment.

"You should go to see it. He filmed all the greats – Picasso, Chanel, JFK, Guevara ..."

"That sounds cool."

"It is, as you say, cool."

He stared at her intently. Reaching out, he put his hand on her waist and pulled her to him. With his other hand, he stubbed out his cigarette on the wall. Her heart accelerated as his face bent down close and he kissed her softly on the lips.

Sure, she had kissed boys in the past. Most of the time it had been open-mouthed slobbery attempts with both heads in fixed positions. Known as the 'shift', it was commonplace at teen discos, normally during the slow songs. She had never understood why the 'shift' was so sought after, as it was more a rite of passage than anything else.

Now, she got it. Raphael kissed her softly at first, nibbling lightly on her lower lip. Then he ran his hands through her hair and deepened the kiss, exploring her mouth with his tongue. She clung to him, exhilarated. It was amazing. She was no longer kissing a boy – she was kissing a man. Arching backwards, she pressed up against him and he enveloped her in his arms. What would Viola say? This sure beat Martin behind the chipper.

He stopped and kissed her nose gently. "You are lovely," he said softly. "I'm staying at the Imperial ..."

"The hotel?" she squeaked.

"*Oui*, the hotel. Will you join me for a drink?"

"A drink?"

"*Oui*." He looked at her in amusement.

"Gosh, I don't know ..."

"Come with me. I'd like to know more about your music. Maybe after another drink you will consent to sing."

Mary bit her lip. Her dad would kill her for taking off with a stranger. She was meant to be staying at Viola's place. She looked up at the brown eyes watching her. He was definitely the best-looking guy she'd ever seen. She'd be mad to pass this up. One drink and then she could take off. She really wanted to stay in his company.

"*Um*, I need to tell my friend."

"Of course."

"I'll be back."

"I'll wait."

She bolted in the main door and climbed the stairs at breakneck speed. Viola was kissing the bearded student in earnest. Mary tapped her shoulder.

"Vi!" she hissed. "I'm leaving."

Viola broke free. "Leaving? Where?"

"To the Imperial with that fine thing. The French guy."

"What?"

"He wants me to go back and have a drink."

"Is he normal? Christ, Mary, he could be a serial killer."

"He's normal. He's an amazing kisser."

"That doesn't make him any less of a psycho." She frowned. "What's his name?"

"Raphael."

"Raphael? Like the Ninja Turtle?"

Mary nodded.

"Will you be home later? I can leave a key under the flowerpot by the garage door."

"Oh, definitely. Just one drink."

"Right." Viola kissed her cheek.

Mary frowned. "Why are you shifting this guy? What about Martin?"

"You snooze, you lose," said Viola airily. "He had his chance. Maybe if he lost the mammy factor, we'd have a chance."

Chapter Three

Raphael was smoking another cigarette when she reappeared.

"Ready?" he asked.

"Ready." She beamed at him.

He took her hand and they walked down the street. Turning right onto Tuckey Street, they ambled towards the Grand Parade. A group of boys were by Hillbilly's Chipper, eating chicken and chips and laughing loudly.

"Will you be a photographer like your grandad?" Mary asked as they crossed the street.

"Maybe. I think I like moving film more. I made a short film about Marguerite Duras last year and it was a success."

"Who?"

He looked amused. "Doesn't matter."

They turned the corner and headed down the South Mall.

"It must help to have a famous name though. I mean, you're lucky."

His face tightened. "I want to be known in my own right."

"Oh, you will," she said hurriedly, aware that she had insulted him somehow. "It's just, look at all the actors out there like Charlie Sheen and Michael Douglas. They must have found it easier having famous dads."

Raphael stopped. "Louis will not accelerate my success. I have known since I was born that I will be great. I will be remembered for my art and nothing will stop this."

Mary rubbed his arm. "Okay, okay. Sorry I said that."

"Soon everyone will know the name Raphael Baptiste. It is my destiny."

The bar in the hotel was closed when they got there.

"Oh, sugar!" said Mary in disappointment. Now the night was over.

"I have a bottle of whiskey in my room." He traced her cheek with his finger. "You are welcome to join me for a glass but I don't want to pressure you."

She smiled joyfully. "I'd love that."

She didn't like the taste of whiskey but that didn't matter. If it meant prolonging her time with him, then she'd take it.

He led her to the stairs. "I'm on the first floor."

"Great."

"Just one drink."

"Just one." She followed him up the steps.

The room was charming with a huge double bed and an armchair in the corner. Raphael immediately walked over to the mahogany dresser and poured Jameson into two tumbler glasses. She took a seat on the armchair and crossed her legs.

"For you," he said, handing her one glass.

"Thanks," she said, suddenly nervous. She took a small sip and nearly gagged. The whiskey was fiery and burned her throat. He took a seat on the end of the bed and drank his with ease.

"This is a lovely hotel. I've never seen the rooms before." Her eyes darted around the room. "The curtains are lovely, aren't they? I mean, for a hotel ..."

He regarded her with amusement. "Do you always talk so much?"

She took a sip of whiskey and coughed. "No."

"You are nervous."

She nodded.

"Don't be nervous. I do not, as you say, bite?"

"It's just I've never done this before. I've never been in a hotel room with a man."

He placed his empty glass on the bedside locker and gestured for her to come to him.

"*Viens*," he said in a husky voice. "Sit beside me."

"I'm okay here," she said in a squeaky voice.

"Come," he said, patting the blanket.

She placed her glass on the dresser and walked slowly towards him. He held out his hand and she placed her small hand in his. Gently, he pulled her down so that she was sitting beside him. He reached out and brushed a lock of hair back from her face and secured it behind her ear. Her chest heaved as he bent his head down and kissed her slowly. His tongue invaded her mouth and she tilted her head.

"You are so lovely," he murmured. "Look, if you want to stop, that's okay. I don't want to pressure you. I told you that before."

"I'm okay."

"You are sure?" He began kissing her neck. "Tomorrow I go back to France and we won't see each other again."

"I'm sure."

"This will be a one-night thing. I don't like commitment."

"Okay. It's just, I'm not on the pill or anything."

"That is fine. I will pull out in time. Do not worry."

"Are you sure?"

"Yes, it has never failed before."

"Okay." She closed her eyes in pleasure as he kissed her neck.

"Don't worry." He pushed her gently back onto the bed. "Let's enjoy tonight and forget about tomorrow."

Mary woke to see Viola's red face over hers. Her friend looked fierce.

"What time did you get home last night?" she demanded. "I was worried!"

Mary rubbed her eyes. "I'm not sure. Around six? It was bright."

"Where did you end up? Jesus, Mary! I thought you'd been abducted."

"I was with that French guy. I told you that." Mary's expression grew dreamy. "He was just lovely. A photography student. He had the most amazing voice."

"And? Any action?"

Mary blushed and Viola gasped. "Tell me all the news and I want every gory detail."

"We went back to his hotel room."

"Room? I thought it was the hotel bar!"

"The bar was closed so he suggested having a drink in his room."

"It's like John Malkovich in that French film we watched. You know, with Michelle Pfeiffer," said Viola excitedly. "The older experienced French dude seducing an innocent young thing."

"Then he started kissing me. Oh my God, Vi! It was so amazing. I couldn't stop myself."

"You hussy!"

"Stop. I went up for one drink. He was really polite. We had whiskey."

"But you hate whiskey!"

"I pretended to drink it. Anyway, we started kissing almost straight away. *Wow*, is all I can say about that."

"Did you, you know ..."

"What?" Mary asked innocently.

"Go all the way? Oh my God, if you've lost your virginity before me, I'll freak out!"

"That's a personal question ..."

"If you're sitting on scandal like that without telling me, I'll explode."

Mary laughed. "Fine. We did it."

"*Jesus!*"

Mary sighed. "He was so sweet. He even walked me back here."

"Pity he wouldn't! It was the least he could do."

"He kissed me goodbye and he gave me a flower he picked out of Mr Minihane's garden next door."

Viola rolled her eyes. "Yeah, yeah. Very *rose-mantic* as my mother would say."

"His great-grandad was a famous photographer. Someone Baptiste or something. Anyway, he was so interesting. He was in Cork to open an exhibition in the Crawford."

Viola digested this. "How old is this Raphael anyway?"

"I don't know. Nineteen, maybe? He's in college."

"An older man." Viola looked impressed. "So, are you keeping in contact?"

Mary shook her head. "We didn't even exchange numbers. He's leaving today."

Viola sat back, shaking her head. "He didn't give you his number? And you're okay with that?"

"He lives in France and he believes in living for the moment."

"How convenient!"

Mary ignored her and pulled a piece of paper out of her pocket. "Look! He drew a sketch of me."

"On the back of a flyer?"

"Yes! It's very good, isn't it?"

Viola had to admit she was right. He had captured her friend's likeness perfectly.

"I thought you said he was a photographer."

"He's good at art too."

Viola sighed. "What's done is done, I suppose. To be honest, I think he's a right mover and shaker to get you to sleep with him without having to ring you. Still, on the up-side, you'll be fierce worldly when you get to college."

Mary sighed. "It was so lovely. He was so considerate. I know it's a bit slutty but ..."

"Enough of the slutty! An older guy with a sexy French accent? It definitely beats Martin!"

Chapter Four

Four weeks later Mary was back at school. She and Viola attended a convent school in the city called Saint Benedicta's, run by the Mercy nuns. The uniform was blue and the skirt, although designed to be mid-calf length, was almost always rolled up by the students.

Sister Cecilia, the principal, would order the girls to fix their skirts when she spotted the offence. "*Ladies!*" she'd shriek. "*Below the knee!*"

The school was an old building dating from the thirties. The desks were wooden with inkwells and some even had storage space. The surfaces were covered in chalk residue from the blackboards and pictures of the Blessed Virgin and the Sacred Heart hung on the walls of each room.

"You'll have a fine convent education," Noel had said on Mary's first day of secondary school. "No harm to teach you some Catholic values."

Mary didn't argue. Nor did she tell her father that the most exciting part of the school day was when the school gates opened at ten to four and the girls spilled out on to the street. There, on the opposite side of the road, stood the De La Salle school – the male equivalent of St. Ben's.

Brother Francis, the principal, would stand in his robes, glaring at the tittering girls as they walked past. "*Move along!*" he'd roar.

Dressed in their dark blue uniforms, the boys lounged against the gates, flicking their hair as the girls walked by. It was definitely the most exciting part of the day, and skirts were rolled up as far as possible for that moment.

Sister Cecilia, patrolling the school gates, would hurry the girls along. "*Go home, ladies!*" she'd call as the girls looked at the boys from under their lashes.

One day at lunchtime, Mary and Viola were sitting in the school yard.

"Did you see that new guy in sixth year? He's the image of Zac Morris from *Saved by the Bell!*"

"No. I haven't seen him."

"Are you still thinking about that French dude?"

"Gosh, no," she lied.

"Well, he did pop your cherry."

"Stop!"

"That's a big deal, to be fair."

The orange leaves from the large oak tree in the school yard blew around sporadically in the breeze. Although still bright, the temperature was dropping and Mary pulled her coat tightly around her.

Viola took an enormous bite of her sandwich. "*Yum*. I love spiced beef. I mean, it's widely known that Cork is the best place in the world, but inventing spiced beef makes it even more brilliant."

Mary felt her stomach heave. "I don't know how you

eat that at this time of the day."

Viola regarded her friend. "Do you have something to eat?"

Mary shook her head. "I slept in this morning and I didn't have time ..."

"Here, I have a spare triangle of this if you want."

"No, no. I'm okay. I think I have a tummy bug."

"Rough." Viola took a swig of water. "So, did you hear about Rachel McGrath? She shifted that Spanish exchange student Antonio at the club last weekend."

"Oh?"

"We were shocked that he even got in. I mean, he looks about twelve and that's being generous. Anyway, they're an item now even though he's gone back to Malaga."

"Absence makes the heart grow fonder." Mary smiled at her words. In her case it certainly did. He filled her thoughts constantly even though she knew it was crazy. She would never see him again – he was so far away and it had been a once-off thing ...

"Out of sight out of mind." Viola interrupted. "There's no way it'll last. She'll be up the walls anyway with her study. Word on the street is that she wants to be a vet."

"That's ambitious."

"Anyway, the pressure is on, Mary. Did you hear old Cecilia today at assembly? Talk about piling on the stress."

"It's always the same at the beginning of the year."

"I'm not overdoing it anyway," said Viola matter-of-factly. "I know exactly what I'm capable of. Let's face it, I'll be lucky to get into Arts."

They walked down the corridor to their next class. It was English with a young teacher called Carmel Moriarty.

Recently graduated from university, Miss Moriarty was bursting with enthusiasm for her subject, and this passion transmitted to the students. She was about twenty-three with bright blue eyes and a warm smile. She was writing '*Macbeth*' on the board.

"Kinsella essays on the desk, please." She kept scribbling with her chalk.

Mary put her four-page essay on the desk and took a seat near the front.

"I must have forgotten to put it in my bag," Viola was saying to the teacher in a meek voice.

Mary smiled to herself. It was always the same story. Viola had used every excuse in the book.

"Fine, but if you don't have it on my desk by tomorrow morning, I won't correct it."

A red-faced Viola slid in beside Mary. "She doesn't believe me," she whispered.

"What happened this time? The goldfish ate it?"

"Ha, ha."

"Right, girls. What do we know about Macbeth?"

"He was Scottish," said a girl called Michaela helpfully.

"Yes, he was. Anything else?"

Michaela shrugged. The rest of the class looked up at the teacher expectantly.

"Right," said Miss Moriarty. "Moving along. Open your books, please."

Mary opened her copy of *Macbeth*.

The vomiting started a week later. Initially, Mary thought it was a bug. There was gastro doing the rounds at school. Even Sister Cecilia had it. Then, after three days of feeling like hell, she told her father who immediately made an appointment with the doctor.

"You poor old sausage," he said kindly. "I can take you if you want."

"No, Dad. You're too busy." She tried to smile. "You can't miss work like that. I'll be fine."

The doctor took a history and checked her temperature. Then, she asked if she was sexually active.

Mary blushed and nodded. "Just once," she admitted.

"May I do a pregnancy test?"

Ten minutes later, it was confirmed. Mary was pregnant.

White-faced, she called over to Viola's house right away. Her friend took one look at her anguished face in the doorway and ushered her upstairs to her bedroom right away.

Mary sat on Viola's bed in a daze.

"What's wrong? What's happened?"

"I'm pregnant."

Viola did a double take. "You're *what*?"

"About seven weeks."

"What? How?"

"The French guy."

Viola stared at her in shock. "Oh my God!"

"I'm dead. My dad is going to kill me."

"Don't mind your dad. You've got bigger problems. Jeez, Mary. You'll have to tell him."

"What?"

"Tell Raphael! He has to know."

"I can't! What will I say to him?"

"*Um*, that he had sex with you and got you pregnant.

He's totally responsible. Why didn't he use a condom? For God's sake!"

"We were drunk. He said he'd pull out in time. He'd done it before, he said. He told me not to worry."

"Spare me the gory details. You've got to find contact details for him."

"How?"

"The internet. We can try at school."

Mary hung her head and started to sob. "My dad will murder me. We can barely look after ourselves, not to mind a baby."

Viola rushed over and hugged her. "Don't even think about that. Maybe if you tell your man, he'll do the right thing and hop on a plane and come over here to marry you."

Mary smiled through her tears. "Hardly."

Viola kissed her forehead. "You never know."

It took three days to track him down. Three days of calls and messages. Three days before he told her to terminate the whole thing. She was so young and it was the best thing to do. How could she raise a child on her own? He was in France and would remain there for the foreseeable future. Abortion was no big deal – people did it every day. A convenient solution to an inconvenient problem.

Viola rubbed Mary's back as she cried. Maybe an abortion was the best thing after all. It would mean going to England as it was against the law in Ireland, but that was possible. They'd come up with some excuse.

Together they downloaded information on a clinic in Wales. The dial-up connection beeped as the internet came to life and Viola yelled at her family not to touch the phone until she was finished. "They always make a call when I'm in the middle of something online," she grumbled. "Then the connection is lost and I'm back to square one."

They printed off information and looked at flights from Cork airport. Mary felt numb. She didn't expect a fairy tale – it was impossible. However, the idea of abortion didn't sit well with her at all. Maybe it was her Catholic education, but she felt that it was the wrong thing to do.

Viola put the sheets of paper in a folder and faced her. "Right, ring up Ninja Turtle and get some money off him. He should send you the costs. It's the least he could do."

Mary couldn't focus.

"I mean, there's the flight for you and me. Then the hotel and of course, the procedure ..."

Mary felt her stomach heave. She had read about the procedure. It frightened her. Abortion was illegal in Ireland. It had always been illegal. Maybe there was a reason for that? Every fibre in her body screamed '*No!*'

"I'm not sure I can do this, Vi," she said quietly. "I don't think it's for me."

"What?"

"I can't go to England. I can't hide something like this."

"But you have to! Your dad will freak out, Mary. Imagine how heartbroken he'll be. No offence but, as you said yourself. you barely have enough to get by as it is."

"I know! Christ, I know." She started to sob. "I don't know what to do."

Viola hugged her close. "Look, we'll take a few days and come up with a plan. There is a solution to this. I know it."

♫ ♫ ♫

"Mary?" Miss Moriarty wiped the blackboard clean. "May I have a word?"

The rest of the class filed out dutifully, en route to the next class.

"Yes, Miss?"

"Your essay on Kinsella was excellent. You really have a flair for writing."

"Thank you."

"However, you seem distracted lately. Is everything all right?"

To her horror, Mary burst into tears. She covered her face with her hands and bawled.

"Mary!" Miss Moriarty got up from her desk and rushed over. "Hey, what's the problem? Tell me. Maybe I can help."

Mary wiped her nose with her sleeve. "It's too awful. I can't."

"Of course you can. I won't judge."

Mary looked into her kind eyes and took a shuddering breath. "I'm pregnant."

The teacher's eyes widened. Walking to the door of the classroom, she closed it.

"You're sure?"

Mary nodded. "I went to the doctor."

"How long?"

"About seven or eight weeks."

"Is the boy local?"

She shook her head. "He's French. I met him during the summer. He's older and ..." Her voice trailed off.

"You told him?"

Mary nodded. "He told me to terminate it. He was quite blasé about it really."

"Abortion is illegal, Mary. You do know that."

"Yes. Viola got some information off the internet. There's a place in Wales ..." She started to cry again. "I don't want to do it. I'm frightened."

Miss Moriarty rubbed her back. "*Shhh,* that's perfectly understandable. *Shhh*, don't worry."

"What am I going to do?"

"I think you need to tell your father."

"What?" Mary's head shot up. "No way."

"Wait, listen. He loves you and will want the best for you. I know you don't believe me but he will know what's best."

Noel stared at his daughter.

"Mary, love, is this true?"

Mary nodded miserably.

"I don't believe this."

"I didn't plan for this to happen ... it was a mistake ..." Mary started to sob.

"God almighty, Mary! What were you thinking? A baby! How the hell will we manage?"

"I don't know, Dad. I'm so sorry. I know that we can't afford a baby. I need to do my exams and go to college. I need to get a good job and look after us. This is a nightmare."

"Who's responsible for this? Will he marry you?"

Mary shook her head wildly. "He doesn't want to know."

"The bastard!"

"He's not from here, Dad. He's not around."

"Well, there's the allowance for single mothers. You could apply for that. It would be desperate, us both being on the dole, but we'd manage."

She shook her head obstinately. "There is another alternative."

Noel inhaled sharply. "Are you suggesting what I think you're suggesting?"

"People have abortions every day. It's all over in a matter of hours and then you can go back to normal."

"*Mary!*"

"What? Then I can go back to school and pass my exams."

"Your mother would turn in her grave. There is no way you're even considering that option."

"Then what? What are my options?"

"I don't know, but there's no way you're doing that. Shur, it's illegal here and everything."

"You can do it in England."

"No, love. I won't hear of it."

"Then what?" Fresh tears fell from her eyes. "*What?*"

His face was grim. "I don't know. I just don't know."

Two days passed. Days of crying and arguments.

"Will I fly over to France and bring this fellow over here?" said Noel. "Taking advantage like that. Shameful!"

"He didn't!" protested Mary. "This is as much my fault as it is his."

"Ah, come on! You're a young girl."

"I am just as much to blame."

"I'm going to ring him," said Noel decidedly.

"Why? He told me to terminate it. He doesn't want to know."

"Then what do we do?"

"I don't know, Dad. I just don't know."

♫ ♫ ♫

The next day at school Mary was summoned to the principal's office. Sister Cecilia was writing in her diary when Mary knocked on the door.

"Come in," said the elderly nun, her pen moving like lightning across the page.

"You wanted to see me, Sister?"

"Yes. Sit down, Mary."

Mary took a seat on the wooden chair that faced the principal's desk. A large grandfather clock ticked loudly as she waited.

Eventually, Sister Cecelia put down her pen.

"Miss Moriarty informed me of your problem," she said matter-of-factly.

'What?" It came out as a whisper.

"She came to me yesterday evening."

"She promised she wouldn't tell anyone." Mary was horrified.

"It's her duty to inform me of something like this."

Mary's eyes filled with tears. "This is so unfair. I didn't want anyone to know."

"Mary, child. It is not a secret you can hide for long."

"I have to go to college. Dad has been on the dole for as long as I can remember. He needs me to do well and support him. The father doesn't want to know. He told me to ..." She stopped herself in time.

Sister Cecilia made a Sign of the Cross. "May God forgive you," she muttered. "Now, who pray tell is the father?"

"It doesn't matter. Just forget about him. He's washed his hands of it."

"So, do you agree with him? Do you think abortion is the way forward? Mary, have you lost your mind?"

"I don't know. I don't think so. Oh, Sister, I don't know anything anymore." She burst into tears.

"There, there." She patted Mary's shoulder. "You're not the first and you won't be the last."

"It's so awful. How your life can change in one second."

"Do you want to keep the baby?" the nun asked quietly.

Mary's rubbed her nose with her sleeve. "No. I can't have a baby now. But I really don't want to have an abortion either, Sister. It scares me."

"There's adoption," Sister Cecilia went on gently.

Mary looked up. "Adoption?"

"Yes. There are thousands of couples who can't have children of their own. You could make someone very happy."

"Adoption?" Mary repeated.

"Then you could get on with your life."

"Would I be able to visit the baby?" Mary asked tearfully.

Sister Cecilia shook her head. "No."

Mary's head was spinning.

"I can help you find a suitable family – a family that can provide your child with the best."

Mary closed her eyes. She couldn't give her baby the best. She was only a child herself. She needed to go to university and get a degree. She needed to live. A baby would tie her down. She was not prepared to be a mother.

Maybe old Cecilia was right. If her child was given to a good family – a family who could provide a proper childhood – then maybe it was the best option.

She touched her belly and felt a surge of emotion. It was all so confusing. It was all very well to think of adoption and things when she looked like she always did. What would happen when she was huge and could feel it kicking? What if she couldn't do it when the time came?

"Pray to God, Mary. He will help you to see that this is the right path. You can take a year to have the baby and recover. Then you can repeat your exams and get on with your life."

Mary clutched the chair handles for support.

"You might change your mind along the way, that's only natural. However, I will be here to set you straight again. You must not give in to your hormones and make rash decisions."

"What about the baby's father? I should tell him about this."

Sister Cecilia shook her head. "Not at all. He would only complicate things. He told you to have an abortion so that's that for him. Better to keep this quiet."

Mary put her head in her hands. "I'm so confused."

"Pray to God. He will guide you. This baby deserves the best chance. Do the right thing."

Later that evening, Mary lay on her bed, sobbing her heart out. She felt like a haze had invaded her brain and she didn't know what was real anymore. It was difficult to process the situation. Like all dilemmas, there was no easy answer. Of the three options she had put on the table, adoption was the sensible path. Like Sister Cecelia said, it would bring happiness to a couple who had been denied a family.

Leaning over, she picked up the drawing he had sketched that fateful night.

In two deft movements, she tore it to shreds.

Chapter Five

Twenty-Three Years Later

"What? An extra date has been added?" Madison glared at her manager, her blue almond eyes narrowed. "Why was I not consulted?"

Ross Curtis inhaled deeply. It felt like he spent most of his life placating her. "Just one more London show, Maddy," he said eventually. "The demand for tickets was so great, the extra night sold out in half an hour. You're a pop legend – an icon. You have to give them what they want."

Madison flicked her blonde hair and scowled at her reflection in the mirror.

"I had plans, Ross. I'm not a machine."

"Look, it's only one more show," he said in his strong Geordie accent. "A drop in the ocean. Then you can take a break, I promise."

Madison sighed. She was almost twenty-three and already she was tired of the limelight. The London shows were the finale of a strenuous European tour. When she had landed a record deal at the tender age of sixteen, she had been ecstatic. Now the gloss had worn off considerably.

Sure, one more night meant huge revenue, but it also

meant one more night of prancing around a stage under hot lights, singing songs that she hated.

"This is the last show, right? No surprises?"

Ross nodded.

"And then we can work on changing my image?"

"Of course, of course. I promised you, didn't I?" He didn't quite meet her eyes.

"Good. I'm sick of this ditzy girl-next-door stuff. I need to grow."

She straightened her dress and her bracelets jangled as her arm moved. At almost five foot seven, she carried herself well. Her head held high, she was praised for her impeccable posture. Her bronzed skin and long blonde hair only added to her beauty.

She picked up her clutch bag. "Now, if you don't mind, I'm going for dinner. Unless you have other plans for me?"

"Sure, Maddy. Have a great time. See you tomorrow." He winked at her. "You're the best."

She stalked out of the room and headed straight for the backstage exit. Her driver was waiting outside as she had a date with an English actor called Tim Kinnear. They had met for dinner once or twice when they were both in London and she liked him because he didn't put pressure on her.

The lights of London illuminated the street as she walked outside. Todd, her beefy American bodyguard, held the door of the Mercedes open and she got in. She had a personal bodyguard with her constantly – Todd and another man called Peter worked alternate shifts. Todd was an ex-Navy Seal and Peter was a retired detective. She also had an ex-Metropolitan policeman called John who acted as her driver.

She had hired protection after her second album went platinum, right after a fan got dangerously close and brandished a knife in her face. Her father had insisted that she ring an agency immediately and look for men with military backgrounds. She needed a visible presence all the time.

Todd was about thirty with biceps as big as her head. John, her driver, was older and had a wealth of experience from his years at Scotland Yard. For dinner dates, shopping excursions and business meetings, John did a quick reconnaissance before her bodyguard got the all-clear through an earpiece. Then and only then, would Madison be permitted to leave the safe confines of the blacked-out car.

For big events like awards ceremonies, concerts and television appearances, a special advance security team was hired to check the venues for potential threats prior to Madison's arrival. They would scour the premises for any threats and liaise with her bodyguard constantly.

Security was big business amongst the rich – Todd and Peter could charge up to one hundred pounds an hour – but Madison didn't mind. Her paranoia increased with every day that passed and she could afford it, so what was the big deal?

Todd sat in the front seat as always. The leather seat could barely contain his huge bulk. She was pretty sure that he could lift her with his pinkie. Her driver looked over his shoulder. "Where to, Miss Ryan?"

"Bouji's," she said curtly, sitting back and flicking her hair. She couldn't wait to have a drink. Anything to unwind after the concert.

♫ ♫ ♫

Madison Ryan was Ireland's pop princess. An only child, she had never wanted for anything and had that arrogant air that only a privileged South Side Dublin child would have.

Comparisons were made to Britney Spears but, unlike Britney, Madison didn't come from a humble background. In fact, she had grown up in one of the most exclusive areas of Dublin – on Vico Road in Dalkey. Her family home was a huge stone Georgian structure with pillars at the entrance. The east wall was covered with ivy and huge bay windows looked out on the sea. It had been in her mother's family for generations and wasn't visible from the main road.

Her father, Kevin, was an independent filmmaker who had struck gold when a low-budget film he made about the Irish Famine won worldwide critical acclaim in the nineties. What followed was a film career that went from strength to strength, culminating in an Oscar. That increased his value immeasurably and offers flooded in.

When Madison was small, he seemed to be always on location. She didn't see him for weeks at a time, except for the odd weekend here and there. A self-confessed workaholic, he gave his soul to his art, and worked long hours to produce the best.

Because of his absence, their relationship was strained. She resented how his work came before her and her mother. She yearned for a normal dad who took her to the park on Sundays and bought her ice cream. It didn't seem fair that they communicated primarily via Skype. As a result, they clashed when they did meet. Kevin was in his sixties and had old-fashioned ideas about things. Madison knew exactly how to wind him up.

Her mother, Louise, opted not to work and instead

stayed at home to look after Madison. After years of disappointments and a series of miscarriages, Kevin and Louise had tried three rounds of IVF with no success, after which they had reluctantly considered adoption. Then, at long last, she had come along – a blonde, blue-eyed baby who was the most blessed thing they had ever laid eyes on.

As a result, Madison had been spoilt from the beginning. Her childhood was one of dreams – trips to Disneyland, ski trips to Switzerland, the latest iPhone, and a sizeable trust fund. Kevin purchased a villa on the Costa Brava so her summers were spent near the charming town of Sitges, just south of Barcelona. On Saturdays she would go to Dundrum Shopping Centre, spending hundreds of euros on Ugg boots, clothes and make-up. Being an only child, she had a whole wing of the house to herself. Thick pile carpet covered the floor of her room and she had a custom-made four-poster bed. A large dressing table had lights all around it, emulating the movie stars of old. She never made her bed as when she got home the room had been cleaned by Mina, the Latvian maid. Anything she wanted, she got. She learned at a young age that tantrums were an effective way to win an argument. So everyone let her get away with being spoilt and entitled for fear of upsetting her.

She entered Bouji's through a private side entrance, her bodyguard Todd by her side. John her driver had performed an advance check, using his contacts within the building. He had learned years before that it was important to build up a good relationship with restaurant, bar and hotel staff by tipping them generously. They knew their businesses inside out and would notice anything odd straight away.

"Maddy!" Her date, the actor Tim Kinnear, was even more handsome than he was on screen. Tall with dark-brown hair, he had a toned physique that required daily two-hour gym sessions. He had just won a BAFTA for his movie about Mick Jagger's early years and was tipped for lots of awards across the pond.

She walked towards him purposefully, her heels giving her added height. He kissed her on the lips and gestured for her to sit down at the table. A glass of champagne was poured immediately.

"You look annoyed," he observed. "How was the show?"

She scowled. "Same as ever. Same set, same type of crowd."

"Sit back and relax now. It's over."

"Oh, no. They've added an extra date. *Cha-ching* for the powers that be!"

"When?"

"Two days. I'm so pissed off. I was planning on flying to New York for the weekend."

"New York?"

She sipped her drink. "I wanted to meet up with some friends and take in a show. It's my birthday next week. I'll be twenty-three."

"Oh?" He looked flustered. "I didn't know, I mean, I had no idea."

"Relax," she said drily. "You're not my official boyfriend. You don't have to do all that chocolate-and-flowers thing."

Tim relaxed. "If you say so."

"Oh, I do." She looked him square in the eye. "What we have is perfect. No strings. No commitment. We meet when we have a spare window. As I said, perfect." She sighed. "I really wanted to see a show on Broadway. It's so unfair."

He rubbed her arm sympathetically. "Just say no. They can't do much about it."

She shook her head. "I can't. They had to go through some serious red tape to get the venue and it would be too much hassle now if I pulled out. I guess it's the price of fame."

"Speaking of fame, I auditioned for that part I was telling you about."

"The Western?"

He nodded. "They said I look too clean-cut for a cowboy. Have you ever heard such nonsense?"

She laughed. "You're too pretty alright."

"I got a call-back, despite their misgivings, so I'm growing a beard."

She made a face. "You'd look weird."

"Thanks."

"Still, it'll be worth it. Is it true Clint Eastwood is involved?"

He nodded. "I've been watching *Unforgiven* constantly. I really want this part!"

Madison's phone lit up with a banner from WhatsApp. It was from Ross, her manager.

Interview, Monday morning, Poporama magazine. They want to do a profile. Call me to confirm.

"Ah, Christ!" She threw the phone on the table.

"What now?"

"A bloody interview with *Poporama* magazine on Monday morning. Do I ever get a break?"

Tim refilled her glass. "It'll take an hour, tops," he said soothingly. "Then you can jet off wherever you want."

Madison slumped back in her chair. They treated her like a commodity – a puppet where they controlled the strings. Signing with Delphi Records had been a whirlwind of excitement in the beginning. They had fawned over her and promised her the world. They had made her believe that she was in control, when in fact they decided almost everything. Every day there was someone to meet or photos to be taken. She was tired of having to look good all the time. She couldn't even pop to the local grocery shop for milk without being followed. There was always a tinted jeep parked outside her apartment in Mayfair, waiting for that all-important photo of her that could be sold to the highest bidder. The paparazzi took it in shifts, all hungry for a shot that would make headlines. The press hounded her and the constant voyeurism was exhausting. She had to have Angelica her stylist and Mona her make-up artist on hand before she ventured out, even to somewhere like the supermarket. Otherwise she paid the price of having awful unattractive photos splashed across social media for the world to see and judge. Hundreds of comments from ordinary people, criticising her outfit or accusing her of creating impossible ideals for young girls. Trolls followed her every move, waiting by their keyboards to tweet or comment maliciously. She had given up reading reviews and rarely used social media. Being judged, often cruelly and unjustly, affected her mental health. The best thing to do was to avoid it. Luckily, her publicist Bethany took care of that side of things. The key to having a large entourage meant that everyone had a role to make her life easier.

Later that night, as Tim lay asleep beside her, she contemplated what she could do. Creatively she was at a standstill. Her fans had grown up with her and the time had come for a change. It was time for Madison Ryan to shake things up. She was no longer the young impressionable teenage girl who hung on Ross's every word.

She bit her lip. She could make enquiries. Surely there were options. The teeny-bopper stage was over. The time had come to seek out other paths.

Tim grunted and changed position. The moonlight illuminated his strong arms as he pulled the duvet up around him.

Her expression softened. She liked Tim. Sure, she had seen the photos of him wrapped around that girl from *Love Island*, but it didn't bother her. Since Cal, she had a real problem with getting close to any of her boyfriends.

Cal Scott, the lead singer of a boyband called The Southsiders, had been her first real love. They had met at a party in Dublin when she was seventeen, one year after her début. The Southsiders had had three number-one singles at that stage and could sell out Wembley arena. Cal, a native of Rathmines, was nineteen and the pin-up of many adolescent schoolgirls. He had kissed her like she was the only girl that existed. Young and impressionable, she had fallen for him completely. The media had jumped on the story straight away, following them when they went out and calling them the golden couple of Irish pop. Madison enjoyed putting photos of them as a couple on Instagram and waiting for the 'likes' that flooded in. She got a sense of validation from that in those early days.

Then the rumours started. Cal had been seen with a girl from MTV. He had laughed it off, saying that it was nonsense. Then she had caught him in bed with her personal assistant. Right before her first big concert at the O2 Arena. Denis Moloney, Cal's manager, had covered it up, paying all the right people lots of money to stay quiet. It would harm their reputations, he said. They would be deemed bad role models for their army of fans.

Her manager had agreed and the relationship limped on for another month or two. Then there were rumours of Cal and a model fornicating on a yacht in the south of France. Incensed, she had dumped him by text, telling him never to contact her again.

There was a privacy injunction taken out against the press so nothing was printed, but rumours spread like wildfire. **#calgotcaught** even trended on Twitter for a while. There was no gagging order that could control the internet. Then the speculation died and she got on with her life.

Her new personal assistant, Emily, was working out well. She was in her thirties, a Size 16, had bad acne and was no threat to Madison at all. She was efficient and organised Madison's life like clockwork. She didn't mind working unpredictable hours but had insisted on having this weekend off as it was her niece's birthday in Bristol.

Tim started to snore. She pushed his shoulder. "Tim!" she whispered. "Tim! Turn over."

He obeyed and the snoring stopped.

Closing her eyes, she willed her brain to go to sleep.

Chapter Six

The interview was due to take place at the Goring hotel at ten a.m. the next Monday morning. Delphi Records had hired a suite for the morning for Madison to meet the journalist from *Poporama* magazine, Corinne Matthews. Ross, her manager, had emailed on Corinne's LinkedIn profile – the professional picture showed a dark-haired woman wearing a red blouse.

Emily, back from Bristol, poured a cup of black coffee for Madison. "You should have seen the cake, Maddy. It was a huge chocolate sponge with fresh cream. I had three slices."

Madison tried to look interested. Two things really annoyed her about Emily. The first was how she never stopped talking and the second was how she called her 'Maddy'. She had corrected her constantly in the beginning.

"Call me Madison, please."

To which Emily replied, "Of course, Maddy. Sorry about that."

Emily had a West Country accent that grated on her nerves as well. She also had zero dress sense, wearing jeans that were too tight for her curvy frame and a blouse that buttoned up to the neck. Her mousy brown hair was straight and thin.

"Did you have a nice date with Tim?" Emily brushed her hair out of her eyes.

Madison scowled and sipped her coffee. "Anyway," she said, changing the subject, "can you book me a massage for this afternoon? I'll need one after this bloody interview. Oh, and call my mother and tell her that I won't make it back for my birthday. I have plans."

Emily took her iPhone out of her pocket and started to type. "Of course. Anything else?"

"Not at the moment."

The receptionist rang at five minutes to ten. "Hello, there is a journalist here to see Ms Ryan. A Ms Corinne Matthews?"

Peter, Madison's bodyguard on duty, said, "Just send her up here."

"Of course, sir." The telephone clicked.

Todd had flown home to Colorado for a few days to see his grandma. Peter had taken over and was working four shifts straight. He was older than Todd – a tall man with greying hair and shrewd eyes. He always wore a suit and spoke with a posh London accent. He had retired from the force three years before and had given his credentials to an agency. Now, he made a fortune protecting Madison. He was only in the game for five years. Then he would retire to Bermuda with his wife.

At exactly five minutes past, there was a knock on the door.

Peter strode over and checked the peephole. "It's her," he said. "She matches the picture."

Madison shrugged. “Let her in.”

Corinne was a small woman wearing a pencil skirt and a white shirt. Her long dark hair was in a high knot on her head and her notebook was in her hand. Peter asked to look through her bag.

“Of course,” she said, opening her small holdall. “A man called John already checked at reception.”

“Well, I’ll check again,” he said coldly. He rummaged inside thoroughly and then gestured for her to pass.

“Hi, my name is Corinne.” She smiled at Madison and held out her hand. “Thank you for seeing me this morning.”

“Would you like a coffee? There’s a fresh pot brewed.” Madison smiled but it didn’t reach her eyes.

She shook her head. “I’m okay, thanks.” She placed her notebook, a pen and a small Dictaphone on the table. “Do you mind if I record this chat?”

Madison shrugged. “That’s grand with me.”

Peter stood sentinel at the door, his arms behind his back. His earpiece was visible above his white collar and every now and then he put his finger up to press it. John was down at reception, keeping an eye on who entered and left the building. Constant communication was vital.

“Will I stay?” Emily looked unsure.

Madison waved her away. “No. Go for a walk or something.”

Emily nodded. “See you later.”

Corinne settled into her chair and pressed the ‘record’ button.

“So, Madison, your career is going from strength to strength.” She beamed at her. “Were you always interested in music?”

Madison stopped herself from rolling her eyes. What a lame question! A miniature Ross Curtis appeared on her shoulder wagging his finger. "*Put on a show!*" he commanded. "*Play your part.*"

"Sure, Corinne," she said brightly. "I've been singing since the beginning. I loved 'Bear in the Big Blue House' and I sang that 'Goodbye Song' with Luna over and over."

"I remember that." Corinne smiled.

"Then at the age of four, I went to the Billie Barry Stage School in Dublin where I learned to sing and dance."

Corinne smiled encouragingly.

"Then I was selected to perform on television," Madison reeled off. "The *Late Late Toy Show* is a national institution in Ireland. It's on at Christmas each year and the whole country tunes in. I sang 'Beautiful' by Christina Aguilera. I think I was nine."

"And then you were noticed by a talent scout."

Madison yawned pointedly. This story had been told a million times before. Surely none of this was anything new.

"He made contact with my parents, suggesting an audition with a record producer."

"And?"

Madison's expression darkened. "My dad put a stop to it immediately. He said I was too young and there were strict rules regarding child performers. He made me go back to school."

She remembered the fights and the tears.

"Why?" asked Corinne.

"There was no way he was allowing me to have such exposure at such a young age. He had worked with child actors in the industry and he saw what fame did to their fragile egos." She looked up. "He felt that I was too young and immature to deal with the pressures of the limelight."

"Where did you go to secondary school?" Corinne moved on.

"I went to an all-girls private school in Glenageary."

"In Dublin?"

"Yes."

Corinne scribbled down the name in her notebook. "Favourite subjects?"

"I studied music for a while, but then I gave it up. All that classical stuff was boring. So, I joined the choir instead. I also played hockey."

"Anything else?"

She paused. "I liked Art. I'm pretty good at drawing actually. I used to sketch my friends and charge them a euro for the picture."

"So, all humanity subjects then?"

She nodded. "What was the point in learning science and maths? I knew I wouldn't need them where I was going. The teachers always complained at parent-teacher meetings that I was wasting time, the usual. Dad went crazy, but I didn't care."

"Were you popular at school?"

"Of course." Madison looked surprised that Corinne had even asked. Of course she had been popular at school – she was pretty and had an air of sophistication that young girls are drawn to and admire. She was a leader – always had been.

"Are you still friendly with any of your school friends?"

"The only girl I still call is Cliona. We're still pretty close."

"Cliona?"

"Cliona O'Connor. She lives down the road from my place in Dublin."

Madison thought of her old friend. Cliona was the opposite to her – she was timid and quiet and preferred to blend in. Where Madison was confident and liked to shine, Cliona preferred the background. With her straight brown hair and dark-brown eyes hidden behind glasses, she suited Madison who liked the fact that there was no chance her friend would steal her limelight.

"She saved my life in secondary school."

"What do you mean?"

"Oh, not literally!" Madison laughed. "We took the same classes: art, music and history. Cliona was great. She was quiet and studious and she helped me write Shakespeare essays to hand up in time, stuff like that. We idolised Justin Timberlake and had posters all over our bedroom walls. Then we actually cried when Westlife broke up." Madison chuckled. "She was more upset than me!"

"Was she your best friend?"

"One hundred per cent. Each September we'd take annual bets on who would win *The X Factor*. We hung out every day."

"So, at what age did your career really take off?"

"Dad organised an audition on my sixteenth birthday. Apparently I was old enough then to handle it."

"And?"

"He had lots of contacts in the industry and he got an appointment with Ross Curtis. He had an office based in Dublin. In the beginning, I was based there."

Corinne wrote something in her notebook. "You dated Cal Scott, the lead singer of The Southsiders. Was it true about him and your personal assistant?"

Madison scowled. "Let's not go there."

Corinne met her gaze. "It was never proved ..."

"Let's get back to my story, okay?"

"If you want."

"Anyway, I sang a cover of Whitney Houston's 'The Greatest Love of All' and Ross was really impressed," continued Madison with a steely expression. "He decided that I was perfect for their target market – teeny-bopper girls. I did two more auditions and then I signed with Delphi Records. Then we made my first album."

"Is he easy to work for?"

Madison thought of her manager. His forceful personality ensured that her diet was strictly controlled and she was encouraged not to drink in public. He was a tough boss and insisted that she keep her squeaky-clean image.

"Yes," she lied. "Of course."

"It must have been advantageous to have a famous dad when you were starting off."

Madison reddened. "What do you mean by that?"

"I mean, it must help ..."

"Dad may have helped things along, but there's nothing wrong with that."

"Right."

"I *am* famous in my own right."

"Of course," said Corinne smoothly. "Right, moving on. That record was filled with covers of popular songs, wasn't it?"

Madison nodded. "The brief was that they'd see how sales went before they hired an official songwriter. They felt that the public were more likely to engage with familiar songs so they bought the rights to classics. Then the radios played my songs continuously." She shuddered. "Cheesy pop versions of The Beatles, ABBA and Cyndi Lauper. Oh my God, when I think of it!"

"So, you regret this stage of your career?"

"Definitely. It's hard to remember it with anything but embarrassment."

"Then you played gigs at the Olympia and then the Marquee in Cork City."

"Yes. Ticket sales were great. All the young girls came to see me and scream."

"Did you like that?"

Madison paused. "At the time I was so overwhelmed I didn't know what to think. It all happened so quickly. I didn't have time to process it. People stopped me and congratulated me, but I didn't really understand why. It was a blur."

"Your first music video was directed by your father, wasn't it?"

Madison nodded. "He flew in specially to take control." She laughed bitterly. "Those three days were the longest I'd ever spent in his company. He wasn't around a lot when I was a child."

Corinne regarded her thoughtfully. "Did you like the video?"

"What was not to like? It was me dancing on a street in a cute pink dress with my hair swinging in a ponytail. The embodiment of the brand."

"Your album topped the charts in the United Kingdom and your YouTube videos began to get millions of hits. Surely that was gratifying?"

"Oh, I got lots of radio air time and then I appeared on daytime shows, singing a song or two and talking about my rise to fame. Then I was asked back to *The Late Late Show*, where I started." She paused. "It was exciting back then. I lived every moment."

"Now?"

"It's all a bore."

Corinne wrote a few lines in her notebook.

"Soon after that you got a songwriter, right?"

"Yep. Album sales took off so Ross relocated me to London and brought in Mike Byrne – do you know him?"

Corinne nodded. "He was a folk singer. Retired now."

"Yes, then he branched into writing easy-listening pop songs for pop artists. The Southsiders owe their greatest hits to Mike."

"And you?"

Madison paused. She could be honest and really throw the cat among the pigeons. Corinne would be sure to print what she said. Did she care anymore? Not really. She had bigger and better plans. Ross would have to engage with her then.

"I don't rate him as a musician," she said finally. "He has no imagination. His magic formula was to create a simple, catchy tune with about three chords that the public could pick up instantaneously."

"What's wrong with that?" said Corinne, surprised.

"It's one-dimensional."

"But your second album went platinum and he penned most of the music." Corinne looked down at her notes. "The first single from the album, 'You and Me', went straight to number one in Ireland and the United Kingdom.

The next song 'Text Me Back' went straight to number one as well."

"I know, but it wasn't me, you know? I hated those songs and I hated singing them even more."

"It made you famous. Your Twitter account has millions of followers, as does your Instagram. Your fans follow your every move. You've released a perfume and a brand of clothing, along with a range of make-up. You were invited to see the president at Áras an Uachtaráin. Then when you tweeted about it afterwards, calling the president 'cute', your army of fans agreed and the president amassed four thousand new followers on Twitter that day." Corinne looked up. "Is that not what you dreamed of? Back in your schooldays?"

Madison fiddled with her bracelet. Did she like the attention? In the beginning it had been heady – she adored when she was recognised and interacted with fans with a huge smile on her face. Now, she resented the constant attention. She couldn't even go for lunch with a pal without someone pointing or asking for a selfie.

Ireland was the only place she could act someway normal. The Irish people didn't really do the whole celebrity thing – they'd nod in your direction, but tended to leave you alone. Bono, the lead singer of U2, often busked on Grafton Street without any hassle.

London and America were a different story. The minute she was recognised, people would swarm around her like bees. She found that terrifying.

However, it was a double-edged sword. If people ignored her, she got paranoid that she was losing her star quality and was fading away.

"Fame is a funny thing," she said eventually. "It's unpredictable and often lonely. Each hotel room morphs into the next and the constant moving around becomes hard."

"Lonely?"

"Yes. The whole world knows your name but no one really knows *you*. You're a sitting duck for people trying to take advantage."

"Like Tariq?"

Madison glared at her.

After the Cal Scott scandal, she had hired a young gay assistant called Tariq. That didn't work out either as he bitched about her spoilt behaviour and demanding ways to anyone who would listen. It was only a matter of time before she heard and he was fired immediately. He wasn't so easily silenced and sold his story to a London tabloid. The article was headed ***MAD-woman*** and didn't hold back in its sensational accounts of her tantrums and outbursts. Tariq then appeared on daytime TV shows, embellishing his tales. The end result was that people began to see Madison as spoilt and entitled. Ross had been furious.

"Sort this!" he demanded. "You need to be a role-model for these young girls."

So, Madison had appeared on *The Great British Bake Off* charity show and appeared on *Strictly Come Dancing*. She was perfectly sweet and polite and the public forgot Tariq's accusations.

"Tariq who?" she said sweetly.

Corinne wrote something in her notebook. "Point taken. So, tell me more about this Cliona. Your friend."

"As I said, she lives down the road from me in Dublin.

That's why I try to go home as often as possible. I meet up with her and we chat like old times."

"How often do you see her?"

"Only when I go home. Not that much, to be fair. She's there for me, you know? She's the one person I can trust."

"She sounds nice, this Cliona."

Madison eyes narrowed. "Yes. She's very nice."

"You should surround yourself with more people like her. Especially in this industry."

"Thanks for the advice, Corinne." Madison glared at her. "Now, can we wrap this up? I have plans."

Chapter Seven

Cliona O'Connor came from a literary family. Her father was the journalist and biographer Aonghus O'Connor. He had written a biography on James Joyce, followed by one on Oscar Wilde. However, it was his work on Countess Markievicz that had really taken off and the film rights were snapped up. The family should have been rich, what with Aonghus's book sales and the lucrative movie deal – however, a hectic social life and a penchant for holidays meant that money was never flowing. When Cliona had won a coveted scholarship to Madison's exclusive all-girls school Loretto Dalkey, her parents had breathed a sigh of relief. It was either pay the school fees or a month's holiday in Greece. Aonghus had already put a down-payment on a house to rent in the hills of Santorini so, when Cliona won the bursary, the problem happily disappeared.

Her mother, Constance, was a retired actress. Now in her fifties, she wrote lifestyle blogs and looked after her cats who roamed the dilapidated old mansion where Cliona had grown up. The old house on the sought-after Sorrento Terrace was badly in need of repair but Aonghus and Constance never seemed to have much money. Constance had inherited the property from her grandmother when she had died. As real estate went, it was worth a fortune, but the family had no intention of selling it.

"I'd love to win the Euromillions," Constance would sigh. "Then we could get insulation and maybe fix the roof."

Cliona had an older brother called Fionn. They were close when they were kids as only a year separated them. "They're what we call Irish twins," Constance would say as she pushed them around Blackrock Shopping Centre in a double buggy. "No one told me that breastfeeding wasn't a contraceptive."

Growing up with Aonghus and Constance had always been interesting for Cliona and her brother: some days they went to school without lunches or without sports gear on days they had a Physical Education class. They came from a disorganised home, there was no denying it. However, with all its disarray, it was a house filled with love. Constance, always demonstrative, showered her children with kisses every day. Aonghus always made it home in time to tell them bedtime stories, embellishing classic mythological myths with accents and extra characters.

Constance was also a keen cook and endeavoured to have freshly cooked meals for her children. The nights she made an effort they dined on dishes like moussaka or homemade ravioli. The nights she was too tired or busy, they ate omelettes or sausages wrapped in bread. Their life moved up and down like a rollercoaster, but they didn't mind one bit.

Madison preferred calling over to Cliona's house when she was in Dublin, mainly because it was the antithesis to her own. Where her house was kept in pristine condition by the army of staff, Constance claimed that she never had time to dust the furniture or clear the cobwebs. She was simply too busy living her life, she'd quip with a wink. Madison was accustomed to arriving at Cliona's to find empty wine glasses on the piano and half-eaten cheese on the bookcase. The large rooms of the old house had plenty of light, but this only served to show up the dust even more. More often than not, Constance would arrive downstairs in the afternoon, wearing a silk kimono and with last night's make-up still on. She would giggle and make a cup of tea, regaling the girls with stories of her youth in Dublin, when she was a well-known actress on the stage.

"Do you miss it?" Madison asked her once. "The attention?"

Constance paused for a moment. "I did at first. But now, I think my priorities were all askew. Self-obsession is a dangerous thing, Maddy darling. Look at poor Narcissus. The simple things are what are important. Love, family and health. You know, it's a pity you don't have a brother. Like Fionn."

At the age of nineteen, Fionn had moved to London to study at the Guildhall School of Music and Drama and eventually joined the band Doctor Eckleburg as a drummer. When he first moved away, Cliona missed him dreadfully. Living with Constance and Aonghus was frustrating at times without his brotherly support. More often than not, she would open the fridge to find the milk was out of date and there was always a mess that was impossible to tidy. Every Saturday she would organise the pile of washing and mop the old tiled kitchen floor, but within hours Constance would dump a new pile of washing by the machine and the cats would walk all over the floor with their muddy paws.

When Fionn did come home, Constance would pull out all the stops. The best meat was ordered from the butcher and roasted, along with all the trimmings. The best wine was produced and Constance would gaze at her son in delight.

"He inherited his musical talent from me," she would say. "I almost got a role in *The Commitments*, you know, but Angeline Ball got it instead."

After graduation at school, Cliona's friends all started courses in various colleges around the country. Some went off to study law; others did English Literature at Trinity College. Cliona attended university in Dublin, studying film and even did her thesis on Kevin Ryan's work in independent film. Living on the south side of the Liffey, she commuted to college every day as she couldn't afford to rent in the city. Plus, it was only a forty-minute drive on the M50. So each day she took off in her trusty old Golf and attended lectures on Cecil Beaton and Roman Polanski. She had a keen eye and a quick brain, and was soon excelling in each module. Being Aonghus O'Connor's daughter was something she didn't broadcast – she wanted to be recognised in her own right. Everyone knew that to make it in the film business you had to work trebly hard.

At night she would take off her glasses and rub her tired eyes. Her naturally pale skin had a small smattering of freckles on her nose and cheeks. She hated those freckles. All her friends at school tried to convince her to use fake tan, but she had politely refused. She had seen what it did to girls her age with their orange faces and uneven applications. She had mentioned it to her mother once and Constance had been horrified.

"You have beautiful skin, my love. Like a porcelain doll. Don't even think about it!"

Cliona looked in the mirror. Beautiful skin was all well and good, but she had nothing else going for her. Her brown hair was straight and unexciting. It fell in the same way every day. How she yearned for some volume! Her glasses were a staple part of her now. They made her look geeky and studious, but she couldn't see without them. She was medium height and slim, so she always wore T-shirts and jeans as they suited her shape. Fashion didn't interest her – her idea of hell was a shopping trip on Saturday. She'd only had a couple of boyfriends over the years as she was shy and preferred to stay in the background. Her longest relationship to date was with a economics student called Gareth. They stayed together for her first year at college. Fionn had immediately christened him 'Nerdy Gareth' because of his glasses and long hair. When they broke up, Constance breathed a sigh of relief. According to her, Gareth was a nice boy, but was terribly boring. Anyone who spoke about GDP at a dinner party would never fit in with their family.

Chapter Eight

Ross Curtis had many famous clients and had all the right contacts. A small man originally from Newcastle, he had made it in the nineties managing a girl band called Lush. Now, he concentrated on solo artists. He was balding and habitually wore black-silk shirts with a gold chain around his neck. Whatever hair he did have, he slicked back with gel. He hadn't lost his Durham accent and reminded Madison of a *bling-bling* version of Jackie Elliot, Billy's dad in the iconic movie.

Madison Ryan was one of his biggest names. Sure, he had smiled and nodded when she went on about changing her style. He had learned years ago that the best way to deal with celebrities was to agree with everything they said. He had no intention of giving in to her demands. What she had was a magic formula: a formula that worked. Her fan base loved her pop songs and he had already given Mike Byrne the go-ahead to write a new album.

Then the *Poporama* magazine interview hit the shelves. He couldn't believe his eyes when he read it. He had been on a well-earned break in Mauritius with his wife when his secretary had emailed it over. He cut his break short, flew home to Heathrow and called a meeting with Madison straight away.

The door of his office opened and Todd appeared, his bulk filling the doorframe. Madison followed, her blonde hair loose around her shoulders. She was wearing a khaki sundress and black espadrilles, her skin as bronzed as ever.

"Why have I been summoned?" she asked in a bored tone. "I didn't think you were back for another week."

"Well, *this* is why I came back!" He jabbed at the copy of *Poporama* magazine that lay open on his desk. "Why did you lambast Mike? What the fuck, Maddy? I had him lined up to write your next album."

"I suspected as much," she retorted. "You never had any intention of letting me change, did you?"

"What you said was pretty fucking obnoxious!"

Madison's eyes narrowed. "I meant every word. I'm fed up of Mike's music. I'm tired of being controlled and restricted. I want to become a real artist."

Ross laughed. "How predictable. Let me guess, you'll collaborate with a rapper."

She glowered at him.

"I'm right, aren't I? That's your plan."

"I want to shake things up. I've exhausted the girl-next-door thing. Madison Ryan has to grow up."

"There's nothing wrong with what you're doing."

"No, Ross! I'm yearning for a change. It's the same old drill day in and day out. If I sing 'Text Me Back' once more I'll scream."

Ross sat back in his leather chair. Madison's face was mutinous. He could tell that she was adamant. Mike Byrne had already called twice saying that he would never work with her again. What choice did he have now?

He eyed the platinum discs on the wall of his office. He earned almost twenty per cent of her income. Because of Madison, he had homes in New York, Sardinia and Bondi Beach. He had to keep her sweet.

"Fine. I'm on your side."

"For real?"

"For real. Let me make a few calls. I'll get back to you later."

Madison stood up. "Good. I'm glad we see eye to eye." She stalked off.

Todd nodded and followed, closing the door behind him.

Ross picked up his phone. "Susan?" he said to his secretary. "Get me Sven Jakobsen on the phone."

Bethany, Madison's publicist, released a statement stating that the young star was taking a well-earned break. She thanked the fans for their ongoing support and promised that it would only be a short hiatus. Tweets flooded in from concerned fans, wondering if their beloved Madison had gone to rehab or had burnt out. Many were well-wishers, praying for her speedy return. Others were nasty, saying that she didn't know what overworked was – just overpaid. Rumours of drug addiction surfaced but were quickly quashed by Ross. Fans stationed themselves outside her London flat, hoping to catch a glimpse of their idol, but there was no sign.

Madison Ryan had disappeared.

♫ ♫ ♫

The truth was that she was hidden away at a wellness retreat in the Austrian Alps. She had flown out with her entourage – Todd, Peter, John, Emily, Angelica, Mona, Boris her personal trainer and Giorgio her personal chef.

Her mother had tagged along for the first week, enjoying the mountain air and stunning views. After a series of arguments, Madison had sent her back to Dublin. For some reason Louise's timid ways annoyed her. She always sat in the background and never contributed. It reminded her of the early days, when her mother used to travel with her when she was on tour and supervise her behaviour. Then, when Madison turned eighteen, she put a stop to it. "I no longer need a chaperone, Louise," she had told her mother firmly.

Ross had found a duo of songwriters to fly out and work with Madison. Sven Jakobsen was a Norwegian DJ who had written bestselling tunes for various popstars. A tall blonde man in his forties, he had retired from the decks in Ibiza and had carved out a successful career writing crowd-pleasing music for a hefty sum. Carlotta Diaz was a Spanish soap star who had a brief pop career in the nineties. When Ricky Martin had gone global, living the *vida loca*, she had jumped on the bandwagon and produced some catchy songs, complete with castanets and lively dance routines. Like Sven, she knew what was trending and worked hard at being on the pulse.

Their first meeting with Madison was tetchy. Sven arrived with bags under his eyes as he had flown from Toronto the day before and needed to catch up on his sleep. Dressed in an oversized T-shirt and wearing frayed jeans, he looked dishevelled and unshaven.

"Who the hell are you?" asked Madison rudely, unaware of who he was. "How did you get past security?"

Carlotta arrived in a tight black top with an enormous amount of cleavage on show and proceeded to shower Madison with praise. "My daughter, she loves your songs," she gushed.

"Let me guess, she adores 'Text Me Back'?" said Madison, rolling her eyes.

"*Si, si,* that's the one." Carlotta beamed at her and started to hum the tune.

"God help me," Madison muttered under her breath.

"Let's start tomorrow," suggested Sven with a yawn. "I need to sleep."

"Your room is on the next floor," said Todd. "Follow me."

The next morning Sven and Carlotta sat at a round table in Madison's suite and discussed her vision. They took notes and made suggestions. They even encouraged her to take part in the process, bringing her own stamp to the songs. She refused, preferring to stay in the background and let them work their magic.

A baby grand piano had been installed and Sven played around with melodies. Carlotta sang various lines in harmony and shook a tambourine in time to the music. Sven asked for a set of decks to be delivered and he started to mix some tunes, his earphones covering one ear. Slowly a new style emerged – the lively pop was replaced by deep bass lines and funkier beats.

Madison flew back to London with a spring in her step. She had to admit that Carlotta and Sven had done a stellar job. She had two days of a break before she jetted off to Montreux to record the first track.

The minute she got back to her apartment, she called Mona.

"I need a makeover," she said without preamble. "Can you come over? My new music doesn't fit my profile at all."

Mona refused as she was on a dinner date and eventually they compromised on the next morning. "Send me a demo," Mona ordered. "I need to get a feel for what you want." Then she hung up.

The next morning, Mona appeared at seven-thirty, armed with her giant bag. A tall, imposing woman from Zimbabwe, she wore traditional tribal clothes with startling colours. Her cheekbones were high and gave her a haughty look.

Madison's stint in Austria had afforded her a well-earned break and she had enjoyed every moment.

"I did some sketches last night when I got home," Mona said, pulling out a notebook full of drawings. "I have an idea for you." She gestured to the leather chair in front of a giant mirror. "Sit and I'll begin."

Madison obeyed, eager to see what would materialise. Mona was the best in the business. She guessed that she was in her forties, but she had an ageless look. She had been doing her make-up for three years now and never once rose to Madison's histrionics. She remained calm, even when one eye was botched or Madison had a giant spot on her nose. Madison liked that about her. She knew that she was notoriously difficult to work with and admired Mona for her sang-froid. Her mother Louise was a different story. She just let her get away with everything and she despised it.

Mona turned Madison's chair away from the mirror. "You must not look until the end," she commanded. Then she pulled down the trademark ponytail and styled the long tresses so that they framed Madison's face. She curled random locks so that they bounced around and looked dishevelled. The famous blue eyes were circled with smudgy dark pencil and the lips were painted a deep red. Blusher accentuated the beautiful cheekbones and false eyelashes made her eyes look huge.

"Now, I think this is more like it." She swivelled Madison around.

Madison gasped. "*Wowee!*" she said in wonder. "I look amazing."

"Yes, you do," said Mona in satisfaction. "No more pastels for you, I think. Dramatic. Dark. That's what we need."

"Gosh, I look like a siren."

"Your fans will be shocked."

Madison's eyes narrowed. "Good."

Chapter Nine

A month later, after a gruelling recording session in Switzerland, Madison flew home. She barely had time to enjoy the spectacular views of Lake Geneva. Every morning she was in the studio for eight and sometimes the session went on until midnight. Sven and Carlotta didn't do things by halves and there were days where she screamed at them for making her sing the same part of the song over and over because it wasn't quite right. However, the end result was a triumph.

The streets of London were a welcome sight as her car sped along. Switzerland had been nice and all, but she had soon grown tired of the food and the alien language. How she wished she had concentrated harder in French class at school. With her musical ear, languages should have been a doddle to pick up. The Swiss had been polite but she could tell they found her gauche and uneducated.

She had sent Emily home the day before to stock the fridge and run a few errands. She couldn't wait to sleep in her own bed. She was dreaming of a hot shower, her pyjamas and a movie on her flat screen. Todd pressed the button to open the gates of her apartment block. A lone photographer waited outside and his camera flashed as her Mercedes whizzed by. Sometimes she didn't know why the paparazzi bothered. She hadn't done anything interesting in weeks. She couldn't remember the last time she had dressed up and gone to a party or an event. It was all work and no play.

Her phone buzzed and she saw a new email notification. It was from Ross, welcoming her back and saying that he had just organised a trip to Stockholm to record an extra track with Sauron, an up-and-coming hip-hop artist.

She nearly dropped the phone. Her flight was booked for the next morning.

"*No way!*" she yelled and Todd looked back in concern.

"All okay, ma'am?" he asked in his deep drawl.

"No, Todd. Things are not okay. Bloody Ross is sending me to Sweden in the morning!"

John looked in the rear-view mirror but said nothing.

"It never stops. I'm so sick of it." She threw the phone on the back seat in a rage. "Have you heard of Sauron? I mean, is he even famous?"

Todd shrugged. "I'm not sure ..."

"Well, apparently he's waiting to record a track with me."

She dialled Ross's number and he answered immediately.

"Jesus, Ross, give a girl a break. I'm just back from Montreux."

"You said you wanted a change – I'm making that happen."

"Yes, but does it have to be so fast?"

"Madison," he said sweetly, "I'm only doing what you demanded. Nothing more. Sauron is tipped to be the next best thing. I pulled major strings to get you this gig. A collaboration with him is the perfect début of the new Maddy Ryan."

She couldn't argue with that.

"It's just four days. He has a demo of the track already. He just wants to play around with your vocals."

"Fine."

The four days flew by. Surprisingly, Madison had fun, despite her qualms. Sauron was a small Afro-Caribbean man with long dreadlocks and a penchant for gold suits. He was in his thirties and hailed from Detroit. His first album was given a stellar review in *Hot Press* magazine and then reached number two in the R&B/Hip-Hop billboard in the United Kingdom. Obsessed with *Lord of the Rings,* Sauron took his stage name from the famous books.

"*You and me – we're gonna make history!*" he rapped with a grin.

Madison, on first meeting him, wasn't so sure. With his tiny size and questionable dress sense, he was sure to look ridiculous next to her on screen. However, she soon changed her tune. The song he had written was gritty and dealt with infidelity. The sample of music Sauron had chosen for her to sing was a chorus from one of The Southsiders' greatest hits 'Don't Leave Me'. Sauron changed it to 'Please Leave Me', slowed down the tempo and had Madison sing it in a gravelly sexy voice.

"This is about female empowerment," he said, his head bopping in time to the music. "I read about this Cal Scott. He didn't deserve you. Now we'll get revenge."

Madison was delighted. It was perfect. The song, with its catchy recognisable hook, would get tons of airtime.

The accompanying music video was Madison wearing black leather and stilettos with a male model on a leash.

Kevin, her father, was furious when he saw the video.

"*You're not releasing that!*" he yelled down the phone.

"Oh, just back off," said Madison calmly. "Stick to what you're good at. Never being around."

After a gruelling three months of promos and interviews, Madison flew back to Dublin. Peter, her bodyguard, had asked for the week off as he wanted to go on holiday with his daughter and her husband, so Todd had agreed to work straight through until his return.

She had given the rest of her entourage a few days off. She didn't need them when she was at home. It was a relief not to have her make-up done or her hair styled.

She had fired Emily two weeks before. She had grown sick of her constant chatter and she had grown sloppy. She needed someone on the pulse – someone who predicted what she wanted before she realised it herself. Dealing with Emily was like dealing with a child. She needed constant instruction.

Wearing big dark glasses and a beanie hat, Madison kept her head down and walked straight through Arrivals at Dublin airport. With Todd by her side, she looked conspicuous and people stopped and stared. A couple of young girls pointed and one squealed when she figured out who it was, but Madison kept walking. Mercifully, no one asked her for an autograph or a selfie. Soon she was sitting comfortably in a black tinted Mercedes, picked up by John that morning, and was heading south on the M50.

♫ ♫ ♫

Her mother was delighted to see her.

"Oh, Maddy, it's not the same around here without you!" She pulled her close, kissing her forehead repeatedly.

Madison allowed her to hug her. Louise always treated her a like a piece of precious china that could break at any moment. She had toyed with staying in a hotel in town but she knew her mother would have a fit if she didn't stay in her childhood room. Her dad was on location as usual so they had the house to themselves.

John had scanned the grounds and checked the CCTV at the gate. Now Todd checked the house before he allowed her inside. Even though people tended to leave her alone in Dublin, both men insisted on being thorough.

"Imagine if some nutcase kidnapped you because we got soft," Todd would say with a frown. "We must give one hundred per cent, ma'am. Always."

Louise Ryan was a pretty woman and spent a fortune on keeping it that way. At sixty-two years old, it meant regular trips to the hair salon for top-ups of dye, weekly facials and a strict regime of Pilates, organic food and a daily walk of three kilometres.

"Cliona called earlier," said Louise, gesturing for Madison to follow her into the sitting room. Bluebell the Labrador was asleep on the long leather couch. The drapes were open and the sunshine streamed in the large bay windows. The sea twinkled in the distance.

Madison flopped down on the couch next to Bluebell and rubbed her ears. "Is Clio at home?"

Louise nodded. "She wants you to ring her."

"Cool."

The Greatest Showman was on television. Madison

hummed along automatically.

"Daddy will be home in a couple of days." Louise brushed a stray lock of dark-brown hair behind her ear.

"That's great."

"He'd like to see you."

"Really?"

"Yes, Maddy. Stop being so difficult."

She raised a perfectly manicured eyebrow. "Don't tell me how to behave, Louise. I'm not thirteen."

Louise reddened. "It's just I hate how you two are around each other ..."

"It's his fault."

"Maddy!"

"I'm going upstairs to ring Clio." She stalked off.

Louise sighed. She was too old for tantrums. She had longed for a baby for so long, and when God finally granted her wishes, she had been so thrilled. She had been thirty-nine and on the verge of giving up. Fast forward over twenty years and she would never have dreamed how hard it would be. Madison had been strong-willed from the start. No matter how many times she had tried to discipline her and refuse her demands, she had always caved in. She simply wasn't strong enough to stand up to her.

Cliona called over to Madison's house an hour later. She lived about a mile down the road and so had walked. The October air was chilly so she wore a large jacket and scarf.

John stopped her at the gate. "Open your bag, please."

She obeyed, smiling.

"Sorry," he said gruffly, rummaging inside. "It's the drill."

"No worries," she said kindly. "I get it."

She walked up the tree-lined drive to the large house. The lights were on in the sitting room and the drapes were open. She could see the movement of the TV screen through the pane of glass.

The door was opened by Mina, the housekeeper, closely followed by Todd.

"Can I check your bag?" he asked.

She sighed. "Sure."

He opened it up and checked it thoroughly. Then, when she handed Mina her coat, he checked that too. He returned her bag just as Madison appeared from the kitchen.

"Clio!" Madison hugged her friend. "It's been ages."

Cliona hugged her back. "Great to see you. Happy belated Birthday. I sent you a message on Instagram but you never replied."

"Oh, I barely check that thing now. Bethany does it for me most of the time. What have you been up to?"

"Well, I did my finals."

"How did that go?"

"Oh, you know, okay." Cliona flicked her long hair over her shoulder. "I just need to find a job now."

"Do you want me to ask Dad?"

"Gosh, no." Cliona blushed. "I'll find something."

"I'm sure he'd let you tag along on some set somewhere."

"No, honestly. I'll make my own way."

Madison shrugged. "Suit yourself. Come into the kitchen. Mum has gone to Pilates so we have it all to ourselves."

There was a solitary glass on the gleaming counter. Madison went to the fridge and took out an open bottle of white wine.

"How was Stockholm?" asked Cliona, taking a seat on

a white-leather high stool.

Madison poured a glass of white wine and topped up her own glass. "Amazing. Sauron is so cool. He doesn't treat me like a teeny-bopper, you know. He sees me as an artist."

"That video is pretty racy."

"Yeah, Dad went mental. I told him where to go."

"You look amazing," said Cliona enviously. Madison seemed to have curves in all the right places, unlike her own body which was very slim.

Madison shrugged. "I work hard at it, Clio. This glass of wine is the first I've had in weeks. Ross is always banging on about calories."

"So, your new look is pretty gorgeous. Did Mona do that?"

"Yep. She's great, isn't she?"

"I'm waiting for you to shave your head. Then you will actually morph into Britney Spears."

Madison made a face. "Oh, whatever. You sound just like the tabloids."

"To be fair, you're mirroring her so far. Good girl goes bad sort of thing.'

"I'm not shaving my head anytime soon."

Cliona sipped her wine. "Fionn's home this weekend. He's back for Daddy's book launch."

Aonghus's new book was a new version of Irish mythology. It had taken him years to research and write but he had finally finished the summer before. Constance had read it over a weekend and, when she finished the last chapter, she took off her reading glasses.

"This is good, sweetheart. So good, in fact, it might pay for the new bathroom."

Madison smiled. "How is Fionn? God, it's been ages."

"Really well. He's in a band. They're doing quite well around London. Playing gigs and that."

"That's pretty cool." Madison looked impressed.

"I sent you YouTube clips of their songs. Did you look at them?"

"Oh, yeah, I did," Madison lied, who frankly wasn't interested in watching anything unless she was in it herself.

"He's taking a two-week break," continued Cliona. "Mum is thrilled. She loves when he comes home."

Madison said nothing but there was a faraway look in her eyes. Cliona's family was like a real family. Sometimes she envied her so much it hurt. If only she had a sibling! Being an only child had its advantages, but there was no one to rub off or argue with. Fionn and Cliona had always been close and, even though they fought like crazy over the remote control, they had each other's backs.

"Anyway, call over on Saturday," said Cliona, interrupting her thoughts. "Mum is cooking a big dinner in honour of his return. I know he'd love to see you. He asks how you're doing, you know. He's thrilled you're doing so well."

Madison paused for a moment. "I was going to go back to London. Dad is due back soon. Plus, there's only so much of my dear mother I can take."

"Maddy!"

"But I might wait. I haven't seen Fionn in years."

"At my 21st birthday party, remember? Before you became mega-famous and moved away."

"Oh yeah." She bit her lip. Life had been a non-stop whirlwind since then. She barely had time to sleep, let alone see old friends. "Fine, I'll stick around. It will be nice to catch up with my old enemy. Remember when he put chewing gum in my hair?"

"He denies it."

"He definitely did. Poor Louise nearly died when she saw it. I was rushed down to a hair salon to fix it." Madison giggled. "He was always mean to me."

"Aw, he loves you really," Cliona reassured her. "Look, you should stay over and we'll make a night of it."

"Todd will have to come too."

"That's grand. He can sleep on the futon." Cliona beamed. "It'll be like old times."

Madison smiled. "Like old times," she echoed.

Chapter Ten

On Saturday evening Madison knocked on the oak door of Cliona's house. Her driver had dropped her off wearing a large hooded jacket to conceal her identity. Her long blonde hair was instantly recognisable so she had it covered. Todd stood behind her, shielding her from the street.

Sorrento Terrace was built in Victorian times and was a row of majestic houses perched on a cliff. The view from each one was simply breath-taking: panoramic views of the Dalkey Sound with mountains in the distance.

Aonghus opened the heavy old door and windchimes blew in the breeze.

"Madison!"

"Hi, Aonghus!" She leaned up and kissed his cheek. Aonghus O'Connor was a handsome man for his fifty-five years. His sandy-brown hair was slightly grey and he had avoided the middle-age paunch that lots of men acquired later in life. Dressed casually in jeans and a blue sweatshirt, he looked younger than his age.

"Todd, I believe," he said, smiling at the burly man at

Madison's side. "Cliona said you would accompany our young star."

"You won't notice me," said Todd gruffly. "I'm good at blending into the background."

"Nonsense. You'll join us. There's plenty to go around. Constance always makes enough food to feed a small village."

He led them into the sitting room which was in its usual disarray. There were piles of books everywhere, empty glasses on the coffee table, crooked paintings on the wall and enormous red-velvet drapes hanging from a huge bay window looking out on the sea. The surfaces were all covered in dust and the old baby grand in the corner was laden down with old magazines.

A fire burned merrily in the grate of the large fireplace and the threadbare Persian carpet was covered in fluff. Constance's two cats – Greymalkin and Paddock – lay asleep on the sofa.

"Where's Cliona?" asked Madison, taking a seat on the armchair.

"She's gone to the DART station to pick up her mother." He pointed to the bottle of whiskey on the dresser. "Would you like one?"

Madison shook her head. "No, thanks. I'll have white wine if you have some."

Aonghus scratched his head. "Now, that's a good question. Our cellar could do with a good replenishing. We need to take the ferry to France and stock up."

He disappeared out the door and returned five minutes later with a bottle of Muscadet.

"It's not chilled. Will it do?"

Madison shrugged. "I don't mind."

Aonghus poured a generous glass of wine and handed to her.

"Todd? Would you like a drink?" Aonghus smiled at him.

"No, thank you, Mr. O'Connor. I never drink."

"God, how I wish I had your resolve." Aonghus took his tumbler of whiskey and sat in the armchair by the fire. "So Cliona tells me that you've just released your third album?"

She nodded. "Yes. The second single will be released next month."

"It's quite different to your usual stuff, isn't it?"

"Yes. It's better. The old stuff was always the same. Meaningless lyrics and a repetitive beat."

"I read that interview in *Poporama* magazine where you lambasted your previous songwriter. My word, you didn't hold back."

"Well, I'm rid of him now."

"I suppose you are." Aonghus regarded her thoughtfully. "You know that Fionn joined a band, don't you? They're doing quite well too. Social media really helps. YouTube is great for publicity."

"I suppose." She sipped her wine. "To be honest, I'm getting tired of all the publicity. I can't go anywhere anymore without being followed. There's always at least one photographer outside my apartment, waiting for me to appear. Even though I make a point of entering and leaving the building in a tinted car, they still wait, hoping to see something scandalous. I wish I could be invisible."

"Yes, fame is odd," he agreed. "You think that all the attention will be wonderful when, in fact, it becomes a real nuisance."

"My manager, Ross, hooked me up with really talented writers."

"Did you contribute?"

"Not really. I mean, I'm not a songwriter. I just sing."

"You should give it a go. Everyone knows that the real money is in the writing of songs. Look at that Adele girl over in England. She's doing very well."

"I suppose."

"You might produce a masterpiece."

Madison laughed. "I doubt that."

The door slammed and Constance, pink-cheeked after a wine-fuelled lunch with pals, arrived into the room with Cliona in tow.

"Winter has descended on us with her icy grip!" she announced theatrically. "I thought the train would never arrive at Pearse Street Station."

Her brown curls were pinned to the side of her head with an enamel comb and were streaked with grey. Once slim, she was now curvier and opted to wear long loose dresses that fell to her ankles. Bracelets and necklaces adorned her wrists and neck respectively, and her blue eyes were warm.

"Maddy, darling! Look at you! The last time I saw you, you were writhing around the ground in scanty clothes on the telly."

"That's my new video."

"Very exciting. I was blushing." She kissed her warmly. "You look thin, sweetie. Are you eating properly?"

Madison shrugged. "I'm not really allowed to eat anything with too many calories."

"Well, tonight will be an exception then. I don't do low-fat, I'm afraid." She accepted a glass of wine gratefully from her husband. "Fionn called. He's getting a taxi from the airport and should be here soon."

Cliona hugged Madison. "This is like old times. I'm so glad you stayed around."

"Me, too."

Fionn O'Connor had the height and stature of his father, but his face resembled his mother. He kept his brown hair short as it had a tendency to curl like Constance's unruly locks, and he shared her smiley blue eyes. Naturally quiet, he had the reputation of being a loner. He had friends but they were few, and he was fiercely loyal.

From a young age he had shown an interest in music. His parents bought him a *bodhrán* traditional drum for his fifth birthday and he had loved it. Constance noticed after a few weeks of incessant banging that he had rhythm and organised a few lessons with a local musician. The *bodhrán* was soon replaced with a drum set and Fionn would spend hours with earphones on, banging away to different songs. Constance would call him for dinner and he'd never reply, unable to hear over the din. She would appear in his bedroom door with a red face from climbing the stairs and pull the earphones from his ears.

Going to Guildhall was the best thing he ever did. It meant moving to London but he found that transition easy. In his first year he stayed in student accommodation and then moved to a small flat with a friend from his class called Dean. He liked city life and enjoyed his course. In those years he really developed his craft and one day he was introduced to a fellow classmate at Guildhall called

Caspian Cole, the lead singer of a band called Doctor Eckleberg which played gigs in local bars. Their drummer had just left and moved to South Africa, so they needed a replacement.

Over a pint, Caspian cajoled Fionn to take the drummer's place.

"Why Doctor Eckleburg?" Fionn asked Caspian.

"It's from my favourite book: *The Great Gatsby.*" Caspian swatted his blonde hair from his eyes. "There's a billboard of an oculist called Doctor T.J. Eckleburg whose huge eyes watch over the characters. He sees the truth in an artificial and shallow world."

Fionn nodded. "I get it," he said.

After a few sessions, Fionn found that he enjoyed jamming with the other talented members of the group: Ethan Hackett the bassist and Alexander Ryder the lead guitarist. Together, they wrote songs about the emptiness and disillusionment after the crippling financial crisis that had taken over the world a few years before. Caspian, a keen piano player, spent hours writing out sheets of music, a pencil in his ear as he amended notes and tried out different melodies.

Fionn stayed in the shadows, not interested in fame and fortune. He liked jamming with the band – that was all. Gigs and groupies and drug-fuelled parties weren't his thing. Caspian, the lead singer, got all the attention and he loved it. With his blonde good looks, he had an army of fans who screamed his name at gigs. His was the name that everyone remembered and it was his handsome face that was splashed across social media after a gig. This suited Fionn just fine. He didn't like being in the limelight. Being a drummer afforded him that privacy as people rarely knew who he was.

Fionn hadn't been home in two months. The band had embarked on a quick tour of England, Scotland and Wales where they had played small gigs in the main cities. Travelling was hard and all the venues rolled into one. Their mode of transport was a banjaxed old Volkswagen van and their equipment was second-hand. However, the tour was successful and they amassed more and more followers. Fans posted videos on YouTube and they got lots of hits and shares. Slowly they started to gain momentum and by the time they played their last gig in Cardiff, radio stations were starting to pick up on them. People wanted to know about Doctor Eckleburg. It was a slow burner, but they were headed in the right direction.

The taxi pulled up outside Fionn's childhood home and he handed the driver a fifty-euro note.

"Thanks, buddy," said the older man with a nod. "I'll just get your change." He reached into his pockets and rummaged around.

"Keep it." Fionn smiled at him and got out of the car. He hoisted his holdall bag onto his shoulder and walked up to the front door.

He lifted the large brass knocker and let it fall. It made a loud noise which reverberated through the house. Thirty seconds later, Constance heaved open the heavy oak front door. "*Fionn! My darling!*" She pulled him into her embrace.

"Hey, Mum!" He kissed her cheek. She smelled the same: patchouli oil mixed with lavender.

"I've missed you!" She ushered him inside. "Just head

in to the fire. It's very cold." The door banged behind them and the sound echoed through the entrance hall.

Fionn dropped his bag on the floor and walked into the sitting room. Cliona was sitting on the couch rubbing Greymalkin's ears and Aonghus was shovelling coal onto the fire.

"I just put dinner in the oven so it won't be long." Constance beamed at Fionn. "I made your favourite: beef stew."

Aonghus got up, brushed his coal-stained hands on his jeans, and pulled his son into a large bear hug. "Good to see you."

"Yeah, you too." He pulled back. "Wait a sec, is that my jumper you're wearing?"

Aonghus reddened. "Maybe. It was thrown in my wardrobe. Blame your mother."

Constance placed a bowl of salted pretzels on the coffee table. "Everyone knows I never do any washing. Cliona is clearly the culprit of this jumper debacle." She took a handful of pretzels. "Help yourselves."

Cliona made a face and Fionn laughed.

"Poor Cinderella. The more you do ..." He flopped down on the couch beside her. "Did you find a job yet?"

"Nope." She sighed. "I need experience. My CV is very basic."

"Then you need to go to London or America," he said practically. "That's where the money is."

"Maybe." Cliona took off her glasses and rubbed her eyes. She couldn't imagine living in Hollywood. Her face looked worried so her mother put a hand on her daughter's arm.

"Our paths are chosen for us," said Constance reassuringly,

sipping a replenished glass of wine. "What will be will be."

"No hurry," agreed Aonghus. "We like having Cliona around, don't we, Connie?"

"Of course."

"So are you all set for the launch, Dad?" Fionn accepted a glass of wine from his mother.

"Ah, yeah," said Aonghus. "It's only to mark the occasion."

"Mark it, my eye." Constance glared at him. "I've invited half of Dublin to this soirée."

"I told you I wanted something low key."

"You want this book to sell, don't you?"

"Maddy is here for dinner," said Cliona smoothly, changing the subject. "She's around for the weekend."

Fionn raised an eyebrow. "Maddy Ryan? God, I haven't seen her in years."

"She's based in London but came home to see her mother. I invited her over."

"God, who would have thought she'd make it so big?" Fionn shook his head. "That new song with Sauron is always on the radio."

"It was inevitable, really. She always had ambition."

Fionn paused to reflect. "You know, the last time I saw her was at your twenty-first birthday, Clio."

Suddenly Madison walked back into the room. She had been in the kitchen talking to Ross. Her hoodie had been discarded and she was wearing a pretty blue dress with black boots. Her blonde hair shone and she was smiling.

"Hey, Maddy!" Fionn gave a little wave from the couch.

"Fionn! It's been so long." She laughed and held out her arms. He got up and hugged her.

Constance laughed. "Would you look! It only seems like

yesterday that you were playing out in the garden with grubby knees."

"Or putting chewing gum in my hair," said Madison drily.

"You can't prove it." Fionn winked at her and resumed his seat on the couch. "I always knew Mads would make it. The way she used to dance around out back singing Madonna at the top of her voice."

"That new song you have out is very good," said Constance. "I'm humming it all the time.'

"That was a collab with Sauron. He wrote it."

"A what?" Aonghus looked puzzled.

"A collaboration, Dad," explained Cliona. "Sauron is the guy in Maddy's new video. He's a rapper."

"Oh." Aonghus raised his glass. "Well, ask this Sauron if you can put in your penny's worth the next time."

"Oh, I probably won't work with him again. It's a once-off thing. Like Jay Z and Rhianna."

"Right," said Aonghus. "I haven't a notion who they are either so let's move on."

Chapter Eleven

They dined on a delectable daube of beef. Fionn's parents were so easy to talk to as, with their laid-back attitudes and apparent *joie de vivre,* they put Madison at ease. She wished her own parents were so relaxed and accepting. Sometimes she felt like she was from another world. Kevin and Louise seemed to have nothing in common with her at all. She couldn't imagine her mother drinking wine and laughing loudly at her own stories. As for her dad? She couldn't remember the last time they all sat down as a family and broke bread together. He was always away.

Her parents had an odd relationship, that was for sure. Her dad was nearing sixty-five and had no plans to slow down. She often pitied her mother who essentially lived alone. She busied herself with lunches and yoga, but each evening she sat on that great big couch with just Bluebell for company. It was a big house with no one to share it with.

"Do you have a picture of this Sauron?" asked Aonghus conversationally, taking a big bite of his food.

"On my phone." Madison picked up her phone and

pressed the screen. Scrolling down, she found a promo shot of her and Sauron in Stockholm. "There, that's him." She pointed to a small black man with long dreadlocks in a gold suit.

Constance put on her glasses. "Oh, look. He's tiny, isn't he?"

"I love his style," said Aonghus. "He's very mod."

Madison giggled. "*Mod!* I love that word. My granny used to say it."

"I suppose the proper term is chic?"

"No, mod is fine!"

Constance took off her glasses. "Well done, darling. You look fabulous in that picture. Now, would you like more potatoes?"

Madison shook her head. "No, thanks. I've put on three pounds already this evening."

"You could do with it." Constance frowned. "You're a veritable Slinky Malinky." She helped herself to more mash. "Fionn, pet? More?"

He patted his stomach. "I'm grand, Mum. It was lovely."

Cliona held up her hand. "Not for me."

"So Fionn, tell me about your band." Madison flashed him a smile.

"It's called Doctor Eckleburg."

"Strange name."

"From *The Great Gatsby*. Eyes on a billboard staring down at the characters, seeing the truth, according to Caspian. He's the lead singer, formed the band about three years ago."

"That long?" she said in surprise. "So why aren't you famous?"

Fionn laughed. "Because we don't have Daddy calling up his buddies and pulling strings."

Madison stuck out her tongue. "Yeah, yeah. Go on."

"Caspian got his two best friends Alex and Ethan together and they started jamming at weekends."

"When did you join?"

"About a year ago. Their drummer left and they needed a replacement."

"They're really good," said Cliona proudly. "Especially Caspian."

"*Wooo!* Who fancies Caspian?" Fionn winked at Madison.

"I do not!" Cliona blushed madly. "I've only met him once for a millisecond. He doesn't even know my name."

"That's probably true," admitted Fionn. "He's on another planet most of the time."

"So, enough of the fancying Caspian talk, okay?" Cliona blushed a deep red.

"Who's your manager?" asked Madison, watching this exchange in amusement.

Fionn laughed. "Me, I suppose. I mean, we don't have an entourage if that's what you're asking."

"What? No agent or publicist?"

"No. It's just us."

"Do you write your own stuff?" asked Madison.

Fionn laughed. "As it happens, we do. Although it's Caspian who does most of it. He's a brilliant pianist. Isn't he, Clio?'

Cliona ignored him and drummed her fingers on the table.

"He plays piano?" Madison scoffed. "How lame! I don't get that instrument at all."

"You don't get it?" Fionn was incredulous. "So Paul McCartney and Elton John mean nothing to you?"

"Oh, leave me alone!"

"Anyway, to answer your question, Caspian does play. He's an unreal singer too. He reminds me of Thom Yorke from Radiohead."

Madison shrugged. "Haven't a clue who that is."

"Oh yeah, I forgot. You only listen to pop." Fionn smiled. "How about Coldplay? Have you heard of them?"

"Of course." She scowled. "I just don't like that depressing alternative-rock stuff."

"Then avoid our gigs then."

"I will." She sat back in her chair with a red face.

"More wine, Maddy?" asked Aonghus with the bottle poised.

"No, thanks." She shook her head. "Do you know how many calories are in one glass?"

Out in the kitchen, Constance spooned a second generous helping of stew on Todd's plate. He had refused to eat with the family, deeming it unprofessional, so she had set a place at the large kitchen table for him instead. Despite two attempts at pouring a glass of wine, he had opted for sparkling water instead.

"I never drink alcohol," he said firmly. "I have to be on the ball, twenty-four-seven."

Constance frowned. "I don't understand this security business. Especially when Madison is at home. Isn't it all a bit de trop? This constant protection? I mean, I saw Gabriel Byrne in the Merrion last week and he was all on his own."

"*De* what, ma'am?" Todd looked confused.

"Oh, of course. I mean, *too much*." Constance smiled. "What I mean is, isn't it all a bit over the top?"

Todd swallowed loudly. "No, ma'am. Not at all. Madison is right to be prudent. There's a psychopath around every corner."

"Really?" Constance looked sceptical. "What a depressing notion."

"Yes, ma'am. Remember when Kim Kardashian got robbed in Paris?"

"Not really."

"That was a bad day at the office for security." He took an enormous bite of stew.

"What's it like to be a bodyguard?" she asked, taking a seat. "It must be so exciting."

"It's a tough job but I love it." He sprinkled some salt on his mashed potatoes. "Madison's safety is my top priority."

"Where does one train to be a bodyguard?"

"Well, you have to have some form of special military training. Peter, Madison's other personal bodyguard, is ex-metropolitan police. I was a Navy Seal."

"Go away!" Constance looked impressed. "Like Steven Seagal in that movie."

Todd's mouth twitched but regained his deadpan expression almost immediately.

"Anyway," he continued, "your experience level is important. Obviously, the longer your resumé, the better. My alarm clock is set to play the James bond theme song, so I'm ready for action right away."

"Golly," said Constance in fascination. "So, have you had any close shaves? You know, with obsessed fans or anything?"

He shook his head. "Just that knife incident. We've only

had groups of teeny-bopper girls so far, so it's been pretty tame."

"Maybe that will change with the new Madison."

"Maybe. I mean, we'd love to guarantee safety, but sometimes it's not possible. There's only so much we can do. Social media is both a godsend and a curse."

"Why?"

"Well, it gives fans an idea of Maddy's location. They can track her. However, we can use it to our advantage too. I can send out fake Instagram posts of where she is, when in fact she's somewhere completely different. It keeps the paps and fans at bay."

"*Constance*?" shouted Aonghus from the dining room. "*When were we in Rome again*?"

"*2013!*" she called back. "*At Easter!*" She rolled her eyes. "Ten euros he's telling his Vatican story."

"Oh?"

"I'll tell you another time. It would take far too long." She winked. "Right. I'd better get back. I just didn't want to leave you out here all alone."

Todd patted his stomach. "Thank you for dinner, Mrs. O'Connor. This beef is awesome. As good as back home."

"Not at all, my love," she said warmly. "I just love a man who eats." She left the kitchen, closing the door behind her.

An hour later, no one could eat another bite. The cheese board had barely been touched and the brie was congealing from the heat of the fire.

"I'll stack the plates and take them to the kitchen," said Fionn, getting up.

"Sit down!" said Constance immediately. "Nothing ruins a dinner party more than cleaning up after it. I have buckets of time in the morning to clear it up."

Cliona made a face. "Yeah, right," she whispered to Fionn as he resumed his seat at the table. "Everyone knows who'll get landed with that job."

"I'll help," he whispered back, patting her arm.

Madison didn't even offer to help. She preferred to eat out when she was in London so she had little or no experience of washing pots or scraping off plates. When she was in Dublin, Mina or her mother did it.

She glanced around the room, taking in the dusty shelves and the black marks on the walls. "Why doesn't your mum hire a housekeeper?" she asked Cliona and Fionn in an undertone. "The place could do with a good clean. There are cobwebs all over the place."

Cliona reddened. "You know we couldn't afford someone every day," she said hurriedly. "Plus, I'm normally around to keep it someway presentable."

"Really?" Madison raised an eyebrow. "Your talents must lie elsewhere then."

"Don't be a bitch," said Fionn mildly. "We can't all be spoilt little princesses like some people around here."

Now it was Madison's turn to blush. "What do you mean by that?" she said in a hurt tone. "I was only trying to be helpful."

"A bit of filtering wouldn't go astray," he said kindly. "You have a sharp tongue sometimes. You've always had. Remember when I went through my rapper phase? You were pretty judgmental."

Madison laughed at the memory. "Oh, yes! I'd forgotten

that. You were like a skinny white version of Fifty Cent."

"Hey, less of the skinny." He pulled up his sleeve and flexed his bicep. "Drumming gives you guns like these."

"Very impressive," said Madison mockingly.

Cliona gently shoved Fionn sideways. "Hey, you're no angel. Remember all the teasing about Nerdy Gareth?"

Fionn guffawed. "Nerdy Gareth! Your first boyfriend! Ah, Clio, I couldn't help myself."

Madison burst out laughing. "Gosh, I'd forgotten about him. Thank God that fizzled out."

"Hey! He wasn't that bad," said Cliona hotly.

Constance raised an eyebrow. "Now, Clio. I don't like mean nicknames as much as the next person. However, it was a godsend that you saw sense there. He was tedious."

"*Mum!*"

Aonghus got up and pulled out a bottle of brandy from a cupboard by the window. "*Digestif*?" he offered.

Cliona shook her head. "No, thanks, Dad."

"Nor me," agreed Madison. "My dad loves the stuff. I hate the taste."

"Too many calories, I suppose," said Fionn innocently.

Madison made an 'L' loser sign on her forehead.

"You two are so cute," said Constance dreamily, accepting a balloon glass of brandy from her husband. "I always fantasised that you'd get married. You'd make a handsome couple."

"Stop that right now." Fionn pretended to choke.

"Fantasy is right," agreed Madison. "We'd murder each other."

♫ ♫ ♫

Aonghus and Constance went to bed half an hour later.

"I must take a pint of water with me," said Constance, rubbing her eyes. "I mean, I've been drinking all day if you count lunch with the girls."

"You're a lush, Ma," said Fionn cheerfully.

"Goodnight, all," said Aonghus with a wave. "Don't stay up too late."

"Put Todd on the futon, Clio," said Constance as she walked out. "Fill a hot-water bottle for the poor boy. He's likely to freeze in this weather."

Cliona saluted like a cadet. "Consider it done."

"Night!" said Madison, waving. "Thank you!"

The door closed with a click.

Cliona got up. "I'd better go and sort Todd out."

"He's in the kitchen," said Madison. "The last I saw he was playing Tetris on his phone."

Cliona automatically began to gather some plates to take to the kitchen.

"He's a saint," said Fionn. "Putting up with you all the time? I mean, it's a tough station being your shadow."

"Todd is devoted to me," she said hotly. "He's well paid too which helps."

"Still, I'm not sure I'd take a bullet for you," he said thoughtfully.

Madison gasped. "Shut up!"

"Would you two stop for a minute? It's exhausting." Cliona kicked the door closed with her foot as she exited the room.

Fionn drummed his fingers on the table and Madison watched him.

"So, tell me about your band," she said, sipping her water.

"I thought I did."

"You didn't say much …"

"There's not much to tell." He shrugged. "We play gigs and hope that someone will notice us." He looked up. "It's not moving fast, to be honest. Caspian is convinced we'll make it – he has unfaltering faith – but I'm not too sure. It's a tough industry, Mads, as you well know."

"Do you want to be famous?" she asked curiously.

He paused. "I don't really mind," he said honestly. "I enjoy playing with the band but I don't like the publicity side of things. In fairness, Alex does all the social-media side of it, but it's non-stop. Instagram, Twitter, Facebook. He's uploading stuff constantly."

"It's a great way to get known though."

"Maybe but, like our bickering, it's exhausting." He grinned.

"Ha, ha." She smiled. "I hope it works out for you."

"See you at the Grammys," he said with a wink.

Chapter Twelve

The next morning, Madison woke and stretched. The old house was quiet, so she stole down the stairs, not wanting to wake anyone. The stairway creaked and she held her breath as she gingerly put one foot in front of the other. Finally she made it to the bottom.

The kitchen was deserted, as was the sitting room. Empty glasses stood on the coffee table with the remnants of red wine at the bottom.

Staring out the large bay window, she congratulated herself for not overdoing it the night before. Lots of water and only three glasses of wine meant that she felt someway normal.

"Morning," said Todd, making her jump.

"Oh, Todd. You frightened me. Did you sleep well on the futon?"

He nodded.

She heard the stairs creaking again and then Constance swept into the room in a red silk dressing gown.

"Morning, Maddy!" she said warmly. "Morning, Todd, darling."

"Hi, Constance." Madison smiled warmly at her.

Todd nodded curtly.

"How's the head, my love?" asked Constance, shielding her eyes from the morning sun.

Madison smiled. "Really good. I didn't go too crazy."

"Ah, you're sensible. Bravo." She gathered the empty glasses and headed for the kitchen. "I was the opposite at your age. My God, the vodka I drank!"

Madison followed and took a seat at the large oak table. Constance filled the kettle with water and switched it on.

"Any sign of Cliona or Fionn? They'd sleep for Ireland, those two."

"No, it's just me down here." The cats meowed under the table, rubbing up against her leg. "Oh, sorry. And Paddock and Greymalkin."

"So, what's on the agenda for you now?" asked Constance, popping a teabag in a mug.

Madison sighed. "Back to London. A meeting with Calvin Harris. He wants to record a track with my vocals. Then on to New York for a concert."

"New York? Lovely."

"Then back here for Christmas, I suppose. Although part of me would prefer to go to the Bahamas or somewhere. Avoid the festivities altogether."

"Why, sweetheart?"

Madison looked away. "I just don't like Christmas."

"Really? Why?"

"It's a time for giving. The time of year you get your heart's desire." She looked up. "But what do you get a girl who has everything?"

Constance didn't answer her. She kept stirring her tea

contemplatively and squeezed the teabag on the side of the mug.

"Exactly," said Madison bitterly.

"So, why did you change your look?" asked Constance, changing the subject. "You're certainly sexier looking than before."

Madison shrugged. "I had to, Constance. I was so tired of the pink and blonde ponytail. I'm not finished yet. I might get rid of the blonde or cut my hair up short. I don't exactly know yet."

"But you're a natural blonde, aren't you?"

She nodded.

"Then don't touch it! God gave you that hair and you should cherish it. Most people in this part of the world spent small fortunes in a vain attempt to emulate such a colour, often with disastrous results. I mean, peroxide sales are booming, darling. You're like a Swedish girl, all exotic with no black roots and dried-out hair. Please don't dye it."

Madison smiled. "Well, if you put it that way ..."

"Maybe change your fashion sense. I mean, that exciting music video with the man on the leash was all very well, but it's been done before. I seem to remember Fionn having a yen for Britney Spears wearing that python around her neck and not much else. It's all expected in your genre, this breaking out and discarding the good girl image."

"So, what do you suggest?"

Constance paused to think. "You would make a gorgeous hippy. You know, long flowing skirts and hairbands. Youthful and pretty."

"It wouldn't suit my music."

"No, but you could steer your music in that direction.

The classics like 'California Dreamin" and 'Mister Tambourine Man' still get played for a reason. People like to idealise the sixties. It was a time of great change and revolution. It was an exciting time to be a woman. Go back, Maddy. Educate the young of today about the *belle époque*."

Madison raised an eyebrow. "I'll think about it."

"You do that. People are bored with seeing women writhing around in half nothing."

Cliona appeared first, without her glasses. She was wearing an oversized pyjamas which made her seem even smaller and her hair was tousled. Madison, who was on her second cup of tea, smiled at her. "You're so sleepy-looking, Clio. My God, you must have had twelve hours."

Cliona took a seat at the table and yawned. "It took me ages to get to sleep."

Madison stared at her thoughtfully. "You know, you're really pretty without your glasses. You should get contacts."

Cliona shook her head. "I'm scared of those things. I've heard horror stories about them getting lost in your eye."

"Lost in your eye? Ah, come on!"

"Yes, they go behind the eyeball and get infected."

Constance looked at her daughter. "Although, the glasses suit her. She looks so intelligent."

Fionn appeared in sweatpants and a T-shirt. His brown hair was untidy and he was barefoot. "I'd forgotten how cold this house gets." He shivered. "If I make money, I'll pay for proper heating to be installed."

Constance blew him a kiss. "So sweet."

He took out a carton of milk from the fridge and poured a large glass. Constance watched him.

"Are you hungry, love?" she asked. "You're looking very thin."

Fionn flexed his muscles. "I'm not thin. I'm in great shape. I just don't eat properly when we're on tour."

"I work out every day," sighed Madison. "After the mashed potatoes and beef stew yesterday, I'll have to do overtime at the gym."

"Poor Madison!" Fionn made a sad face. "Do you ever listen to yourself?"

"What do you mean?"

He rolled his eyes.

"I have lovely bacon and sausages from the market," said Constance, interrupting them. "Let me whip up a fry for you all."

"Nice one, Mum," said Cliona.

"Not for me," said Madison regretfully. "I'll stick with some fruit."

"You're doing overtime at the gym anyway, Mads. You might as well," Fionn teased.

"Nah, I'm going to go before the smell makes me crazy. I can resist most things, but bacon isn't one of them."

"Todd? Can I tempt you?" Constance smiled at him.

"No, ma'am. I'm perfectly fine."

Madison got up. "I should go anyway. I need to get back to London."

"Text me," said Fionn suddenly. "We should meet up. I live near King's Cross. You should come and see us play."

"Yeah." Madison smiled. "Maybe. I mean, it might do you some good to be seen with me. Raise your profile a little."

He grinned. "I'm in a reputable rock band. I can't be associated with a teeny-bopper Britney wannabe."

Madison stuck out her tongue. "I'm not a Britney wannabe!" She waved. "Bye, Constance. Thanks for all the food and company."

"Bye, Maddy. Mind yourself, okay?"

They hugged tightly.

Todd held up her bag. "I have your things," he said. "The car is outside."

"Great."

Cliona walked her out to the front door. "When are you flying back to London?"

Madison shrugged. "Tonight? Tomorrow morning? My manager booked it. I'll check my emails in the car."

"Keep in touch. I'll be here, unemployed, looking after my wayward parents."

"You should come and visit. We could take in a show."

Cliona sighed. "I'm skint, Mads. There's no way I'll be going anywhere for a long time. I have college debt and everything."

"Really? Jesus, your parents need to sort their lives out. They should be loaded and footing the bill for your studies. That's what parents do."

"I know, I know, but Mum wanted to go on a cruise around the Baltic and Daddy had to replace the car."

"Maybe he'll give you money from his new book sales."

"Maybe."

"Well, bye." She turned and walked down the footpath. Suddenly she stopped dead.

"Cliona!" she said, turning back abruptly. "Why don't you come with me?"

"What?"

"Be my PA! God knows I need someone trustworthy."

"PA? I don't know, Maddy. What would I have to do?"

"Organise my life. Travel with me. Keep me on the straight and narrow."

"Gosh, I don't know."

"Come on! We'd have a right laugh. I'd pay you well."

"I can't just up and leave."

"Sure, you can. You're perfect for the job. Remember how organised you were in school? I need you, Clio. I need the company." Her blue eyes beseeched her. "Please?"

"I'll think about it." Cliona bit her lip. "Give me time."

A dark cloud passed over Madison's face. She wasn't used to being refused.

"Maddy, I'll text you later." Cliona smiled reassuringly at her. "I promise. I just need to think."

"If you say no, you'll regret it." Madison turned and got into the car.

Todd banged the door, then got into the front seat and John drove off.

Cliona walked back inside the house and met Fionn in the hallway.

"Maddy just asked me to be her PA."

"What?"

"Her assistant."

"I know what a PA is." He whistled. "I'd say you'd earn it. She's spoilt rotten."

"It's not that. I'm used to her moods. It's Mum and Dad. Who would look after them?"

Fionn took her shoulders in his hands and shook her gently.

"Mum and Dad can look after themselves. You need to get out and live your life, Clio. No more baby-sitting them.

Take the job and travel. It would do you good."

She nodded. "You're right."

"You need to get out and live a little. Stop worrying about everyone else."

Chapter Thirteen

Caspian Cole led a charmed life. With his shoulder-length blonde hair and his dark-brown eyes, he was the perfect face for Doctor Eckleburg. Girls screamed his name at gigs and he had thousands of followers on Instagram, despite being relatively unknown. He had that star quality – that undefinable magnetism that some have without effort – and everything seemed to fall into place.

The only son of George and Prudence Cole, Caspian had been named after Prince Caspian in C.S. Lewis' famous Narnia series. His mother had loved the books as a little girl and had chosen the name, despite her husband's protests.

"Caspian? It's a poof name," he argued. "Call him a strong name like Arthur in honour of my father. He'll be teased with a name like Caspian."

But Prudence had been firm. "He is our little prince," she said. "It is a name worthy of him."

So Caspian it was, despite George's misgivings.

George Cole was the owner of a bus company who spent his time between London, Birmingham and Liverpool.

Originally from Sheffield, he was the son of a steel worker. He worked long hours to provide for his family. Prue hailed from County Tipperary in Ireland and was a former air hostess. Pretty and vivacious, she was the opposite to her staid husband. She enjoyed the theatre and devoured books; he liked to play golf and tend to his garden. Despite their differences, they were devoted to one another.

Prudence gave up her job when Caspian came along. He was their only child and she doted on him. When he woke at night crying for a bottle of milk, she was on hand to give it to him. When he fell and grazed his knees, she was there to clean it and put a plaster on the wound. She prided herself on being a hands-on mother and, as a result, she and Caspian were very close.

When Caspian was at school, he excelled at history, art and music. When the time came to choose a university, he agonised over his choice. His father wanted him to try for Oxford or Cambridge. He wanted the best for his son and expected him to read History or English Literature. However, Caspian had other plans.

As long as he could remember, he had loved music. His adoring mother had bought him a xylophone when he was a baby and he had banged it incessantly. Then, at the age of seven, he started piano lessons with a family friend. Within months he had skipped grades and received top marks in his music exams. At school, he loved music and got involved in the school shows and concerts. He auditioned and got the part of Jean Valjean in a production of *Les Misérables* in year eight, wowing the crowds with his haunting rendition of 'Bring Him Home'. He wasn't interested in reading History or English with toffs at a prestigious university. He was going to be famous.

His father had been disappointed. Caspian had so many more opportunities than he had as a boy and he couldn't understand why he would waste his time playing piano. He had worked every hour he could to provide a good life for his son and he was throwing it back in face, insisting on becoming a musician.

Prue had been more understanding. She realised that Caspian was strong-willed and would never back down. She gently encouraged George to let their son alone. "He'll find his own path," she said softly. "His talent is a gift from God and we should nurture it."

"He'll get nowhere playing piano, Prue. For God's sake, woman!"

"He'll be fine." She was adamant. "He's got to be happy."

So Caspian applied for the Guildhall School of Music and was accepted with flying colours. George, although disapproving, patted his son on the back. "Good luck with it," he said gruffly.

"I'll make you proud of me," Caspian replied, his brown eyes earnest. "Just wait and see."

Guildhall had been a fulfilling experience for Caspian. Naturally talented and full of energy, he had thrown himself into his course. Everyone noticed when he walked into a room. He had a presence that attracted attention straight away. When he, Alex and Ethan had first played music together, it was accepted that Caspian would be the lead singer. He had charisma and a confidence that emanated from him. Piano was his first instrument, but he could also play guitar. His voice had huge range and the music Doctor Eckleburg produced in the early days ranged from soul to hard rock. They experimented with different genres until they found their niche: alternative rock. Then Fionn came along – a talented drummer who was laid-back and easy to get along with.

After a whirlwind tour of England and Wales, they had all taken a couple of weeks off. Alex had gone home to his family home in Kent. Ethan had flown to Gdansk with his Polish girlfriend. Fionn had gone home to Dublin for his father's book launch. Only Caspian had stayed in London, writing songs until the sun rose, scrunching up sheet music only to smooth it out again. He was bursting with ideas – songs filled his mind constantly – and he just had to write them down.

His flat near King's Cross was on the fourth floor of an old red-bricked building. It had been renovated but still maintained that Victorian feel – high walls, a big bay window and a chiselled fireplace still remained. His father paid the rent, of course. Just until the band got settled. His mother had insisted. Caspian was happy with that. If he had a part-time job in some restaurant or bar, he wouldn't have time to write. A new dawn was beckoning – he could sense it.

The winter sunshine filtered through the half-closed curtain of his sitting room. It was a small room consisting of a two-seater couch, a multi-coloured rug on the floorboards and a piano crammed between an old mahogany dresser and the wall. He played the notes again, just to be sure. Then he scribbled down the melody in his notebook. Sitting back, he rubbed his neck. It was cramped after hours of bending over the keyboard and playing the same tune over and over again until he was pleased with it. The door opened and a girl walked in. She was wearing nothing except an old T-shirt of his she had found in his wardrobe. Her long black hair swung from side to side.

"I woke up and you were gone," she said in her posh voice.

He made an '*mmmm*' sound.

"I hate waking up alone in a strange place."

"Sorry," he said distractedly, rubbing out a B flat and replacing it with a G.

"It's nearly eight so I'd better go."

"Right, right." He tore his eyes away from the notebook. "Can I get you a cup of tea?" He prayed that she would refuse.

"No," she said tightly. "I'll just get my things and leave."

Caspian noticed the tone of her voice and jumped up. "God, sorry, Lila. I just lost track of time."

"Right."

"Let's go back to bed."

"I can't. I have an appointment in town."

He flicked his hair back. "I had fun last night."

She narrowed her eyes. "Fun? I guess you won't call me then."

"Don't be like that. I told you, it's impossible with the band and all."

"Sure. Impossible." She left, slamming the door.

Caspian turned back to the piano. He couldn't focus on anything else. Lila would have to realise that nothing came before his art.

At the next band practice, Caspian produced his new songs.

"They're in their infancy, but I think they have potential." He sat at the piano and played an arpeggio, his hands moving effortlessly over the keyboard.

"What are they about this time?" asked Ethan, tuning his guitar. "Global warming? Brexit? It has to be something about saving the world."

Caspian ignored him. "Right, this is it." He started to play gently with his right hand. Then he started to sing. Fionn sat back in his chair and listened as Caspian's voice soared above them all. The song seemed to be about combat. After the first verse, Caspian stopped.

"What do you think?"

"Is it about war?" asked Alex.

"Yes, but metaphorically about the internal battle we fight every day." Caspian ran his fingers through his long hair. "You know, trying to be good people."

"Right." Alex caught Ethan's eye and they smirked.

"I like it," said Fionn. "It's catchy."

"It's how we deal with the conflict – how we survive – that's the key." He played the melody again. "Good must overcome evil."

"On what level? Is it like when you're on a diet and you see a doughnut in the shop but you resist and get a quinoa salad instead?" asked Alex.

Caspian waved him away. "Stop taking the piss."

Fionn picked up his drum sticks and tapped them together. "Right, let's figure this out. Play it again, Caspian."

Caspian played the opening notes. Alex joined in with a basic riff and Ethan started to play around with harmonising. Fionn waited until the chorus before he started tapping the cymbals gently. The song ended.

"That wasn't too bad actually," admitted Alex, tuning the E string on his guitar slightly.

"It's really good," said Fionn. "Nice one, Casp."

Caspian shrugged. "It's a beginning. We have a long way to go for perfection."

Chapter Fourteen

Cliona's first week was hectic. Madison insisted that she stay at her apartment in Mayfair which was a large three-bedroomed penthouse.

"You take the guest bedroom for the moment," she said. "It's not as big as my room, but it'll do."

Cliona's eyes widened when she saw her room. It was all white with a huge bed. The sheets were soft and there was a palatial bathroom attached. Compared to her draughty cold room at home, it was luxurious.

"This is amazing," she said in awe, gazing at the smart TV on the wall and the walk-in wardrobe.

Madison shrugged. "It's grand. I just got the place renovated so at least it looks fresh. Right, I'm going to bed. I've a meeting with my manager first thing and I need you with me."

Cliona smiled. "No problem."

"Be prepared, Clio. My life is a whirlwind and you'll have to keep up. Your job is to keep things running smoothly. Our friendship will not be a factor – this is strictly business, okay?"

"Okay." Cliona smiled. "You're a bit scary though, you know."

Madison laughed. "You must be used to that by now. We've been friends forever, Clio. You know what I'm like."

Madison immediately bought her the most up-to-date iPhone and a pager.

"Never turn these off," she ordered. "I might need you at any time."

Cliona nodded. "I won't."

"Todd or Peter are assigned to me at all times. There's John the driver and a woman called Agnieszka to clean. Giorgio is my chef. You've met Mona and Angelica. They're in and out, depending on my schedule. I also have a security team that I hire to travel with me to big events. For example, if I have an interview on telly or whatever, they'll put the studio in lockdown until it's deemed safe."

"Really?" Cliona looked surprised.

"Yes, really. There are nutjobs out there, Clio. The best advice my absent father ever gave me was to hire a professional team of heavies to protect me. It helps me sleep at night."

"How is your dad?"

"God knows. He messages me once a fortnight if I'm lucky."

"Where's he filming at the moment?"

"I don't know. Cambodia or somewhere?" She looked at her suspiciously. "What do you care? Don't even dream of leaving me to go volunteer on his set, okay?"

"I won't, Mads. I'm just interested. Film is my thing."

"Not anymore. My happiness is your thing. From now on you have to live and breathe my life and make it as problem-free as possible."

"Of course." Cliona blushed. "Forget I mentioned anything."

"Anyway, I'm due to fly to New York next Tuesday to meet with James Corden. He wants me to do *Carpool Karaoke*."

"What?" Cliona clapped her hands. "Brilliant!"

"Oh, he insisted I fly to LA. but I said no. We eventually agreed on New York. Pack a bag as you'll be coming with me."

"Cool! I love that. Are you excited about singing with him?"

"I'm not sure." Madison frowned. "Do I really want to sing 'Text Me Back' and all those stupid songs? I think I should wait for my newer, cooler stuff but Ross won't listen. He thinks the time is now. All the greats have sat in his car – Adele, Mariah, Bieber. I have to join the list."

"Well, people know your old songs," said Cliona carefully. "That's what they want to hear. Would it be so bad to sing them?"

"Yes. They're awful and not what I want to sing."

"Look, see how it goes."

Madison raised her arms and started plaiting her hair.

"We'll be staying at the Plaza. Make sure they put white orchids there and only Evian water. I also want a treadmill, cinnamon Oreos and a full body massage as soon as I arrive."

Cliona typed furiously on her phone.

"I don't want a fruit bowl and make sure the sheets are over 1000 thread count."

"Right."

"And I want Arpeggio Nespresso capsules – decaff ones,

too. And the fridge to be stocked with cubed melon pieces in biodegradable cartons."

"Anything else?"

"A room looking out on Central Park. It has to have a view of the park."

"Is that it?"

Madison paused to think. "For the moment."

They flew to America in a private jet. Ross, her manager, rang Madison and bawled her out for such an extravagance. "You've got to be eco-friendly," he told her. "It's hot right now. Private jets are something you should avoid. Global warming, Maddy. We've got to harness its potential to sell records."

Cliona had never been on a private jet before and was enchanted by the champagne and the leg-room. There was a huge bathroom and a bedroom with a double bed.

"Mum and Dad are budget airline people," she said, gazing at the leather seats and the enormous flat screen television. "We don't even pay for priority boarding and we never book in a bag."

"How awful!" Madison rubbed her hands with lavender cream. "I can't get over your parents sometimes. I mean, they're always broke. What the hell do they do with their money? They must be so clueless."

"*Hey!*" said Cliona loyally, her cheeks reddening. "Don't talk about them like that."

"Sorry, Clio." Madison patted her arm. "I just feel sorry for you, that's all. I mean, my parents aren't perfect but at least they didn't make me fly on a budget airline."

Cliona grinned. "Fair enough."

Todd was sitting near the cockpit, his huge body almost too big for the seat. Mona, Angelica and Bethany sat together, all reading magazines or books on an iPad.

Madison got up and picked up her eye-pads. "I'm going to take a nap, okay? Don't let anyone disturb me." She headed into the bedroom and shut the door.

Cliona nodded. "I'll just watch a movie." She pressed the remote control and accessed the menu.

Watching films was her idea of heaven. She saw it with a director's eye – she understood the mise-en-scène and why certain props were put in specific positions. She noticed small things like the lighting and the music and the subliminal messages conveyed through camera angle. It gave depth to anything she watched – the conventions of each genre easily recognisable.

Her years at university had been wonderful. Even though she had lived at home with her parents, it hadn't made a difference. She was never one for social events, preferring to stay in and read a book than head to a nightclub in town. She was nerdy and she liked that. She wasn't interested in shots of tequila and wearing heels. She was comfortable in her own skin.

It was obvious that she would never look as good as Madison. She was unremarkable with her straight brown hair and bespectacled eyes. Why try to compete when there were a million other girls who looked so much better?

A steward appeared.

"All okay, ma'am?" he asked, flashing brilliant white teeth.

Cliona took a sip of champagne. "Perfect!" she said, really meaning it.

Chapter Fifteen

Six weeks later, back in London, Cliona woke one morning and stretched. Automatically she reached for her phone to check if Madison had texted or called during the night. The screen was mercifully blank. She relaxed and placed the phone on the bedside locker once more.

The double glazing kept out the hum of traffic from the street outside so she luxuriated in the soft bed, closing her eyes and sighing in contentment.

Working for Madison was unpredictable, tiring and stressful, but she loved the excitement. One day they could be watching Netflix on the couch – and the next? An impromptu trip to Berlin. She had a gruelling schedule and was always on the promotion train.

Privately, Cliona felt sorry for Madison sometimes. There never seemed to be any time to enjoy herself. Even when she did have down time, she was under strict instructions not to eat too many carbs and to be well-behaved in public. The constant voyeurism of social media was exhausting – Madison refused to leave the house without styling her hair or without make-up.

"It would be the one day a pap would take a horrible photo and splash it across the world," she said grumpily. "They just love to catch you off guard."

Cliona rarely had a day off as her timetable was as haphazard as Madison's. Wherever her friend went, she went too. She missed her parents a lot – Constance texted her constantly, sending her pictures of the cats and asking questions like how to work the hoover. Aonghus kept asking her to pop home for a weekend but, such was her job, she couldn't commit.

The first few weeks were the hardest. She didn't have any contacts and had to learn all Madison's quirks on the job. How she liked her latte, how she hated black pepper on anything. Frantically she took notes and tried to remember all the little details but inevitably she made a mess of things in the beginning.

"*Clio!*" Madison screamed down the phone. "Why the hell am I having a facial when I clearly stated that I needed a pedicure?"

Fionn had called and called, inviting her over for dinner or to a gig. He was delighted that his little sister was in the same city as him. Again, she couldn't accept. Any night off she had could be disrupted by Madison. Did it annoy her? Sometimes. However, she had been warned about that aspect of her job and she didn't say anything.

London was a great city – she enjoyed zipping here and there, getting to know the streets and shortcuts from A to B. Madison paid her well and encouraged her to buy new clothes and get her eyebrows done. She quietly refused, quite happy with her jeans and T-shirt. Her eyebrows were thick but not bushy and she couldn't face waxing the sensitive skin. She didn't get the lengths people went to for grooming purposes. Fake tan, threading, body wraps. It was all a mystery. Being comfortable was her main objective.

She stretched. Sunday morning should mean a relaxed day off, but she steeled herself for a change of plan. She wound her long brown hair into a messy chignon and tied it with a black bobble. Her oversized tartan pyjama pants and Fionn's old Nirvana T-shirt made the perfect bedtime ensemble. Opening her bedroom door, she headed for the kitchen, her stomach rumbling. Unbeknownst to Madison, she kept a stash of brioche and real Irish butter in a small cupboard over the fridge. She had hidden it behind the porridge oats. A cup of coffee and a slice of buttery sweet toast sounded great.

Madison was sitting at the breakfast bar of the enormous kitchen when she walked in. She cursed silently. Now she would have to wait for her secret treat.

"Morning," said Madison, eating cubes of melon and drinking iced water. "I hope I didn't wake you when I got home last night."

The previous evening, Madison had gone out for dinner with Tim Kinnear so Cliona had availed of her free time and had watched the latest season of *Game of Thrones* on Sky boxsets.

"Nope, I slept like a baby. How was the date?"

Madison made a face. "It's not working out."

"Oh?"

"He's just so one-dimensional, you know? All he talks about is himself."

Cliona hid a smile and poured a glass of orange juice.

"Where did you go?"

"To a club. I ended up faking a tummy-ache and leaving."

"So, bye bye, Tim?"

Madison nodded. "For sure. There's room for only one superstar and that's me."

Suddenly they heard the ringtone of Cliona's phone from her bedroom. She jumped up.

"I'll just get that."

It was Fionn.

A few minutes later she went back in to Madison.

"That was Fionn. He's invited me to a gig tonight. His band are playing. Do you think you'll need me?"

"I shouldn't think so. I mean, it's Sunday and I've nothing on."

"I've only ever seen him play once so it would be great."

Madison frowned. "Where's it on?"

"Soho."

"Maybe I'll come with you. Then you'll definitely have a night off."

Cliona raised an eyebrow. "A night off? With you around?"

"Ha, ha." Madison stuck out her tongue. "Look, I'll dress down. You know, jeans and an oversized T." She giggled. "Like you, actually."

"Thanks."

"Todd will have to come but I'll tell him to blend in. It'll be exciting." She beamed. "Don't tell anyone, and I mean, *anyone,* that I'm coming with you. We can't risk a security breach."

"It's just a gig. I'm sure it'll be fine."

"Clio!"

"Fine. I'll say I need three tickets for me and some pals, non-specific of course."

"It'll be fun."

"And you won't be bossy?"

"I promise." Madison crossed her heart.

Borderline was an alternative music space tucked away on Manette Street in Soho. John parked the Mercedes on Tottenham Court Road and, leaving Todd in the front seat, he vacated the car and disappeared up the street.

"He knows the owner," said Madison. "He called there today and had a chat with her. Now, he's just checking one last time."

Cliona said nothing. She just stared out the car window. Sometimes she wondered if it was all a bit much. She was pretty sure that no one at the gig would recognise Madison and if they did she didn't think they'd really care. Doctor Eckleburg's music drew a different type of crowd to Madison's fans.

Cliona had opted for the comfortable look – her hair was scraped back with an elastic band and she was dressed in jeans and a Harry Potter T-shirt.

Madison had berated her during the car journey. "You look about twelve!" she complained. "With the glasses on, you really take the biscuit. There's no way you'll get served, not to mind get into the club."

Fifteen minutes passed and then John reappeared. "All clear," he said to Todd.

"Okay." Todd got out.

Madison pulled up her hood and pulled her scarf up around the bottom half of her face. Her jeans were tucked into tall Ugg boots and her blonde hair was completely concealed.

Todd held open the door of the car as she and Cliona got out. The streets were packed with people and London glowed with streetlights and neon. No one noticed as they walked up the street, Madison with her head down in case anyone recognised her.

"It must be such a buzz for you to go incognito," said Cliona as they turned towards Orange Yard.

"I can think of other words," she replied drily.

Cliona approached the woman selling tickets.

"Hi, there," she said smiling. "There should be an envelope with three tickets there for me. Cliona O'Connor."

"Here you are," she said in a Yorkshire accent. "Complimentary."

"Where are the band?" Cliona peered into the darkness of the club.

"They're in the back," answered the woman. "They'll be starting soon."

The venue was small and dark with strings of fairy lights illuminating the stage. Long red drapes concealed the back stage area and a guitar on its stand was lit up. A keyboard was on its right and a drum kit was at the back. There were about twenty people standing around drinking beer and chatting.

Todd scanned the room and ushered Madison behind him. "I'm not sure I like the clientele here," he said gruffly.

"Oh, relax, Todd. John checked it out." Madison took out a twenty-pound note and pulled at Cliona's sleeve. "Look, I know I said I wouldn't boss you around, but will you go to the bar?"

Cliona nodded.

"I'll just melt into the shadows until the music starts."

"Grand. Do you want a beer?" Cliona looked at both Madison and Todd.

Todd shook his head. "I don't drink."

Madison shook her head. "Just a soda water. Beer is so fattening."

"Maddy!" Cliona put her head to one side. "It's our night off. Have some fun, for God's sake!"

"Fine, I'll have a gin and tonic then."

"Okay, that's better."

"*Slimline tonic!*" she added, calling after Cliona's retreating back.

Fionn peered out from behind the curtain. "Ah, my little sis is here. Cool." He narrowed his eyes. "And someone with their hood up, looking conspicuous." He grinned. "It's Maddy! I guessed the extra tickets were for her."

Alex looked up. "Maddy?"

"Madison Ryan. Remember? I told you that Clio's her new PA. I should've guessed that she'd come."

"*Text me back! Baby, baby ...*" sang Alex in a high voice.

"Exactly." Fionn started to laugh.

Caspian was warming up his voice in the corner.

"Madison Ryan is here, incognito," Ethan informed him, but Caspian took no notice. Instead, he focused wholly on his vocal scale.

The woman who gave Cliona the tickets popped her head in the door. "Ten minutes?"

Ethan gave her a thumbs up. "Casp! Did you hear that? Ten minutes."

Caspian nodded.

"I'll just pop out and say hi to Clio." Fionn disappeared behind the curtain and bounded down off the stage. Cliona was just back from the bar and sipping a bottle of Heineken.

"Hey, it's great that you made it." Fionn punched her playfully on the shoulder. "I didn't think you would."

"Well, it's my first night off in ages."

"Who's your friend?" asked Fionn, winking in Madison's direction.

"Shut up, Fionn," said Madison, making a face.

"Anyway, we're starting in five minutes," said Fionn. "Scream loudly and make us look popular."

Cliona kissed his cheek. "No bother."

Madison half-waved. "Try and play some upbeat stuff. I can't handle too much doom and gloom."

"Like 'Text Me Back'?" he said innocently.

She pulled down her scarf indignantly. "Don't mention that!"

"See you later." Fionn ambled off and then turned back.

Cliona sipped her beer. "Don't mind him. Let's enjoy the music."

"I'll try my best."

Chapter Sixteen

Ethan was first on stage. He picked up his guitar and adjusted the strap so that it rested comfortably on his shoulder. His dark-brown hair was tousled and his beard needed a trim. He had studied finance for while at King's College, but then had dropped out, hating the course. His parents had been suitably annoyed – they had wanted an accountant for a son – and when he agreed to play guitar in Caspian's band, their annoyance had turned to fury.

"*A band? Are you joking?*" his father had yelled. "Make your own way, son. This gravy train is finished."

So, he had moved in with Alex, the bassist, and he worked in a coffee house in Chelsea to make ends meet. His Polish girlfriend, Stella, spent most of her time in the flat too. They had been inseparable for two years. He had invited her to the gig but she couldn't make it, as she had to work instead.

Alex walked out next, his auburn hair gleaming in the lights. He didn't have pale skin and freckles like the quintessential redhead – instead, he had sallow skin and brown eyes. The Titian colour of his hair made him stand out and he was popular with the opposite sex. He had studied music with Caspian and Fionn at Guildhall and was the original founding member of the band. His parents were one-hundred-per-cent supportive. They owned a small farm and Alex had grown up with homegrown food from the garden, moon charts on the wall and free-range eggs in the morning.

Fionn appeared next, his sweatbands on his wrists and around his temple. He flexed his biceps as he took a seat at the drum kit, preparing them for the workout that was to come. He picked up his drumsticks and waved one at Cliona and Madison. With his right leg, he pressed the kick drum, checking the sound. The bass sound echoed through the room.

A crowd started to gather at the foot of the stage and the buzz of conversation hummed loudly. Madison, huddled close to Todd, sipping her gin and tonic furtively. People gave her strange looks as she was still hooded, but she didn't care. Anything was better than being recognised.

Ethan checked his microphone. "*Testing, one, two.*"

"Is he the lead singer?" Madison asked Cliona curiously.

"No. The lead singer is blonde. Remember? I sent you clips from YouTube."

"Oh, yeah. Right."

"*Testing, one, two.*"

"You saw them play in Dublin a few months back, didn't you?" asked Madison.

Cliona nodded. "At Vicar Street. It was so good."

She had only met the band once, that time Doctor Eckleburg played in Dublin. Fionn had invited her along but she had only stayed for a couple of hours as she had her finals coming up at college. After a brief introduction where she was called 'Fionn's little sis', she had melted into the background, content to watch Fionn's friends from a distance. Alex had been friendly, asking about her film work and telling her about his Dad's old Nikon that he used for birdwatching. Ethan had asked her for a light and then disappeared outside for a cigarette. However, when she was introduced to Caspian, she didn't know what to say. He was like someone from a movie – she searched for a flaw but couldn't find one. She blurted out that she loved C.S. Lewis and Prince Caspian was her favourite character, and he had smiled absentmindedly and walked away, forgetting her existence immediately. Fionn, noticing her red face, immediately started to tease her – "*Clio and Caspian up a tree, k-i-s-s-i-n-g*" – and she had reddened even more. Of course she didn't fancy him. She was a four and he was a ten plus on the gorgeous scale. There was no point even dreaming about it.

Suddenly the curtain on stage was pulled back and Caspian walked out. His blonde hair was slicked back, showing his beautiful bone structure. He was dressed in black jeans and a purple T-shirt with *I Am The Walrus* printed on the front.

Cliona stared up at him as he dislodged the microphone from its stand. Again she was entranced by his beauty.

Madison was equally as gobsmacked. She pulled back her hood to get a better look.

Todd immediately stood in front of her, but she pushed him away.

"*Who the hell is that?*" she whispered to Cliona.

"Caspian Cole. He's the lead singer."

"Is he the guy you fancy?"

"*No!*" Cliona almost shouted. "For the millionth time, that was just Fionn messing around."

Madison stared up at Caspian. The way he carried himself was so haughty – like he was a king. Instantly she was attracted to his arrogance.

"Good evening," he said in his deep voice. "Great to be here at Borderline."

The crowd whooped and he nodded at Fionn. After three counts of the drumsticks, Ethan took the cue and played a melody. Alex joined in and then Caspian started to sing. His voice was gentle to begin with and battled with the instruments. However, when it got to the chorus, it gained momentum and soon he was walking back and forth across the stage. Madison was enraptured and she gazed at him as if she were hypnotised.

"You must introduce me," she said in awe. "As soon as possible."

Cliona sighed. It was inevitable that she would want him. He ticked all the boxes.

"Of course. Anything you want."

After the third song, Caspian took a seat at the keyboard.

"Right, a real piano is preferable, but I've got to make do." He smiled and it transformed his face.

Madison couldn't take her eyes off him. Cliona bought another gin for her and she drank it without thinking.

The melody was in a minor key and Caspian's fingers flew up and down the keyboard before he started to sing. The remainder of the band remained still, clothed by darkness.

"*You seem uneasy, you seem upset, it's been the same, since we met.*"

Soon he was singing in falsetto.

"*Question marks, align with the stars, where will we go from here?*"

Cliona watched him intently. His voice made her hairs stand on end. Even though he had gelled his long hair back off his face, an obstinate lock broke free and fell over his eyes. Every now and then he'd flick it away only to have it fall back into place almost immediately.

There was a piano solo in the middle, one where he bent his head in concentration and his fingers moved like lightning. One particular part was thundering, lots of bass notes and fortissimo. Then, with his right hand, he crept up and played a series of treble notes only, and started to sing once more.

"*I would stay here, I would follow you, don't walk away, don't be so cruel.*"

The song came to an end. There was a moment of silence and then the crowd erupted.

"*Bravo!*" shouted one enthusiastic woman on Cliona's right.

There was a young Indian girl right up the front, clapping madly. "*Well done, Caspian!*" she called, her pretty face beaming at him. He stood up and bowed. Then he bent down, took the Indian girl's hand and kissed it.

The crowd roared in response. Alex raised his eyes to heaven and Ethan did the same. Fionn slammed the High Tom drum with his stick and Caspian jumped.

"Get up and sing, for God's sake!" said Alex. "Chat her up later."

"Yeah, move it, Casanova," agreed Ethan. "We've a big set list to get through."

The gig ended after two encores. The crowd started to disperse as the band packed up their gear.

"Great, boys!" said the owner. "You sounded great. Let's talk about another booking, yeah?"

Caspian zipped up the bag that held his keyboard and placed it carefully on the ground. Then he stacked up his sheet music and slipped it into a side pocket.

Madison watched the young girl Caspian had singled out. She was loitering by the stage, her face earnest and hopeful.

"Give me a hand there, Casp," said Fionn, heaving the kick drum.

"Sure, of course," he answered, walking towards him.

"My kid sister's waiting for me outside," said Fionn, heaving the drum. "I told her that we'd get a drink somewhere. Do you want to come?"

Caspian eyed the Indian girl who was standing shyly by the door.

"I've other plans, mate. Some other time."

"Cool. Thanks for the help."

Caspian walked away and jumped down off the stage. He sauntered up to the girl and smiled.

"Are you waiting for someone?" he asked.

She shook her head wordlessly.

"I'm Caspian."

"I know," she said in a soft voice. "I'm Preeta."

"Preeta? Pretty Preeta."

"Oh!" She giggled.

He smiled lazily. "So, maybe we could ..."

He didn't get to finish his sentence. Todd tapped him on his shoulder and boomed, "Someone would like a word."

Caspian looked surprised. "And you are?"

"She's over here."

"Just one moment," said Caspian apologetically to Preeta. "I've no idea who this guy is ..."

Madison walked up and pulled back her hood, revealing her long blonde hair.

"Hi," she said with a bright smile.

"Madison Ryan," said Preeta in astonishment. "Are you the real Madison Ryan?"

"Your gig was great," said Madison, ignoring her and talking directly to Caspian. "Fionn is an old pal of mine actually."

Caspian stared at Madison for a moment. "Are you that singer with Sauron?"

"Well, Sauron is that singer with me actually," she said with an edge to her voice.

"Right."

Madison stared at him, unsure of what to say. He didn't look remotely star-struck or intimidated.

"Anyway, nice to meet you," said Caspian politely and then he turned back to Preeta. "Let's go and get a drink, shall we?"

Madison watched open-mouthed as he walked off with the other girl. She couldn't quite believe it. She stalked off towards the back door, past a surprised-looking Ethan. She found Cliona and Fionn outside, heaving the drum kit into the van. Both of them were laughing as they struggled to get it inside.

"What's the deal with Caspian?" she asked, interrupting them.

Fionn raised an eyebrow. "Well, hello to you too."

Madison scowled. "He's so rude."

"Oh?"

"He barely spoke to me and then took off with this other girl."

"So?"

She paused. What was her problem exactly? Was she angry because he didn't fawn all over her like everyone else? Did it irk her that he seemed uninterested?

"It's just ... it's just ..."

Fionn regarded her thoughtfully. "You fancy him and you're mad because he didn't fall at your feet, am I right?"

"No!" said Madison, blushing madly.

"My God, the Caspian Fan Club has increased by one. First Clio here and now you, Maddy."

Cliona pushed him gently. "I don't fancy him. Stop it."

"Nor do I," said Madison haughtily. "He's rude and arrogant and thinks he's God's gift."

"*Whoa*, you've only just met him."

"I know his type." She turned around and put up her hood. "Todd? Let's move. I need my full eight hours." She put on her shades once more. "Cliona? Are you coming?"

Cliona shook her head. "I'll stay with Fionn for a while."

"Suit yourself. See you tomorrow."

She walked away purposefully, Todd in tow.

Fionn locked the door of the van. "How do you put up with it on a daily basis? Maddy's cool and all, but full time? I'd go crazy."

♫ ♫ ♫

Alex and Ethan joined them for a drink in a late bar. Fionn bought three beers and bottle of Heineken for Cliona.

"How's Mum and Dad?" he asked when he sat down.

"Fine, I think. Mum calls me every night, asking me for a detailed account of my day. Dad is busy with his biography on Beckett. They're off to Tunisia for a week next month."

"They call you a lot more than they call me," he said.

"Count yourself lucky. It feels like I haven't left. One minute Mum is texting about the neighbours, the next she's live-texting through *My Kitchen Rules Australia*, asking my opinion. She has to realise that I have a life now."

"She just misses you, that's all."

Alex took a long drink of his beer. "The gig was good. Not our best, but good."

Ethan nodded in agreement. "We were off towards the end."

"Yeah," agreed Alex.

Fionn shrugged. "I thought it went well."

"I thought it was amazing," said Cliona honestly. "I loved it."

Fionn grinned. "Ah, but Caspian could be singing 'Old McDonald Had a Farm' and you'd think it was worthy of a Brit award."

Alex laughed. "What is it about Caspian? He's a lady-magnet."

Cliona blushed furiously. "I don't fancy him at all. Fionn is always messing around. Don't take any notice."

Ethan's phone started to ring. "Stella? Yeah, we're almost finished. Yeah, see you soon."

"Is she at our place?" asked Alex.

Ethan nodded. "She's just back from work."

"What does she do?" asked Cliona.

"She's a waitress at TGI Fridays." He finished his beer. "I'm going to head back. I'm pretty tired and I've an early start."

"I'll have another here," said Alex. "Three's a crowd back at the flat, if you get what I mean." He got up. "Fionn? Cliona? Another round?"

They nodded.

Ethan waved goodbye. "See you again sometime," he said to Cliona.

"Bye!" she said warmly.

Fionn's phone pinged. He checked the screen. "It's Mum. She wants to know if we met up."

Cliona pulled out her phone. "There are about ten messages! Damn! I didn't check my phone all night."

"Let's send her a selfie," he suggested. "Take off your glasses. They'll reflect in the flash and you'll end up looking like a Jawa from *Star Wars*."

Cliona did as she was told and placed them on the table. "Gosh, I'm blind without them," she said. "You're a fine big blur."

Fionn stretched out his arm and put his head close to Cliona's. "Say Caspian!" he called mischievously and she shoved him sideways.

"Stop!"

"Fine, say Cheese!"

"*Cheese!*"

The camera on his phone flashed, just as Alex arrived back. "Selfies? Really?"

Fionn nodded. "For my ma. She misses us."

Cliona squinted at the photo. "*Ugh*, it's not the best."

"Let me take it," offered Alex. "Pose for me." He lifted up the phone and aimed it at them. Suddenly he stopped. "Just one second," he said, reaching out and pulling Cliona's hair from its elastic so that it fell around her face. "There, much better."

She blushed furiously as the camera flashed.

"You should wear your hair down more often," he said. "It suits you."

She took a big sip of beer. "Thanks."

"And get contacts. I mean, your glasses make you look smart, but you have lovely eyes that no one sees."

Fionn held up his fist. "My baby sis is off limits, Ryder. Back off."

Cliona smiled, delighted. It felt nice to be talked about. She wasn't used to being the centre of attention. She toyed with putting her hair up again, but decided against it. Even though she could barely see Alex's face, she left the glasses on the table too. Just for a little while.

Fionn bought another round after that and she did too – she found that she liked chatting to Alex. He was funny and sweet, regaling her with stories about the band on their various tours around Britain.

She was fascinated to hear that Fionn had just split up with a girl called Jules and teased him for the rest of the night about it.

"If Mum knew she had competition," she said with a big grin.

"You tell Mum and you're dead," Fionn had threatened. "I'll never hear the end of it. She's always on about grandchildren and I have no plans in that department."

"Fine, no more Caspian teasing then."

They all shared a cab in the end, dropping Alex first. "Night, you two," he said as he got out of the car. "See you soon, Clio."

She smiled radiantly. "Bye, Alex."

The door slammed shut.

"Do I sense a bit of frisson?" said Fionn as the car took off down the dark street.

Cliona put her head in her hands. "Just leave me alone! If it's not Caspian, it's Alex. Maybe, just maybe, I can have male friends? Now, no more or I'll FaceTime Mum and tell her everything about your break-up with Jules."

The next morning, Madison arrived into Clio's bedroom at seven-thirty. "Up and at 'em," she said cheerily, opening the curtains. "Crikey, Clio, this place smells like a brewery! What time did you get home?"

Cliona rubbed her eyes groggily. "I'm not sure – around two?"

"Well, I hope you hydrated before bed as we've a big day ahead. I want to go shopping."

"Right."

"So, Harrods are closing one floor for an hour while I browse."

"That's great."

"I want you to book lunch somewhere nice and get Todd a birthday present. His birthday is tomorrow."

"Anything in mind?"

Madison sat down on the bed. "No, I don't have time to think about those things. That's your job."

"But Todd is a tough one, Maddy. What does he like? James Bond?"

"Look, this is what I pay you for, okay?" She glared at her. "You shouldn't go out drinking like that on a work night."

Cliona sat up straight. "*What?* Wait a second. I never go out. I'm always at your beck and call. Then the one time I have a night off and, God forbid, a little bit of fun, you act like this."

"I always act like this."

"Yes, but you could be a bit kinder. My head hurts."

Madison looked away. "Okay, I'm sorry. Look, have a shower and get dressed. I'll meet you in the kitchen." She stood up and walked to the door. "Oh, and Clio?"

"*Hmmm?*"

"Did that blonde singer turn up again?"

"Caspian?"

"I can't remember his name," she lied.

"No. Why do you ask?"

"No reason." The door slammed.

Caspian arrived back to his flat late the next afternoon. Preeta had been sweet and all but, in the end, a little immature for his liking. She kept going on and on that she'd met Madison Ryan in the flesh. This annoyed him as he felt that he was more than enough for anyone.

Turning on the shower, he stripped off his clothes, discarding them on the bathroom floor. A song was playing on his mind and he hummed along as the water cascaded down. His shoulder-length blonde hair stuck to his back as he rinsed it clean. He had toyed with cutting it, but had decided not to in the end. It was sort of like his trademark. It gave him an edge as everyone had it cropped or shaved nowadays.

Madison's image crept into his thoughts. He didn't like bossy women, especially arrogant ones like her. Just because she had sold millions of albums, didn't makes her an artist. He heard her music on the radio and didn't really rate it. It lacked depth and soul in his opinion.

Stepping out of the shower, he rubbed his body dry with a threadbare towel. Naked, he walked over to the piano and played a few notes.

You think you're more important

You feel like you're the best

Don't get too comfortable

Because life is designed to test ...

You ... Stuck-up you ... yoooouuuu ...

He smiled. Closing the lid of the piano, he set about getting dressed.

Chapter Seventeen

The next few weeks were hectic. Madison was invited to appear on *The Jimmy Fallon Show* and played a Christmas themed gig at the MGM Grand Garden Arena in Las Vegas. Cliona dutifully accompanied her everywhere she went, trying her best to make life easier.

Her show in Las Vegas was a triumph and critics called it her best to date. Sauron was unable to join her so a huge screen was erected on the back of the stage and a pre-recorded video of him rapping was played. Madison sang with the virtual version and the crowd went wild. She had an outfit change for every song and even had a real lion in a cage for her latest track 'Pride'. Bethany, her publicist, posted official pictures on Instagram and the amount of 'likes' hit two million in half an hour. After the show, Mona and Angelica went for drinks with the light and sound crew, but Madison refused. She was so exhausted, she could barely stand up. No one understood how aerobic it was – how singing live while prancing around a stage is one of the hardest things you can do.

"Run me a hot bath and put a 'Do Not Disturb' sign

on my door," she told Cliona wearily. "I need to wind down."

On the twentieth of December they both flew home to Dublin. Madison had toyed with flying to the Bahamas for the holidays but her mother had insisted that she come home as Kevin, her father, was due back for the break.

"So, I definitely have holidays until the second of January?" said Cliona in the car as they sped south on the M50.

"Yes," answered Madison, typing furiously on her phone. "I promise I won't need you. I'm off to Madrid on the twenty-eighth anyway."

"It's so lovely to be home." Cliona stretched happily. "I can't wait to see Mum and Dad."

"*Hmmm*," said Madison, who didn't feel the same way. She hadn't seen her father in over six months. The last time had been for lunch in London where he had berated her for not going home to Dublin for her birthday.

"Your mother was looking forward to having a party for you, Mads. She called me up in tears when you didn't turn up."

"I told her a million times that I was going to New York. I had plans, Dad. I mean, aren't I a little old for a party and a cake? I mean, really!"

"You should have made the effort ..."

"Were you going to be there?" Her eyes flashed.

Kevin looked uncomfortable. "No, I was tied down on set. You know that."

"Same old story then, isn't it? I can count on one hand how many of my birthday parties you've bothered to attend."

"Maddy ..."

"So, shut up, you hypocrite, and leave me alone!"

So, their lunch had ended in a row, just like it always did. Now, he was due home for Christmas and she didn't know how that was going to pan out. He always looked like a stranger in his own house – someone who didn't belong.

John dropped Cliona home first.

"Bye, Maddy," said Cliona, hugging her tightly. "See you at some stage. Bye, Todd!" She patted his huge shoulder in the front seat.

"Bye, Cliona," he said formally. "Happy Holidays."

John had already taken Cliona's bag out of the boot of the car and was standing on the kerb.

"Bye, John. Thanks for the lift."

John smiled. "Happy Christmas."

The door slammed and the car sped off.

Cliona walked up to the old door of her family home and knocked. She heard a squeal and then the door opened to reveal a beaming Constance. "She's here!' she called in excitement. "Aonghus, our baby Clio is home!" She pulled her daughter into her arms and kissed her face repeatedly. "Oh, Clio! I've missed you so. Daddy just lit the fire so come in and put your feet up. I just made a batch of mince pies and there's some leftover punch on the hob."

The door closed behind them.

The Mercedes pulled up outside Madison's family home. She waited until Todd gave her the all clear. Then she vacated the car and walked into her house. The hall gleamed and there was a smell of polish.

Louise walked out of the kitchen and opened her arms. "Maddy, darling. Welcome home!"

Madison paused and then reluctantly walked towards her mother. They hugged awkwardly and stood back from each other.

"Is Dad here yet?"

"Yes, he just popped down the village for the paper."

"How is he?"

"Good form. They wrapped the film three days ago."

"Great."

Bluebell bounded out of the sitting room and jumped on Madison joyfully.

"Hey, Bluebell, hey!" She rubbed her head and scratched her ears. "I've missed you."

"Happy Christmas, Todd," said Louise graciously. "I hope you're not too disappointed about having to work through the holidays."

"No, ma'am." He stood erect. "It's my job."

Madison yawned. "What's for dinner?"

"Well, Daddy and I are going out. We're meeting the Ronans. Daddy hasn't seen them in so long, he wants to catch up."

He hasn't seen me either! Madison wanted to scream. It was just typical that they'd leave her alone.

"So, you can order in if you want."

"Thanks." Madison turned on her heel. "I'll just go to my room."

Kevin Ryan liked to be busy. He immersed himself in his work and thrived on being under pressure. Normally, he would only take a week off at Christmas, rushing back to whatever project he was working on. This year he had more time as the film he was working on had come to a natural end a week before. Flying home to Dublin, his mind was filled with his next project and he disappeared almost immediately to his study to research it.

He and Louise had met when they were students at Trinity College Dublin. He had studied English Literature and she was a business undergraduate. They married young and she supported him through those early days when scripts got refused and he was told to give up on his dream. She never bossed him around and always encouraged him. She didn't complain when he was away for months at a time. They understood each other.

Madison was another story. She was forceful and opinionated. She challenged him on almost everything. She didn't understand that he needed space. She called him selfish and self-obsessed, and called him out on his remote parenting.

She was the child that he and Louise had longed for. After years of disappointments, she had arrived into their world and he had really believed that everything would be idyllic. Fast forward twenty-three years and things were far from that. He kept an eye on her career – he had been instrumental in those early days – but he avoided confrontation with her as much as possible. She brought out the worst in him and upset his creative spirit. He hated to admit it, but sometimes it was very hard to love her.

Fionn arrived home three days later.

Constance was just icing the Christmas cake she had made when he sneaked up behind her and hugged her.

"Oh!" she said with a jump, knocking a plastic Santa off the surface of the cake.

"Happy Christmas, Mum."

She dropped the palette knife and hugged him fiercely. "Fionn, you rascal! You nearly gave me a heart attack. Oh, it's so wonderful to see you."

"It's great to be home. I've been dying for some of your mince pies."

"I've just put a fresh batch in the oven."

"Nice one." He walked into the utility room and started emptying his bag. "Can I put on a wash?" he asked, stuffing clothes into the machine.

"Of course. We can put them by the fire and they'll dry in no time."

"Where's Clio?"

"In town with Aonghus. I sent them in to pick up the turkey and get a last few bits."

"I've some interesting news for her."

"Oh?"

"You know you said we were having a New Year's party?"

"Yes. I know I said we wouldn't but it's almost a rite of passage at this stage."

"Well, I sort of invited the band last weekend. We'd had a few drinks and I suggested they come over ..."

"Your band?" Constance clapped her hands. "Wonderful, darling. I'd love to have them. I'm still miffed that they didn't stay here that time you played Vicar Street."

"Ah, there was a party in town that night. We live too far out ..."

"Anyway, no matter. We'll show them some proper Irish hospitality." She sprinkled some silver balls on the cake and then paused. "Why would Clio be interested?"

"Oh, she has a crush on Caspian."

Constance smiled. "Oh, leave her alone. You shouldn't tease her. She's such a shy little thing."

"Still, I want to see her face when she hears the news."

Cliona's face didn't even flicker when Fionn told her about the new guests.

"So?"

"It's a chance for you to seduce him."

"Seduce who?"

Aonghus put his arm around her shoulder. "You leave my best girl alone. She'd find it very hard to find anyone as good as her dad here."

Cliona kissed his cheek. "That's exactly it." She sauntered out into the hall, closed the door of the kitchen and then bounded up the stairs. It was only when she closed her bedroom door that she punched the air in delight.

Caspian Cole was coming to her house. He was going to be in her sitting room, drinking her mother's famous cider punch. He would be there when the clock struck twelve. It was perfect.

She opened her wardrobe. Piles of T-shirts and jeans stared back at her. She didn't have any decent dresses. Her mother always chided her for not dressing up for parties. She had never wanted to before.

Madison would have something. She had tons of nice dresses.

She was also going to Madrid for New Year which meant she wouldn't turn up and take all the limelight. Cliona immediately felt ashamed of herself.

Was she scared that Madison would run off with Caspian? There was nothing she could do about that. However, her friend being abroad when the party was on certainly helped.

Over on Vico Road, Madison drank her pomegranate juice and hummed along to Taylor Swift on her iPod. She liked sitting at the breakfast bar after her run, letting her breath come back to normal. Todd had accompanied her as Boris, her personal trainer, had flown home to the Ukraine for Christmas. The cold December weather added pep to their step as they pounded along the coast roads, the bay a murky grey with white horses visible in the distance.

Madison's reunion with her father had gone as expected. The arguments had started almost immediately when Kevin had reprimanded her for making Todd work through Christmas.

"You're not going to be abducted here, Madison. Give the poor lad a break."

Madison had flipped, screaming at Kevin for his hypocrisy. "*It was you who suggested I hire security in the first place. Leave me alone!*"

So, the past few days had been frosty. Kevin avoided her, spending hours in his study or disappearing into the city for a few hours. Louise tried to placate them but failed.

When Cliona texted looking for a dress, she instructed her to call over right away. She used to love giving her Barbie dolls makeovers when she was a child. Cliona was an adult real-life version. She was also curious as to why she wanted to break tradition and wear something so radical, in Cliona terms. She had been sparse with information in her texts.

She went upstairs and had a long shower, standing under the powerful jet of hot water for longer than normal. Her song with Sauron had hit over fifteen million downloads in the States alone. Ross was putting pressure on her to collaborate with someone else in the New Year but she didn't want to risk it. It would be very hard to match the success of that track. Plus she wanted to try something new.

She dried herself with a towel, admiring her supple body in the mirror. She was in great shape and she looked better than ever. Why then was she single? There had been no one since Tim Kinnear. She simply didn't have the time. That Caspian played on her mind a bit, mainly because he had snubbed her. Of course he had seen her at her worst – dressed down in jeans and a T-shirt – so that would explain a lot of it. She rarely didn't get what she wanted so when the initial rage had faded, it had been replaced with a desire to win. She would have him. There was no way he was having the upper hand.

She found herself looking him up on Instagram and gazing at his face. He really was something else. They would look beautiful together – like a model couple.

The doorbell rang and she hurriedly put on her robe.

"*Send Clio up here, Todd!*" she called. Her parents were out so they had the house to themselves. John had gone back to England for Christmas so Todd and Bluebell were her only company.

Cliona appeared at the door a few minutes later. "Todd checked my bag again," she said, shaking her head. "I mean, how long have I been working for you at this stage? Will he ever trust me?"

Madison smiled. "Nope. He's the best. Never slips up."

Cliona took a seat on Madison's enormous bed. "So, can you help me look pretty?"

"*Um*, I'm not sure ..." She put on a worried face.

"Maddy!"

"Of course, I can. But you have to one thing."

"What?"

"Go into town today and get some contact lenses."

"They won't be delivered in time."

"They will. Pay for express service. Now, do it or I won't help you. Glasses will not go with my clothes."

Cliona ended up with a green dress with a full skirt. Madison zipped up the clothes bag and handed it to her.

"Now, this is Dolce and Gabbana so mind it, okay?"

"Okay."

"I mean, it doesn't fit perfectly, but I can't help the fact that you're flat-chested."

"Wow, thanks."

"What do you need it for?" asked Madison airily. "You never said."

"Mum's New Year party," said Cliona impassively. "Okay, see you."

"But you wore jeans last year." Madison pressed on. "Why the effort this year?"

"I just wanted to jazz things up a bit." She started to walk away.

"Clio! Tell me what's going on."

Cliona cursed silently. "Okay, okay, Fionn's band are coming over. I just wanted to look sophisticated."

Madison said nothing but her mind was racing.

"So, thanks, Maddy. Have a great Christmas. Text me before you head to Madrid."

"I will."

"Bye."

"Bye."

Cliona arrived back to find her mother having tea with her old friend, Diana McCarthy. The two women were seated at the oak kitchen table, both with china cups in front of them. There was a plate of madeleines and some chocolate biscuits in a tin. Diana lived in Killiney, not far from Sorrento Terrace.

"Hello, Cliona," said Diana with a small wave.

"Hi, Diana. Happy Christmas." Cliona walked over to her and kissed her cheek. She smelled of Chanel.

Diana was a year older than Constance but she looked younger. Her blonde hair was cut in a chic bob and her large brown eyes dominated her face. She always wore beautiful clothes, impeccably cut and expensive. Both she and her husband Oscar were barristers and they lived in a huge mansion on the coast, a few doors down from Enya.

"You know Di's a granny now, don't you?" said Constance to Cliona, dipping a chocolate finger into her tea. "Colin's adoption finally went through."

Colin McCarthy, Diana's only son, had been thrilled when gay marriage was voted in by the Irish people. In 2017, he married his partner Val in a Humanist ceremony at his parents' place. Aonghus and Constance had been guests and it was still deemed the wedding of the century by some in the area. Crates of Cristal champagne were flown in from France and the wedding party all wore original gowns by the famous designer, Gabriella.

"Oh, congratulations!" said Cliona in delight. "Colin must be delighted. Is it a boy or a girl?"

"It's a boy. He's six months old and from Portugal. He's a cute little thing."

"I thought he tried India," said Cliona with a frown. "That's what he told me the last time we met."

"Oh, he tried China and India but they wouldn't entertain a same-sex couple. So, he opted for Portugal. It's taken months and buckets of money, but it's finally come through."

"What did he call him?"

"Orlando. They're over at our place actually. We normally spend Christmas in West Cork, but we decided to stay in Dublin this year and have a low-key affair. Colin wants us to get to know the baby."

"How's Britney holding up?" Cliona asked, referring to Colin's adored pooch. A Pom named after his idol Britney Spears, she was the apple of his eye. She only ate free-range chicken fillets and drank Evian from her doggy bowl.

"Oh, Colin made sure that Orlando brought a present for Britney, just to curb any jealousy. He had read up on the best way to introduce a new baby to a sibling, that sort of thing."

"A sibling!"

"Yes, indeed. Well, Orlando brought a baby doll for Britney. Colin was hoping that Britney would bond with it and, in turn, bond with Orlando."

"What happened?"

"Britney tore it to shreds. Colin was distraught."

Cliona giggled. "Britney'll come around."

"Is she at your place too?" asked Constance.

Diana nodded. "So is Val, Colin's husband. They arrived two days ago with everything but the kitchen sink. You know how organised Colin likes to be. The child is like a model, dressed in the best clothes. He has two buggies – one big one and a light one for the city centre, a baby monitor with three cameras wired to different rooms in the house. Oscar keeps tripping on developmental toys scattered around the place. We're just not used to small people around the house."

"You're so lucky!" said Constance enviously. "I can't wait to be a granny."

Cliona held up her hands. "Don't look at me."

"So, are you sorted for Christmas?" asked Constance, dipping a madeleine in her tea.

Diana nodded. "Oh, Colin insisted that he cook the turkey on Christmas Day. You know he thinks he's Heston Blumenthal, but I've hired caterers. He's frazzled as it is."

"Good idea,' said Constance approvingly. "I remember when Fionn was a baby, I didn't have time to brush my hair."

"Absolutely," agreed Diana. "He just can't juggle everything. What with Orlando and Britney, he's exhausted."

"I'd love to see him," said Constance wistfully. "He always makes me laugh."

"Yes, he's a ticket," agreed Diana.

Constance clapped her hands together. "We must wet the baby's head! Are you planning to go to abroad for New Year?"

"Well, we normally go skiing but Oscar hurt his back three weeks ago so we'll be on terra firma."

"Great! You must come to our little soirée. Fionn's band are flying in so it should be a good night."

"Really? Are you sure you'll have space?"

"What's another few? Aonghus will be delighted. He's been dying to open this rare bottle of Midleton we've had stashed in the cupboard. Oscar's penchant for whiskey will give him the perfect excuse."

Diana laughed. "I'll say it to Colin. He'll be delighted to get out. Since Orlando has arrived, he's been curtailed on the social front."

"I'm sure that Davis girl next door to you is a good age for baby-sitting."

"Yes, of course. I'll ring her mother and ask. I'd better check if she's okay with dogs."

"Dogs?"

"Oh, she'll have two kids to look after – Orlando and Britney."

Chapter Eighteen

Christmas came and went. Constance went all out with the turkey, serving it with two types of stuffing, homemade cranberry sauce and four different vegetables. Her roast potatoes were crispy on the outside and fluffy in the middle, and champagne and wine flowed all day.

At one stage, Cliona ventured into the kitchen and bolted out again.

"Fionn!" she said in alarm. "In all my years I've never seen such a mess. I'll be three weeks cleaning up after her."

"I'll help," he said with a laugh. "Judging by the amount of vino Mum has consumed, we won't see her at all tomorrow."

They played Scrabble and had their annual quiz. They drank port and watched some Christmas television. Aonghus got emotional and made a heartfelt speech where he thanked God for such lovely children and paid special tribute to his wonderful wife.

More wine was opened and Constance made turkey and ham sandwiches. Fionn opened a box of Roses and they watched home videos of when Fionn was three and Cliona was two, toddling after him in her nappy. Then it was Constance's turn to get emotional.

"Time passes so quickly," she said with a sniff. "When you two were little, it felt unending – the sleepless nights, the early mornings, the nappies. Now it seems like a fleeting moment. I miss having you sleep on my breast, your little eyelids flickering."

"That's quite enough of that," said Fionn, taking the brandy glass from his mother's hand. "Stop being so maudlin. Come on, let's sing some carols."

Madison's Christmas couldn't have been more different. Louise had booked the three of them into the Merrion Hotel for a five-course traditional menu in its Garden Room.

Madison had objected at the start. "I don't want to deal with fans," she moaned.

"Oh, I asked for discretion and the guest list doesn't seem to be your target audience."

"Well, Todd is coming too, just in case. He can sit at a separate table."

"That's fine, darling."

So, the three of them sat around a table, eating delectable food. Kevin on his iPad, Madison on her iPhone and Louise barely touching her food. Madison opted for sparkling water, as did her mother, and Kevin had a half bottle of red. The room was decorated festively with crackers and garlands, however this atmosphere did not transmit to the Ryan table.

"Can we go? I don't want dessert." Madison picked up her bag.

"Sit down and wait until we're all finished," ordered Kevin.

Madison slumped back in her chair. "Fine," she said, glowering at her father.

The New Year's Eve forecast was for rain and wind but, mercifully, the weather was bright and dry.

"Thank God," said Constance. "I felt bad about banishing the smokers to the garden in bad weather."

Cliona and Fionn spent the morning cleaning the drawing room and the hall. Cobwebs were swept away with the top of the brush, the piano was dusted down and the windows were gleaming thanks to the Windolene and newspaper that Cliona used to clean them. Aonghus hoovered the floor and Constance busied herself making canapés in the kitchen. Boxes of wine were set up on the dresser, along with bottles of vodka, whiskey, brandy and rum. Mixers were lined up next to that, along with glasses and napkins. Constance's famous cider punch took centre stage on the dining-room table in a huge glass bowl.

"What time are the boys arriving?" asked Constance, heaving a large joint of ham out of a huge pot.

"About six," answered Fionn. "I told them to take a cab from the airport."

Cliona tried to hide a smile, but inside she was buzzing. It was going to be a magical night. She could feel it in her bones.

There was a knock on the door at about ten past six. Cliona darted upstairs. She didn't want anyone to see her dirty jeans and sweaty face. Her contact lenses had finally arrived the day before and, surprisingly, they had been easy enough to insert.

"*I'm using the shower!*" she called downstairs, bolting into the large bathroom at the top of the stairs.

Of the three dresses she had borrowed from Madison, she had chosen the green one. It was the simplest – it had a scooped neck, a nipped waist and a full skirt that fell just below the knee. The colour suited her brown hair and the cut of the material gave curves to her slim body. Madison had texted the day before, wishing her a Happy New Year and photos of the Plaza Mayor in Madrid.

Cliona had smiled in relief. She had been half-afraid that Madison would change her mind and stick around for the party. Caspian had intrigued her friend that last night and his indifference must have driven her mad. Throughout all the years she had known Madison, she knew that she always made a point of getting what she wanted. She suspected that Caspian Cole was on that list.

The remaining members of Doctor Eckleburg arrived by taxi at six.

"I love your home," said Ethan in awe. "That view is amazing." He gazed out the bay window at the ocean. "Look, Stella, isn't it incredible?"

His girlfriend nodded. "Incredible," she echoed.

Fionn shrugged. "You get used to it. So, how was Christmas?"

Ethan made a face. "Awful. Dad is still angry with me about the band. He holds it together until he has a few drinks and then *boom*! It all comes out."

Stella kissed his cheek. "He will come around. Don't worry, *mój kochany.*"

"How was your Christmas, Stella?" Fionn smiled at her.

"Good, good. I went home and had a good time with

my family." She smiled and flicked her blonde hair. "I miss the food in Poland. It was great to have *pierogi* and see my grandmother."

Alex, who had been in the kitchen with Constance, walked into the room. "Love this house, Fionn. It's amazing." His red hair clashed gloriously with his pink shirt but, oddly, he pulled it off.

"Where's Caspian?" asked Fionn. "I thought he was with you."

"Gone out to the cliff with your dad. He wanted to feel the wind on his face."

Ethan rolled his eyes. "Cue a new song about life rushing past you like a gale."

Alex laughed. "Or standing steadfast against the elements."

Constance appeared with a red face. "Those blooming tartlets are a labour of love! Why do I insist on making them?"

Fionn kissed her forehead. "Because you're famous for your tartlets, Mum. Your guests would riot without them."

"I suppose," she agreed.

The door opened and Cliona appeared.

"Clio!" said Fionn in surprise.

The occupants of the room turned around.

"My baby girl!" Constance's hand flew to her mouth. "You look beautiful!"

Cliona hung her head in embarrassment. Her long brown hair had been brushed until it shone and fell around her shoulders. Her eyes had a touch of shadow and a thin line of kohl. Her lips glistened with gloss. The green dress was becoming and her pale arm was adorned with a single gold bangle. She looked around the room and tried to mask her disappointment when she realised that Caspian wasn't there for her big entrance.

Alex smiled at her warmly. "Hi," he called, waving.

Ethan waved too.

Constance hugged her tightly. "You're a vision," she said, ruffling her hair. "Gorgeous."

"Mum! Stop making a big deal," she said, blushing.

"I'm not! It's just not often that you make an effort." She stroked her cheek. "You know, some girls would give their left arms for your skin. It really is fabulous."

"I'm too pale."

"Not in the slightest. It was a sign of prestige back in the old days. Only the finest ladies had alabaster skin like yours."

"Right." Cliona accepted a glass of white wine from Fionn. "So, what time is this starting?"

"I said from seven," said Constance. "I'm expecting around forty but you know there'll be a few extra."

"Have we enough booze?" asked Fionn with a frown.

"Of course," she answered. "There's at least four more boxes of wine in the garage. I also expect people to bring a bottle. You know, it's mannerly."

Aonghus and Caspian arrived back at that moment. "There's a fine wind blowing," said Aonghus with a shiver. "You'd better light the heat lamp in the garden for the smokers, Connie."

"Cheers! I appreciate that," said Ethan, who smoked Marlboro Red.

Caspian's blonde hair was dishevelled from the breeze. "This place is inspiring!" he said, his eyes shining.

"Oh, here we go," said Ethan to Alex in an undertone. "I feel inspired by nature and her power."

Fionn clapped his hands for attention. "Casp? That's great, man. I'm thrilled. But tonight's a party, not a song-writing session. Dad? I'll set up the heat lamp and I'll stash some rugs by the door too. Mum? Sit down. You've done enough in the kitchen at this stage. The rest of you? Help yourselves to Mum's cider punch. There's enough for the whole of Dublin."

Guests started to arrive at around seven, just as Constance predicted. Aonghus's publishing friends and colleagues, along with Constance's group from choir and yoga. Neighbours from the Terrace and friends from the golf club. The old house started to fill up and sixties classics played on the stereo.

Caspian, enchanted with the bookcase and paintings on the wall, drifted around the room, reading blurbs of books and standing back to appreciate a work of art. Cliona watched him furtively, sipping her wine. Every now and then their eyes would meet and her stomach would flip over. Then he'd look away again and she wondered if she'd imagined it. She wished she had the courage to approach him and dazzle him with her wit and beauty.

I wish, she thought dolefully. Why would Caspian Cole be interested in her?

Constance replenished plates of canapés on the dining room table, filled bowls with homemade mayonnaise and salsa, dressed some salad leaves and refilled bowls of nuts and crisps.

Diana and Oscar arrived with their son Colin in tow. He and his husband Val couldn't have been more different.

Colin lived for his style – he adored designer clothes and drank Prosecco by the gallon. Val preferred check shirts, jeans and cans of beer.

"Evening, all," said Diana gaily. "Thanks for having us." She was dressed in a beautiful silk dress and her blonde hair was newly streaked.

Oscar, her husband, was tall and haughty. Dressed in a white shirt and navy pants, he had his iPhone in his hand and accepted a glass of whiskey immediately from Aonghus. His hair had gone mostly grey, but he carried it well with his sallow skin. "My dad is a total silver fox," Colin would boast.

Colin was carrying the baby in a Baby Bjorn sling.

"Colin!" Constance rushed over to him. "Congratulations, my love. Let me see the precious bundle." She gazed at the sleeping baby on his chest. "Oh, he's so dinky and cute. Are you in love?"

Colin nodded. "Totally in love." He kissed the sleeping baby's head. "I was so relieved that he's so good-looking, Constance. I mean, adoption is a gamble and someone as gorgeous as me would have to have a stunner of a kid."

Val appeared behind him, also wearing a sling.

"Twins?" asked Constance, puzzled. "Diana never said ..."

There was a bark and she focused in on the brand name. "*Doggy Bjorn*," she read aloud.

"Yes," said Colin breezily. "I hope you don't mind, but we just had to bring Britney. She promised not to chase your cats but we put her in the sling to be safe. She's been acting up no end since Orlando came along. All to be expected, but a pain nonetheless."

Diana laughed. "Britney has a highchair too."

"And why not?" Colin looked fierce. "It's important that she feels included at mealtimes."

Fionn appeared. "Colin! Great to see you. Would you like a white wine?"

"An enormous glass," said Colin, wiping his brow. "It's been a long day. Orlando here doesn't understand naptime and if I see *Peppa Pig* once more I'm going to scream."

"What happened to the baby-sitter idea?" Constance asked. "I suggested the girl from down the road."

"There was no way on earth I was leaving my baby with a teenager I barely know." Colin's brown curls bounced as he talked. "Val is going to have one drink and then he's taking them home. It's my turn to have a night off."

Val raised his eyes to heaven. "Says he who stayed out until seven in the morning at his Christmas party. Says he who met friends for lunch yesterday and arrived home at midnight."

"*I'm the social one, Val!*" shrieked Colin. "You knew that when you married me."

Fionn handed Val a beer. "Good times, Val. Good times."

"Tell me about it," said Val with a sigh.

The party grew louder. Baby Orlando, woken by a raucous rendition of 'It's Now Or Never' by Aonghus's editor, cried and cried.

Val put Orlando in his sling and Britney on a leash.

"Do you have the nappy bag?" asked Colin. "Remember, check the temperature of the room. It must not be too hot or too cold. I have three bottles sterilised in the kitchen and there are extra vests in the chest of drawers by our bed."

"Colin, this is not my first rodeo," said Val patiently. "Just enjoy your night, okay?" He kissed him and swung the nappy bag onto his shoulder. "Can you bring Britney's sling home? I can't manage everything."

"Of course, honey." Colin waved. "See you later."

The front door slammed shut.

Cliona handed Colin a full glass of wine. "Do you miss Orlando already?"

Colin sighed. "Well ... maybe just a little ..." He laughed. "Not at all. Now, let's get this party started!"

Chapter Nineteen

Alex sidled up to Cliona and nudged her arm. "Are you having a good night?" he asked.

She smiled. "I am actually. Stella is really nice. We've been having a great laugh."

"Yeah, Ethan adores her." He sipped his beer. "Have you anyone?" He stared at his feet. "You know, a boyfriend?"

Cliona, who had uncharacteristically had five glasses of Pinot Grigio, sighed. "No, I don't have a boyfriend. I do fancy someone though."

"Oh?"

She hiccupped. "Don't tell Fionn, okay? He's always teasing me."

"I promise."

"I really like Caspian."

Alex's face betrayed nothing. "Really?"

"He's just so gorgeous and cool and talented."

"Have you made a move?"

"Gosh, no." She put her face in her hands. "He'd never bother with someone like me."

"Why not?"

"I'm boring and frumpy."

"You don't look frumpy tonight." His brown eyes stared at her.

She shook her head. "I thought I was the one who needed glasses. Anyway, I'm going to admire him from afar and yearn."

"That seems like a waste." He put his beer bottle on the bookcase behind them. "Nothing ventured and all that."

"Oh, no. I'd never have the courage." She gazed across the room at Caspian who was talking to Aonghus, gesticulating madly. "He's in another league."

Alex said nothing.

Constance clapped her hands for attention. "Right, midnight is fast approaching! Have you all someone to kiss when the clock strikes twelve?"

Cliona stared at Caspian.

Alex got up. "You should head over there and chance it."

"You think?"

"Yes." He backed away. "Then at least you'll know and can move on with your life." He winked at her. "There are plenty more fish in the sea, young Cliona, goddess of the waves."

"Hey, how do you know that?"

"I know lots of things." He smiled. "So does Google."

"Why did you google my name?" She stood up. "Alex?"

He walked away.

"*Five minutes!*" called Constance.

"I love this part!' said Colin in excitement. "I've got to FaceTime Val for the big moment."

He took out his phone and accessed his contacts. "Hi,

Val? Hey, honey, it's me. All okay? Do I hear Britney? Val, it's hours past her bedtime! How's Orlando? He's there too? Ah, stop! Why am I always the bad cop and you're the good cop?" He walked out into the garden.

Cliona took a deep breath. Maybe Alex was right. Maybe she should make a play. Alcohol gave her new-found courage and she started to walk purposefully towards Caspian. Her father waved at her as she approached and she held her head high.

Caspian's eyes locked with hers and he smiled.

"Clio! I was just telling Caspian here about your film career."

"My what?"

"How you've given it all up to be Maddy's PA."

"Oh. Well, it's not forever ..."

"You should never give up on your art," said Caspian definitely. "I mean, my dad wasn't too pleased when I told him I wanted to be a musician but I did it anyway. I knew I was going to be great and he wasn't going to stop it."

"I haven't given up," said Cliona, blushing furiously. "This is just a job ..."

"Just be careful," went on Caspian, his brown eyes sincere. "You could lose sight of what's important."

Aonghus nodded. "I hate to say it, Clio, but he's right. Don't get too comfortable being her skivvy. You need to make one of my new books into a film and then we can all retire comfortably."

"I'll write the score," said Caspian with a wink.

Constance turned off the speaker and clapped her hands.

"*Let's say goodbye to 2018!*" she called to the crowd.

She turned up the television as clock started to countdown.

"*Ten ... nine ... eight ...*"

Caspian moved closer to Cliona so that his arm was touching hers. She gazed up at him in wonder.

"*Six ... five ... four ...*"

"Have you any resolutions?" he whispered and she shook her head.

"*Two ... one! Happy New Year!*"

Bending down his head, he kissed her softly on the cheek. "Happy New Year," he said in her ear.

Cliona felt herself sway. He smelled of musk.

Then he walked over to Ethan and Stella.

Aonghus pulled her into a hug. "2019 will be your year, pet," he said, kissing her on the forehead.

Fionn appeared and gave her a big bearhug. "I saw Caspian making his move," he teased. "Mrs. Cliona Cole. Lovely alliteration there."

"Stop it," she said, beaming in delight.

Aonghus kissed Constance full on the lips. "You are my muse, my life, my greatest love!"

"That'll be Caspian next year," went on Fionn with a grin. "*Oh, Cliona, you're my muse, my life, my greatest love!*" he repeated in high voice.

She shoved him forcibly so he toppled sideways. "Stop! He'll hear you. Anyway, he didn't make a move. He just kissed my cheek."

"I know what I saw. This is your chance, little sis. Go in for the kill."

Everyone in the room was cheering and hugging. Constance started to open champagne bottles with a 'pop'. "I got these in Aldi," she said, the glasses overflowing.

"Not exactly Dom Perignon, but drinkable."

"Everyone is too pissed to notice, Mum," said Fionn. "I'll help dole them out."

Aonghus started to sing 'Auld Lang Syne'. The crowd joined in, forming a circle and crossing their hands until Caspian held up his hand. "Please," he said loudly. "Let me accompany you." He walked over to the piano and took a seat. Playing the intro, he started to sing from the beginning again. The crowd joined in again, some out of tune.

"God, he's no joke at the piano," said Colin to his mother, Diana. "Look at those fancy arpeggio things thrown in. I usually hate this song but tonight it's almost decent."

"Yes, he's quite good," she agreed. "A bit like that Coldplay guy."

Suddenly a powerful female voice drowned out everyone else. Caspian's head swung around in surprise.

Madison stood in the doorway, looking sensational in a short silver dress and stilettos. Her long blonde hair was sleek and fell down her back and her skin was bronzed.

Closing her eyes, she sang the end of the song, giving it all she had. Caspian harmonised with her and played the last few notes. There was a pause and then rapturous applause.

"*Bravo!*" said Aonghus, clapping loudly. "*Maddy!* We didn't know you were coming."

Constance walked towards Madison and opened her arms. "Maddy, darling, come in! I thought you were in Madrid."

"I was and it was boring so I decided to fly back and surprise you. I hope you don't mind an extra person."

Cliona couldn't believe it. She felt herself shrink backwards.

Caspian swivelled around on the piano stool and stared at Madison. His brown eyes betrayed nothing, but you could see that his interest was piqued.

Colin burst out of a small crowd of people and shook her hand. "Love your work," he said earnestly. "I mean, I have a dog called Britney ..."

"So?" Madison regarded him icily.

"It's just you're so like her. You know, in style and music and stuff."

Madison removed her hand from his grip and turned away.

"Champagne?" asked Aonghus, thrusting a flute in her hand.

"Why not?" Madison beamed at him. "For the night's that in it."

"Is that Todd I see lurking in the hallway?" Constance narrowed her eyes. "Shall I offer him a glass?"

Madison shook her head. "He never drinks."

She scanned the room and her gaze rested on Caspian who was now standing by the fireplace. Then she saw Cliona by the bay window, looking pretty in her green dress.

"*Clio!*" called Madison loudly so that everyone could hear. "*I just love my dress on you! So pretty!*"

Cliona gave a half-wave and blushed furiously. Caspian looked from Cliona back to Madison.

"You should wear my clothes more often." She smiled sweetly. "So much better than the jeans. Oh, and you took my advice about the contacts. Again, a huge improvement."

Fionn, who was standing to the right of Cliona,

squeezed her arm. "She's just feeling threatened that you look so lovely," he whispered. "Ignore her."

Madison walked towards them, her earrings sparkling in the lights. Someone pressed 'play' on the stereo again and music filled the room.

"Hi, Fionn!" Madison smiled at him.

"Hey, Maddy, this is a surprise." Fionn gave her a brief hug. "Clio said you were in Madrid."

"Oh, I was," she said airily. "Then I thought, why am I missing the party of the year?"

"How did you get a flight back?" he enquired.

"Oh, I hired a private jet. Ross will have a heart attack but I don't care. I can't be Miss Perfect all the time."

"Right."

She smoothed her dress and flicked her hair. It was obvious that she was on edge. She kept glancing at Caspian to see if he was watching her, and was gratified when he approached the group.

There was a shout from outside and a large crash.

"Christ, I'd better check that out," said Fionn, rushing off.

"Hello," Caspian said with a smile. "Thanks for helping me out there."

"Singing?" Madison gave a little laugh. "That's my job."

"You have a good voice."

"I know," she said with an edge to her tone.

"It's just not so obvious with the tracks you release."

"Oh?"

"You should project more. Lose the frills."

"Thanks for the advice." She bristled. "How many albums have you sold exactly?"

Caspian put his finger to her lips. "*Shhh*," he said softly.

"Don't fight so much."

Cliona watched this exchange with a sinking heart.

"I must use the bathroom," she said, but they didn't notice. She passed Colin and Diana.

"Doesn't Madison look amazing with Caspian?" she heard Colin say approvingly. "Like movie stars."

Rushing out the door, Cliona felt sick. It was like she had lost the glass slipper and her coach had turned back into a pumpkin. The spell had been broken.

"More?" Aonghus held up a bottle of whiskey.

Ethan shook his head. "Not for me. I'm going to hit the hay."

"Fionn, put some blow-up beds in the spare room so pick whichever one you want," said Constance.

Ethan took Stella's hand. "Thanks for a great evening," he said genuinely. "You hear about the Irish and their hospitality but I never expected this."

"Yes, we're very good at parties," agreed Aonghus.

Alex yawned. "I might join them. Where's Fionn? I need to say goodnight."

"Outside, I think." Constance yawned too. "Oh, Alex, you've started a yawn epidemic. I feel myself fading."

"Say night to Fionn for me, man," said Ethan, leading Stella out into the hall. "See you all in the morning."

Madison's silver dress gleamed in the moonlight. When Caspian had suggested a walk in the garden, she had been thrilled. A small voice in her head chided her for her insensitivity regarding Cliona, but she ignored it. *All's fair in love and war.*

She had intended to turn up at the party ever since Cliona had told her that the band were coming over. It was the perfect chance to reset the balance. The first time she had met Caspian, she had been at a disadvantage with her baggy T-shirt and faded jeans. Tonight she looked amazing and she knew it. No one could resist her. She was sure of it.

"What's it like to be famous?" he asked as they strolled along the grass.

"Good and bad. Good because everyone sucks up to you and you can pretty much do what you want. Bad because it's lonely."

"Lonely? How?" He looked surprised.

"Everyone thinks that they know you, but they only know the public you." She sighed. "When the crowd goes home and the lights go out, you've no one but your ego."

"I didn't expect a response like that."

"Why? What did you expect?"

"A glowing description of life in the limelight."

"Well, it wouldn't be true." She stopped and faced him. "Do you want to be famous?"

"I will be famous. Whether I want it or not is irrelevant."

"How can you be so sure?"

"I just know. I've known all my life."

She laughed. "Well, I'll see you on the red carpet then."

He smiled. "Maybe."

She shivered, her silver dress a flimsy barrier from the cold. He noticed straight away.

"Come here," he said huskily, pulling her into his arms. She rested her head against his chest and she could hear the steady rhythm of his heartbeat. Closing her eyes, she relaxed.

"Your hair smells like roses," he murmured.

"That's my shampoo."

"It's nice."

They stood like that for five minutes, wrapped around each other for warmth. Madison hadn't felt so alive in years. Not since Cal. Surely he would kiss her. The moment was perfect. The moonlight, the crashing waves. Surely ...

"We should get back," he said suddenly.

She pulled back. "Go back to the house? Why?"

"Well, I'm cold for one and I'm not really into kissing you in front of that beefy guy in the shadows over there."

"Who? Todd?"

"I suppose. Biceps the size of watermelons?"

She giggled. "Yes. That's him."

He held out his hand. "Let me take you back."

She grasped his long fingers and allowed him to lead her back to the house.

Cliona woke the next morning to a barrage of texts from Madison. Refusing to read or engage with them, she threw her phone in a drawer and shut it. She didn't want to know. There was a pain in her chest when she thought of them together.

Constance was adding painkillers to a glass of water when she entered the kitchen. There was a fizzing noise and a groan from her mother.

"I'm going to die, Clio. Please cremate me and scatter my ashes out on the ocean."

"You'll be fine."

"No, no. This time I've really done it."

"Where's Dad?"

"Sleeping." She put her head on the table. "Colin was the only one left in the end. He was pissed, singing 'Rocketman' at the top of his voice and talking about it being a metaphor for his own life or something."

"What time did Maddy leave?" Cliona poured a cup of juice.

"After Fionn and Caspian went to bed, she called her driver and left almost immediately."

"Really?" Cliona brightened. "So, Caspian didn't leave with her?"

"No, I'm sure he didn't. I think I met him coming out of the loo at half six this morning. Fionn ended up giving Ethan and Stella his bed in the end as he didn't want her sleeping on the floor. Such a gentleman I've raised. Anyway, he had to take a lilo on the floor with the others."

"So, Caspian is here?"

Constance nodded. "Sound asleep, I suppose. He's a bit of a dreamer, isn't he? Kind of ethereal. I'm not sure what to make of him."

But Cliona had gone. Bounding up the stairs, she pulled off her glasses and picked out her best T-shirt and jeans. She brushed her hair and added some lip gloss. She wanted to look pretty but like she hadn't really tried.

There was a knock on the door, just as she sprayed some perfume on. "Clio?"

It was Fionn.

"Hey," he said, closing the door behind him. "God, my back aches. There's definitely a hole in that blow-up bed. I was flat on the ground this morning."

"Are the others up?"

"Just Alex. He's gone down to have a cup of coffee."

"How's your head?"

Fionn shrugged. "Not too bad actually. I stopped drinking at around two. Right after Mum tried to set me up with her beautician."

"No interest?"

"No. I mean, all I could think of was her and Mum and wax. Quite the turn-off."

Cliona giggled. "What time did Maddy leave?"

"Around three." He paused. "You know the way I tease you about Caspian. Is it true? I mean, do you genuinely fancy him?"

Cliona shook her head. "Not at all."

"Good." Fionn looked relieved. "I think that he and Maddy had a moment. She was on cloud nine and he looked like the cat that got the cream."

"A moment?" She forced a smile.

"Yeah. They went for walk and arrived back hand in hand. I can only assume."

"Oh." She sat back, deflated.

"Watch this space."

"Right."

"Anyway, are you coming down? Mum promised that she'd make a fry."

"A fry? Right, of course. I'll be right there."

Fionn left and she grabbed a tissue. With one quick movement, she removed her lip gloss.

Chapter Twenty

Three weeks passed. Madison's good mood after the party quickly evaporated when Caspian made no contact at all. Even though she had given him her private number, there hadn't been one text or call. Cliona clammed up when she mentioned it so she stopped talking about him. It baffled her. He had almost kissed her in Dublin. Why then had he not been in touch?

Then, out of the blue one Tuesday morning, her phone buzzed. She was in the middle of a pedicure and didn't check it until afterwards.

You free later? C

She didn't recognise the number.

C.

It had to be Caspian. Typical he would assume she'd know it was him.

She debated what to do. She didn't want to seem too eager. He had left her to stew for three weeks and didn't deserve an answer straight away. She put her phone in her bag. She was Madison Ryan. Not some love-struck teenager, desperate for attention.

An hour later, she checked her phone again. There was another message:

???

With a smirk, she set about replying.

Yep. What's the plan?

She waited five minutes and then ten. Finally her phone buzzed.

Come to my place. Leave the bodyguard at home.

Seconds later, he sent another text with his address.

"Todd?" she called.

"Yes, ma'am?"

"I'm going out."

"I'm ready when you are."

"No, no. I mean, I'm going out alone. John can drive me."

"But, Madison ..."

She smiled. "I'll be fine. Go and catch a movie or meet up with some friends."

"This is against all protocol, ma'am." He stood up straight. "My brief is to protect you at all times. From everyone."

She grinned. "It's fine, Todd. I mean it." She didn't want to be protected from Caspian. Not in the slightest.

Cliona, who had gone for a walk, arrived back to the apartment, just as Madison was leaving.

"You're going out?" she asked in surprise. "I thought we were going to watch *The Notebook* and cry our eyes out."

"Something came up," said Madison vaguely. "I'll see you later."

"See you." Cliona looked suspicious.

The door slammed.

Cliona wandered down the hall. The door of Madison's room was open and she could see that her bed was covered in different dresses and tops of all colours. Strolling in, her eyes widened at the mess. It looked like she had pulled out every item of clothing she had.

Angelica appeared behind her and tutted. "I'm her stylist, right? Not her maid. I hope she doesn't expect me to put all these back."

"I thought you'd gone home," said Cliona in surprise.

"Oh, I had gone home," answered Angelica tartly, "until Miss Princess calls and demands that I come back right away to help her dress for a date."

"A date?"

"Yeah. She called Mona too, to come and do her make-up, but she told her to go jump. I wish I was as brave as her sometimes."

"Yeah, Mona takes no prisoners," agreed Cliona. "Did she mention a name?"

Angelica shook her head. "Nope. Just that he was drop-dead gorgeous and she had to look amazing."

Cliona backed out of the room with a sinking heart. It had to be Caspian. Who else could it be? She walked into her room and closed the door.

The Mercedes pulled up outside a block of apartments on Phoenix Road near King's Cross. John looked back at Madison. "Do I need to check this place?"

She shook her head. "No. I told him that I'd come alone."

"Do you trust him?"

She nodded. "Yes."

"Will I wait out here?"

She shook her head again. "No. Go home. I'll be just fine."

John shrugged. "If you're sure, Madison. I mean, this is a big security breach, I've got to say."

"It's my call."

"Fair enough."

"I told Bethany to post a picture of me going into Raffles, so I'm covered. The paps will more than likely follow that up."

She pulled up her hood and opened the door. "I'll call you when I need you to pick me up. Goodnight, John."

The street was quite deserted as she pressed the buzzer of a flat on the third floor.

"Hello?" Caspian's voice crackled on the intercom.

"It's me."

The buzzer sounded and the door opened. Inhaling sharply, she entered the building. An old man passed her blankly.

She opted for the lift as she didn't want to be red-faced and breathless from climbing three flights of stairs. It took a few minutes to arrive and she was gratified to find a mirror inside. Hastily, she checked her hair and her make-up. The lift pinged and the doors opened. She walked down the corridor until she came to his door. She knocked twice.

She waited patiently. Then she knocked again.

Finally the door opened to reveal Caspian barefoot, wearing faded jeans and a green T-shirt. His blonde hair was dishevelled and his brown eyes looked straight into hers.

"Welcome," he said with a smile. "It's not a palace but

it's home." He opened the door wider to reveal wooden floors, a Victorian fireplace and a piano in the corner. Some abstract pictures hung on the wall, splashes of paint on canvas.

Madison walked into the sitting room and fiddled with her handbag.

"Those paintings look interesting," she said nervously, desperate for conversation. "Did you paint them?"

Caspian took a seat on the old couch and shook his head. "My ex was a painter. She studied Fine Art at college."

"Oh, right." She cursed herself for asking.

"Would you like a drink?" he asked.

She nodded. "Yes, please."

"I've beer or wine. Maybe some vodka, but I'm not sure." He got up and opened a cupboard door. "Yes, I've some cheap Polish vodka that Stella brought back at Christmas. It's pretty harsh but effective."

"That sounds perfect." She perched on the armchair, crossing her legs elegantly. The outfit she had chosen in the end was a simple black dress, tights and boots. A large silver pendant hung around her neck and her eyes were smudgy and black. With her blonde hair falling around her shoulders in waves, she looked really pretty. He gazed at her for a moment.

"Right, vodka. I'm on the case." He disappeared into the tiny kitchen and she could hear cupboards being opened and closed, the clink of glasses and then he reappeared with two tumblers of vodka and what looked like orange juice.

"That's the only mixer I have, I'm afraid," he said apologetically. "I meant to go to the corner shop and stock up, but I spent the day writing songs and lost track of time."

"It's fine, it's fine," she said hurriedly. "I like orange juice." She accepted the glass from his outstretched hand and took a huge gulp.

He watched her in amusement. "Why are you so jumpy?"

"I'm not."

"Yes, you are." He resumed his position on the couch. "What's the matter? Are you nervous of me?"

"Nervous?" she squeaked.

"Well, I invited you over here so you must be expecting something, right?" He grinned lazily.

Madison went a deep red. "No, I did not."

"Liar."

He got up and placed his glass on the mantelpiece. "Madison, you're not a child. I can tell that you want me to take off all your clothes, one by one."

She stood up. "You're so arrogant! Honestly. I mean, I could have anyone I want. I don't have to sit here and listen to this."

"The tigress roars," he said with a small laugh. "You really have the worst temper." He took her glass from her hand and placed it next to his own. "Stop fighting with everyone," he whispered. "I think I preferred you when you were nervous."

She opened her mouth to protest but he was too quick for her. Putting his strong arms around her waist, he drew her to him and kissed her passionately on the mouth. Madison felt her legs sway and she clung to him. Picking her up easily, he walked towards his bedroom and kicked open the door. Seconds later, they were on the bed. Her dress disappeared, followed by her boots and tights. His clothes were discarded too and soon they were naked, clinging to each other, blonde entwined with blonde.

They remained wrapped around each other for the rest of the night. He held her close, letting her sleep on his chest, trailing his finger up and down her arm. At one stage she woke up and jumped, unsure of where she was, and he kissed her lips. "It's okay," he whispered. "You're with me."

She relaxed.

"This is like that movie *Notting Hill,*" she murmured.

"I've never seen it."

"Julia Roberts plays a famous actress who sleeps with an ordinary guy. She mentions Rita Hayworth saying, *'They go to bed with Gilda; they wake up with me'*." She looked fearful for a moment. "Was it a disappointment, sleeping with the star and realising that she's just a girl?"

He sat up straight. "What do you *mean*, an ordinary guy?"

Dawn broke over the rooftops of London, the limited winter light giving a bleak feel. Madison got up and stretched. Caspian was still asleep, his beautiful face peaceful. She walked into the sitting room and checked her bag for her phone. There were three missed calls from Ross and an urgent message to call him. Todd had texted four times, asking if she was okay. Bethany had called too, asking about the press release for her new single. Another day at the office.

She rang Ross and spoke in a low voice so as not to wake Caspian.

"Where the hell are you?" he asked in his Geordie

accent. "I've been calling everyone asking where you are, like."

"Nowhere. What's up?"

"I've been on to Jeremy and we have to get planning that tour, Maddy."

"Isn't that what I pay Jeremy for? He's a tour manager, Ross. That's his job."

"Yes, but we need your input. Remember last time when you kicked up and things had to be changed, *yadiyadiya*? I don't want a repeat performance of that."

"Give me a couple of days."

"What?"

"I'm taking a couple of days off."

"You're what?"

"You heard me. Don't call me. I'll let you know when I'm back." She hung up the phone.

Caspian was awake when she re-entered the bedroom.

"All okay?" he asked.

She nodded. "I just told my manager that I'm taking a couple of days off."

"Oh?"

"Yes." She jumped onto the bed next to him. "Can I stay here with you?"

He reached up and took her face in his hands. "Of course." He kissed her. "But you'll have to put up with my music. Sometimes I put it first and I'm warning you in advance. If a song comes into my head, I'll think of nothing else."

"Maybe I could help? Sing along or something?"

He smiled. "Maybe." He pulled her back onto the bed. "Although, I like to work alone."

He kissed her neck and nibbled on her ear. "Tell me

about your childhood. I want to understand you."

Madison closed her eyes in pleasure as he trailed his tongue down her breast. "There's not much to tell. I got famous singing silly songs. The end."

"And now?"

"I'm changing my image. I'm sick of being a good girl."

He laughed. "Judging by last night, you're not a good girl at all."

She laughed too. "You like my moves?"

He nodded. "To be fair, this was a lot better than anticipated."

She punched his shoulder. "What the hell is that supposed to mean?"

"Exactly that." He pinned down her arms. "I didn't expect you to be so giving. You seem like a spoilt brat who expects everyone to play to your tune."

She struggled but he was too strong for her.

"Yet you're surprisingly sweet in bed. I mean, it was nice."

"Nice?"

He nodded and kissed her slowly, biting her lip gently. "Very nice."

They stayed in the flat until the next day, eating takeaway pizza, drinking wine and making love. They took a shower together around noon the next day and Caspian hummed a song.

"What's that?" she asked, picking it up and humming along with him.

"Oh, it's called 'Stuck Up'."

"Who's it about?"

"No one," he said blandly.

She harmonised with him easily, adding in a few 'oh yeahs'. "I like it. It's catchy."

Caspian had the grace to blush. "Right," he said changing the subject. "Let me shampoo your hair."

She closed her eyes. "Massage it in really well, okay? I love head rubs."

Later that day he suggested that they go out.

"No," she said immediately. "It's too risky."

"Madison, you need to get a grip." He pulled on a T-shirt. "You won't be recognised and if you are, just ask people to leave you alone. The chances of you meeting a maniac are slim."

"You're not famous," she retorted, her eyes flashing. "You don't understand."

"Yes, but there are plenty of people more famous than you that just get on with their lives. They live like normal human beings. You look for trouble with all the heavies and drama."

"What did you say?"

"You heard me. You are not handling your fame properly."

She pulled the blanket up around her breasts. "I handle it just fine," she spat. "Again, I repeat that you have no idea what you're talking about."

"Is this because someone waved a knife in your face?"

She nodded.

"Once?"

"Yes."

"But it was blunt, am I right?"

"So? I didn't know that." Her eyes flashed. "It's different

for actors and people like that. They are protected by the screen. Their job doesn't rely on contact with fans. I could have eighty thousand faces in front of me at one time. People try to touch me."

He tied his jeans. "Look, if we're going to be something, you're going to have to get rid of all that nonsense. I want to hang out, walk down the street, have dinner in a restaurant, without people looking over my shoulder."

"My dad advised me …"

"He's being over-protective."

"You don't know my dad," she said bitterly. "More like guilt."

"Look, I want to take you to an art gallery today. Just us. Will you come?"

"How will we get there?"

"The tube? I don't know."

"No way," she said vehemently. "I'll go but only if John can drive us."

"John?"

"My chauffeur."

Caspian ran his fingers through his hair. "Fine. You win."

She smiled. "I'll text him there and ask him to bring over some clothes. I didn't bring anything with me."

"I prefer you without any."

She made a face and dialled John's number. "Hey, it's me. I need you to pick me up. Yes, same place. I'm going to text Clio and ask her to pack a bag. Bring that with you. Sure, sure. See you soon."

She hung up. "All done." She smiled. "Now, have you a beanie hat I could borrow? A big one to cover my hair."

Chapter Twenty-one

Cliona read the message twice. It consisted of a list of clothes, shoes, toiletries and a phone charger. It ended with: **Give the bag to John and enjoy your days off xxx Mads xxx**

There was no mention of what she was doing or with whom she was staying.

She dialled Fionn's number.

"Hey," she said in a bright voice. "Are you busy? I've a few days off and would like some company."

"Hey, Clio. That sounds good. I don't have any plans."

"Oh? No gigs or anything?"

"Nope. Caspian has gone AWOL. He texted a couple of days ago and said he needed some time to write. So Ethan headed to Gdansk with Stella for a few days and Alex is gone back to Kent to see his parents and pet pig Bella."

"His what?"

"His pig. He's had her since she was a piglet. His parents wanted to send her to the abattoir but Alex chained himself to the fence and refused to let it happen. Now she's the family pet."

"That's so cute." Cliona smiled briefly before resuming her sombre mood. Caspian was on the missing list. So was Madison. It didn't take a genius to work out where they were.

"Text me later and we'll meet up." Fionn sounded cheerful. "We could take in a show or a museum."

"Great. Talk then." She hung up the phone.

Wearily, she packed Madison's bag as instructed. One of the items on the list was lacy underwear. Opening Madison's drawer, Cliona pulled out some flesh-coloured granny knickers instead. She debated whether she should pack them, but baulked in the end. It just wasn't worth the hassle. There was nothing she could do anyway.

Half an hour later, John called.

"Thanks, Cliona," he said formally, taking the bag. "See you."

The Mercedes dropped Madison and Caspian as close to the Tate Modern as possible. She pulled Caspian's beanie hat down around her ears. Dressed in jeans and an oversized hoodie, she kept her head down and walked towards the tall red brick building. Caspian, dressed in a dark brown overcoat and skinny blue jeans, held her hand.

They entered the building. "Stand here," he said. "I'll get the tickets."

She glanced around furtively, expecting someone to approach her, but no one did. Everyone passed by without a second glance.

Minutes later they were upstairs. "Pierre Bonnard. Have you heard of him?"

"Yes," she said enthusiastically. "I read about him at school."

"You took Art at school?"

"Yes. I loved it."

"Me too."

"Have you seen his work before?" he asked.

She shook her head. "No."

"Then you're in for a treat." He led her to the first painting. "He captures moments in time. I love the intimacy of his domestic scenes."

Together, they walked through the different rooms, pausing in front of some paintings. Caspian pointed out different aspects, commenting on Bonnard's unconventional use of colour. "This is *Le Jardin.* He painted it in 1936."

"You know a lot about him," she said in wonder.

"This is my third visit," he admitted. "I've read up on him too."

"Still, you're impressive." She smiled. "You could give tours."

Someone tapped her on the shoulder. "Excuse me, could I have your autograph?"

It was a young girl of about seventeen. She had a piece of paper and a pen. Caspian squeezed Madison's hand in reassurance.

"Sure," she said eventually. "What's the name?"

"Jennifer."

Madison scribbled something and signed her name. "There you go."

"I'm a huge fan."

"Thanks."

"Can I have a selfie too?"

"There's no photography allowed in the gallery. Sorry." Madison turned away.

The girl pulled at her sleeve. "Can you come outside for a minute? I really want to put this on Instagram."

Madison shook her head and walked away.

"*Madison!*" the girl called. "Come on! I'm such a big fan."

Madison kept walking.

"*Please!*" she shouted.

Madison left the room and pulled up her hood. Caspian followed. They walked out into the cold air.

"She was insistent," he said, falling into step beside her.

"Yep."

"Does it annoy you?"

"Now, it does. I mean, in the beginning, I lived for the attention. Now, all I want to be a normal person."

"Really?" He looked dubious. "You wouldn't miss it?"

Madison smiled. "Well, maybe a small bit. I just want to go to a gallery with my boyfriend and not be pestered."

"Am I your boyfriend?" He grabbed her arm and stopped her in her tracks.

She blushed. "Sorry, that just slipped out. I mean ..."

"It's fine with me." He traced her cheek with his finger.

"Really?" Her blue eyes searched his.

"Yes." He bent his head and kissed her on the mouth. In the distance, a camera flashed and the next day the internet was covered with the breaking story of Madison's new love.

Cliona stared at the paper. There they were, kissing each other, two blonde heads together. The headline was: **Maddy's Mystery Man**

She turned it over. She was trying to be happy for her

friend. She really was. She knew she had no claim to him – he had barely spoken to her for a start. However, she was hurt that Madison didn't even acknowledge the fact that her feelings might be bruised. Instead, she carried on like nothing had happened.

She sighed. Life was life. She had to accept that girls like Madison wiped the floor with girls like her. If she were Caspian, she'd pick her blonde, beautiful boss too. It's just he filled her thoughts all the time and she felt a little bit heartbroken for her dream that would never be realised.

Her phone pinged and Madison's name appeared.

Take the next few days off! X Will be in touch x Mads xx

Cliona accessed the Ryanair app straight away. There was no way she was sticking around London, mooning about him and her and imagining them together. She would go home and spend time with her parents. No one could cheer her up like them. Constance with her mindfulness spiel and Aonghus treating her like his 'best girl'. She found a flight straight away. Typing in her PayPal password, she purchased a flight for the next morning. Then she texted Madison to say that she was going to Dublin for three days. Home was where the heart was. That was for sure.

Two days later, the whole world was asking: **Who is Caspian Cole?**

People started following him on Instagram and Twitter. Pictures of him were shared and printed. Doctor Eckleburg's tracks on YouTube got thousands of hits. Caspian received a direct message from a radio station, asking if he had a track they could play. He called the band to his flat immediately. Madison had gone home to collect a few things so he was by himself.

"This has gone crazy," he said, pacing the floor. "We're not ready for this."

Fionn twirled his drumstick in his hand. "It's fast but I think it's good. We're going from nought to sixty in a matter of days."

"I agree," said Alex. "What we badly need to do is hire a studio and record a few tracks."

"It will be rushed," argued Caspian. "We'll just produce sub-standard work and sell ourselves out."

"So?" said Ethan. "I'm cool with that. Stop being so moral."

Caspian shook his head. "No, no. It's not going to happen like this, guys. We have to make it on our own. We *will* make it on our own."

"It's not just your band!" said Fionn practically. "I mean, I for one am delighted that you've bagged yourself a famous girlfriend if it means we get lots of cash and fame."

Alex laughed. "Don't say that to him, mate."

Caspian stopped and held up his hands. "Well, I'm not buying into it. End of story. I need to write some new songs and we need to take this slowly. Maybe gig a bit more but that's it. We've got to have integrity."

Ethan stood up. "Look, integrity or not, I don't think you'll be able to control this. However, I do agree that we need new material. We also need to find a manager and record a few tracks. Fionn has been doing an admirable job but it's time we had a professional."

"That's grand with me," said Fionn cheerfully.

"Who?" asked Caspian.

"Ask Maddy," suggested Fionn. "Her manager might know someone suitable."

"Yeah, he could point us in the right direction," agreed Alex.

"I don't know," said Caspian dubiously. "I don't want to use her ..."

"Oh, come down off your high ground," said Ethan irritably. "Ask Madison to recommend someone and let's get this moving."

When Madison got back, the band had left. She dumped a huge suitcase in next to the couch and threw herself on Caspian.

"Did you miss me?" she crooned, kissing him.

He wriggled free. "I'm all over the internet," he began.

"Yeah! I know. Bethany texted me." She beamed at him. "It's great, isn't it? Your band will get airplay in no time."

His expression darkened. "I don't want airplay. Not yet. We're not ready."

"Really?" She took off her coat. "How else will people hear your stuff?"

"At gigs."

"How many people turn up to those things? One hundred? You need to put yourself out there. Radio is so effective. Then it will lead to other things like television and stuff. That's how it works in this business. One thing leads to another."

"No." He was firm. "We're not ready. I don't want to rush greatness."

Madison made the mistake of laughing. "Caspian, you're something else. You need to take a serious chill pill."

He glowered at her.

"*I don't want to rush greatness,*" she mimicked. "You're not Tchaikovsky, you know. Or Brach ..."

"It's *Bach.*"

"Whatever. Look, our relationship might speed things along. Just go with it. Your so-called greatness will overshadow it in the long run."

Caspian looked mutinous. "Let's change the subject. How long are you staying over?"

"I don't know, a couple of days. I told Ross I wanted time off."

A few days turned into two weeks. Madison turned off her phone and spent a lot of time at Caspian's flat. She preferred it there as it felt like a different world.

One time she brought Caspian back to her apartment and the next morning they saw Cliona on her way out. Madison was wearing Caspian's T-shirt and they were kissing and giggling on the couch. The look on Cliona's face was telling. It was obvious her crush hadn't abated. Madison didn't do guilt, but she felt bad for Cliona. She knew it wasn't easy for her to see Caspian like that, so she opted to stay in King's Cross to avoid confrontation.

As she was off the radar so to speak, her staff were at a loose end most of the time. Cliona's pager and phone remained silent and Mona took the opportunity to go skiing. There were no big events to attend in January, so Angelica also went on holidays to Mexico. Boris kept calling Madison, warning her that she shouldn't let her fitness regime slip, but she turned off her phone. She liked eating pizza and drinking beer. She found that Caspian preferred the natural look so opted not to wear make-up anymore.

Instead, she let her long hair fall loose and she liked wearing his clothes as they were baggy and comfortable.

They argued a lot too, mainly about going out. Madison would insist on Todd or Peter being in the vicinity if they were going to a public place and Caspian would object. In the end, they rarely ventured outside to avoid confrontation.

The band called over a few times to practise when she was there and she found that she loved hanging out with them. Ethan was so witty and Alex was so nice. They accepted her into the fold without any fuss and never really mentioned her day job. What Madison especially loved was how the band acted so normally around her. Never once did they make her feel like a star and for that she was grateful. It had been years since she had really been herself, abandoning the act and allowing herself to relax. Once Ethan asked her about some famous people she had been photographed with and what they were like in real life. She proceeded to regale them with scurrilous stories about the rich and famous, embellishing parts to add to the drama.

One night, Stella made a traditional Polish meal – *bigos*, which was a cabbage stew, and *golonka*, which was pork. The band joined them and they drank bottles of red, smoked some weed and played card games until three in the morning.

Madison often thought of Ross and how he would react if he knew she was stuffing her face, drinking as much alcohol as she wanted and getting high. That thought made her feel rebellious and she liked it.

She also enjoyed how they teased Caspian for his lofty ideas and artistic temperament. During the short time they had been together, she had often woken up to find his side of the bed empty, and he would be at the piano, gently playing melodies and humming along. She picked up the tunes quickly and sometimes she would sing with him. However, he didn't like that and would often tell her to stop as she was distracting him. A fight would inevitably follow.

"I can't concentrate with you warbling in the background, making it sound like a stupid pop song."

"Warbling? Are you for real? Just remember that I'm the star, not you."

"Like you ever let me forget."

Soon the band grew restless. Caspian's place was the main venue for practising as he had a proper piano. In the beginning, Madison's presence had been a novelty. She would sit and watch as they played around with riffs. However, after a while, she became a huge distraction. Caspian hadn't produced any new material, despite his promises, as all his time was taken up with her.

"Look, I'm all for you having a girlfriend," said Alex. "She's certainly something, Casp. But we have to keep up the momentum. We are so close, I can feel it."

So, Caspian asked Madison for some space as he felt guilty about his lack of productivity. Insecure, she lashed out and accused him of going off her. What ensued was a screaming match where she stalked out and he threw a shoe at the wall in rage.

When they eventually made up two days later, a subdued and apologetic Madison explained that she was notoriously jealous and that Cal Scott's betrayal during her formative years had scarred her. Caspian held her in his arms and reassured her that he was faithful but that he needed to work.

Chapter Twenty-two

They spent time apart naturally in the end. Ross, fed up of Madison playing hooky, called her up and demanded that she come down to his office. The Grammys were two weeks away and she was supposed to perform with Sauron.

"You need to dazzle at this, Maddy," said Ross. "You've taken your eye off the ball. That Ariana Grande is wiping the floor with you. I want you to work the red carpet, the works. Then your performance with Sauron better lift off the ceiling, do you know what I mean, like?"

She couldn't argue with him as she knew it was true. Hiding from reality was fine until you had to face it again and pick up the pieces.

"Fine, fine. I'll get back to work." She glared at him. "I just needed a break."

"How's your new fella? He's a singer, right?"

She nodded. "He's in a band called Doctor Eckleburg."

"Any good?"

"Yeah, pretty good. A bit like Coldplay."

"Have they signed with anyone?"

She laughed. "They don't even have a manager. Caspian

is very slow to push them into the limelight. He's too busy writing songs."

Ross drummed his fingers on the table. "He's getting a lot of press coverage because of you. It might be something we could work with. Celebrity couples are revenue gold. Especially from two different genres. Your fans and his future fans would merge and *bam*! A powerhouse."

Madison bit her lip. "He's allergic when I offer to help things along. He has way too many morals. We couldn't be obvious about it."

"I'll make a few calls."

"Make sure it's not linked back to us. He'd never forgive me."

"Fair enough." He smiled. "So, back to the grindstone, Maddy. I'll call you later."

She stood up and gave a little wave.

"Oh, and you're looking a bit well-fed, if you know what I mean. Lay off the chips and booze for a week. You can't afford to attract body-shaming attention."

She blushed furiously. How dare Ross make a comment on her weight? She went straight home and frantically looked in the full-length mirror in her bedroom. She looked healthy and happy. Didn't she? Sure, her jeans were a bit tight, but they still tied. She turned sideways and sucked in her stomach. Was that slight paunch there before? She didn't remember it …

She called Boris right away. "Meet me at the gym," she said grimly. "I need to do double time to get back in shape."

Cliona, who had had a relaxing few weeks, found that having Madison back was a huge shock to the system. Her phone pinged constantly and she found herself running here and there. There was huge organisation for the trip to LA. If she packed the suitcases once, she packed them ten times as Madison kept changing her mind. She researched the weather in California in February and tried to prepare accordingly.

The apartment was buzzing with life. Angelica was constantly on the phone to all the major fashion houses, trying to secure a gown for the big night. She had contacts in Valentino, Chanel and Stella McCartney, and was trying to get the best gown for the red carpet.

Bethany was tweeting constantly, preparing America for Madison's trip. Already she had secured five invitations to after-parties. The challenge was to decide which one to go to. The opportunities to visit Caspian became fewer and fewer. This gave the band much-needed time to practise and reconnect.

"Did you ask about a manager?" Alex demanded one evening.

Caspian shrugged. "I didn't have time ..."

Ethan banged his fist on the amp. "This is a band, Caspian. A democracy. Sort it out or I swear I'm done with it."

Three days later a man called Jax Mastrano from Odyssey Management contacted Caspian and asked to meet at his office on Camden Street.

He showed the message to Madison.

"Is this anything to do with you?" he asked directly.

"Jax Mastrano," she read aloud. "Never heard of him."

Later that evening, Caspian showed the message to the band.

"What do you think? Maddy had nothing to do with it. He has contacted us on his own."

Ethan googled him. "Right, it says here that he's a member of the MMF."

"The what?" asked Alex.

"The Music Managers Forum," explained Ethan. "Thirty years old. Second generation Italian. Sharp dresser."

"Does he manage anyone we know?"

Ethan frowned. "I don't think so." He read on. "Oh, wait. He used to manage Quantum, that indie band from a couple of years back."

"Oh yeah, they played Glastonbury."

"I say give him a chance," said Fionn. "He might organise us properly."

"They can take up to a twenty-per-cent cut," warned Caspian.

"Twenty per cent of nothing is fine with me," said Alex cheerfully.

"Hey, I've been sort of managing us and I didn't get any cut," mocked Fionn. "I'll make out an invoice."

"Look, I say we meet him. I think he'd be a good bet," said Alex. "We're at a standstill, guys. We need something to happen."

Fionn contacted Jax and arranged a meeting at his offices. They took the Northern Line to Camden Town and walked the short distance down Camden Road. The brightly coloured houses looked cheerful in the winter sun and the bustle of the people heading to and from the famous market gave an upbeat atmosphere. The canals that lay adjacent to the street gave the place character and the Odyssey Management building was covered in street art.

The secretary, a young girl of about twenty, looked up when they walked in through the glass door.

"Can I help you?" she asked.

"We're Doctor Eckleburg. We're here to see Jax."

"Ah, okay. He's expecting you." She pointed to the stairs. "Second storey. The lift is broken so you'll have to go on foot, I'm afraid."

They climbed the two flights of stairs and stopped in front of a door with Jax's name on it.

Alex knocked and waited. The door opened to reveal a small, dark-haired man wearing a beautifully cut suit.

"Doctor Eckleburg!" he said warmly. "Come in, come in!"

He led them into a spacious office with a large mahogany desk and a big bay window overlooking the busy street. A huge Mac was perched on the desk along with a framed picture of Jax and a small boy on the desk, and a withered plant in a ceramic pot.

"I think you boys have something," he said, taking a seat on his leather chair. "I've been reading about you." He pointed at Caspian. "So I checked out your songs. Not bad. Not bad at all."

"Have you represented a band like us in the past?" asked Caspian.

"Not exactly, no." Jax smiled showing brilliant white teeth. "I started with a jazz musician called Smokin' Frankie, have you heard of him?"

The band shook their heads.

"I'm not surprised. Jazz is too niche, too select. So I moved on to an indie band, Quantum, and that was going great until the lead singer got too big for his boots and they split." He stared at Caspian. "No chance of that with you, I hope."

Caspian stared back haughtily.

"Look, I'm interested in giving this a go." Jax sat back in his chair. "Because you're the next best thing. I can feel it. I've been watching those clips on YouTube and I've got to say you're smoking."

"Right." Caspian looked dubious.

"Plus those headlines with Maddy Ryan help a bit too."

Fionn looked at Caspian in alarm. "But that's not why you want to manage us, right?"

Jax shook his head. "No, I genuinely believe in you. I think you'll be huge."

Ethan glanced at Alex. "How does this work exactly?" he asked Jax.

"Well, I act as an agent and manager. I get you gigs and press coverage. We build up a fan base."

"You'll take care of all that?" said Fionn.

"One hundred per cent. That gives you time to write new songs and record an album. I've a mate with a studio and he'll let us have it when you want it."

"A studio?" repeated Caspian. "Just like that?"

"Yeah, just to get you started." Jax smiled. "We need proper demos."

"And then?"

"We sign with a record company. That's a given."

"You make it sound so easy," said Alex. "Like a walk in the park."

"With me behind you, it will be." He sat back in his chair. "We've got to trust one another. Give me a chance to show you what I can do."

Fionn looked at the other members of Doctor Eckleburg. "That sounds fair enough."

They nodded.

"Right, let's get the ball rolling," said Alex.

"For sure," said Jax. "I'll get on it right away."

Caspian looked at him suspiciously. "You don't know Ross Curtis, do you?"

Jax shrugged. "I've heard of him. I mean, he's pretty big in my line of work."

"He didn't call you or anything?"

"Not at all. Why do you ask?"

Fionn pulled Caspian out the door. "Don't mind him, Jax. Keep in touch."

Madison called over to Caspian's flat that night. He was playing piano and writing on sheet music with a pencil.

"Hey, you!" She sat on the couch. "I'm exhausted. Boris made me run ten kilometres."

Caspian looked at her and frowned. "Why?"

"The Grammys are next week. I have to be in great shape." She sighed. "Sometimes I wonder if it's all worth it."

He hummed a tune and then played it with his right hand. Then he hummed it again, replacing the major key with a minor.

"How was your day?" she asked, resting her head backwards.

"We met with that manager."

"Oh?"

"I'm unconvinced. He seemed a bit too earnest."

"*Hmmm*. They tend to be like that. It's that kind of world."

He played the left hand, his fingers moving like lightning. She closed her eyes for a moment.

"Caspian?" she said suddenly. "Will you be my date to the Grammys?"

He stopped playing immediately. "What?"

"It's next weekend in LA. I mean, it's no big deal."

"I'm not sure ..." He brushed his blonde hair out of his eyes. "I shouldn't really take off now. That Jax guy is pretty enthusiastic. He wants to get recording next Monday."

"It's an important night," she said earnestly. "Ross is freaking out because I've been so lax lately. I mean, just because I've taken a small break."

"What night is it?"

"Sunday."

"When will we be back?"

"Tuesday? I mean, it'll be a quick visit."

Caspian rubbed out a crotchet on the sheet music and replaced it with a minim. "Okay. I'll check it out with Jax and the band." He looked up. "Now can you be quiet while I finish this song? I need silence."

Jax clapped his hands together in delight. "The Grammys? Go for it. Publicity gold."

"Really? I thought we were booked to record some tracks next week."

"We can start and take a small break while you jump across the pond. It's a great opportunity to network. I insist that you go."

"If you're sure."

"I'm sure. Now, see you at the studio on Monday morning. I think we'll record 'Mosaic' first. It's the most accessible one; it's our first single."

"I disagree ..."

"Caspian," interrupted Jax. "You do what you're good at, which is writing songs, and I'll do what I'm good at, selling your music. 'Mosaic' is the song, don't argue."

Jax was waiting for them at Atlantis Music Studios near Richmond the next Monday morning.

"You all look like death warmed up," he said with a grin.

Fionn yawned. "It's before eight, Jax. I'm never up before ten. Plus I've only had three coffees. Give me a break."

Alex had his bass guitar slung over his shoulder. "Morning, Jax. I'm from a farm so I'm used to early starts." He grinned cheerfully.

"Did you source a grand piano?" Caspian asked immediately.

"It's all good, boys. It's all good." Jax opened the double doors. "Welcome to where the magic happens."

They took the lift to the second floor and Jax used a tag to enter two sets of sound proof doors. Finally they entered the control room where they found a sound engineer called Carly and a producer called Pat. There were three chairs, a huge multitrack mixing console and massive studio monitor speakers.

"Hello, there," said Carly with a broad smile. "Jax says we're in for a treat. I'm Carly."

She was a pretty woman in her forties with peroxide blonde hair and a nose ring.

"Hello," said Ethan with a little wave. The rest of the band mumbled a greeting.

"I'm Pat," said the other occupant of the room. "I'm going to produce this track. Have you worked with a producer before?"

They shook their heads.

"Well, I'm here to advise you on how to arrange the tracks and possibly improve them."

Caspian's face tightened.

"We have to collaborate and compromise, boys." He smiled. "Now, time is precious, so head into that room over there." He pointed to the live room. "Get set up and we'll get cracking."

Madison called Caspian at lunchtime. "Hey, baby. Are you free this afternoon? I've a tailor booked from Armani. He's going to make you a new suit. Custom-made."

Caspian, who had spent most of his morning in an isolation room singing, couldn't process what she was saying.

"A tailor? What?"

"He's only over from Milan for two days and Angelica pulled strings so if you could meet me at around three, that would be great."

Caspian took a deep breath and counted to five.

"Maddy?"

"*Hmmm?*"

"You know I'm recording today, right?"

"Yeah."

"I can't go for a fitting of any kind. The studio is costing a small fortune and we've just nailed the vocals to 'Mosaic'. We recorded a guide track and now we have to overlay separate instrument takes. Then harmonies and fills. I'm tied up."

"I know what it's like to record a song," she said icily.

"Not this kind of song. My vocals and piano are separate. All you do is sing."

"Look, Caspian, it'll only be an hour. Two, tops."

"No, Maddy. Not today. I'm focused on the song. Sorry."

"Caspian! Alessandro is only here for two days! You'd better jump ship and come down ..."

He hung up the phone.

They finished the song late that night. Pat and Carly stayed with them throughout.

"We'll mix it in the morning," said Carly with a big yawn. "I'm out of here."

Caspian was reluctant to leave. "If only we could try the piano once more," he said ruefully. "That last take was rubbish."

Fionn propelled him out the door. "Tomorrow, Casp. Now go home and get some sleep."

Madison left five heated messages on Caspian's phone, but he didn't bother to listen. He didn't care about a stupid suit. She didn't understand that he couldn't focus on anything now except his music.

Recording his voice had been intense but mind-blowing. He had never dreamed that it could sound like that. Walking down the street, he gazed up at the stars. 'Mosaic' was going to be a triumph. He could feel it.

Carly sent the edited track to a specialist company to be mastered. "That gives it the professional polish so that it can be released," she explained. "Well done, boys. That's a great song right there."

"Shall we start on another one?" Caspian held up some sheet music. "I have an idea. I think we should bring in a harpist."

Jax nodded. "The plan is to produce an EP. Then we'll send it to some record labels. Are your social media accounts linked?"

Alex shrugged. "I don't think so. I've been pretty lazy with that lately."

"Then hand it over to us. We'll do the publicity side from now on. The first step is to interlink Instagram, Facebook, Twitter, YouTube, your website ..."

"We don't have a website," said Fionn.

"You will." Jax smiled. "By close of business today." He typed something into his phone. "Now, we've got to look at branding. We need ideas for the cover. Anyone good at art?"

Caspian held up his hand. "I'm not bad."

"Right, can you envision something for the front cover? We can always change it later."

"Right."

"Maybe a mosaic? Or is that too kitsch?"

Caspian looked thoughtful. "I'll sort it out."

"We need a pitch that sets you apart from the rest. I'll work on that and we'll collaborate before we finalise." He picked up his car keys off the desk. "Back to work, boys. Talk later."

At three o'clock, just as Alex finished his instrumental, there was a big commotion in the control room. Caspian looked up from his piano.

Madison was behind the glass, gesticulating madly, with the Italian man by her side.

"Who the hell is that?" asked Ethan.

Pat spoke through the microphone. "Caspian? Have you got a few minutes?"

Madison made a pleading gesture.

"What does she want?" asked Fionn. "Casp?"

"That man is here to measure me for a suit." He stood up slowly. "I don't believe it."

Alex started laughing. "Tell me you're joking."

"No, no. I'm perfectly serious. His name is Alessandro and he's from Armani."

"Good God." Ethan put down his guitar. "Well, get to it, lover-boy. We'll wait."

Caspian walked into the control room and Madison rushed into his arms. "Sorry to disturb but Alessandro's flight is at six and we just have to get you suited and booted for the ceremony."

Carly leaned back in her chair and put her arms behind her head. "Don't mind us."

"Madison, I ..."

"Come on, we can do it in the bathroom." She kissed his cheek. "The sooner you get it done, the sooner you get back to your song."

Chapter Twenty-three

By Thursday, they had the EP in the bag. Four original songs by Doctor Eckleburg.

"Let's hit the pub and celebrate," suggested Alex. "We deserve it."

Fionn nodded. "I'm in. We need to mark the occasion."

"I'll call Stella,' said Ethan. "She's off tonight."

"Do you want to call Maddy?" Fionn asked Caspian.

He shook his head. "She's on a health binge for the Grammys. Strict bedtime routine and no alcohol. Plus we fly to LA tomorrow so she'll be busy getting ready for that."

They walked along Camden Road.

"It's a good record," said Ethan. "Not blowing our own trumpet, but it has something."

"Yeah," agreed Alex. "This time next year things might be so different."

Fionn's phone started to ring. "Hey, Clio. Yeah, we finished. No, I don't have a copy for Mum and her buddies yet." He rolled his eyes at the band. "Yeah, yeah. I promise I'll call her."

Alex grabbed his sleeve. "Ask her to come for drinks," he said.

Fionn nodded. "Hey, are you free to meet up? Yeah, now? Just for a few. Okay, okay. We're heading to Waxy's near Piccadilly. Cool, see you there." He hung up.

Waxy O'Connor's was a bustling Irish pub in Soho. It had three different bars, all with a different vibe. Its interior was famous – six levels of extraordinary features such as timber carvings, stained-glass windows and a labyrinth of staircases.

Cliona was waiting outside the arched door when Doctor Eckleburg arrived. Her cheeks were rosy from the cold and she wore a big padded jacket and a long woolly scarf.

"Clio!" called Fionn as he crossed the street.

"Hey!" She waved.

Alex and Ethan waved back. Caspian, who was texting on his phone as he walked, didn't notice her presence until they came to a stop on the pavement.

"Hi, Caspian," she said shyly.

He focused in on her face. "Oh, hello," he said absentmindedly. "How have you been?"

"Great." She blushed. "I hear you're coming to LA tomorrow."

He nodded. "That's Madison on the phone. She sent me a list of things to bring." He put it in his pocket. "I'll pack in the morning."

"Have you been waiting long?" Fionn asked as they walked up the steps and entered the bar.

"Not really."

The pub was crowded and they meandered their way through the different groups. Finally they found an empty table underneath a giant preserved tree.

"Beers all around?" asked Fionn.

The group nodded.

"Stella should be here soon, Cliona," said Ethan. "Just in case you're feeling outnumbered amongst all the guys."

"Oh, I'm fine," she said happily. "It's no problem at all."

Alex took the stool next to her. "So, is this Waxy a cousin of yours?" he asked with a grin.

"Sorry?" She tore her eyes away from Caspian who had resumed texting on his phone.

"Waxy O'Connor. He's a relative, right?" Alex's brown eyes stared at her.

"Oh, I get it." She smiled. "No, no. No connection at all." She flicked her hair nervously, willing Caspian to look up from his phone. His brow was furrowed as he typed. She guessed that it was Madison again as every now and then he would audibly sigh.

Finally, he threw the phone on the table.

"She's such a control freak!"

Ethan laughed. "Get used to it, mate."

"Seriously, does it matter what colour shirts I bring? I mean, will the world end if we're not coordinated?" He started shredding a beermat. "I wish I didn't have to leave, guys. We're really tight after this week. I wish I could skip LA and write."

"No!" Cliona almost shouted. "I mean, no. Maddy would be so disappointed."

Caspian said nothing.

Fionn appeared with a tray of beers. "You could've helped, lads." He threw his eyes to heaven as he carefully placed the tray on the table.

"Sorry!" Cliona's hand flew to her mouth. "You're some man to carry all those pints down here."

"Drummer's muscles," said Fionn, flexing his bicep.

Stella arrived, pushing through a group of men holding pints. She blew on her hands. "It's so cold!' she complained.

Ethan helped her to take off her jacket. "Would you like a beer?"

She shook her head. "A vodka, please."

"Coming right up." Ethan kissed her nose and walked off to the bar.

"Jax is like a tornado, isn't he?" said Fionn. "We've known him for such a short time and look at us now."

"It's great to have someone take over the other stuff," agreed Alex. "Now, we can just concentrate on our music."

Ethan arrived back and placed a glass in front of Stella. "Enjoy," he said, kissing her lips and resuming his own seat at the table.

"Right, a toast!" Alex held up his pint. "To Doctor Eckleburg and our first EP!"

Everyone clinked their glasses.

"This is the beginning," said Ethan seriously. "I can feel it."

"I think we should thank Caspian here," suggested Fionn, with a wink. "Without his dashing good looks and his love affair with Maddy, we would never have gained as much momentum."

"Stop," said Caspian. "Of course we would. Conversation over."

"Maddy did help, mate," said Ethan. "You being splashed across social media on her arm definitely put us on the radar. That's where Jax heard about us."

"Maybe she sped things along, but there was never any question of us not making it." He drank his beer. "We will be famous for our music, not my personal life."

"Your self-belief is something else," said Alex. "It's unfaltering."

Caspian shrugged. "I've known all my life that I will be …"

"Great." Alex cut him off. "We know."

"Madison is separate to all this," he continued. "Whether we're together or not, our music is what matters. It's the quality of the songs that will catapult us into the stratosphere."

Caspian left after one beer. He was desperate to play his piano as a tune had crept into his head and he could think of nothing else. The pub was like a blur to him. He could hear various conversations, but he didn't process it. Not when he could feel the notes of the music coming out his fingertips. Not when the melody drowned out everything else.

He walked to the Piccadilly tube station and bounded down the steps. He followed signs for the Piccadilly Line and took the train to King's Cross St. Pancras. It was still relatively early. All he needed was some peace and quiet and a keyboard.

Cliona tried not to look dismayed when Caspian announced that he was leaving.

You'll have him for an entire trans-Atlantic flight tomorrow, she chided herself.

Still, it was disappointing that he took off. She never saw him without Madison by his side.

"How's life in the fast lane?" Alex nudged her gently and she came back to earth.

"Oh, fine," she answered, pulling herself together. "Hectic, but fine."

"Is Maddy hard to work for?"

"No," she said loyally. "I mean, she's a star and used to getting what she wants all the time."

"Including your crush." His eyes were filled with compassion. "I presume she was aware of your undying love for Caspian?"

"Hey!' She looked around nervously in case the rest of the table heard. "Don't say that."

"But she knew, didn't she?"

"It was never confirmed."

"Still, it can't be easy."

"It's fine." Her eyes met his. "I never stood a chance anyway."

"You don't know that."

"Oh, I do." She looked bitter for a moment. "I mean, I dressed up tonight." She pointed to her red dress and boots. "I never wear dresses. Oh, and I'm wearing contacts. All in a sad attempt for him to notice me." She faced him. "You see, I'm no better than Maddy. He's her boyfriend and I'm trying to impress him."

Alex dismissed her with a wave of his hand. "All's fair in love and war," he said.

Fionn balanced a beermat on his nose. "Check this out, lads. I'm a talented young fella!"

Cliona giggled. "Well, I'll always be cooler than my big brother here."

Alex laughed. "Immeasurably."

♫ ♫ ♫

The next day Madison and Caspian flew to LA in a private jet. Her whole team went too, even her chef.

"I hate American food," she said, making a face as they boarded the steps. "Giorgio is a genius in the kitchen. Especially with low-fat stuff."

Caspian, who had never really experienced Madison in this context, didn't say much. He just drank it all in – the bodyguards, the personal trainer, the stylists. He tried not to look that impressed with the private jet and the endless champagne.

A blushing Cliona took a seat opposite him.

"It's pretty amazing, isn't it?" she said, buckling her seatbelt. "I had never travelled first class before I started working for Maddy, not to mind fly in a private jet."

"Yeah, it's cool,' he said, stretching out his long legs.

"Did you write that song last night?"

"Some if it." He looked pained. "I'd love to have spent all day today at it, but here I am."

He put his head back, closed his eyes and fell asleep almost immediately. Cliona stared at his face in wonder. She searched for a flaw but couldn't find one. She had steeled herself to act cool in his company. A whole week of him in close proximity filled her with joy, even though he'd be on the arm of Madison. Pathetic as it was, she was delighted to be in his presence, irrespective of why or how.

Caspian was woken up by Angelica talking loudly to Mona about the rep at Chanel.

"I asked her for three samples," she said, chewing her

gum noisily. "She was all weird about it so I said 'Do you realise how lucky you are that Madison is even considering wearing Chanel to the ceremony?' and she got all huffy."

"Bloody reps," said Mona, making a face.

"So I said, 'We need a gown for Sunday night and it looks like we'll go with Valentino' and then I hung up."

"That told her," said Mona approvingly.

"She needs to realise that we celebrity stylists can make or break a trend. She should've kept me sweet."

"For sure."

Boris was rubbing Deep Heat on his calf, humming along to a song on his iPod. His boot camp with Madison had paid off and she was in good shape. He thanked God that she had seen sense when she did. Every minute of that two weeks had been necessary to get her back on track.

Bethany, although a publicist for three celebrities, had opted to come as it was a chance to network. A small dark-haired girl, she always wore stilettos to give the impression that she was taller. She was never without a phone in her hand and spent her days finding angles to promote her clients and gain a wider audience. Madison was her biggest name and she worked hard at keeping her sweet. She had warned the media of Madison's arrival and was expecting a good turnout. Then there was a short interview at the Beverly Wilshire, followed by a rooftop meet and greet. She had already leaked the time and place of this appearance so she expected thousands. Lots of young fans with banners and smartphones, desperate for selfies with their idol. The cops had been informed too as public order had to be maintained. Railings would be set up to corral the crowd, just in case there was a stampede. Madison would smile and wave from the safety of the roof as they screamed her name from below.

She had three celebrity photographers on speed dial and she had nurtured a symbiotic relationship. She gave them classified information when she wanted media coverage and, in return, they backed off when required. Some newer members of the paparazzi were harder to control, but she was working on it. Most of the time, Madison's 'tweets' were in Bethany's hand. The photos posted on Instagram were carefully chosen and edited by Bethany also. Harnessing the power of social media was her trade and she was damn good at it.

Mona gave Madison a pedicure and a manicure halfway across the Atlantic. They conducted this grooming session in the bedroom of the plane. Using a pumice, she rid her feet of dead skin. Then she buffed and filed her nails, applied some lotion and finally painted them a deep red. Just before landing, she blow-dried Madison's hair and touched up her make-up. Madison sat motionless for the whole thing, letting Mona work her magic.

Madison's outfit had been carefully chosen by Angelica back in London. It was a navy skirt and a white shirt. On her feet she wore navy kitten heels and on her arm she had an oversized Louis Vuitton holdall. At the last minute, Angelica added a large red belt and tied it around her small waist. It gave a splash of colour and finally she was ready to face the world.

They touched down in LAX at around four local time. Both Todd and Peter had accompanied Madison as maximum security was needed. An extra security team had been hired for the Grammys as it was such a high-profile event.

Madison took Caspian's hand as they walked through the airport, her eyes concealed by enormous glasses. Cameras flashed and people called her name. One photographer got too close and Todd pushed him back forcibly with his huge arm. Madison kept walking with her head down. They reached the doors and John was outside, standing next to a Range Rover. He opened the door and she stepped in. A bemused Caspian followed and the door shut. Todd got in the front seat. There was another Range Rover behind them for the staff who followed suit.

Madison took off her glasses. "How do I look?" she asked Caspian worriedly. "I'm always stressed when the paps are around."

"Good, fine."

"Thank God. I want those photos to be decent." She sat back in the leather seat as the car pulled away from the kerb.

"I found that a bit odd," said Caspian after a few minutes. "I've never seen you like that before."

"Like what?"

"I don't know, a superstar, I guess."

She leaned over and kissed him lightly so as not to ruin her lipstick. "Welcome to the Bigtime," she said with a wink. "Bethany made sure they knew I was touching down at that time. The paparazzi are annoying most of the time, but sometimes you need to use them to your advantage. Now, the whole of America knows I'm here and I'll get maximum coverage."

"So, it's like a game."

She nodded. “Hence the carefully chosen outfit and flawless make-up. I was prepared.”

The car indicated left and entered the freeway. “We have a quick stop in Beverly Hills. I hope you don’t mind.”

“Why?”

“A short interview with MTV. Just a few questions. Then a brief appearance for the fans and then home for the night.”

“So, where are we staying?” asked Caspian as they sped along, staring at the palm trees and the hills in the distance.

“Sauron’s producer has a house he doesn’t use so we’re taking that for the week.”

“The week?” He sat up straight. “You said a few days.”

“A few days, a week. What’s the difference? I have a few things I need to do over here.”

“Maddy, I can’t stay here for a week.” He faced her. “I have to get back to London as soon as possible.”

She looked affronted. “Are you serious? You’d give up a week in the Hollywood Hills to go back to London?”

“I’ve a lot to do, so yeah.”

“Thanks for telling me.” She narrowed her eyes. “I have a few parties to attend. I was hoping you’d be my date. I mean, that’s what boyfriends do, isn’t it?”

“You didn’t mention parties. You said the Grammys. You insinuated that we’d take the long weekend and head back. The next couple of weeks are huge for us. We’ve sent off the EP to different labels. What if we get a call and I’m swanning around over here?”

“You can just reschedule. Simple.”

“What? Christ, Maddy. You know I can’t do that. These labels get hundreds of demos a day. They don’t mess around. We'll have one chance and that's it."

She bit her lip. He didn't realise that it was in the bag already. Ross was itching to promote them as a power couple. A signing and an album were only around the corner.

"You see the crap I get from the boys over not being around?" he continued. "You take up all my time. They're getting so annoyed with me and I don't blame them."

"Look, it's only a week. You have to stick around. The media have shipped us, like Brangelina or Kimye. We're now called *Madian*."

"Bloody stupid name," he interrupted.

"I can't go alone or they'll think we've split up."

"Jesus, Maddy. Who cares what they think? Seriously."

"Fine," she said angrily. "Go back if you have to. Just get your own flight. My jet is staying put until I decide to go home."

She turned away and accessed Instagram on her phone. Bethany had tagged her in a beautiful shot of her walking hand in hand with Caspian through the airport. They looked amazing together. Her face softened.

"That's a fantastic photo," she said, holding up her phone. "This skirt was a great choice."

He ignored her.

"You're in it too! You look great."

He pretended he didn't hear.

"There are hundreds of comments already." She read them like lightning. "They're all about you!" She started to read them out loud.

"Who is this hot guy?

"It must be serious!"

"Prince Caspian."

"MAD about the boy."

She looked up. "You're a sensation. How cool is that?"

"Whoopee."

"What do you mean by that?"

"I don't give a monkeys if I'm a sensation or not. You see, Maddy. I'm not a sensation for my art or for my work – I'm a sensation because of you. So excuse me for not jumping for joy."

She threw the phone at him and turned her back. "Bet your poxy band will get something out of this."

"I don't want it."

"Oh, you want it. I know that you crave it. And remember that you'll always have me to thank."

Chapter Twenty-four

Sauron's producer, QT, was a retired rapper turned music mogul who had property all over the world. The house Madison was given was a seven-bedroomed villa in Beverly Hills. It had an infinity pool, a gym in the basement and a tennis court.

Madison and Caspian took the master bedroom which took up most of the top floor. It had huge French windows that opened out onto a balcony with an ocean view. She stripped off her clothes straight away and walked into the huge marble bathroom. Caspian could hear the shower being turned on and the door closed.

He walked out onto the balcony and gazed at the panoramic view in front of him. The temperature was about nineteen degrees Celsius which was about average for LA in January. He had discarded his jacket and only wore a long-sleeved T-shirt and jeans. Leaning on the railing, he saw Cliona wandering down the path to the pool. She was wearing her glasses and a denim jacket and her long brown hair blew in the breeze.

He could see that she fancied him. She blushed anytime

he even looked at her. She was a sweet little thing with her earnest face and soft voice. The polar opposite to his current girlfriend.

Cliona dipped her hand into the pool and sat on her haunches for a few minutes, tilting her head upwards. Then she stood up and walked back into the house. Caspian watched her until she disappeared from view.

The next morning, Caspian woke up to find Madison gone. Yawning, he grabbed a pillow and hugged it, willing himself back to sleep. The night before they had gone out for some fusion food in a trendy eaterie downtown. Madison had been followed by fans, her bodyguards stood sentinel all night, so in the end he had drank too much rum and passed out when they got home. Madison, on a health binge, didn't touch a drop of alcohol and chided him for his drunkenness as he lay on the bed. The last thing he remembered was her angry face before everything went black.

He heard shouts from outside and groaned. He just wanted half an hour more.

Five minutes later, he was sitting up, drinking water thirstily. The shouting was a male voice. He sounded foreign.

Getting up, he padded out onto the balcony and looked down.

Boris was standing at the top of the pool, shouting at Madison to speed up.

"*One more lap, faster this time!*"

He had a stopwatch in his hand.

Madison was doing a stylish crawl up and down the pool, her arms pulling her body forwards at speed. She reached the top of the pool and Boris pressed the button.

"*Good, good. Three seconds faster, now again!*"

Caspian turned away. He needed coffee and painkillers.

He turned on his phone and a barrage of messages came through. Two were from Fionn, saying that Opus Records had emailed, asking to meet, followed by lines of happy emojis. Three were from Ethan, asking for the sheet music to the new song they were practising. Alex didn't text; instead he left a voicemail asking when he'd be back and if they could meet to practise their pitch.

All these jobs he had planned to do before he left. In the end, he had thrown himself into writing that song and didn't have time. Madison had marched him out the door to go to LA, severing him from his piano.

He sat down on the bed gloomily. The band would kill him if he stayed for the whole week. And rightly so. Here he was, messing around LA when he should be preparing with them for their big break.

Grabbing a pair of jeans and a T-shirt, he walked down to the kitchen in his bare feet. Mona and Angelica were seated at the breakfast bar, both reading books on their iPads. Cliona was eating pancakes made by Giorgio the chef. She squealed in delight when he flipped one high into the air.

Caspian watched her and smiled. "Morning," he said, giving a little wave.

"Pancakes?" asked Giorgio.

"Not for me." He walked straight to the coffee machine and pressed the button. "I don't eat a lot in the morning."

Cliona poured some syrup on her breakfast.

"Did you sleep well?" she asked politely.

"I think so." He grinned. "I was pretty wasted when I got back last night."

"Oh?"

"Yeah, I hit the rum. It was Cuban stuff. Probably not the best idea." He added sugar to his coffee and took a sip. "Ah, that's good."

"The ceremony is tomorrow so you'll be well recovered by then." She played with her pancake. Suddenly she wasn't so hungry anymore.

"Yeah." He had a faraway look on his face. "Cliona?" he asked suddenly.

"Yes?"

"Does Fionn ever mention me?"

Mrs. Cliona Cole flashed through her mind and she tried not to laugh. "No. Not really."

Caspian put his fingers through his hair. "It's just I sense that they're annoyed with me. You know, since I got with Madison."

"Ah, no," lied Cliona, who had heard it all from Fionn the week before. "All's good."

He stared at her. "You'd tell me, right?"

She nodded.

"Good." He smiled at her. "Because you're my buddy. You're the one I rely on."

She nodded again, her heart brimming.

"Keep me updated because I have a tendency to get lost in my own world."

Caspian called Fionn and told him that he wouldn't be back until the following Monday.

"She wants to stay for the whole week," he said

apologetically. "I'm sorry, man."

"Caspian! I was about to call. Opus want us there on Friday. Jax called to confirm this morning."

Caspian rubbed his forehead. "Fuck! Should I try and get a flight back? Would Jax cover it?"

"I'll text you later."

Fionn told the rest of the band that afternoon.

"*What?*" Ethan shouted. "He won't be back? Tell me you're taking the piss. How arrogant will it look if we postpone?"

Alex looked grim. "I can see us splitting up over this, guys. She's like Yoko Ono. I mean, Caspian is the face of Doctor Eckleburg. We can't risk losing him."

Fionn nodded. "I get what you mean. We'll have to deal with this properly."

They called Jax and asked if they could reschedule.

"Sure, sure. I'll work it out," he said smoothly. "I mean, they'll have to understand. He's at the Grammys. That's all good."

Jax hung up the phone and dialled Ross's number straight away.

"She's staying out there for the week? Thanks for letting me know. I got them a meeting for Friday."

"News to me," said Ross. "She told me she'd be back by Wednesday. Look, it's in the bag. Just reschedule for next week."

"Got it."

"We've got to speed this along. There's only so long he'll put up with her, like."

♫ ♫ ♫

Madison found a sombre Caspian by the pool, drinking a bottle of beer.

"What did you decide to do?" she asked.

"I'm staying here," he said gloomily. "Apparently we had a meeting with Opus Records next Friday that they'll have to postpone."

She bit her lip. "Look, I have to meet Sauron for a rehearsal this afternoon but I'm free after that. Do you want to go for dinner and drinks?"

He shrugged. "I don't mind."

"Caspian!' She shook him gently. "It's only a meeting. They'll want you more now as you're playing hard to get. Being on my arm over here is worth its weight in gold publicity-wise. Just enjoy it."

He got up and walked away.

"Caspian?" She stood up. "What did I say?"

The 61st Grammy Awards took place in the Staples Center in Los Angeles. Security was amped up around the event, with metal detectors that everyone, celebrity or not, had to walk through as well as fifty police officers. Todd and Peter collaborated with the team inside the Center, making sure of maximum protection.

Madison wore a full-length red Valentino gown and had piled her hair on top her head. Her lips were painted the same red as her dress and her eyes sparkled. Two drop diamond earrings dangled from her ears and on her right hand she wore a two-carat ruby ring.

Seated in the back of the limo with Caspian, she squeezed his hand. "This will be epic," she promised him.

The limousine pulled up next to the red carpet and she took a deep breath.

"Here we go," she said, her heart pounding. She lived for moments like this: the adrenaline pumped through her veins, the crowds screaming her name.

John opened the door and she carefully swung her legs out. Standing up, she straightened her dress and squinted slightly as the cameras flashed. Caspian followed and took her hand once more, looking handsome in a black tuxedo.

"*Madison!*"

"*Maddy!*"

"*Look this way!*"

She walked slowly up the carpet, stopping sporadically to pose. Caspian held up his hand to shield his eyes from the flashing, unused to such a barrage.

"*Caspian! Look here, Caspian!*"

"*Madian!*"

The noise was deafening. Journalists called her name and she stopped every now and then to speak with them.

"Madison," said one girl from E! News. "Who are you wearing this evening?"

"Valentino," she answered with a smile. "It's lovely, isn't it?" She did a small pirouette.

"Caspian?"

He looked bemused.

"Who are you wearing?"

"It's Armani," said Madison. "Custom-made."

They moved on.

"What a silly question," said Caspian.

"No, it isn't," she hissed. "That's why we get stuff for free."

"Madison! Do you think Sauron will win?" It was a presenter from MTV.

She nodded furiously. "Without a doubt. He's the best."

They moved on again. Madison could see Jennifer Lopez in the distance wearing a hat. She was posing for the photographers.

"Caspian, are your band here tonight?" asked one reporter. He looked down at his notes. "Doctor Eckleburg, isn't it?"

Caspian's face tightened.

Madison pulled him along. "Smile," she said in an undertone. "Just until we get to the top. Then I'll pose for photographs and we'll head inside."

Sam Smith, dressed in a bold green suit, waved at Madison.

"God, he looks amazing," she said to Caspian. "Look, he has a white rose pinned to his lapel as a show of support for the anti-harassment movement. I should've done the same."

"Indeed." He stood back and let Madison pose for the cameras alone. Then they walked through the front doors.

The Staples Center was a huge auditorium with rows and rows of seats looking down onto a stage adorned with lights. Each seat had a picture of a celebrity with their names printed underneath. Lady Gaga was next to Mark Ronson, and Miley Cyrus was on the left of Dolly Parton.

Sauron spotted her straight away. "Madison!" he called. "How you doing?"

He bounded over and hugged her.

"Hey!" she said warmly.

"Is this your man?" Sauron smiled at Caspian. "I've seen pictures of you two."

"Yes. Caspian? Meet Sauron."

They shook hands.

"Delighted," said Caspian.

Sauron's bodyguard, a huge Jamaican man, only served to make the rapper look even smaller. He had long dreadlocks and a bulletproof vest.

"No guns in the Center," said Sauron. "There's a real crackdown this year."

"Yeah, Todd and Peter got the memo." She gestured to her bodyguards behind her.

"I don't know if I'm cool with that," said Sauron with a frown. "I mean, what do we do for protection?"

"We don't have many guns in Ireland," she said, "and we get along just fine."

"But the cops got them, right?"

She shook her head. "Nope."

"Holy shit." Sauron looked genuinely horrified. "I've a gig coming up in Dublin."

"You'll be fine," she reassured him with a smile. "The Irish tend to prefer partying to drive-by shootings."

An official-looking man in a suit appeared with a clip board. "They're ready for you backstage," he said in his California drawl.

Sauron nodded. "I'll be right there." He kissed Madison's cheek. "Meet you backstage. For warm-up."

She nodded. "See you later."

"So, do we sit together?" asked Caspian, looking around.

She shook her head apologetically. "No, not for the

show. I have to perform and they tend to put all the celebs together."

"Great."

"You'll be further back," she said reassuringly. "Then we'll go to an after-party."

He walked away. "See you later then."

The ceremony opened with the host Alicia Keys bringing out Jada Pinkett Smith, Lady Gaga, Jennifer Lopez and Michelle Obama onto the stage. They talked about how music had transformed their lives to huge applause. Then after numerous awards and performances, it was Sauron's turn. Madison, who had changed out of her red dress, was now wearing a skin-tight gold suit with gold boots. Her hair was loose and backcombed, and her lips were painted dark red. Sauron walked on stage first to rapturous applause. He jumped round, rapping at speed, almost swallowing the microphone. The crowd danced along to the bassline, some clapping in time. Then came Madison's turn. She arrived on stage, standing on a moving float of men dressed in loincloths with chains around their necks. Her earpiece was concealed by her blonde hair and she started to sing with all her might. The float was placed on the floor and she started to dance. The men lined up behind her and together they moved in unison.

Caspian couldn't take her eyes off her. Sure, he'd seen her on stage before. Snippets of concerts on television screens, but nothing like the sheer power and magnetism of a live performance. She stomped, she sang, she gave it her all. Sauron gave her centre stage, rapping on stage left, harmonising with her towards the end. There were lasers beaming upwards and strobe lights flicking from purple to white. The performance ended and they got a standing ovation. Madison stood erect, holding her arms up, as her peers stamped their feet and clapped loudly. Then she took Sauron's hand and they bowed simultaneously. Waving her dance troupe forward, they bowed too.

Then it was over.

Caspian was waiting by the limo when Madison finally appeared. She had changed into a small black Jean Paul Gaultier dress with strappy Jimmy Choo sandals and a Prada clutch.

"All complimentary," she said with a smirk. "I love being famous sometimes. Angelica is a wiz at getting the best freebies."

Todd shielded her as she got into the car.

"Sauron is surprisingly cool about not winning. He was expecting Cardi B to get it. He reckons it was a given." She started to read some messages on her phone. "So, Sauron is off to a party in the Valley. I wonder where Dolly Parton is headed. Wasn't that tribute to her lovely? She's such a classy lady."

Caspian let her ramble on. She was as high as a kite and he understood that it took hours to wind down. He was still reeling from the whole experience.

Holed up in his flat in King's Cross, he had spent time with the Madison he thought he knew. The past few days had shown him a different side to her. She was like a stranger – a public figure that he had to share with the world. He wasn't really sure where he slotted in. She seemed elusive, like a goddess to his mere mortal, and he felt overwhelmed. Gone was the girl he held in his arms, wearing one of his T-shirts and talking about what to eat for dinner. She had transformed into the superstar she was and he felt intimidated.

"Maddy?" he began slowly.

"Did you see Gaga? She's such a legend. I mean, what a voice!"

"Madison!"

"Yeah?"

"Can we just go back to the house?"

She looked at him in shock. "The house? Why? This is a big night. Bethany got us five different invites to all the best parties."

He took her face in his hands and kissed her gently on the lips. "I want you all to myself. I'm not interested in talking nonsense to famous people with enormous egos. I don't want to share you. I just want to take you home. You and me alone. With no flashing cameras or people screaming your name. Just us."

She stared at him for a moment. "Just us?"

He nodded.

"But you could network …"

He shook his head. "I've no interest. It's been a long night. Let's go home."

She looked torn.

"Please?" He kissed her again.

"What do you want to do? Play a game of Monopoly with Clio and have hot chocolate with marshmallows?"

"Don't be mean."

"I just texted Sauron and told him that we'd hook up."

"Well, if you do, I'll pass."

"What?" She glared at him angrily. "This is an important

night, Caspian. It's what you do when you're famous. You network, you say 'darling' a lot because half the time you don't remember people's names. You go to A-list parties and get your photograph taken. It's the price you pay for being adored."

"Then I don't want that."

"What?" She looked incredulous. "Then what's the band about? Why the gigs?"

"It's the music I care about, Maddy. Just the music. Recording an album and sharing my vision with the world. Fast cars, big houses and designer clothes don't really matter. All I want is to be respected for my art."

"Oh, here we go!" She threw her hands up. "Mister Integrity!"

"We're different, that's all." He turned away.

"Well, I'm off to Mark Ronson's bash. Gaga is going to be there and I want to butter her up so that she'll let me use a sample of 'Shallow' for my next track with Frazier Q."

"You're doing more rap? Why, Maddy?"

"Because it's cool and it combines our fan bases."

"You're selling out."

"Don't get on your high horse with me. God, I'm glad you're going back to the house."

She leaned forward and tapped John's shoulder. "Can we run by the house? Caspian wants to go home. Then we'll head to Studio City."

"Of course." John indicated into the left lane.

Cliona was listening to her iPod in the kitchen when Caspian walked in, pulling off his bow tie and throwing it on the ground.

She jumped and pulled off her earphones. "Hey! I didn't expect to see you back so early. Where's Maddy?"

He went straight to the fridge and grabbed a beer. "Gone to a party."

"Alone?"

He nodded. "It's not my scene." The can hissed as he pulled the tab. He drank thirstily, wiping his lips afterwards.

Cliona played with her hair and regarded him warily. He looked really angry and she didn't know what to say.

"How was the ceremony?" she said eventually. "We watched you arriving on E! News."

"Long."

"It was a shame Sauron lost out to Cardi B."

"I suppose."

She bit her lip. He didn't look remotely interested in the conversation.

"I wish this house had a piano," he said broodily.

No one spoke for a minute.

"Cliona?" he said suddenly. "Do you think it's weird that I don't want all the trappings of fame?"

"How do you mean?"

"The money, the cars, the jets. I don't want all that pomp. All I want is to write and play music."

"No, I don't think that's weird."

"Madison does."

"Maddy is different," she said carefully. "All her life she's been searching for something to fill the void."

"The void?"

"She has major Daddy issues. She doesn't really get on with Kevin, her father. He's never around and that really affects her. She won't admit it, but it does."

"She doesn't talk about her parents."

"Yeah, that sounds about right." Cliona sighed. "She thinks money and fame will make up for feeling like an outsider in her own home. I feel sorry for her sometimes."

Caspian's eyes met hers. "You're a wise little thing, aren't you?" he said with the hint of a smile. "Thank God she has you to keep her grounded."

"Oh, I'm not sure about that."

"No, really. It's true." His expression darkened. "We spend most of our time fighting. She's always trying to control me. I suppose we have two strong personalities that are constantly vying to be on top."

"Maybe."

"I'm getting tired of it. All the drama. We've only been together for a month and already I can see the end fast approaching."

Cliona couldn't believe her ears.

He traced his finger down the beer can. "Maybe I need someone quiet. Someone who will let me be me." He looked up and their eyes connected again.

Cliona felt her stomach flip over. With little or no experience with men, she didn't know what to do except blush.

They heard the front door slam and Angelica and Mona arrived in.

"We had the best time," said Angelica to Cliona. "I met so many people I haven't seen in years."

"Me, too." Mona took a seat at the breakfast bar. "I love award ceremonies. The buzz backstage was electric."

Then they noticed Caspian. "Oh!' Angelica's hand flew to her mouth. "I didn't realise you guys were home."

"It's just me."

"Thank God," said Mona. "We were planning on cracking open a bottle of vino and it's much better fun when the boss isn't here."

"I get it." Caspian winked. "I'm tired so I'll head upstairs. Enjoy your evening, ladies."

He strolled away, his jacket slung over his shoulder.

"*Wowee*, but he's fine." Mona put her head to one side and whistled.

"Gorgeous," agreed Angelica.

Cliona couldn't focus. Did she imagine that conversation?

"I'm going to bed," she said, gathering her things. She needed to analyse what he said and she needed to be alone.

"Sleep well," said Angelica.

"Night, Clio." Mona blew her a kiss.

Cliona's bedroom was in the basement so she descended the stairs. Switching on the light, she fell on her bed, her heart racing.

Caspian's face filled her thoughts as she replayed their conversation over and over in her mind. He had basically said that he and Madison were on the rocks. They were too alike, he said. He needed someone quiet.

A huge smiled played on her lips. He had looked at her then. On purpose.

The next morning, Clio woke up at nine. The house seemed quiet so she put on her robe and glasses and headed upstairs for a cup of coffee. She didn't bother with brushing her hair as she knew Caspian wouldn't surface until at least eleven. She knew his routine by heart.

The coffee machine hissed as she filled a cup and she

added a splash of milk. The morning sunlight streamed in the huge windows.

Suddenly she heard a shriek from outside and then laughing. Strolling over to the window, she peered outside. Madison was in the pool, her blonde hair trailing down her back.

"*Stop tickling me!*" she screamed, splashing water everywhere.

"*Maddy, come back here!*" came a male voice.

Cliona knew that voice.

Then she saw Caspian's strong arms lifting Madison onto the edge of the pool and kiss her passionately. Then his head bent down and kissed her neck, his hand disappearing into the bikini top. Madison threw her head back in pleasure, wrapping her legs around his waist.

"What the hell?" Cliona backed away. They didn't look like a couple who were fighting, on the brink of breaking up.

Rushing down the stairs, she bumped into Boris who was on his way to the gym.

"Morning," he said, moving out of her way.

Cliona stifled a sob and banged her bedroom door closed. She had never felt so silly in her life.

Chapter Twenty-five

Amiens, France

"Raph? Raph? Wake up."

He could hear a soft voice.

"Raphael? We have to go. Our flight is in a couple of hours."

Raphael groaned and turned over, taking the duvet with him.

"Raphael!" Her tone grew sharp. "Get up! Man, you're impossible in the morning."

He opened one eye and turned his head. His wife Isabelle was kneeling on the bed next to him, her hands on her hips.

"What time is it?" he asked huskily.

"Eight fifteen." She got up. "The car is on the way."

"Okay. Okay, I'm up." He threw back the blanket and sat up, his muscles rippling.

At forty-three years of age, he looked well. He was in good shape and his signature long hair still retained its dark brown colour. His film career was back on track after a dip a few years before. A stint in rehab had almost ruined his career, but now he was back on top, having conquered fickle Hollywood once more. He no longer drank alcohol or took drugs. Instead, he smoked a bit too much, but he had to have one vice or he'd explode.

His new wife Isabelle was twenty years his junior. Tall, with long red hair and pale skin, she was a retired model who had given up the limelight. After a few years as one of the most famous supermodels in the world, she had developed a drug problem and had given it all up to live in France with Raphael. Both replaced their previous addictions with each other and subsequently were inseparable.

They were due to fly to London to meet with studio executives about marketing the new film. He hated all that side of it, preferring to be on set, but it had to be done. His great friend, the award-winning actor Bertie Wells, had offered to put them up at his mansion in Belgravia, so at least they wouldn't have to stay in an impersonal hotel.

"How long do we have?" he asked, pulling his new wife down on to the bed. "I simply must make love to you before we go."

Isabelle wrapped her arms around his neck. "Twenty minutes. We have time."

Raphael's new film was about the Empress Josephine, chronicling her early life and her marriages, notably to Napoleon Bonaparte. When the script had finally been completed the year before and presented to Canal +, the task of casting had begun. Raphael had heard that Aurora Sinclair was destined for greatness. He watched her on screen and decided that she was right for the role. With her long dark hair and beautiful face, she embodied his vision of the title role and he set about securing her for the part.

Harry Finkelman, her agent, played hardball, asking for an extortionate amount of money. Her people had talked to his people and the whole affair had dragged on for a month. Finally, a compromise was reached and Aurora signed on the dotted line.

Initially, it didn't work at all. Aurora was talented, there was no denying it, but she seemed too innocent to play the Empress. The first scene they shot was the initial meeting between Josephine, or Rose as she was known, and Napoleon. After fifteen takes, Raphael threw down his coffee cup in rage and started to shout.

"Your first husband was guillotined, you have two children, you had many affairs with politicians, why then do you act like a coquettish child around Napoleon? He wrote that you gave him memories of intoxicating pleasure. Instead, you seem like a neophyte débutante who has never kissed a man in her life!"

Aurora, warned by Bertie about Raphael's notorious temper, had remained calm. "I will amend my portrayal," she said in her posh voice. "Please don't shout."

"You must be worldly and sexy. You're an older woman with lots of experience. Seduce him."

Dexter Macauley, who was playing Napoléon, clapped his hands. "*Woohoo!*" he said to the crew with a wink. "That's cool with me."

"Shut up," said Raphael rudely. "Now." He took Aurora's shoulders in his large hands. "Look at me, Aurora."

She did as he said, her brown eyes meeting his.

"You have known love, have you not?"

She nodded.

"You have experienced passion?"

She nodded again.

"Good. Now channel this. Bring this to Josephine. Napoleon once said that he won battles, but his Josephine won hearts. We need to see this charm, this magnetism in you."

Dexter sidled up close to her and put his arm around her waist. "Come on, wifey, let's heat things up."

"Please wait until the camera is rolling," she said coldly, removing his arm.

"You heard the boss ..."

Raphael watched this exchange in silence. His eyes moved from Aurora to Dexter and then back to Aurora. "This is all wrong," he announced suddenly. "There is no chemistry between these two. He is not suitable."

"What?" Dexter swung around. "What do you mean, not suitable?"

"I mean, you're fired." Raphael stalked off.

"Fired?" roared Dexter. "You can't do this. We have a contract ..." He ran after him.

Two days later, an American actor called Jasper Dale auditioned and got the part right away. He was fresh from a stint on television, starring in a Netflix Original series about the Cold War. Attractive, he was of medium build with dark hair.

"Is he short enough?" asked Isabelle when she saw the rushes.

"For the millionth time, Napoléon was not that small. He was average height for his time." Raphael rewound the last minute of the scene.

"Fine, Jeez." Isabelle backed away. "You need to relax, baby. You get too stressed. It's only a movie."

"Only a movie!" repeated Raphael, rolling his eyes.

♫ ♫ ♫

So, with the change of actor in a leading role and Aurora's amendments, the film started to take shape. They shot in various locations – Martinique for Josephine's early years, the Tuileries Palace in Paris and the exterior of Malmaison, her stately home near Paris. The famous actor Bertie Wells played the small part of Josephine's first husband, Alexandre de Beauharnais, and relished the role, prancing around in his tights and making the crew laugh. He and Aurora were old friends and she adored having him on set.

When Raphael roared at them for making a mistake, Bertie diffused the situation, often playing the fool until even the angry director would relent and smile.

Filming took eight months and Raphael was utterly consumed by the project until he shouted, "*It's a wrap!*" Isabelle, although patient, found it difficult. It was hard being second best. Even though he had warned her of his all-consuming nature when it came to his art, she was unprepared for the loneliness that ensued when he worked late at the studio or didn't come home at all. Being in France with a limited grasp on the language, she missed her family and friends. There were days when she walked the grounds of the Baptiste estate, wandering aimlessly, wishing she were back in Philadelphia with her parents watching HBO and eating Twinkies.

They arrived at Heathrow that afternoon and were picked up by Bertie's driver. The Bentley travelled smoothly along the road, eating up the miles effortlessly.

Raphael hated London. In fact, he loathed cities full stop. When he got an idea for a script in his head, he could think of nothing else. It consumed him and he lost track of time as he put it on paper. His family home near Amiens in Picardy is where he loved to be. It was there he could indulge his creative side, sitting in peace by the river that traversed the estate, surrounded by trees and flowers. He had written the script of *Josephine* in such a setting, imagining Napoleon's loved one standing by the willow tree that trailed its branches in the water. Isabelle had been so patient during this time. He had worked such unpredictable hours, unable to engage with anything else. She had been so supportive, even when her family had flown over to visit and he had refused to meet them.

Elaine, her mother, had been horrified. "He's goddamn rude, honey," she said in her American drawl. "Genius or no genius, he could at least eat some steak with us."

Isabelle was delighted that they were staying with Bertie in London. He always cheered her up. They had met years before when they had starred together in a perfume commercial together. He had supported her throughout the bad times, namely her drug addiction, and she had never forgotten that.

The car pulled up outside Bertie's elegant mansion in Belgravia, an exclusive area of London near Hyde Park. He had bought the property for seven million pounds in 2001, changing it from offices to a beautiful residence with a sizeable garden out the back.

"Raphael! The beautiful Isabelle! Welcome, my darlings!" Bertie held out his arms wide and hugged them both. An Oscar-winning actor, he had been in the film industry since the eighties. Plummy, funny and kind, Bertie was extremely popular amongst his contemporaries. He had worked with Raphael many times throughout the years and had been one of his only friends during his time at rehab. They remained close and visited each other when they could.

Raphael smiled broadly and it lit up his face. Isabelle beamed at Bertie, delighted to see him.

"Oh, Bertie, it's so good to see you! It seems like ages since the shoot."

"It certainly does," he agreed. "Come in, come in. I have lunch ready."

"You cooked for us?" asked Isabelle in amazement. "This I've got to see."

"Good Lord, not at all. Anytime I've ventured near an oven, disaster has ensued. No, I asked my wiz of a chef to make us some seabass."

They walked through the large hallway and into a huge room with large glass doors looking out onto a manicured lawn.

"So, the film is finished?" Bertie went to the drinks cabinet and poured two glasses of San Pellegrino for his guests and a glass of white wine for himself.

"Yes. I'm pleased with it now." Raphael took a seat on the leather couch and crossed his legs. "Aurora really worked."

"Didn't I tell you? She's a star, that girl. I adore her. So like her mother Grace. I knew she'd be perfect."

"Jasper worked out well too."

Bertie snorted. "You know, I wish old Beauharnais hadn't been guillotined. I was a far better husband to her. I have to admit, I'm a bit sore you didn't let me audition for the role of Napoleon."

"You're too old now ..."

"I am not! Plus I've had a teeny tiny bit of work done to combat the ageing process."

"You have?" said Isabelle in amazement. "Gosh, I'd never have guessed."

"Oh, my surgeon? He's a genius. I can't reveal his name as everyone wants him. I used every contact I had to get an appointment. He's the best in the world."

"I'm good for now, thanks." Isabelle grinned. "I'm still in my twenties."

"Of course you are, my sweet. Such loveliness I don't see every day. Don't even contemplate it for at least another five years."

"Five?"

"Well, seven. You know how this industry works." He winked.

"I'm retired now. No more modelling for me."

"Pity. You were only getting started."

She sighed. "I know, right? I miss it sometimes. It's hard having nothing to do."

"I can imagine." Bertie turned to Raphael. "Do you look after your new wife?"

Raphael put his hand on Isabelle's knee. "Of course."

Isabelle raised an eyebrow. "Sure you do."

"Come, come. Let's eat. I have a table set in the conservatory."

They followed him out to a huge glass extension, filled with exotic plants and a round table. White cloth covered it and it was set for three people. Isabelle took a seat on the right and Raphael on the left, leaving Bertie sitting between them.

A young man appeared with three plates balanced on his arm. He placed them carefully in front of each diner. There was a fillet of seabass, pan-fried with samphire and a butter sauce.

"This looks awesome," said Isabelle. "I love France and all, but you sure get sick of baguettes."

Chapter Twenty-six

Doctor Eckleburg's rise to fame was meteoric in the end. Their first single 'Mosaic' reached number eight in the charts and they played as many live venues as they could to promote themselves.

When they came off stage, they were greeted by hordes of fans, all wanting to take selfies. Caspian got the most attention as he was the face they all recognised. However, some approached the others and they politely did what was asked of them.

Fionn found it all amusing. He made funny faces in the pictures, sticking out his tongue and crossing his eyes, and never once refused to sign an autograph. Alex, with his red hair and dark eyes, was a big hit with the ladies. His mother rang him and told him that three young girls had turned up at their farm, asking to take photos of his childhood home.

Ethan got the least amount of attention, much to Stella's relief. She found the pace unsettling and pleaded with Ethan to stay grounded. He reassured her by saying that he was the Meryl Streep of the music world and his private life would remain private.

The album they recorded in Wales was a thirteen-track debut called *Colourless.* Jax listened to it and urged them to release the fourth song 'Charisma' as their first single.

"That's the one that will get airplay. I'll look into a music video. Put out a few feelers."

The resulting music video was shot near Alex's home place in Kent. Caspian was filmed walking through a field with the band close behind. As he walked, the seasons changed from winter to summer and back to winter again. He kept walking, through the snow and the rain, then as the sun shone and the clouds cleared.

"It's fantastic," enthused Jax when he saw the rushes. "Symbolic, guys. Time passing and all that."

Caspian didn't like it, of course. He had volunteered to direct the video himself but Jax had refused.

"I've told you time and time again to stick to what you're good at. Write me some songs, Caspian. We have another album planned for 2020."

The single 'Charisma' went on to reach number three in the UK charts. Reviews flooded in from well-known music journalists, praising Caspian's voice and urging fans to download the album. They called it 'beautifully simple' and 'touching', and Jax was bombarded by calls from magazines and newspapers, all wanting an exclusive interview. Caspian refused – he wanted to keep his private life separate – and Madison went ballistic.

"*How can you have a private life when you're going out with me?*" she yelled. "*For God's sake, give an interview!*"

In the end, he agreed to meet with a journalist from the *Guardian* and proceeded to speak awkwardly, clearly uncomfortable. The resulting interview portrayed him as a shy genius, who preferred to communicate through music than words.

Madison threw the paper at him in disgust. "How are we together?" she asked. "Talk about chalk and cheese."

Jax hired a publicist straight away. "You need a professional," he told the band authoritatively. "Someone on the pulse who will maximise every opportunity. There's off-line publicity and on-line publicity. It's a twenty-four-hour job, guys. We need someone on top of it constantly. Someone to liaise with celebrity journalists and the general public."

The publicist was a young cockney called Tommy. He was second generation Haitian and hailed from Walthamstow. For eight years, he had worked in America – three years of that on E! News – and subsequently was a close friend of Perez Hilton. Through this alliance, he had built up many contacts and had created a company called Bow Bells Media.

The first time he met the band, he made it quite clear that he was to be told everything.

"If I don't know about it, I can't cover it up, right?" he said. "It's all about damage control, boys. I've got to make sure your reputations stay untarnished."

Caspian found all this aspect of fame mindless and found Tommy's constant chatter tedious. Why did it matter what he wore in public? Why did he strategically warn the paparazzi of certain locations? It all seemed so contrived.

Jax took Caspian aside one day and shouted at him. "*Tommy thinks that you don't like him!*"

"It's not that I don't like him. I don't need him."

"Watch it, Caspian," said Jax warningly. "It's like health insurance. You're bloody glad when you have it when the shit hits the fan. Tommy is a godsend. He'll coordinate public events, network, do press releases, work on your overseas public image. Then you don't have to worry your pretty head about it."

"It's all just fluff," said Caspian haughtily. "Our music will transcend all of that. We don't need someone like Tommy coordinating us."

"Well, tough, because you do." Jax glared at him. "Now, cut the crap and be nice to him, okay?"

When Caspian and Madison ventured out in public together, the world couldn't get enough. Both beautiful and powerful, they seemed to be made for each other. One Sunday they took a walk in St. James' Park, both wearing hats and glasses. Within ten minutes, a crowd had gathered around them, asking for autographs and selfies. Todd ushered them back to the car and they sped off. Madison, used to such things, took no notice. Caspian was the opposite. It troubled him. he didn't like the constant voyeurism and yearned for some space.

Like anything, it was a novelty in the beginning. He liked the attention and the sense of importance. But that all changed. There were some days when he wanted to be left alone. Then someone would tug at his sleeve or shout his name and he couldn't escape.

Madison had warned him about it but he'd always laughed it off. Now, he understood her over-zealous approach to privacy. Now he got it.

Finally, the album, *Colourless,* was released. It debuted

at number four and became an overnight success. They were tipped to be nominated for a Mercury Award and Jax had to take the phone off the hook, such was the barrage of calls looking for dates and performances.

Doctor Eckleburg started to play gigs all over the British Isles, night after night of venues.

Then Jax collaborated with a tour manager for a sell-out European tour. What followed was a whirlwind of organisation. A logistics crew of about one hundred people was hired – electricians, carpenters, drivers, riggers, chefs and roadies. The sets had to be built, dismantled and packed away again. Two sets of identical gear was boxed up in custom-made steel cases, rolled onto pallets and packed into trucks with padded walls for protection.

Gear A was set up in Paris while Gear B went on to Amsterdam to avoid any delays with concerts. The crew worked like clockwork. There was a predetermined sequence of rigging. The stage set came first, followed by the lighting and then the video and audio. The band's instruments were the last to go on stage and the first to come off. Customs clearance was set up well in advance to allow smooth movement from France to Switzerland.

Everything was done in meticulous detail.

Over two months Doctor Eckleburg played all the major European cities, delighting fans with their haunting melodies and infectious beats. They mostly stayed at hotels, living out of a suitcase. They were mobbed outside venues and followed by professional photographers in black jeeps. Long lenses were pointed at them from all angles. Tommy attempted to put the press off track by posting photos on Instagram of the band in another location. However, these photographers knew all the tricks and it was virtually impossible to avoid them until they were safely behind enormous electric gates.

Caspian found this oppressive. He disliked being curtailed. Being Madison's boyfriend only made him more famous and out of the four members of Doctor Eckleburg, he was followed the most. When he complained to Madison about the invasion of privacy, she would redirect the conversation to herself and how aggressively the press followed her. She never listened to him as she was only interested in herself. So, he texted Cliona. She always let him rant and offered support in her gentle way. She let him talk about himself incessantly and never judged.

Madison, back from a short tour of Australia, flew to Berlin to surprise Caspian. As Doctor Eckleburg played the last song on stage at Huxley's Neue Welt, a concert hall in the city, Madison appeared from the wings, looking gorgeous in a short gold dress and heels, and walked up to a surprised Caspian. The crowd went crazy, screaming their names.

"Hey, baby," she drawled, kissing him on the lips. Their faces appeared on the giant screen behind them. She took the microphone from his hand and started to sing the chorus of 'Mosaic' acapella. Alex glanced at Ethan and they adjusted the key so as to play along. Fionn beat the kick drum and suddenly it was Madison prancing around instead of Caspian. When she had finished, the crowd cheered. She handed a bemused Caspian the microphone and kissed him again. There was a tsunami of flashes as thousands of phones took photos and the story was splashed across the internet within minutes.

When they got off-stage, Caspian shouted at her for being so self-obsessed. "Why did you come and take over?" he fumed. "How dare you sing my song like that?"

"Oh, get over it," she said in a bored tone. "I've done you a favour. Just look at Instagram. The 'likes' are coming in steadily."

When the tour ended, Jax suggested that Caspian hire a personal assistant, but he refused. He wanted to keep it real. He didn't need someone to organise his life like that. He still rode his bike around London and popped to the shop for some milk. He still went to Tesco and went for a pint in his local pub. The rest of the band felt the same; they didn't want the trappings of fame and vowed to keep things as normal as possible.

"We must not get notions," Fionn said with a grin. "My granny always condemned people who acted above their station."

The band also pledged to act as a democracy and made that very clear from the beginning. Even though Caspian wrote most of the songs, the rights were split four ways. He also insisted that five per cent of their profit went to charity. Jax had objected, but Tommy took him aside and showed him the benefits of such a move. "In this day and age, mate, people love this philanthropy stuff. Let them do it. It will sell more albums."

After a huge royalty cheque came in, Caspian moved out of his flat in King's Cross and rented an apartment near Knightsbridge. It had three large bedrooms, one of which he used as a studio, and a huge open-space living room and kitchen. It was also about two miles from Madison's place. Fitted with top-of-the-range security cameras and alarms, he felt safe when he closed the door. He had refused to get a full-time bodyguard like Madison – he didn't want someone looking over his shoulder all the time. She had insisted that he hire someone, but he had stood firm. He would try to retain some sense of normality. Getting full-time security would be crossing the Rubicon and he wasn't ready for that. All he wanted to do was write music and share it with the world.

When Doctor Eckleburg played Dublin, they stayed with Constance and Aonghus. Fionn tried to convince his mother that they would be better staying at a hotel, but she was firm. "I bought some fold-up beds in IKEA. I insist."

She cooked a huge roast lamb with all the trimmings and listened to their tales of being on the road. At one stage, Caspian related how he had read a particularly awful review of their album by an American music critic who had ended his piece with: *Here's hoping Doctor Eckleburg don't try to come Stateside.*

Constance snorted scornfully. "What a beastly man!" she said. "Don't give it a second thought, my love. Stravinsky once said that all music critics are like rats with padlocks on their ears. Don't ever read reviews. Just plough on and keep doing what you're doing."

Early in the morning, when the rest of the house was asleep, Caspian strolled around the house and paused in front of a communion photo of Cliona. She had glasses, two braids and a white veil. Her hands were fastened together as if she were praying and her face was solemn. Caspian thought it was adorable and took a photo with his phone.

Later that evening he sent it to Cliona on WhatsApp, with lots of laughing emojis.

Madison noticed Cliona's face when she accessed the message and asked what was going on.

"Oh, it's Mum," lied Cliona. She knew how jealous Madison was and didn't want to explain her relationship with Caspian. There was nothing to tell anyway. It was just an innocent friendship where they would text each other periodically about silly things. Madison didn't need to know that she lived for his texts. That they made her heart race.

After a few months of constant promotion and seemingly endless gigs, Caspian went through a crisis: he felt overwhelmed and exhausted, lost in a chaotic world of paparazzi, fans and publicity. Madison, who was on tour in America, barely checked her phone and when he did get to talk to her, she didn't listen. Instead she told him about Detroit and how she brought the house down with a cover of 'You're So Vain' by Carly Simon. "I thought of you when I sang it," she quipped.

She just didn't get him. She went on stage, sang her heart out and then headed out to a party, unmoved by the whole experience. He was different. He tended to go through the entire gig in his head, cringing at the parts he deemed weak and being his own worst critic. He relived every moment, good and bad, and often didn't sleep with the enormity of it.

Some people loved Doctor Eckleburg's work, deeming

them the greatest band that ever lived. Others hated them and ridiculed them on public forums. Fionn took no notice nor did Alex and Ethan. It was impossible to please everyone, they mused sensibly. Perfection didn't exist.

It was Caspian who took every bad word to heart. It felt like a dagger had been plunged into his chest and every bad review of his work twisted it around and around. He had bared his soul to the world and some didn't understand it. He didn't know if he was resilient enough.

Feeling lost, he began to text Cliona in earnest. She always listened and gave good advice. She never tried to overshadow him and encouraged him to keep going. She reminded him of a little mouse, timid and shy, hiding from the world. Where Madison barely listened and tried to talk about herself, Cliona was the opposite. In those early days, she kept him sane.

He knew she fancied him; most women did. He knew it was crass to lead her on, but he needed her support. Madison was never going to be that person.

One day Caspian met his mother for lunch in St. John's Wood.

"Caspian," she said, kissing his cheek. "I've missed you so."

"Hey, Mum." He had purposely covered his blonde hair with a hat.

She looked worried, her brow furrowed and he noticed immediately. "Is everything okay?"

She sighed. "Well, not really."

"Oh?"

She twisted her napkin around and around. "Lots of

people come to the house, Caspian. Lots of girls, asking about you. Dad and I are at our wits' end."

"What?" He took her hand. "That's awful, Mum."

"I mean, in the beginning it was a novelty. Dad went out to bring in the bin and a young girl asked for his autograph. He was delighted."

"I'll bet."

"But then it became a nuisance." She looked up. "I'm sorry, darling, but we can't even go to the shop now without someone pointing or following us."

"Gosh, Mum. I had no idea."

"Well, you haven't been home in so long."

"I know, I know."

"And then this horrible man came and started asking questions about you when you were little …" She took a shuddering breath. "You must stop it, Caspian. I hate it."

"Of course, of course." He gave her a hug. "I'll sort it. Maybe we could install some security cameras and a gate. My new flat has all that as standard and I've got to say, I feel safe."

She sniffed. "I just want my life back. I don't want people snooping around."

"I understand."

Caspian arrived home to find a furious Madison in his sitting room, brandishing her phone at him. A photographer took a shot of him and his mother together and the world was asking if he was cheating on Madison with a woman thirty years his senior.

"That's my mum," he said in shock.

"Well, I wouldn't know," she retorted icily.

"What do you mean by that?'

"You know exactly what I mean." She banged the door of her bedroom.

Caspian sighed. He knew she was sore about the fact that he'd never introduced her to his parents, but he kept putting it off. Maybe because he didn't know what they'd make of her. If it was just Madison, it would be fine. However, the circus that followed her might intimidate them.

"Maddy," he began, following her into the room. "I'll sort this out."

"I don't care," she said, her eyes flashing. "Do I look like I care?"

That afternoon, Tommy released a statement, clearing up the whole thing. Caspian and Maddy were as much in love as ever. They were due to appear on *The Graham Norton Show* and perform. All was well.

Caspian, despite being told not to, tweeted that the press should back off and leave him alone. There was an immediate backlash from fans and journalists, lambasting him for being two-faced.

Without #presscoverage, you're nothing!

Fans deserve to know what you do #thepriceyoupayforfame

"I told you not to do anything without my saying so!" shouted Tommy down the phone. "They'll hound you more now."

Much to Caspian's dismay, Tommy was right. Everywhere he went, people followed. Every move he made in public was analysed and judged. He was seen drinking from plastic straw and condemned in the media. Then he was photographed exiting Madison's private jet and his song about global warming was parodied straight away where he was ridiculed for his hypocrisy.

"Why can't people leave me alone?" he said desperately to his bandmates. "It should only be about the music. Why are they so obsessed?"

"Mainly because of Maddy," said Fionn simply.

Soon after, Caspian met Cliona for a coffee in a café near Hyde Park. He wore the habitual beanie hat to conceal his blonde hair and large Police glasses covered his eyes. Suddenly he noticed a lens pointed right at them. The photographer was standing behind a newspaper kiosk, snapping at random.

"Fuck this," said Caspian, standing up. "I've had enough." He stalked over to the man and yanked his lens out of the way.

"*What's so interesting about my putting sugar in my coffee?*" he yelled. "*Just back off!* I'm sick of you all. What's so interesting about my having a coffee with a friend? There's nothing to see here."

The man sneered at him. "Sorry, mate, but photos of you put food on my table."

"Have you any shame?" Caspian grabbed his black jacket.

"No," he answered, calmly removing his hand. "Now, touch me again and I'll have you for assault." He laughed. "What's the problem anyway? Doing the dirt on Maddy then, are we?"

"*Just go away!*" howled Caspian. "*Fuck off!*" He shoved the man backwards.

"Caspian!" Cliona appeared behind him and pulled him backwards. "Stop!"

"Get used to it," shouted the photographer, walking away. "I'm on your case."

Madison was having a facial when Caspian called to her apartment that night. Mona was in the bedroom when he walked in.

"What a day!" he exclaimed.

Mona placed a second slice of cucumber on Madison's left eye. "I'll leave you to it," she said. "I'll be in the kitchen if you need me." She closed the door quietly.

"Oh?" Madison lay flat on the bed, her face covered with white goo. "What happened?"

"I had an altercation with a photographer."

"Why?"

"I was having a coffee and he kept taking shots. I just lost it."

"Having a coffee? With whom?"

"Cliona."

"My Cliona?" She sat up straight, causing the cucumbers to fall off. "Why were you having coffee with her?"

"She's my friend. We hang out sometimes."

"Oh, you do?" Madison threw up her arms. "Thanks for telling me."

"There's nothing to tell ..."

"Oh grow up, Caspian. You know she fancies you. A blind man could see it."

"Maddy, stop."

"I can't believe the two of you, going behind my back like this."

"We're not! Stop."

She grabbed a tissue and started to wipe off the cream on her face. "Stay away from Clio. Not only is it leading her on, she's also a brilliant PA. I don't want to lose her."

Tommy was furious when he heard. "You'll be lucky if we don't have a law suit on our hands," he fumed. "Why are you constantly pushing it?"

Caspian scowled. "I don't care about law suits. If I'm having a coffee with a friend, I shouldn't have to deal with a giant lens in my face. The press need to be brought to task. They ruin lives."

"They are necessary," said Tommy angrily. "People like you depend on them. Don't forget that. We have to keep them sweet or they'll make you and your band a laughing stock. You're not established enough to fuck around with them, Caspian."

Caspian held up his hands. "Forget I said anything."

Chapter Twenty-seven

Esquire magazine called and asked to do a 'Behind the Scenes' feature of the golden couple of the music world. Tommy hired a luxury apartment and two photographers took photos of Madison and Caspian in domestic scenes like lying together on the couch or cooking in the kitchen. Both dressed in designer clothes, with both hair and make-up done, the photos were a supposed insight into their private life. It couldn't have been further from the truth – it was all fabricated and contrived. The public didn't care – they couldn't get enough of them. Both blonde and beautiful, with youth, talent and fame.

They didn't see the reality. The arguments. The competition. Madison was jealous of every girl he spoke to. She constantly kept tabs on his conversations.

He was a faithful boyfriend – most of the time. Sometimes there were girls around after a gig, when he needed to let off steam. They were willing and available and didn't nag him about every single thing. He didn't allow phones or photographs and kept his trysts to dark rooms. He never saw them again so he conveniently forgot it ever happened.

Madison didn't know so what was the problem? He needed that outlet. She had refused to tour with him so he had no choice.

He got that she was busy with her own career. It's just he wished she'd prioritise him for a change. Instead they met for nights here and there, in different cities around the world, packing their relationship into a few hours.

Eventually, he asked her to take a weekend break with him away from the city. He wanted to write and he found London too noisy. He mentioned the Lake District and she agreed. Feeling guilty after a tour filled with girls, booze, drugs and almost no sleep, he wanted to reconnect with Madison and rekindle their love affair. The only stipulation was that Todd was not permitted to come. It had to be them and them alone.

She refused, saying that she had to have a bodyguard nearby.

"Sorry, but those are the terms and conditions of being my boyfriend."

"Then we're not going."

"Fine." Her eyes flashed. "Suit yourself."

"*How can we be a proper couple with people hanging around all the time?*" he shouted. He grabbed her shoulders and forced her to look at him. "We need to be alone."

"You knew what you were getting into when you met me," she retorted. "Now, go home. I don't want to deal with this right now."

Caspian released her and stalked off. "I can see the end, Maddy. It's coming."

"*Good!*" she shrieked, throwing her shoe at him.

He slammed the door.

♫ ♫ ♫

Mercifully, fate intervened. That evening, Prudence Cole called her son.

"Caspian?"

"Hey, Mum." He was weary. Fighting always upset him and it seemed to be all he and Maddy did lately.

"I was hoping you'd come home for the weekend. It's been so long since we've seen you."

"Sorry, Mum. I'm busy," he lied.

"I want to meet Madison properly," she continued. "It's shocking that I have to read about the two of you in the paper to know what's going on. My friends at the Flower Club keep asking me what she's like."

"She's busy too."

"I can do a roast dinner. Please, darling. Dad misses you. Since you installed all the cameras and locks, it's like Fort Knox here. You'd both be safe."

"Oh, okay. I'll check with Maddy and let you know."

"I'm so glad. I'll make your favourite roast beef."

Madison agreed immediately to the change of plan. She had been dying to meet Caspian's parents for ages, deeming it the next big step on their relationship. It had irked her that he had never suggested it. Their earlier argument was forgotten straight away.

"Should I bring a gift?" she asked. "Would your mum like chocolates or perfume?"

"Just bring yourself."

"No, I have to bring something. I'll send Clio to Harrods before we go."

"No, no. Mum would be embarrassed. Just bring yourself."

Madison laughed. "Don't be silly. I'll think of something."

Caspian's family home was in Banbury, an hour and a half from London. Madison packed ten outfits ranging from skinny jeans to demure dresses. She ordered John to drive them up there and insisted that her other bodyguard Peter come too as Todd had been working for twelve days straight.

Caspian knew better than to argue and texted his mother to make up the spare room. He sauntered outside to see John heaving a huge Louis Vuitton trunk into the Mercedes.

"It's only one weekend," he said incredulously. "Blimey, Maddy."

"I want to make the right impression so I've prepared for all eventualities."

Madison gave the rest of her staff the weekend off. Cliona tried not to be annoyed at the short notice. Last minute flights cost a fortune. However, she decided to go home to Ireland anyway. She missed her parents and wanted to breathe in the sea air of Dalkey Bay.

She rang her mother as she threw some clothes in a bag.

"Mum? It's Clio. I was thinking of coming home for a few days. Maddy's gone off with Caspian so I'm at a loose end."

"Oh, darling! Daddy and I have just taken off to Sligo for a week. It's his annual pilgrimage to Lissadell, you know the way."

"Oh."

"Sorry, sweetie. You could always get a bus and join us."

"It's okay." She plonked on her bed in disappointment. "I'll find something to do over here."

"Text me later!"

Cliona ended the call and sighed. She had been looking forward to going home. She texted Fionn.

"Hey, are you free tonight?"

He texted back immediately saying that he was packing a bag for a few days in Italy with his current squeeze, Mariana. "Caspian is taking a few days so we all followed suit," said Fionn cheerfully. "So, I'm off to Lake Como."

Cliona threw her phone away. It was only four o'clock in the afternoon. She was sick of Netflix and the apartment seemed huge without Madison and her entourage. Only Todd remained, sitting at the table doing a crossword.

She walked into the kitchen and switched on the kettle. Her mother always said that a cup of tea cured everything.

"Would you like a cup of tea?" she asked Todd.

"No, ma'am," he replied. "I'm good with my barrocha."

An hour later, her phone rang.

"Clio? It's Alex."

"Oh, hey, Alex."

"I'm outside."

"Outside?"

"Yeah. Can you come down and meet me? That building is like the Pentagon. I'm not even going to attempt to get in."

"Okay."

She hung up the phone, checked her reflection in the mirror and headed for the door.

"Clio!' Todd was by her side in a flash. "Will I come with you?"

"It's fine." She smiled up at him. "No one will bother with me."

She took the elevator and pushed open the huge front doors of the building. Then she walked to the electric gates and punched in a code. The pedestrian access opened and she walked out onto the street. Alex was standing next to the band's van, a huge grin on his face.

"Caspian is in Banbury with Maddy, Fionn is loved up with Mariana in a posh Italian hotel and Ethan's gone to Gdansk to see Stella's granny."

"And?"

"I was with Fionn when you called so I thought, we're both alone so why not join forces?"

Cliona bit her lip. "Join forces?" she repeated warily. "How exactly?"

"I'm heading home to Kent for my mother's birthday. Do you want to come? There will be cake."

"Oh, I don't know ..."

"It's only for a couple of days. I'll drop you back afterwards."

Cliona looked doubtful. "I can't just impose on your parents like that."

"Oh, Mum will be delighted. She loves guests." He ushered her back towards the building. "Pack some wellies. We live on a farm."

"I don't have any ..." she protested.

"I'm joking. Just grab some things and we'll go. I want to beat the traffic on the M2."

Alex talked the whole way down.

"So, my dad is a retired QC."

"You mean, a barrister?"

Alex nodded. "Anyway, he took early retirement and he and Mum moved back to her family farm."

"Did your mum work?"

Alex nodded. "She was a nurse for a while but she gave it up when the twins were born."

"Twins?"

He nodded as he indicated left. "My twin sisters: Maia and Daphne. They're eighteen. The poor sods had their A-Levels this summer and are waiting for the results."

"Nice names."

"Anyway, Mum always wanted to move to the country so they took over the farm and make a nice living from it now. They have a small vineyard and an apiary."

"That's amazing," said Cliona impressed. "Are they self-sufficient?"

"Pretty much. They even make their own cider." He grinned. "Although, I've caught Mum eating a burger from McDonald's a few times. She loves Big Macs."

The van sped along the road. Soon the spires of Canterbury Cathedral appeared in the distance.

"I've always wanted to visit the cathedral," said Cliona in excitement. "Dad is always going on about Chaucer and how he was one of the first to write in English rather than French. Dad loves his revolutionary soul."

"Crikey, I didn't know that," said Alex.

"When the Normans invaded, French became the language spoken by those in power. Chaucer challenged this." Cliona blushed. "Sorry, I'm boring you."

"On the contrary." Alex nudged her arm. "I love brainboxes. Keep going and educate me. Then I'll spout all of this at dinner and Mum will be so proud."

Chapter Twenty-eight

The farm was situated three miles outside Canterbury. Alex drove up a wooded lane and came to a halt outside a charming building with a thatched roof and small windows. The walls were whitewashed and there was a rusty plough outside the door. Cliona opened the door of the van and stepped out. She could hear chickens clucking in the coop and large oak trees stood next to the large barn to the right of the house.

"Mum? Dad?" called Alex as a Golden Retriever ran up to him and jumped on his legs. "Hello, Elvis, hello, boy! He scratched his ears. "I've missed you, boy!"

"Elvis?" said Cliona in surprise.

"Dad is a massive fan of The King," explained Alex. "He goes to Graceland every couple of years.

Cliona giggled. "That's gas."

"Gas?" Alex frowned.

"It means funny. It's an Irish expression." She grinned. "Hiberno-English."

"Oh, right. It's like when you told me to pass out that bus on the way down here."

"So? That's what we say in Dublin; we pass out cars on the motorway."

"*Overtake*, Clio. I only pass out when I've had too much to drink." He opened the front door. "Mum? Dad? Anyone here?"

The kitchen was empty, as was the sitting room. Both rooms were spotlessly clean with lows beamed ceilings. Alex had to duck his head as he travelled from room to room.

"Odd," he said, throwing his bag near the dog basket. "Maybe they're out on the fields. Come on."

He exited the house via the back door and opened a gate. Cliona followed, trying to avoid muddy puddles in her espadrilles, and gasped when she saw the expanse of green fields.

"This is beautiful," she said in wonder.

Cows grazed in a paddock to the right of a small brook. A small orchard was on the left and in the distance, she could see a fenced-off area with small trees in perfectly symmetrical lines.

"That's our vineyard," said Alex, following her gaze.

"Amazing," she said.

"Come on, I think I know where they might be."

She followed him out into the field, breathing in the clean country air. It was so lovely not to have high-rise grey buildings and a smoggy atmosphere. The open expanse of ground and the green grass reminded her of Ireland.

They reached the small orchard and Alex jabbed his finger towards the trees. "And there they are," he said. "My parents."

A pretty red-haired woman of about fifty was filling a

sack with apples that had fallen on the ground. A taller man of a similar age was reaching high into the branches, plucking fruit he deemed ready for harvest.

The woman looked up and her face lit up. "Jeff!" she said to her husband. "Alex is back!"

She dropped the bag and ran over to her son.

"Hey, Mum," he said, hugging her close. "Happy Birthday."

She kissed his cheek. "It's so good to see you, darling."

Jeff followed her and gave Alex a big hug. "We didn't expect you until later, son. We're just picking the first batch of apples for the chutney."

"And the cider of course," added his mother. She turned to Cliona. "Hello, I'm Nancy and this is Jeff."

"I'm Cliona." They shook hands. "I hope you don't mind my being here."

"Not in the slightest," said Nancy cheerfully. "Jeff is cooking his famous roast pork and he usually makes enough for a small army."

"Roast pork?" Alex looked at them in alarm. "I hope Bella is still around."

Jeff laughed and turned to Cliona. "Alex bonded with one of our pigs and named her Bella. Then he went on a hunger strike until we promised not to send her to the abattoir."

"So naturally I get paranoid when pork is on the menu," explained Alex.

"Oh, Bella is far too old for slaughter now," said Nancy. "She's ruling the roost in the sty, bossing the piglets around."

"That's my girl." Alex smiled. "I presume the twins are at work?"

Jeff nodded. "They'll be back at six."

"Our girls work at a strawberry farm," explained Nancy. "Now, let's go inside. I made a fresh gooseberry pie this morning. Let's have tea and a chat."

Jeff ate a plate of pie and made his excuses. "I just need to dig some potatoes for the feast later on," he explained.

"No problem, Dad. I'm looking forward to it." Alex gave him a thumbs-up.

Cliona sipped her tea and her gaze travelled around the kitchen. A large dresser filled with pottery plates stood by the giant Aga. The tiled floor was a deep red colour and the small windows afforded little light. They sat a huge scrubbed oak table with a ceramic tile in the centre for the tea-pot.

"You're Irish, right?" said Nancy after they had consumed a big plate of pie and custard.

"Yes, I'm from Dublin."

"Are you a musician too?"

Cliona shook her head. "No, I studied film at university. At the moment, I work as Madison Ryan's PA."

"Ah, now I get the connection." Nancy placed her fork on her plate. "She's going out with Caspian. Is that how you two met?"

Alex glared at his mother. "Enough of the interrogation, Mum."

"I just didn't realise you were seeing anyone, Alex ..."

"Oh, he's not!" said Cliona immediately, blushing furiously.

Alex put his hand on her arm. "Calm, Clio. I'll handle this." He turned to his mother. "We're good friends, Mum. That's all. Plus, she's Fionn's little sister and I'm pretty sure he'd hunt me down if I ever made a move."

Cliona blushed even more. "No, he wouldn't," she said in mortification.

"Fionn's sister!" said Nancy in delight. "Oh, I adore Fionn. Such a considerate boy. He always brings me flowers when he visits."

"Fionn is the golden boy at home too," said Cliona. "Mum thinks he's God."

"We know better," added Alex. "Right, Clio?"

"Right."

The twins arrived home just after six, arguing about who would get the shower first. They barely greeted Cliona and rushed upstairs, screaming at each other until a door slammed. Then a sombre-looking Daphne appeared.

"Maia's such a cow," she complained to her mother. "She always gets her own way."

Alex put his arm around her shoulder. "Cheer up, Daph," he said. "Meet my friend Clio."

"Hi, Clio," said a pouting Daphne.

"Hi."

A delightful smell of apples and onions wafted around the kitchen. Jeff checked the meat as it had been slow-roasting all day. "Almost done," he said in satisfaction.

Nancy had changed her clothes and looked pretty in a blue dress. Her hair was plaited and hung down her back, red mixed with grey. Cliona could see Alex in her face – both had similar eyes and bone structure. However, he had Jeff's height and build.

The door opened and Maia joined them, her hair wet from the shower. Both twins looked like blonde versions of Alex.

"Did you use all the hot water?" asked Daphne fiercely.

"I hope not." Maia accepted a glass of wine from her father. "What's this? Your homebrew?" She took a sip and grimaced. "I love you, Dad, but this is hard to drink."

"I like it," said Cliona, who was on her second glass.

"Just be careful," warned Maia. "It's deceptively strong."

"This is Clio," said Alex.

"Hi," said Maia. "I'm the alpha twin."

"Oh?" Cliona raised an eyebrow.

"Yes, I was born first, I was bigger at birth and I'm better at sport."

"You also have the bigger ego," said Nancy. "Right, dinner will be ready in ten minutes. Maia, finish setting the table outside. It's not too cold and we should avail of al fresco dining before autumn descends properly."

"What about Daphne? Why does she get away with doing nothing?" Maia put her hands on her hips.

"Well, you are the alpha twin," quipped Alex. "Plus, you took the shower first. Suck it up."

Jeff placed a platter of pork on the table. Having been slow-roasted for five hours, the meat fell off the bone. On the side he had roast potatoes, stir-fired kale and mashed celeriac with butter.

Cliona had two helpings of everything, unused to such food at Madison's place.

"This is incredible," she enthused. "Honestly, my diet consists of sushi and pizza most of the time."

"More?" asked Nancy, holding up the bowl of kale.

"No, I'm stuffed." Cliona sat back with a red face. "I couldn't eat another bite."

Alex held out his plate. "I'll have a bit, Mum. We didn't eat properly on tour at all."

"Tell us about it," said Jeff. "Your messages were uninformative to say the least."

"I put all your photos on my Insta story," said Maia. "I loved that one of Caspian pouring the bottle of water over his head."

Alex forked up some kale. "Touring is fun but really tiring," he said, after swallowing. "I'm not sure I could do something that intense again. It was night after night. Jax wanted us to fit it all in to coincide with the album release."

"Understandable," said Jeff. "It's your debut. They'll want it to make a splash."

"Yes, but night after night? It was hectic."

"Were you followed by fans?" asked Daphne in excitement. "Like, to the shops or to restaurants?"

"Only when I was with Caspian," said Alex. "He's the face of the band and the one everyone recognises. I mean, the lead singer is always the one. Look at Chris Martin or the Gallagher brothers. Would you recognise the drummers of those bands? Or the bassists?"

"Not really," said Cliona.

"Exactly. I'm still incognito to the masses." He smiled. "Although, I bet I have dedicated fans who love me."

"Maybe two or three," agreed Maia. "Mum being one of them." She turned to Cliona. "Are you one of his fans?" she asked mischievously. "Mum says you're only friends but I don't buy it."

Cliona blushed again and Alex held up his hand. "Leave her alone! She's my friend, Maia. She was at a loose end and I invited her down. No big deal."

"Right," said Maia, sitting back. "Sure."

"Back in a sec," said Jeff, leaving the table.

Nancy started to stack the plates.

"No, Mum," said Alex immediately. "It's your special day. We'll handle it. Won't we, girls?"

Maia stuck out her tongue. "We were working all day, Alex, unlike some people I know."

Daphne gathered some plates. "I'll help," she said quietly.

Cliona glanced from one twin to the other. It was like watching her and Madison. Two different personalities clashing. Bold, confident Maia and timid little Daphne.

She stood up to help but Alex pushed her back down. "You're a guest," he chided gently. "You spend your life looking after Maddy. Let us look after you."

"No, really, I ..."

"Sit." His brown eyes were warm.

Suddenly they heard a deep voice singing 'Happy Birthday' in a style akin to Elvis Presley. Jeff appeared out of the house, holding a cake with lit candles, their flames dancing in the breeze.

Nancy gasped and held her hands up in delight. "Oh, darling! Chocolate cake, my favourite."

"Beetroot cake," he corrected. "From the garden."

"Even better." She took the cake from his hands.

"Make a wish, Mum," said Alex.

She closed her eyes and blew out the candles. "Oh, Jeff. I love it," she said genuinely. "Thank you."

"A toast!" said Jeff, holding up his glass. "To my beautiful wife. Every moment with you has been a joy. I'm so lucky to have found you. You're always on my mind! Promise to love me tender forever."

"Enough of the Elvis puns, Dad," said Maia. "We know you love him more than life itself."

"*To Nancy!*" shouted Jeff.

"*To Nancy!*" said Cliona with the others, raising her glass.

An hour later, Cliona tried to suppress a yawn but failed. Alex noticed immediately.

"Come on, I'll show you your room," he said, getting to his feet.

"Night, everyone," said Cliona with a small wave. "Thank you for a lovely evening."

"Night," said Jeff and Nancy in unison.

"Sleep well," said Daphne and Maia saluted.

To her surprise, Alex led her to the barn, not the house. "This is the guest quarters," he explained. "It doesn't function as an actual barn with hay and things." He opened the door and led her inside.

There was an open-plan kitchen and sitting room on the lower level. Then there was a bedroom on a mezzanine floor which looked like a loft. There was a ladder leading up to it.

"There's coffee and tea in the cupboard," said Alex, pointing to the wooden unit in the corner. "There are extra blankets next to the bed."

"This looks amazing!" Cliona looked around in delight.

"Yeah, the band stay here when we come down here. Caspian loves the tranquillity."

Her face changed at the mention of his name.

"Sorry, I shouldn't have mentioned him."

"Gosh, no. It doesn't matter. I've given up on that."

"Really?" He looked like he didn't believe her for a second.

"Yes." Cliona tried to be firm. "We're good friends, that's all. I'm over him."

Alex raised an eyebrow but said nothing. "Right, sleep well, little Clio. I'll see you in the morning."

Cliona woke at three o'clock in the morning, disorientated. For a moment, she didn't know where she was. She could hear noises and creaks and pulled the woollen blanket up around her chin. Used to having street lamps outside her bedroom window, she wasn't accustomed to the darkness of the countryside. She activated the torch on her phone and shone it down on the kitchen area. It was deserted.

Go back to sleep!

Closing her eyes, she thought of Caspian. He had warned her in his last message that he would be turning off his phone for the weekend, but that he would be in touch when he got back. She accessed her previous texts from him and scrolled backwards. This was her normal practice before going to sleep. She would reread messages and analyse them. It made her feel close to him.

Oh, how she yearned to call him her own. She thought about him incessantly. She knew it was wrong, but the heart didn't play by the rules. She couldn't help her feelings for him. Initially, it had been because of his looks but now, it was deeper than that. She felt like she knew him better than anyone. She put the phone away and willed her brain to go to sleep.

Her thoughts drifted to Alex. He was so nice to her, making sure she wasn't left alone. She suspected that Fionn asked him to watch out for her while he was in Italy, but that didn't matter. He was still really nice to even bother watching out for her.

His family were sweet and welcoming. They reminded her of her own – the bickering, the closeness. Jeff's meal was like something her mother would produce on a Sunday and made her feel homesick.

Mercifully, she fell asleep eventually and it was ten when she opened her eyes. She could hear noise outside and the sound of a tractor engine. Sitting up straight, her mouth felt dry. All the wine the night before had taken its toll. Gingerly she descended the ladder and took a glass from the cupboard. She filled it with ice-cold water from the Belfast sink and gulped it down thirstily.

There was a knock on the door. "Are you decent?" came Alex's voice.

She glanced down at her oversized pyjama bottoms and T-shirt. "Yeah!" she answered.

Alex opened the door and walked into the barn. He was wearing jeans and a black top.

"Come on, we've got some farming to do."

"Farming?"

"Yes, you don't get your bed and board for free, you know." He winked. "Move it, Clio. We've lots to do."

"Like?" She eyed him warily.

"Collect eggs from the hens, feed the pigs and replenish their water trough, pick some courgettes ..."

"All of that?" She rubbed her temple. "I'm quite hungover to be honest. Maia was right about that wine."

"The fresh air will sort all of that," he said cheerfully. "Now, I'll meet you by the gate in ten minutes."

♫ ♫ ♫

They started at the chicken coop. Alex reached into the hen house and extracted five eggs. Carefully, he placed them in the basket hanging off his arm.

"Have you ever had proper free range farm eggs before?" he asked.

"Mum gets them at the market."

"Not the same," he said dismissively. "Wait until you have these."

They moved on to the pigs. A large sow approached them.

"Hey, Bells," said Alex, scratching her behind the ear. "Cliona, meet Bella, the love of my life."

Cliona smiled. "Hello, Bella," she said. "So delighted to meet you." She bowed formally.

"Bella is the best," said Alex. "She's seen me through a lot. Break-ups, my disastrous A-Level results, my Justin Bieber phase."

"What?" Cliona looked shocked. "You were a Belieber? A fan?"

He nodded. "Guilty as charged. I blame the twins. They played his songs over and over."

Cliona patted his arm. "I wouldn't broadcast that if I were you."

"A real man can admit such things." He grinned. "Hand me that bucket of slop, please."

She picked up the brown bucket by the fence and grimaced. "What the hell is this?"

"Leftover beetroot cake and vegetables." He threw it into the trough and the pigs started to eat with fervour. "Not the pork though," he added. "That would be unethical."

After feeding the animals, they went to the vegetable garden and picked some courgettes. Using a knife, Alex cut the stem and put yellow and green varieties in the basket next to the eggs.

"The stems are really prickly," he said, grasping her hand and forcing her to rub the truncated plant.

"*Ow!*" she exclaimed, pulling back. "That hurts."

"I'll make a farmer out of you yet." He stood up and brushed soil from his jeans. "Now, let's go into Canterbury. The twins said we can borrow their bikes."

"Cycle into town? Are you crazy?"

"It's only a stone's throw away. Come on! I'll buy you lunch." He put his head to one side, his brown eyes pleading with her.

"Oh, fine. Let's cycle." She threw up her hands. "I'm just not very fit."

"Nor am I, but I'm convinced we'll make it."

As planned, they cycled into Canterbury, taking country lanes rather than main roads. Alex tried to do a wheelie to impress her. Instead, he fell flat on the ground. She laughed out loud until she realised that he was lying on the ground, not moving. Discarding her bike, she rushed to his side, kneeling close by him.

"Alex!" she said urgently. "Alex, are you okay?" She shook him gently. "Alex!" She stroked his red hair. "Wake up, please wake up."

His eyes opened and he smiled. "Aw, you care! You really care."

"How could you!" She started to pummel him but he was too strong for her. He caught her wrists and kept smiling infuriatingly.

"Look, my near death aside, that wheelie-fail was seriously embarrassing."

"You could have been badly injured."

"Would you have looked after me?" His brown eyes connected with hers and she blushed.

"Your mum would do a better job ..."

He released her wrists. "I guess you're right. Come on. Let's keep moving."

The famous cathedral, a site of medieval pilgrimage, had tall spires that stood over the rooftops of the town. Its stained-glass windows were a sight to behold, with the multi-coloured glass illuminated by the light passing through them. After visiting the cathedral, they climbed the Westgate Towers and gazed at the view of the city. Then Alex took her to the Chocolate Café, a chic place to have coffee and cake.

"I have to stop eating," said Cliona, munching on carrot cake. "I'll be fat."

"You could do with a few pounds," said Alex. 'You're a skinny little thing."

"No!" She shook her head. "Madison would probably fire me. She is such a fattist."

"Madison is shallow," he said. "We all know it."

"Don't."

"She is spoilt and entitled. I don't know how you put up with her."

"Alex!"

"I mean, we've had a little taste of fame and it's great and all, but it shouldn't change your life completely. She lives in an alternate universe that revolves solely around her."

"She's my friend," protested Cliona. "Please don't bitch about her."

"We call her Yoko." He grinned. "You know, because of Caspian."

Cliona couldn't help but smile.

"Fionn told me you love film," he said, dropping the subject. "Why did you give up on your dream?"

She put down her fork. "I haven't given up. I just needed a job. Dublin is a closed shop for someone like me. I need to travel and make connections."

"Have you made connections?"

"Not really," she admitted. "No one notices me."

"What about Madison's dad? Isn't he a filmmaker? Why doesn't she put in a good word?"

"She doesn't want me to leave."

"But it's your life."

"I know, but she depends on me."

"Cliona," he said gently, taking her hand. "Before Maddy, your parents depended on you. Fionn told me. You have to start putting yourself first."

"I do! I travel the world with Madison. I get well-paid. I live in Mayfair."

"So? That doesn't fulfil you."

"It's better than most."

Alex sighed. "You're too sweet for your own good. I swear, there isn't a bad bone in your body."

"Oh, I have my moments."

"Oh?"

"Like when people pretend they're unconscious after a disastrous attempt at a wheelie."

"You were angry?" he asked, surprised.

"Yes! I was worried. I mean, you could've really hurt yourself."

"Aw, shucks!"

She touched his arm. "Seriously though, thanks for bringing me here. I love your farm and your family are so nice."

His eyes burned. "What are friends for?"

Chapter Twenty-nine

Prudence placed the platter of roast beef carefully on the table. She was extra careful as she had used her white lace tablecloth. George, her husband, was waiting beside her to carve.

Madison sat at the other end of the table wearing a high-necked blouse and black trousers.

"Help yourself to the vegetables," said Prudence, pointing at the china bowls of mashed parsnip, potatoes and carrots.

"Thank you, Mrs. Cole," said Madison demurely.

"Call her Prue, for Christ's sake." Caspian rolled his eyes.

"So, Caspian tells me that you're from Dublin." George sat down at the head of the table. "I knew a man years ago from Dublin."

"That's nice," said Madison, smiling.

"I like your song 'Text Me Back'," said Prudence. "I looked it up. It's catchy."

"Really?" Madison looked pained. "My new stuff is so much better."

"I must check it out."

Madison ate a small piece of beef. She tended to avoid red meat, but she didn't want to appear rude.

"So who did Caspian inherit his talent from?" Madison smiled brightly. "Who's the musician?"

George glanced at his wife. "Prue's dad played the harmonica," he said. "He was quite good."

"That's nice."

Caspian reached for the bowl of roast potatoes. "Mum, this dinner is ace. I don't know how you do it."

"Thanks, lovey."

They ate in silence for a few minutes. Madison ate some carrots and half a potato, but avoided the parsnips.

"Have you had enough?" asked Prudence, noticing her knife and fork laid out sideways on her plate.

"Oh, loads," said Madison. "I don't really eat a lot. It's the pressure of fame."

"How awful!"

"Caspian will have to watch it too," Madison joked. "Three helpings of roast potatoes are a *no-no* when you're famous."

"Is it terribly hard?" asked Prudence. "It frightens me sometimes. One can attract all manner of fans, stalkers included."

"Well, I have security, as you know." Madison pointed to Peter who was standing outside. "My dad insisted. It's the only way to protect yourself."

"I'm not at that stage," protested Caspian.

"You will be," she went on. "You see how they hound me. How they're constantly digging into my past, looking for something to print."

Prudence's hand flew to her mouth. "How intrusive!"

"My mum has electric gates and cameras everywhere," Madison sighed. "For peace of mind. It got to the stage where she was accosted at the supermarket by yobs asking about my schooldays or what my favourite food was as a child. Seriously, the world is mad."

"Oh, George!" Prudence grasped her husband's hand. "I don't want that."

"It'll be fine," said Caspian. He squeezed her fingers in reassurance.

"Look, guys. I think we're overreacting. My life to date has been uneventful to say the least. If there are no skeletons in my closet, then interest will wane. Now pass the gravy, Mum. I think I'll have more beef."

That night, as they lay in Caspian's childhood bed, he stroked her bare arm, humming a tune.

"That's nice," she murmured. "What is it?"

"A new song I'm working on."

"I like it."

He sighed. "It's so hard to write in London. There's always somewhere I have to be or someone I have to talk to."

She snuggled closer to his bare chest.

"Maddy?"

"*Hmmm?*"

"Will you come away with me next week? I'm think of heading somewhere quiet to write. I want you with me."

"I don't know. I'd have to check my schedule."

"Please. I like when it's just us. I mean, tonight was great. You were like the Maddy I first fell in love with."

She rested her head on the crook of her arm. "Where are you thinking?"

"Norway? A friend of mine hired a log cabin there and he said it's amazing."

"Norway?" she repeated. "No way."

"Come on," he pleaded. "You, me and the forest. You deserve a holiday before your world tour kicks off."

She contemplated what he said.

"When you start touring, we won't see each other at all," he said.

"Of course we will."

"No, we won't. I hate meeting for a night here and there in an impersonal hotel."

She kissed his shoulder. "Okay, okay. Norway it is. I'll talk to Ross."

"We need to reconnect."

"I get it." She kissed his cheek. "Oslo, here we come."

A week later, Madison shook Cliona awake. "Clio!' she said in excitement. "Ross called. We have to go to his office right now. He has big news."

Cliona yawned and rubbed her eyes. "What? Why?"

"Just hurry. He said it can't wait."

"Okay." She got out of bed and opened the blinds.

Madison had been in a great mood since her trip to Banbury and talked about it constantly. How Prue adored her and how Caspian was so sweet to his parents. Cliona plastered a smile on her face and tried to be happy for her friend. Meeting the parents was a big step and by all accounts it had gone well.

Not once did she ask you about what you got up to over the weekend, said a small voice in her head. Alex's words resonated in her brain and she started to see the reality.

Madison was shallow and self-obsessed. Maybe she should quit and follow her dream. Film was her talent and she was wasting time being a PA.

"*We leave in ten!*" shouted Madison from the kitchen.

Cliona picked up her toothbrush. "*I'll be ready!*" she yelled back.

She didn't understand why she had to go too. It was as if Madison couldn't survive alone.

John picked them up as usual and the Mercedes sped along the streets of London. The traffic lights near Regent Street turned red and the car came to a halt. It was raining and the droplets travelled slowly down the window. Cliona gazed out at the pedestrians hurrying along the wet pavements, most of them with their hoods up and others holding newspapers over their heads and grimacing. There was a Robbie Williams song on the radio and Madison hummed along.

After twenty-five minutes, they pulled up outside the Generation X building on Holloway Road.

As per usual, John got out and disappeared into the building. Cliona drummed her fingers on her knee, accustomed at this stage to the wait time. She peered out the window at the grey sky and saw John in deep conversation with the security guard at the door of the studio. Then he strode back to the car and got in.

"All's well," he said in his deep voice.

Todd got out and automatically scanned the area. Then he magically produced an enormous umbrella and opened the back door. "Let's go," he said, holding up the umbrella for Madison to walk under. He escorted her to the door.

Cliona followed, yanking her hood up over their hair. Her glasses got wet so she had to wipe them clean with a tissue in the foyer.

The receptionist smiled at Madison. "Ross is waiting for you."

They took the elevator to the third floor. There was a ping and the doors opened. Todd and Cliona took a seat outside on a leather armchair respectively. Cliona reached out and took a magazine from the table in front of her. A large yucca plant gave a splash of green colour to the white walls which were covered in framed photos of discs – various accolades of Ross's success with famous artists.

Over by the window was the most recent addition: Madison's new album had just gone platinum.

Madison walked straight up to a door with '**Ross Curtis**' on it. She knocked and entered. "Hi, Ross," she announced.

"Maddy!" He sat back in his leather swivel chair and smiled. "You're looking well."

She took a seat in the large leather chair. "So, what's the big news?" she asked.

Ross smiled. "Well, I got a call yesterday from a film studio."

"*A what?*" She sat up straight.

"They want you to record a song for a film that's coming out soon. It stars Aurora Sinclair."

"Seriously?" Her eyes widened in shock.

"They're looking for something fresh. The film is out in five months so they want this in the bag pretty quickly."

"What's the film?"

"*Josephine*. It focuses on her relationship with Napoléon."

She closed her eyes. That was it.

"Have we a song?"

Ross nodded. "We have two. Both written by Savannah Morris."

"Really?" Madison looked impressed. "I thought she'd retired. She hasn't released music in years."

"Yeah. She's friends with Raphael Baptiste, the director. He pleaded with her and she caved. Lucky for us she did."

"Can I listen?"

"Sure. She sent me a demo. She's playing piano and singing. You'll put your own stamp on it, of course, but they're good tracks." He leaned forward and pressed an icon on his Mac. The room filled with Savannah's voice and the chords of a song. Madison closed her eyes and listened. "This is really catchy."

Ross nodded. "I think so. Wait, listen to the second one." He pressed another button. The second one was slower with an instrumental cello solo.

Madison tapped her knee in time to the music. "*Wow*, that's brilliant!"

"I know. I'm torn between the two of them."

"Why isn't Aurora Sinclair singing?" she asked suspiciously.

"Baptiste doesn't want it. It distracts from the film."

"Gosh, this is big, isn't it? I could go down in history."

"That's exactly it. This will be your legacy." He clicked on his emails. "Savannah lives in Norfolk and she'd like to meet you."

"When?"

"Well, next week if you can. I've freed up your schedule."

Madison bit her lip. "I was supposed to fly to Oslo with Caspian. We decided it over the weekend. We need to spend more time alone together."

"That's nice, Maddy. My heart bleeds for you both, but can you reschedule?"

"I suppose."

"Great. I'll let her know that you'll be there around lunchtime on Monday."

"It'll be so cool to meet her. I mean, she's iconic."

"She's not the easiest," he warned. "Just be prepared. A friend of mine managed her for three months and then quit. She was a right diva in her day."

"She retired young, though, didn't she?"

"Yes. She walked away from the industry. Said it was empty and shallow. She bought a farm and lives there with her horses, her dogs and runs an aviary. She must be seventy if she's a day."

"How did Raphael convince her?"

"He's a charmer, that Baptiste. She's an old family friend, apparently. Her mother knew his great-grandad or something like that. Anyway, it doesn't matter. All we care about is jumping on this lucrative bandwagon. With Aurora Sinclair as Josephine and Baptiste on the director's chair, this is going to be massive, love."

"I'm sorry, Caspian. It's just I have to meet Savannah."

"You promised that you'd come with me. I need you there. I hired the log cabin especially. You, me and nature."

"Next time."

"We had such a great time with my parents, the blouse aside. You promised that we'd never let things get so bad again."

"I have to go ..."

"This is getting harder and harder, Maddy. We made a pact ..."

"Look, I can follow you to Oslo in a few days."

"The cabin is in Rauland which is miles from Oslo. You'd never find it."

"There is a thing called Google Maps, you know. Of course I can follow you."

"You never fulfil your promises. Remember the last tour?"

"I couldn't go with you, you know that."

"Yes, but it gets lonely on the road. Now, you're blowing me off to meet an ageing hippy?"

"Caspian! This is huge for me."

"I wanted us to spend time together, without the internet. I wanted to write music with you by my side."

"I'll follow you! I just need Monday to go and see Savannah and then I'll take the first flight out of London."

"Don't let me down."

"I won't, Jeez."

"If you do, I'll find some hot Scandinavian girl to replace you."

"Don't say things like that."

He hung up the phone.

Chapter Thirty

Madison's Mercedes arrived in the small town of Aylsham in rural Norfolk the next morning. Todd and Cliona accompanied Madison, along with John her driver. Ross had squeezed in at the last minute, rendering the backseat crowded.

"My Porsche is at the garage," he explained. "Let's carpool and help the environment."

Cliona pressed herself against the window and Madison begrudgingly moved into the middle of the backseat to accommodate him.

"Drive like the wind," she muttered to John. She couldn't understand why Ross was coming along. He was surplus to requirement.

Savannah lived in a farmhouse three miles outside the busy market town. The entrance to her house was a long road filled with potholes and John did his best to avoid them as they approached the house.

Two dogs ran towards the car as it pulled up, barking madly.

A woman followed, wiping her hands on an apron. She

had long white hair wound into a chignon and her face was wizened from being out in the sun. She wore loose pants, a woolly cardigan and wellington boots.

"*Pozzo! Lucky! Come here!*" she yelled at the dogs. They scampered back and circled her legs.

"Is that Savannah Morris?" asked Madison in shock. "She's so old! I googled her last night and she looked completely different."

"Well, she is in her sixties, like, " said Ross.

John stopped the car and hopped out, opening the door for Ross to get out.

"Thank God," said Madison to Cliona in an undertone. "That journey was way too close for comfort."

Todd opened the other back door and Cliona got out, followed by Madison. Then he approached Savannah and asked could he check the premises.

"You must certainly cannot," she said coldly. "How dare you even suggest such a thing?"

Ross waved Todd away. "It's cool, it's cool. I'm sure there are no threats here."

Todd looked at Madison for confirmation and she nodded. "Just leave it."

He stood back, his arms crossed defensively.

"Welcome to my home," said Savannah, addressing Madison alone. "Did you bring some things?"

"Some things?" she repeated.

"Yes, some clothes, a toothbrush, that sort of thing."

"Why?"

"Well, you'll have to stay here for a while. I need to see if you can do this to my satisfaction. I'm not giving my songs to just anybody."

"*What?*" Madison looked thoroughly shocked.

Ross stood in front of her and held out his hand.

"Savannah, I'm Ross her manger. Ross Curtis. We spoke on the phone?"

"Yes?"

"You didn't mention staying here. Madison has commitments."

"Cancel them. She's got to stay here and work with me."

"Stay here?" Madison wrinkled her nose. "On a farm?"

"Yes." Savannah regarded her frostily. "Alone. Without this circus of hangers-on."

"Alone?" Madison burst out laughing. "Well, that's not going to happen. I mean, Todd is with me all the time. And Clio is my PA. I need her with me too. John drives me everywhere so he can't leave." She glanced at Ross. "I can live without you, Ross. No offense."

"None taken," he said, holding up his hands.

"Either you rid yourself of these people or leave." Savannah met her gaze. "Those are my terms. Take them or leave them."

"What? Are you crazy?" Madison's eyes narrowed. "I'm not staying here all by myself. Forget it."

"Fine. Goodbye." Savannah turned on her heel and walked back into the house, banging the door behind her.

"*Maddy!*" Ross shouted. "Don't piss her off, like. You have to get this gig. Go in there and tell her you'll stay."

"I will not," said Madison hotly. "How dare she boss me around like that? I don't care who she is. I'm Madison Ryan, not some nobody from nowhere. She can stick her two songs where the sun don't shine."

Todd nodded in agreement.

"John, let's go. I'm going back to London." Madison turned around and walked towards the car.

Cliona ran after her and pulled her sleeve gently.

"Maddy! Don't go. Wait a second. She's not so bad. She just wants you to work with her and have no distractions. I get that."

"Todd is not a distraction, he's a necessity. I mean, I could be abducted up here."

"No, you won't," said Cliona. "Bethany just tweeted an old photo of you in Bermuda. Everyone thinks you've jetted off on holidays. No one knows you're here."

"She's right," interrupted Ross. "We made sure to put the paps on the wrong trail."

"Mum texted last night and was so excited that you were working with Savannah. She's an icon. You'll regret it if you don't."

Madison bit her lip. "But stay here alone? What will I do, Clio?" She took out her phone. "There's barely any phone coverage up here and I bet she doesn't have Wi-Fi."

"Sing. Learn from her. Enjoy nature."

"But a farm?"

"So? I had a blast on Alex's farm. It was really nice. Milk a cow if you have to. Just relax and let it happen. This is the right path for you. I can feel it. Imagine your name on the credits of that film. Up there with Aurora Sinclair and Raphael Baptiste. You might even get to the Oscars."

"*Hmmm*, maybe."

"Come on, Maddy. I'll only be a phone call away."

"You just want a few days off."

"Well, there's that too." Cliona smiled. "I'd like to fly home and see Mum."

"Fine. I'll go back and suck up to the old bag. Maybe I can show her a thing or two about modern music." She paused for a moment. "Clio? Will you do me a favour?"

"Of course."

"Will you call Caspian for me and tell him that I'm stuck up here for a few days? He was so angry last night, I can't face it."

"No problem."

"He thinks I'm going to join him in Norway but it's not looking likely now."

"Sure. I'll handle it."

Caspian hung up the phone when Cliona told him the news.

Then, a few minutes later, he called back.

"Sorry, Clio. I just get so angry with her sometimes."

"She said to apologise."

"Like she means it!" he said bitterly. "Her career will always come first. I really thought we'd turned a corner and reconnected."

Cliona felt uncomfortable. "Look, good luck with the songwriting. I have to go."

"Wait! You're at a loose end. Why don't you join me?"

Cliona sat down on a chair, her heart racing. "Join you?"

"Yes! We could just hang out. It's a short drive from Oslo."

"I don't think Maddy would approve ..."

"So? It's her loss. I'd like the company. Please, Clio! I'm currently staring out at coniferous trees and not much else."

Cliona closed her eyes and imagined being holed up in a log cabin with Caspian Cole. It was a heavenly image. However, she knew it was wrong. Madison was her friend and it would be inappropriate. She steeled herself.

"I'm flying home, Caspian. Sorry. Maybe ask one of the band?"

"Fine, I will." He sounded annoyed. "Talk soon." He hung up the phone.

Cliona felt deflated. How she wished she was spontaneous sometimes. Deep down, she knew she couldn't behave that way. It just wouldn't be right.

After John had driven away, it was just Savannah and Madison sitting at the large kitchen table. It was a huge wooden affair, scrubbed clean with a few burn marks from hot pots being put down without protection.

"I like the songs," began Madison, reddening slightly. The other lady's silent stare was unnerving.

"What is your motivation?" asked Savannah suddenly. "With regard to your work?"

"My motivation?"

"Yes."

"To sell albums and be famous, I suppose."

"Do you like your music?"

"I do now."

"Why?"

"It's cool and it's funky. People seem to like it."

"I don't like it." Savannah played with a silver ring on her index finger. "It's repetitive and boring. It's been done before."

Madison stood up, her chair falling backwards. "Now

wait a second," she said angrily. "Who do you think you are?"

"I'm Savannah Morris. Seven time Grammy winner, multi-million-selling songwriter, musical legend and horticulturalist."

"Well, I'm Madison Ryan, Grammy winner, VMA winner and ... and ..."

"Exactly. Now sit down."

Madison obeyed.

"I contacted Ross because despite your appalling choice of music and your questionable dress sense, I think you have something. I think you need someone like me to pull you out of a rut. You've spent the last few months reinventing yourself when, in fact, you're doing what all the other pop artists have done before you. It's so predictable."

"No one has ever spoken to me like this," said Madison in a small voice. "Like, ever."

"Maybe if they had, you wouldn't be such a prima donna." Savannah got up. "I'm going to make some tea. Would you like a cup?"

"Yes."

"Yes?"

"Yes, please."

Savannah smiled. "Good. Now, let's discuss the film and then the angle I want you to try with the first song. This is not teeny-bopper stuff, Madison. This is grown-up. You must listen and learn."

"Okay."

"You have to put everything into this song. Love, loss, sex. It will not be like your usual work."

"I get it." She resisted rolling her eyes. Something told her that Savannah would not appreciate it.

"Good. Now, let's have tea and then we'll move to the studio."

Three days passed. Madison quit twice before rejoining Savannah at the keyboard. They came to blows over the key, the tempo and the projection.

Savannah won most of the arguments but allowed Madison a small victory when she conceded to change the lyrics in the second verse.

"*Cherish me, never stop.*" Madison made a face. "Cherish me? It's so dated. Like, she's an antique or something."

"So, what do you suggest?"

"How about '*Possess me, never stop*', or something? I think it's better. More direct."

Savannah adjusted her glasses and peered at the sheets of music. "Possess? I'm not sure."

Madison put her hands on her hips. "You know it's better, you just won't admit it because you're so stubborn."

Savannah took off her glasses and a rare smile formed on her lips. "Yes, you might be right about that."

Madison smiled too.

"*Possess* it is then." Savannah scribbled something in pencil on the sheet music. "Now, back to the bridge."

They spent the mornings working on the songs. Then, in the afternoon, Savannah would take her on a walk around her land, showing her the different trees and hills.

"Most of the trees are beginning to lose their leaves," she said in her gravelly voice. "You should see this place in spring. It's joyous."

"I'd love that," said Madison, really meaning it. She

nearly had to pinch herself. She couldn't remember the last time she'd been so content. Madison Ryan didn't wear wellies and walk through muddy fields, looking at trees and scenery.

Savannah's life was so simple. She made her own bread, ate poached eggs each morning from her two hens out in the yard, and listened to classical records on her old player in the evenings with her eyes closed. There was no evidence of her success anywhere. No discs on the wall or bling to be found. Despite her millions in the bank, she didn't flaunt it. Her car was a fifteen-year-old Saab that she barely used as she had an old Raleigh bike with a basket that she rode into town for groceries.

In the evenings, Savannah took her time making dinner. She would often opt for vegetarian dishes, using produce she had from her garden. She picked vegetables like purple-stem broccoli, tomatoes and beetroot. Using spices and herbs, she created flavoursome dishes that Madison devoured.

Savannah watched her in amusement. "So, you like kale pizza?"

"It's unreal," said Madison, helping herself to another slice. "Who'd have thought?" She chewed thoughtfully. "I'm always under pressure with my weight. It's really hard."

"Then don't do it. No one can force you."

"I beg to differ. The minute I put on a pound, I'm targeted. It's exhausting."

Savannah poured some elderflower cordial into a glass and added some water. "You need to decide what's important. What do you want from your life?"

Madison paused. "Love, money, success."

"Love? Are you in a serious relationship?"

"You must have seen pictures of me and Caspian."

"The blonde man?"

Madison nodded. "He's a musician too. We've been together for eight months."

"I'll ask again, are you in a serious relationship?" Savannah sipped her drink. "Or is it for the attention?"

"I love Caspian."

"*Hmmm.*"

"I do love him." She put down her fork with a clatter. "He's everything I want."

One evening, over a cold glass of limoncello, Madison asked Savannah why she gave up the limelight.

"Oh, there were a few reasons." Savannah took a small sip of her liquor.

"How did you do it? I mean, I complain about fame but I don't think I could live without the attention."

"Oh, but you could." Savannah looked up. "It's a terrible life. It's all fine when you're in the spotlight and everyone wants to be around you and talk to you. When I was on stage, I felt like a queen. I felt powerful and invincible." She sighed. "Then the comedown, that inevitable crash, became harder and harder to cope with. The darkness of those in-between times was all consuming and I felt so lost."

Madison's eyes widened. She had an inkling of that feeling and it had frightened her.

"So, are you happy now?"

"Oh, yes. The darkest hour I've had since I moved here is my potato crop failing or that day I ran over my best hen with my car." She smiled. "I'm so content here."

"How are you not lonely?"

"I was married for a time. You know that."

Madison nodded. When she had googled Savannah before coming up to Norfolk, she had read that she had been happily married to the artist Andreas Sharman until his death seven years ago. Their marriage had been short-lived – they had found each other when they were in their fifties – but the five years they had lived together had been the happiest time for both of them. Then, when he was diagnosed with lung cancer, she had nursed him to the end.

"Andreas was everything I ever wanted. He was intelligent, sexy, fun, caring, kind. He was perfect. However, life does not allow one to enjoy perfection for too long. I often think it's for fear of tarnishing it. Cruel fate snatched him from me and I've been alone since."

"You poor thing."

"Yes, I used to think like that. I wallowed in self-pity for months, cursing the gods for stealing him away." She met Madison's gaze. "But now I realise that I was far from poor. I had five wonderful years with him. I was rich and privileged and incredibly lucky. That got me through it. That brought me into the light."

"Do you have any pictures of him?"

Savannah nodded. "Just a few of him when we first met. I wanted to remember him in his prime, not as the broken man he became when the cancer ravaged his body." She opened a drawer in the old oak dresser by the window. Riffling through, she found three faded photographs of a handsome man with his shirt open at the neck. He was laughing and holding a brush in his hands. Then the second photo was one of the two of them. Savannah looked years younger, her hair braided down her back. The third was of Andreas again, painting a picture. There was the form of a woman on the canvas, a painting in its infancy.

"Me," said Savannah softly. "That painting hangs in my bedroom now. It's probably worth a fortune."

"Wow." Madison looked awestruck.

"You see, Andreas and I worked because he was the opposite to me. He was quiet and reserved. He complimented my ego, allowing me to shine. Then, when things became too much, he was stable one in the background, there to pick up the pieces."

Madison said nothing but she had an uncomfortable feeling. Her relationship with Caspian was the opposite. They were both vying for attention all the time.

"So, enough about me," said Savannah, bringing her back to earth. "I think we're almost ready to record those tracks. You've softened, Madison. You've blossomed."

"Really?" She blushed with pleasure.

"Really. Now, would you like some more limoncello? I must admit I tend to drink too much of it. I rather like the sweet taste."

"Why not?" She held out her glass.

Chapter Thirty-one

One day in late September, Raphael was in the garden reading a newspaper when Isabelle appeared. She looked nervous and unsure, her long red hair in a loose braid.

"How was town?" asked Raphael, taking off his glasses.

"Interesting," she said slowly. She took the newspaper from his hands and sat on his lap. "I have some news."

He kissed her shoulder. "Good news, I hope."

"Well, I think so." She kissed his lips. "I'm pregnant," she whispered.

Raphael sat up straight. "What?" He looked shocked. "How? When?"

She stroked his hair soothingly. "I'm about three months. That's why I was so sick. I didn't realise until we were in London but I wanted to wait until we got home to see a doctor." She looked up at him shyly. "I think it's awesome."

"It is, it is." He took her face in his big hands and kissed her repeatedly. "It's wonderful."

"Are you sure?" She looked terribly young and unsure.

"Of course," he said, his brown eyes staring into hers. "This child will be a prince amongst men. I don't doubt it."

"Or a princess," she corrected.

"Maybe." He stood up with her in his arms and swung her around. "I love you," he said, placing her back on the ground. "You are my everything."

Late that night, he watched his wife sleeping. Her chest moved up and down and her eyelashes fluttered. Her breasts looked full; he couldn't believe he hadn't noticed it before. She looked so different – even more beautiful than ever. His expression softened. She was carrying his child, like a sacred vessel.

Suddenly an image floated into his mind. The image of a young blonde girl.

Mary.

He hadn't thought about her in years. He remembered the phone call. The tears. He told her to terminate it without a second thought.

He put his hand on Isabelle's abdomen and let it rest there. How he had changed. The baby growing inside his wife was now the most important thing in the world. He was ready for this. He was ready to continue his legacy.

He pushed Mary's image from his mind. His life would have been so different now if that pregnancy had come to fruition. He definitely made the right decision at the time. This was his second chance. His opportunity to make amends. He would love this child like no other.

Madison listened intently until the last bar of music had been played. Then, taking off her earphones, she looked up at Savannah. "It's perfect," she said joyously. "It's the best song I've ever recorded."

Savannah smiled. "Yes, I think you're right."

"I never knew I could sing like that."

"You had to believe in yourself and cut away all the frills. You have a great voice but you don't use it enough."

"Thank you." Madison got up and hugged her. "Thank you for teaching me."

"You're most welcome." Savannah regarded her fondly. "Now, hopefully Raphael will like it."

"What's he like?" asked Madison curiously.

"Domineering, volatile, demanding, but wonderful." Savannah's expression softened. "I knew his parents in the seventies. That's how we met. I used to holiday in Amiens with the family. Raphael was only a child back then."

"I'd love to meet him."

"I'm sure you will at some stage. If not soon, then at the première."

Madison couldn't stop smiling. She was breaking into the world of film. She would be on the red carpet with superstars of the silver screen. The song might even be nominated for awards. It was heady and exciting.

"Now, I must leave you. I've been in London far too long."

"What? It's only been three days." Madison looked desolate for a moment. "Will I see you again?"

"Someday."

"At the première?"

Savannah laughed. "Now, Madison. Do you really think I'd show up at that?" She hugged her briefly. "Look after yourself."

"I'll miss you."

"You'll be fine." She walked away. "Remember what's important!" she called as she left the studio.

♫ ♫ ♫

Ross called her three days later.

"Baptiste? He likes the song. He wants a music video right away. You've got to go to Paris."

"Wait, what?"

"He wants you in front of the different locations in the movie. Then they'll edit in scenes from the film."

"Is he going to direct it?" she asked in excitement.

"Yes. He's a control freak."

"*Oh my God!*"

"Just pack a bag. It'll take three to four days. Possibly a week. There was talk of Martinique, but Baptiste vetoed it. He doesn't have time."

Madison closed her eyes in ecstasy. "This is going to be big, isn't it, Ross?"

"Huge. You're about to go stratospheric."

Caspian watched her zip up her bag.

"So, how long will you be gone this time?" he asked sulkily.

"A week? I'm not sure." She tied her hair up into a ponytail. "The video has to be wrapped as soon as possible as they want to release the song. It'll add hype to the film." She leaned down and kissed him. "This is the biggest moment of my career. I'm so excited."

"Will you be back for our gig at the Empire?"

"When's that again?" She threw her hair straightener into the bag.

"Friday."

"Gosh, that's cutting it a bit fine. I'll try to be."

Caspian sat up straight. "Look, I realise you're on cloud nine, Mads, but this is a big deal for me. It's our first arena gig. I want you to be there."

"I'll try," she promised, her blue eyes wide. "I mean, music videos only take a few days." She leaned in and kissed him on the lips. "I'll call you tonight."

"Watch that Baptiste. He's a lady's man."

"Oh, stop. He's old enough to be my father."

"Maddy?" Caspian stared up at her.

"*Hmmm?*"

"I love you."

She paused for a fraction too long. "I love you too."

Raphael sent an email with an itinerary for the first day of the shoot. All members of the cast and crew had to be on set for six o'clock in the morning.

Mona groaned when Madison told her.

"We'll have to be up at four in the morning," she said. "I'll need all that time to do your hair and make-up."

Madison didn't care. She was buzzing at the thought of meeting Raphael Baptiste. She had googled him and after reading at length about his past, she decided that he was intriguing. Catapulted into fame in his late twenties, he had partied with the rich and famous. With his then girlfriend, the model Sylvie Marot, by his side, he was photographed with politicians, film stars, musicians and artists. With his shoulder-length dark hair and his brooding brown eyes, he was a pin-up for many. Then, after things spiralled out of control, he went to rehab. Sylvie left him and his career went down in flames, only to be revived when he directed an advertisement for Allegra Starr. Now, he was back on top, making Oscar-worthy films and happily married to the retired supermodel, Isabelle Flynn.

Madison gazed at photos of Isabelle, entranced at her beauty. She was tall with pale skin and had vibrant red hair that hung down her back. Together, they were a stunning couple. Despite Raphael's age – he was forty-three now – he still looked as good as ever.

Cliona printed off another email that Raphael sent and gave it to Madison. It was a storyboard of the proposed shoot. It showed sketches of Madison walking in front of Malmaison, then entering the Tuileries Palace and opening a book. Notes filled the margin, saying that the pages of this book would be stills from the film. These pictures would come to life, transporting the viewer to Martinique and then back to revolutionary Paris. There was also an extensive note on Madison's costume, saying that he wanted her to be all in black. Her hair was to be worn loose and she wasn't permitted to wear jewellery.

Angelica frowned when she saw the brief. "Talk about underwhelming," she said, wrinkling her nose in disgust at the black shirt, trousers and pumps. "No imagination."

It was still dark when Madison was woken by her alarm clock. Groggily, she reached for the light and switched it on. Her suite at The Four Seasons was luxurious and perfectly central. John was waiting for her outside in a hired black Mercedes. Cliona and Todd accompanied her in the car, with Mona, Angelica and Bethany close behind in a Land Rover.

They travelled through the streets of Paris to Rueil-Malmaison, west of the city. The sun was starting to appear as they drove up the long driveway.

"This was Napoleon and Josephine's home," said Cliona in awe. "Isn't it stunning?"

It was certainly a beautiful mansion. It had ivory walls and immaculate gardens.

Raphael and the film board had gained permission to film the exterior of the house but the schedule was tight. They had one day to get the rushes they needed. Just one day. This only served to make Raphael even crankier than usual.

At six o'clock on the dot, a large car pulled up and the door opened. Raphael himself got out, his dark brown hair blowing in the wind. His haughty face scanned the crowd that had assembled. There was a sizable crew waiting with cameras, sound booms, monitors and lights. Most were drinking coffee and speaking in French. Then there was Madison and her entourage, along with security and a hospitality table.

Raphael gave orders to a small man for a black coffee and then shouted at another man to find him a chair.

Madison gazed at him and felt winded. She had seen lots of pictures, but seeing him in the flesh was a different matter entirely. She watched him stride up to the cameraman and speak in rapid French. Cliona said something to her but she didn't hear it. She didn't know why, but she had a strange feeling. Like she had seen him before.

"Maddy! Wake up!"

She came back down to earth.

"Yeah?"

"We have to go and meet the boss." Cliona pointed at Raphael.

"Fine, fine." Madison stood up straight. "Let's do it."

They walked over to him. Madison cleared her throat and he turned around.

"Yes?" he asked curtly.

"I'm Madison Ryan."

"Who?" he asked rudely.

"The singer?"

"Oh. Good. Stand over there and I will be over in a minute. I need to explain my vision." He turned away again and continued his conversation with the cameraman.

Madison blushed and stumbled backwards.

"Are you okay?" asked Cliona in concern.

"I'm fine," she snapped, embarrassed.

Ten minutes later, Raphael walked up to her and kissed her on both cheeks. Slightly disarmed, she was at a loss for words. The sheer magnetism of him was overwhelming.

"You sing well. I am pleased with it."

"Savannah was a great help."

"Yes, she is wonderful." He smiled. "You studied my storyboard, *non*?"

She nodded.

"We have very little time here so we must get going. I have asked the camera to film you entering the house. The sun is suitable now as it is dawn. Then we will move inside." He regarded her outfit. "Good, you listened to my brief. I want you to blend in as otherwise you'll distract from the film itself. Anyway, less is more, *non*?"

Madison thought of her habitual ostentatious outfits and reddened. "Yes – yes, it is."

"*Bon*, we will begin." He drained his coffee and threw the empty cup into a cardboard box.

The shoot took three days in total. The first day started well, but ended up in chaos. Both Madison and Raphael had fiery tempers and clashed over silly things. However, the peak was when Madison refused to gaze wistfully out a window, even though he had explicitly instructed that she do so.

"*I look lame!*" she yelled. "*It's so kitsch!*"

"*Kitsch?*" he roared. "*How dare you call my work such things? You're fired. Get out of here now!*"

"Fine! I don't want to be in this stupid excuse for a music video anyway."

She stalked off only to be calmed by Cliona.

Raphael was pulled aside by his assistant who gently told him that they were out of time and that starting again with someone new was impossible.

He apologised grumpily and she accepted.

Then they compromised. Madison stared at the pages of the book, her blonde hair falling around her face. Raphael got his wistful expression and she didn't have to gaze out the window.

When he watched the rushes that night, something niggled at him. With her blonde hair, she reminded him of that girl in Cork all those years ago. That sweet young girl he had taken to his room. Strange that he should think of her again. Shaking his head, he put it down to Isabelle being pregnant. It was bound to make him think of the past.

♫ ♫ ♫

When Raphael shouted, "It's a wrap!", the crew cheered.

Madison, who was exhausted from the early starts, couldn't wait to sleep in her own bed. It was Thursday so she would be back for Caspian's gig at Shepherd's Bush Empire. However, the thought of a noisy concert with screaming fans and an after-party did not appeal. She debated what to do. She could just stay on in Paris and relax. He need never know the shoot wasn't finished.

"Clio!" she said later that evening. "Let's stay for one more night. I want to go for *macarons* in Ladurée and do some shopping."

"What about Caspian's gig?" Cliona looked shocked.

"He'll be fine."

"He's quite nervous actually. It's their first arena gig."

"Oh? And how are you so knowledgeable?" Madison's eyes narrowed.

Cliona reddened. "Fionn told me," she lied.

"Right."

"Fionn has a ticket for me," went on Cliona, "and I'd really like to go."

"So, go." Madison shrugged. "Take the Eurostar this evening if you like. I'll manage."

"Really?"

"Yeah. Just organise my trip back for Saturday morning. Not too early. And please don't say anything to Caspian. I'll call him later."

When Raphael got home to Amiens, Bertie and Isabelle were in the garden drinking iced tea. Bertie had flown over for Paris Fashion Week and had called to see his old friends.

"Raph!" Bertie got up and shook his hand. "How did the shoot go?"

Raphael kissed Isabelle and sat down. "It went well, in the end. That girl Madison surprised me."

"Oh?"

"She worked hard and gave it her best. I respect that."

"I adore the song!" Bertie hummed it. "Savannah was the right choice."

"Yes, I think so."

Isabelle had her legs raised on a stool. Raphael reached out and rubbed her feet. "How are you today?" he asked lovingly.

"Tired," she admitted. "It's hard being pregnant."

Bertie nodded. "One would imagine so. Making a baby from scratch? There's huge work in that." His eyes twinkled. "It will be a gorgeous baby, no doubt. What with your face, Isabelle, and your cheekbones, Raph. A stunner."

"How's Gabby?" asked Isabelle, referring to her best friend and fashion designer who was in Paris for Fashion Week. "I hope she wasn't mad that I didn't come to her show."

"She was too busy to notice, my love. She and Oberon collaborated for the final show. It was an amazing spectacle. Like the master and his apprentice."

"I should've gone," said Isabelle regretfully. "I was just so tired."

"Gabby understands. Anyway, her wedding isn't too far away. We'll all meet up then."

"Some bridesmaid I'm going to be," said Isabelle, rolling her eyes. "The dress will barely fit."

"Nonsense," said Bertie. "You're like a fertility goddess. You will never look so beautiful again."

♫ ♫ ♫

Madison called Caspian from her hotel room in Paris and informed him that she wouldn't be back in London for the gig. She pretended that she had a meeting with the film studio in Paris the next afternoon. What followed was a screaming match where Madison hung up the phone and stalked out of the room, Todd in tow. Then she stalked back in and told Cliona to cover for her and back up her story.

"I'm just too tired to face it," she said with a pained look.

"Don't worry, I won't say anything," Cliona promised. "Will you be okay without me?"

Madison waved her away. "I'll survive. I know you have to go for Fionn. I'll be fine."

Privately, Madison needed some space. Her head was spinning from the shoot and the excitement of meeting Raphael. His world and indeed the world of Savannah Morris was a different place to what she was used to. She liked having grown-up conversations and using her voice properly. She needed time to think. She was no longer the coquettish popstar singing about break-ups and texting. She had grown up.

Caspian would be fine without her. Once he went on stage, he forgot everything else. She always came second to his music; now he had to come second for once. She needed time on her own and she was going to have it.

Chapter Thirty-two

Cliona took the Eurostar from Gare du Nord to King's Cross St. Pancras.

Caspian texted her all the way from Paris, asking why Madison put everyone else first and if she really had a meeting. Cliona answered vaguely, staying loyal to her boss, but she could sense Caspian's anger and bitterness.

His last message was: **At least you'll be there x**

That thrilled her to the core. She knew it was wrong, but he filled her thoughts constantly. Life was never easy and matters of the heart were rarely fair. She held her phone to her chest and closed her eyes. Their epistolary relationship was what kept her going. She felt she knew him better than anyone. He told her all his problems and she prided herself on being a good listener. He relied on her and she loved being needed.

As she exited the train, she felt a pang. Caspian used to live nearby in the old days. She always thought of him when she saw the street sign on the old brick wall.

Hailing a taxi, she got in and gave the driver Madison's address.

♫ ♫ ♫

Fionn called her the next morning and told her to come backstage before the gig.

"I'll put you on the list," he promised her. "Come early so we can hang out."

She took the tube to Shepherd's Bush and made her way to the arena. There were crowds of people hanging around the entrance, drinking beer from plastic glasses and chatting. She introduced herself to the bouncers at the stage door. She was ushered through, given a backstage pass to hang around her neck and brought to a small dressing room.

Ethan was sitting on a couch with Stella by his side and Fionn was drinking a beer while texting someone on his phone.

"Hey, Clio," he said with a wave. "Just on to Mum. She's wishing us luck."

"She's so disappointed that she can't make it."

"I know," he said with a frown. "Dad's operation comes first."

"Operation?" asked Stella curiously.

"A hernia," explained Fionn. "Nasty."

Ethan pointed to the armchair. "Take a seat. We're not on for an hour."

Stella handed her a bottle of beer. "You look nice,' she observed, noticing the absent glasses and the flattering cut of the dress.

Cliona went pink. "It's just a dress."

"No, I like the colour," said Stella. "Green suits you."

"So where the hell is Maddy?" asked Fionn when he

was finished texting Constance. "Don't feed me that crap that she's busy."

"She is," lied Cliona. "Anyway, are you nervous?" she went on, changing the subject. "There are about two thousand people out there."

"Nah," said Ethan with a grin. "We've got it down."

Their manager, Jax, walked in the door and clapped his hands. "I've just seen two journalists from *Rolling Stone*. Make this count, boys."

Fionn held up his thumb. "No problem."

"This is a big night for you," went on Jax. "We need some nominations in awards season next year."

"We'll do our best," said Ethan. "Do you want a beer?"

Jax patted his stomach. "No, I never touch the stuff. Goes straight to my gut. Right, see you outside." He disappeared again.

"Where's Caspian now?" asked Cliona casually.

"Oh, on the phone to Yoko," said Ethan. "She called five minutes ago to wish him luck."

"And Alex?" She moved hurriedly on.

"He's with his new squeeze, Vivienne."

"His what?" Cliona stopped short.

"Alex is in love," said Fionn. "They met a while back at a *GQ* party. He's smitten."

"Yeah, he took her to the farm and everything." Ethan laughed. "There'll be a ring by next week. We're taking bets."

Cliona felt her stomach flip. She didn't know why, but the thought of Alex with a girl made her feel strange. He was always there in the background, making her laugh. Now, he was with someone and happy.

"That's nice." She smiled brightly. "Good for him."

She walked out and flashed her badge at security.

"Follow me," said the man, leading her to the stalls right next to the stage, It was filled with family and friends, all drinking from bottles of water. Jax waved to her and she veered towards him.

"What happened to Maddy?" he asked straight away. "This could have been publicity gold. Like that time Chris Martin ran up and kissed Gwyneth Paltrow during a gig in Miami. It was all over the media."

"She's busy."

"Ross called, saying she's turned off her phone. He's pretty mad."

"She couldn't make it," she said blandly.

"Still, I thought she'd support him."

Cliona gestured to the other occupants of the stand in an effort to distract him. "Who are these people?" she asked conversationally.

"Mostly family." Jax pointed out Ethan's mother and Caspian's parents, along with some childhood friends. Then Nancy and Jeff arrived with the twins and waved madly at Cliona.

She waved back. "Great to see you!" she called.

Then a beautiful girl walked in and joined them. Cliona gazed at her. She had to be Vivienne. She had jet-black hair cut into a bob and beautiful green eyes. Her four-inch stilettos gave her added height and she had an enviable figure poured into a black dress. She looked up and her eyes met Cliona's. Then she looked away.

Nancy walked over to Cliona and gave her a hug. "How are you?" she asked warmly. "Busy, I'd expect. Alex told me about Madison's song by Savannah Morris. You must be running here, there and everywhere."

"Yes, it's been hectic lately." Cliona smiled. "You're so good to come all the way up here to support him."

"Oh, we're very excited. This is a big night for the band."

"Yes, Fionn's acting all cool but I can tell he's nervous."

"He said your dad had an operation. I hope all's well?"

"He's fine. He's had a hernia for years and he finally got it sorted. My parents don't have private health insurance so when you get the call on the public list, you take it."

"I understand."

"Mum was gutted though. Fionn is the undisputed apple of her eye."

"At least you're here."

Cliona smiled. "That I am. I have my phone ready to video them so I can send it to Mum and Dad."

Nancy took a swig of water. "Vivienne is a nice girl," she said, stealing a glance in Cliona's direction. "She's a model."

"Oh?" Cliona kept a neutral face.

"Yes. A bit skinny for my liking. She wouldn't touch Jeff's apple pie. In fact, she avoided most of his cuisine, deeming it too fattening."

"What a shame."

"I guess it's the price you pay to be so stunning."

"*Hmmm.*"

"I was surprised when he brought her home." Nancy looked her square in the eye. "I had hoped you two would make a go of it."

"Really?" Cliona's voice came out as a squeak.

"Yes. Then Alex said you have feelings for someone else."

"I don't, I mean ..."

"Oh?" Nancy gave her a knowing look. "That's interesting."

"Mum!' called Daphne. "Auntie Julia is on the phone."

Nancy kissed Cliona's cheek lightly. "See you later, my love."

"See you."

The support act – a guitarist from Leeds – finished up to rapturous applause and the lights dimmed. Cliona felt her stomach flip and took out her phone, ready to video the opening for her parents.

The crowd screamed and stamped their feet. A large screen at the back of the stage began to show some graphics – lots of colours moving in sync and creating a spiral effect. Fionn appeared first, his drumsticks in his hands. He held them up by way of a salute. Ethan followed and then Alex.

They picked up their respective guitars and put the straps over their shoulders. The crowd roared in response.

Then Caspian walked on, his blonde hair slicked back off his face. He grabbed the microphone and said, "Great to be here in London."

The crowd screamed in response and Ethan played the intro to "Mosaic". Caspian sat at the upright piano to the right of the stage, and played along. Then he started to sing.

Two thousand voices sang along as he reached the chorus. Fionn, his ears covered with headphones, played the steady beat in perfect time. Then, with a nod from Caspian, the band stopped playing their instruments. Caspian's voice was all that could be heard over the speakers. He stood up and held up his microphone, asking the crowd to sing the chorus. With their arms swaying in the air, they sang together, with Caspian joining in at different times. Then Fionn beat the drums, signalling to Ethan and Alex to resume playing, and the end of the song was a crescendo of voices and the twang of guitars.

Cliona clapped loudly and shouted, "*Brilliant!*"

Nancy looked as proud as punch and the twins were jumping up and down.

Alex looked up and blew a kiss at Vivienne who reciprocated with a smile. Cliona averted her eyes, unable to decipher the horrible feeling she had in the pit of her stomach. Alex's new relationship shouldn't matter. She should feel happy for him. Instead, she felt waves of jealousy.

Caspian held up his arms and clapped for the crowd. "You guys were amazing," he called into the microphone. "Now, we'll play 'It's Over'."

Towards the end of the set, the lights dimmed. Two stools were brought out and only Caspian and Ethan stayed on stage.

"Now, we're going to play a new song," said Caspian, adjusting the microphone to suit his seated height. "It's called 'Your Shell'."

Jax, who was texting on his phone, looked up. "No one told me about a new song. They should discuss this with me first."

Cliona made a "*Shh!*" noise.

Caspian put his lips close to the microphone and spoke softly. The crowd quietened down so as to hear what he was saying.

"This is a song about a shy girl: a girl who stays in the background." He smiled. "If she only came out of her shell, she'd understand what love was all about."

Cliona felt her knees give away.

Ethan picked out a melody and moved his head in time to the music. Lights appeared as some of the audience lit lighters and held them above their heads.

Then Caspian started to sing.

"*Shy girl, my girl, always blending in,*

It's time, girl, to shine, girl, you make my world spin

Cliona strained to hear every word.

Come out of your shell, my love,

Come out and be free,

Take a chance on me, girl,

Give your heart to me."

Cliona felt her cheeks heat up. What was it he said that time? He needed someone quiet – someone who wouldn't compete with him. Maybe this was his way of telling the world. Judging by his angry texts about Madison, it was only a matter of time before that relationship was over.

The song came to an end and there was silence. Caspian raised his head and opened his eyes with a huge smile. The crowd erupted, screaming his name and whistling.

Cliona waved her pass at a security guard backstage, but he refused to let her through. "Sorry, no can do, love. Strict orders."

"But I'm Fionn's sister."

"They all say that, love."

"Look, I have a pass."

"I don't care if you've the crown jewels, darling. You

ain't getting through until I get the green light."

Journalists and photographers were milling around, along with fans and crew. She shrank back into the shadows and rang Fionn, but he didn't answer.

Suddenly she saw Jax walking past, behind the barrier. He was talking on the phone and laughing.

"*Jax!*" she screamed. "*Jax!*"

His head swung around and he spotted her. "You okay?"

"Get me in!"

He nodded. "Oi, mate. Let her through."

The security guard glowered and waved her along impatiently.

"Thanks," she said, squeezing past.

A girl behind her started to wail. "How come she gets in and I don't?"

Cliona pushed through crowds of people and spotted Fionn. He was sitting on an amp, surrounded by three girls.

Cliona rushed over. "Fionn, where's Caspian?" she asked.

"Well, hello to you too. You're here to congratulate me? Aw, you shouldn't bother."

"Sorry," she said blushing. "You were great. Now, where's Caspian?"

"No idea."

Cliona groaned and turned around. She had to find him. She scanned the room desperately.

"Ask Alex," suggested Fionn helpfully. "He's over there."

She looked around and saw Alex standing about six feet away.

"Alex!" she said, walking purposefully towards him. "Great show."

"Thanks."

"Have you seen Caspian?"

"Not recently." He took a swig of beer.

"I just need to see him."

"Oh?"

Cliona went red. "That song he sang, you know, with Ethan. It was lovely."

Alex regarded her thoughtfully. "The one about the shy girl?"

She nodded.

"You want to find him and thank him because you think it's about you."

"No, no, I wouldn't dare think that."

"No, you're right. It *is* about you."

"Really?"

He stared at her. "Yes."

"So, have you seen him?"

Alex's brown eyes connected with hers.

She inhaled sharply, such was the intensity of his gaze.

"Check the dressing room," he said eventually. "Caspian likes to wind down alone after a gig."

"Thanks." She leaned up and pecked his cheek. "Vivienne is beautiful by the way."

"Yes, she is." He turned away. "See you around."

Cliona ran off in the direction of the dressing room. She imagined Caspian sitting in there alone, rubbing his neck and relaxing after the gig. It would be the perfect time to talk to him. Without the band, Madison or fans getting in the way. Alex had confirmed that the song was about her. Now was the time to ask why.

She stopped outside the door and fixed her hair, shaking

it back off her shoulders. Then she knocked. There was no answer so she knocked again. Still no answer.

Gingerly, she opened the door and walked in. The dressing room was deserted. Just empty bottles and cartons scattered around the room.

She tried not to feel disappointed.

It's for the best, she consoled herself. Looking for Caspian like this is bound to attract bad karma. Turning around, she exited the room and walked down the corridor towards the others. Suddenly, she heard a noise. It sounded like a moan. Then she heard it again. Louder this time. It was coming from behind a door that was slightly ajar. Gently she pushed it open, slowly revealing a storeroom filled with boxes. The light was dim so her eyes struggled to adjust. Peering into the gloom, she gasped. Her hand flew to her mouth and she stumbled backwards. Caspian was having sex with a brunette against a pile of crates. His jeans were around his ankles and her legs high in the air. Such was their passion, they didn't notice her presence. Horrified, she backed away. All she saw as she closed the door was the girl's bright red nails scratching his golden back.

Later that night, she lay awake in bed, her thoughts muddled. She couldn't figure him out. There were three texts on her phone from him – three breezy texts asking if she had enjoyed the gig, if he had sounded okay, and if she had heard from Madison. She didn't reply. She couldn't even process what she'd seen. It filled her with disgust.

Miserably, she rearranged her pillow, plumping it up and lying on her side. She had to step back and get on with her life. Caspian blew hot and cold and clearly didn't know what he wanted. Madison was her friend and she deserved better. She had always felt guilty about texting Caspian behind her back, consoling herself that the texts were innocent and they were 'just friends'. Now she saw the light. She had been disloyal and selfish, putting herself before others. That song was inappropriate – how dare he write a song about her when he was still linked to her best friend? She hated to admit it, but he was stringing them all along.

Not any more, she vowed.

She had finally woken up and realised that Caspian only thought of himself.

Chapter Thirty-three

Two days later, Cliona woke up at nine thirty. Grabbing her glasses, she jumped out of bed, surprised that she hadn't been roused earlier. She found Madison in the kitchen, dressed in her gym gear.

"Hey, Sleepyhead! I let you have a lie in."

"Thanks." Cliona opened the fridge and took out a carton of juice.

"That restaurant last night was amazing."

"Oh?" Cliona kept her head down.

"Caspian insisted that we go there."

The red nails scratching his golden back flitted through Cliona's mind. "That's great, Maddy," she said mechanically.

"To be fair, Caspian was a bit mean at first. He was really angry that I missed the gig."

"Really?"

"Yeah. I was surprised. I didn't realise I meant so much to him."

Cliona went bright red.

"We went home and had the nicest time." Madison beamed at her. "We needed to reconnect physically. It definitely bonds you."

"Do you need me to do anything while you're gone?" asked Cliona, desperate to change the subject.

"Not at the moment." She stretched her calf muscles. "God, Boris nearly killed me this morning. I feel achy all over."

"You're in amazing shape."

"Yes, but it's hard looking this good." She sighed. "I have a meeting with Ross at twelve. He wants to talk about the new album."

"Do you need me to come with you?"

Madison shook her head. "Not at all. We're just going over some technicalities. I want to change things up again. Maybe release some songs like 'Possess Me'."

"So no more rap then?"

"Not for the moment." She released her blonde hair from its bobble. "Right, I'm off for a shower. See you later."

Cliona was brushing her hair when her phone rang. She glanced down and saw Caspian's name flashing. She debated what to do. He almost always texted her so it had to be important.

"Hello?" she said guardedly.

"Clio, thank God. I wasn't sure you'd answer."

"Are you looking for Madison? She's out."

"No, no. I was looking for you."

"Oh?"

"Why are things off between us? You barely answer my texts and I get the feeling you're angry about something."

"I'm fine."

"Fine? That bloody word. It generally means the opposite."

"I don't know what you want me to say."

"I want to know why you're so distant. Did I do something to upset you?"

"No."

"Clio!"

"No."

"Tell me."

"Okay, fine. You're unfaithful. You screw around on Maddy and it's unfair."

"What?"

"She was positively glowing this morning, all loved up. Why do you do it?"

"Do what?"

"Have sex with other girls?"

"I don't."

"Yes, you do. Don't deny it."

"Fine. Maybe once or twice. It's just to let off steam after a gig. It doesn't mean anything."

"It's not right, Caspian. Poor Maddy."

"You haven't said anything to her, have you?"

"No, of course not."

"Please don't. It's not worth mentioning."

"I just don't understand you. I don't get why you behave like that."

"What's with the moral high ground?"

"I'm just disappointed in you."

"Cliona, you're not my mother."

"Yes, but I don't agree with it."

"Point taken."

"What really pisses me off is that you don't know what you want!" Her voice rose. "*You write beautiful songs about people and then behave like that?*"

"Beautiful songs? What do you mean?"

"You know what I mean. Alex told me."

"Alex? Cliona, I don't get what you're saying."

"Look, forget it, things are cool between us. I just don't want to blur the lines anymore."

She hung up the phone.

Later that evening, she cooked some pasta and watched Madison as she painted her toenails.

"God, I hate doing this myself," she complained. "I'm all for Mona going on holiday but I really miss her when she's not here."

Cliona tried to smile but she was feeling so glum. Caspian had sent her a lengthy text that afternoon, apologising and asking that their friendship continue as normal. Then he had texted again about a new song he was writing and wondering if they could meet for coffee. She had responded in a curt manner, not wishing to engage in the lengthy texts they enjoyed in the past. She was sick of the emotional rollercoaster. How he played with her emotions. How he could write a song like that and then never refer to it again.

It was odd but she felt protective of Madison. Seeing his infidelity made her feel sorry for her friend. She knew it was hypocritical – after all, she had had an inappropriate texting relationship with him – but she was angry at him for betraying her friend.

The best thing to do was to establish some boundaries.

This was the wake-up call she needed.

Madison screwed the top on the varnish and sat back on the couch.

"Now that I've had a taste of film, I want to meet people like Robert Downey Junior and Leonardo," she said. "This is a fabulous new direction for me, Clio."

"Sure." Cliona struggled to focus.

"I mean, Dad has met a fair few movie stars but no one mega-famous. I mean, he's an indie director and doesn't like the limelight."

"That's nice."

"Clio? Are you okay? You seem a bit spaced."

Cliona took off her glasses and rubbed her eyes. "I'm grand altogether."

Jax sent Caspian an email asking him to come to his office for a noon appointment.

Begrudgingly, he agreed. He hated going across town during the day but Jax had emphasised that it was urgent.

The receptionist smiled at him as he passed, twirling her hair around her finger.

Jax was sitting at his desk with Tommy standing to his right when he entered the room.

"Take a seat," said Jax with a nod. Tommy stood with his arms crossed.

Caspian sat on the leather chair and raised an eyebrow. "Wow, this looks serious. Is everything okay?"

"There are rumours," Jax began slowly.

"Oh?"

He looked him straight in the eye. "Damaging rumours."

"Rumours about what exactly?"

"Other girls. I don't know. There are some reports going around."

Caspian waved his hand dismissively. "That's just gossip."

"*Hmmm.*"

"So ignore it."

Tommy snorted. "Ignore it? Are you having a laugh, mate? You're going out with the golden girl of pop. How do you think people will react when they hear of your cheating?"

"I have never cheated on Madison." Caspian raised his head. "So, there's nothing to say."

Tommy laughed out loud. "Right."

"Yes, but you need to be prepared," said Jax smoothly. "Some girls are selling their stories to tabloids. They're out to make a few pounds out of it. I just had to warn you."

Caspian looked him square in the eye. "Look, Mads and I aren't perfect but I wouldn't do that. Sure, we fight a lot but who doesn't? I'm bound to be targeted by these freaks, wanting to make a few pounds. I'm not even going to give it a second thought."

"She didn't turn up at your gig at the Empire. People are talking."

"She was stuck in Paris."

"Right."

"Look, I'm just busy. It's hard when we both travel a lot."

"Fair enough." Jax sat back. "Just make a public appearance soon. Reassure your fans that it's all lies."

"Fine." Caspian got up. "Is that all you wanted to say?"

Tommy glared at him. "Just try and keep it in your pants until we sort this, okay? People don't like cheaters. Your sales will suffer if this becomes public knowledge."

Caspian saluted him like an army officer. "Yes, sir!" He scowled. "Now, if there's nothing else, I'll head home."

Jax waved him away.

Bethany, Madison's publicist, was waiting at her apartment when she got back from the gym.

"Hey, Bethany! What brings you here?" She pulled her sweatband from her head and shook out her hair.

"I think you should see this." She held up her iPhone.

There was a picture of Caspian talking to a voluptuous blonde girl backstage. His face was inches from hers and she had her hand on his arm.

Madison peered closer at the picture.

"So? What's the big deal?"

"Tommy rang. They're trying to quash the rumours but you need to be prepared."

"Prepared for what?"

"Caspian and his other girls."

Madison's blue eyes widened and she laughed. "Caspian and his what? Are you for real?"

Bethany nodded. "It's circulating. Four girls have come forward saying that they've slept with him." She looked uncomfortable. "I mean, it's probably not true but ..."

"Of course it's not true." Madison raised her eyes to heaven. "As if he would."

Bethany shrugged. "Anyway, we've got to be prepared. You should appear in public together. Get Clio to book a fancy restaurant somewhere and I'll inform the press."

"Tonight?"

"Yes. Let me know the details later." She slung her bag over her shoulder. "Now, I've got to fly. Talk later."

***

Madison called to Caspian's apartment that afternoon. Bethany's words played on her mind and, even though the idea of his cheating was ridiculous, she still had to ask.

She took out her pocket mirror and checked her reflection. Satisfied, she replaced it in her bag. There was no way anyone would cheat on her. Cal Scott floated into her mind but she pushed his image away. That was years ago – she had been a child. Things were different now – she was a superstar. Yes, she didn't think about him all the time. Yes, she should prioritise him more, but relationships always ended up like that. The first stage was heady and exciting. Now they were in the comfortable phase. It was a natural evolution. She cared about him – of course she did – she just had a lot on her plate.

Caspian was playing piano when she arrived.

"Just give us a minute, Todd," said Madison.

"Of course, ma'am." He went straight to the kitchen and shut the door.

"Maddy?" Caspian eyed her cautiously. "Why are you here?"

She walked straight over to him and kissed him on the lips. "I just wanted to say hi."

"Oh?"

"And ask you about the rumours."

"Rumours?" He sat up straight. "What rumours?"

"Oh, it's splashed all over Twitter. About you and some girl. There's a picture of her and everything. I mean, there's no way you'd cheat on me with someone like that."

"Where did you hear this?" He stood up. "From Cliona?"

"No." Her eyes narrowed. "Why did you mention Clio?"

"No reason," he said blandly.

"Caspian? You look strange. Should I be worried about this?"

He took her in his arms and kissed her forehead. "Not at all. My God, no way."

"I mean, you'd never cheat on me, would you?" She stared up at him, her blue eyes wide.

"Never," he lied, holding her close. "Never ever."

"Good." She pushed him backwards. "Now, I must tell you about my new look. It's going to be epic."

"Yes, tell me all about it." He exhaled slowly.

"I'm going all hippy-dippy. Sort of Marianne Faithful." She wrapped her arms around his neck and kissed him. "It's going to be so cool."

Her good mood didn't last long. Pictures of wanton-looking girls with enormous breasts and lips were printed alongside photos of a sullen-looking Madison with headlines such as:

Was Mads Left Out in the Cole-d?

Naughty Caspian

His alleged infidelity remained trending on Twitter and everywhere Madison went, people shouted at her – some in solidarity, some in pity. She tried to ignore it but story after story started to circulate until she was inundated with proof.

On evening, she was sitting on the sofa in her apartment. He was fiddling with the giant flat-screen TV, adjusting the contrast.

"Have you been lying to me?" she asked him quietly, staring at the ground.

"Of course not, baby." He was by her side in a flash. "These girls are trying to get famous. They'll make up anything to get their names in the paper."

"It's just after Cal ..."

"I understand." He stroked her hair.

She tried to feel better, but she could feel it in her bones. Caspian was lying.

"Can I stay over tonight?" he murmured into her hair.

She pulled back. "Not tonight."

"Maddy?"

"I've a lot on for the next few weeks." She didn't quite meet his eyes. "It might be a good thing."

"What?"

"To take a break from each other for a while."

"What?"

"Just until things die down."

Caspian grabbed her shoulders and shook her gently. "That's a terrible idea and you know it."

"Is it?" She felt weary.

"Yes."

She got up. "I need to sleep. Just see yourself out. I'll call you when I'm free."

"When will that be?" He looked genuinely shocked.

"I'm not sure."

"Madison!"

She walked away.

Chapter Thirty-four

Two weeks later, Madison received a letter in the post. It was a crisp white envelope with beautiful gold writing. Cliona found it in the post box and brought it to her directly. However, Todd intercepted it immediately.

"This has to be checked, ma'am," he said formally. "It may be contaminated."

Madison, who was having her breakfast, sipped her pomegranate juice. "Crikey, I never get snail mail anymore. My interest is piqued." She tried to muster up a smile, but failed. She was in terrible form and she knew it. She just couldn't pull herself out of it. She hadn't seen Caspian since that night– he had flown to Berlin almost immediately to film a music video with the rest of the band. She welcomed the break from him. She needed to gather her thoughts. If he was indeed guilty, then a break-up was imminent. However, it had to be handled correctly.

Todd came back and handed the envelope to Madison. "All clear."

"Thanks, Todd." She tore it open and pulled out a white card. It read:

Mister Albert Wells requests your company at the celebration of his birthday on Saturday 5th October. Dress Code: 1980s. Please RSVP to the following address.

There was an address in Belgravia.

Madison clutched the card in delight, Caspian forgotten. "What did I tell you? I'll be mixing with Hollywood greats from now on. This has to be because of that song. Oh my God!"

"Will I RSVP for you?" asked Cliona.

Madison nodded. "Definitely. What will I wear? It's only a week away. I'll have to look amazing."

Caspian got back from Berlin two days later and called Madison straight away.

"Jax called. We've been invited to a party at Bertie Wells' place."

"*We?*" she repeated. "What do you mean, we?"

"The band. Plus partners if we like."

"*What?*" she shouted. "Why were you invited?"

"I don't know. Bertie included a handwritten note, congratulating us on our success. He must like our stuff."

"That's great, babe." She injected brightness into her tone. "I've been invited too."

"You have? That's good. I was going to take you as my plus one."

"No need," she said icily.

"Great. Any thoughts on a costume?"

"Not really," she lied.

"Well, I thought we could go as a famous couple from the eighties."

"Such as?"

"Well, I googled them. We could go as Johnny and Baby, Han Solo and Leia, ET and Gertie ..."

"ET? You're a bit tall."

"JR and Sue-Ellen," he continued, "Diana and Charles ..."

"*Stop!*" She cut him off. "Leave it with me."

"Want to call over tonight?"

She closed her eyes. "I can't tonight. I have plans."

"Oh?"

"Boring stuff. I'm picking outfits for my world tour."

"Can't that wait? I haven't seen you in so long."

"Not really. They have to be ordered and made ..." She trailed off.

"Right."

"But we can definitely go as a couple to that party. I'll text you when I come up with a plan."

"Fine." He hung up the phone.

Cliona stared at the message on the screen. Fionn had texted, asking her to be his date to Bertie's party. Things had turned sour with Mariana and he needed someone uncomplicated to bring along.

Uncomplicated.

She sighed. Boring was what he meant. Good old Cliona. The doormat. The one everyone used to make themselves feel better.

She hadn't sent a reply as she wasn't sure if she even wanted to go. She felt silly mixing with the rich and famous as she had nothing to bring to the table. Her true love – making films – was what she truly wanted to do. However, she was stuck in a rut, working for Madison. If only she was doing what she loved. Then she might feel interesting.

Instead, she was just Madison's PA or Fionn's little sister.

Her phone pinged with a message.

Come to the party, Clio! You owe me for not telling Mum that you broke her Waterford Glass bowl in 2015.

She smiled in spite of herself.

Fine. I'll come. Give me some costume ideas.

The day of Bertie's party dawned.

Caspian looked in his full-length mirror and smiled. His costume was pretty good. He was going as Westley from *The Princess Bride*. His outfit consisted of black boots, black pants, a black shirt and a scarf around his head that covered his eyes. It resembled that of a pirate. He carried a long sword which he swished around like Zorro. Madison was dressing as Buttercup, Westley's true love in the famous film.

True love.

He glowered. Their relationship didn't know the meaning of the word anymore.

Since his return from Berlin, he had seen her twice – briefly. She was always too busy; his schedule always clashed with hers.

He was supposed to call over to her place in an hour, then they were to travel to the party together. Jax had called to remind him. There would be photographers outside her building and it was crucial that they pose for a shot as they exited the building. Bethany was on hand to upload the photos and show the world that they were united and happy.

He was glad that he was wearing a mask. It hid his face from the world – he wasn't sure if he could pretend anymore.

♫ ♫ ♫

He arrived at Madison's place early, hoping that they could spend time together before she got dressed up. However, when he asked where she was, Angelica told him that she was with Mona her make-up artist.

"Is Cliona here?" he asked.

"No," said Angelica. "She's gone to Fionn's place."

He sat down on the leather couch and drummed his long fingers on the arm rest. Idly, he leafed through a *Vogue* magazine and read a few paragraphs about the various fashion weeks that were taking place. There was a large picture of a black bald man wearing a snakeskin suit with 'Oberon' written beside it. His pose was haughty and he almost sneered at the camera. One of the world's leading fashion designers, Oberon had just showcased his Spring/Summer collection in Paris.

After twenty minutes, Madison arrived out of her bedroom fully dressed.

"You're early," she said brusquely. "I specifically said seven-thirty."

"I was hoping that we could spend some time together before you got all dolled-up."

"Well, it's too late now." She smiled sweetly. "My make-up cannot be messed up."

"You look great," he said, regarding her long red dress and loose blonde hair. "Just like Buttercup."

"To be honest, I've never seen the film. I just did what you ordered."

"Hey, I didn't order you to do anything."

"Really?" Her eyes flashed. "I wanted us to go as Baby and Johnny. I had a curly-haired wig and everything."

"I hate that movie."

"That's blasphemous! Everyone knows that *Dirty Dancing* is a classic – one of the greatest films of all time."

"Christ!" Caspian rolled his eyes. "If you really believe that, then I don't know what to say."

"Don't insult my taste!" She glared at him. "Look who I'm dating."

"Oh, is that what it is? *Dating*? You see, I wasn't sure. I mean, I see more of my mother than I do of you. And she lives miles from here."

Todd cleared his throat. "We should make a move, ma'am."

She nodded. "Of course. Right, let's face the paparazzi." She scowled at Caspian. "Now, try and look happy. Just while the lenses are on us."

"I'm wearing a mask, Maddy. No worries there."

There was a group of photographers waiting by the electric gates, their long lenses poking through the grille.

"*They're coming out!*" shouted one and they sprang into action.

Caspian walked out first, Madison trailing behind. They were hand in hand.

"*Oi! Maddy! Look this way, darling!*"

"Caspian! What's the costume, mate? Long John Silver?"

"It's that movie from the eighties. That one about the princess and a giant."

"Oh yeah! '*My name is Inigo Montoya, you killed my father. Prepare to die!*'"

They all laughed. The cameras clicked as they walked past.

"*Caspian?*" called a man from the crowd. "*Ever heard of Bronwyn Evans?*"

Caspian stopped dead.

"I had a lovely chat with her. She seems to know you very well."

Madison looked back. "What's he talking about?"

Caspian ushered her towards the car. "Nothing."

"*Maddy!*" called the man. "*I think you should meet her.*"

"Who? What?" Her blues eyes looked confused.

"*Caspian! Yoohoo!*" The man's face hardened. "*Don't ignore me. I know so much about you.*"

"*Fuck off!*" Caspian roared. "*You know nothing!*"

"Caspian! What's he talking about?" Madison pushed him back.

"Miss Evans likes to meet you after gigs, am I right?" The man sneered.

"After gigs?" Madison felt her heart constrict. "What's he saying? Caspian?"

"Nothing, he's a liar. Now get into the bloody car."

Raphael kissed Isabelle lovingly on the lips. She had dressed up as Madonna from *Desperately Seeking Susan.* Her long red hair was concealed by a frizzy blonde-streaked wig and large hoop earrings dangled from her ears. Her swelling stomach was hidden by a loose T-shirt and a pink tutu, worn over black leggings, purple leg-warmers and stilettos. Raphael had opted for John from *The Breakfast Club,* wearing a red-check shirt over a white long sleeved top, jeans and black fingerless gloves. His long brown hair hung loose, just like Judd Nelson in the iconic film.

"You look wonderful," he murmured, kissing Isabelle on the temple.

She picked up her lipstick and reapplied it. "Let's go down. Bertie will be wondering where we are."

He took her hand in his. "We don't have to stay very long, okay? I know how tired you are."

"We'll have a couple of Pellegrinos and take it from there."

"If it is too much for you, just tell me. I'm happy to leave."

She kissed his nose and then wiped off the residual red mark with her finger. "Come on. Let's go and party."

Bertie was in the garden, bare-chested and wearing a red velvet cloak, white trousers with red stripes down the side and a crown on his head. He was also sporting a black moustache and was holding a bottomless microphone stick.

"Isabelle, darling! Who are we this evening? Madonna or Cyndi Lauper?"

"Madonna."

"Stunning. I love the wig."

"You look amazing," she said genuinely. "Freddie to a T."

"I met him in the eighties. What a star. I just had to pay homage to him tonight."

Raphael refused a flute of champagne from a passing waiter.

"Bring me two mocktails," said Bertie smoothly to the young man.

"Water will be fine," said Raphael, turning his back to the waiter.

"Wait a second, mister," Isabelle interrupted. "Maybe I'd like a mocktail?"

"Yes," said Bertie. "Stop being so bossy."

"I'd like a mojito without the rum, please." She flashed him a brilliant smile.

"Of course," said the waiter, blushing.

Isabelle turned to Bertie. "How many people have you invited?" she asked, watching the waiting staff lay platter after platter of canapés on a large banquet table.

"About one hundred. Fewer souls than the last time."

"The last time?"

"The last party I had at home was my James Bond themed bash."

"Oh, I missed that."

"More's the pity. Aurora Sinclair sang all the iconic songs from the films. It was stupendous."

"Will there be music tonight?"

"Not live music," he admitted. "I wanted some disco so I hired a DJ. Prepare yourself for Wham!, Bronski Beat and Boy George!"

"Excuse me, sir," interrupted a waiter. "The chef needs a word."

"Duty calls, Zsa Zsa my love. Enjoy your mojito and I'll see you in a sec." He tipped his crown in salute at Raphael. "Lighten up, old boy. This is a party after all."

Isabelle and Raphael wandered out into the garden where a large marquee had been erected. A sign saying '*The Breakfast Club*' hung over the door and there were disco lights emitted from a ball hanging in the centre. The DJ, dressed as Adam Ant, was testing the sound and playing intros of songs like "Come On, Eileen" and "Careless Whisper".

She smiled at an Indiana Jones as he walked by. As yet, the garden was quite empty as the majority of guests had yet to arrive.

Chapter Thirty-five

An hour later, the marquee was full. Well-known faces dressed as celebrities from the eighties mingled and chatted, all availing of the limitless champagne. Isabelle spotted a Ferris Bueller, two David Bowies, a Grace Jones, three Michael Jacksons and an Axel Foley. All the costumes were top-notch and very convincing.

A blonde girl in a long red medieval-style dress stalked in with a tall man in tow. He was dressed in black, carrying a sword and wearing a black scarf over his eyes and head.

Buttercup and Westley, thought Isabelle with a smile.

The girl stopped and swung around, shouted something and ran off. He headed straight for the bar and drank a shot of whiskey straight. Then he asked for another, his face unsmiling.

Isabelle had only seen Madison Ryan on screen. Raphael had shown her the music video for "Possess Me" before it was released. She had to admit that Savannah had written a corker. It suited the film perfectly. Madison had surprised all her critics by nailing the vocals.

Madison was now talking to a group of men with an

angry expression. She jabbed her thumb in the direction of the man in black and made a face.

He must be Caspian Cole, surmised Isabelle. She had read about their relationship. There was definitely trouble in paradise by the look of things.

Madison walked off, her blonde hair flying. Caspian ordered another drink and leaned against the bar.

Cliona, dressed as Molly Ringwald, watched Fionn as he chatted to a woman. He had come as Marty McFly, dressed in a red gilet, a shirt, blue jeans and a baseball cap.

He had forced her to accompany him and within half an hour of arriving had taken off and left her alone. She sipped her champagne and fiddled with her wig, securing it in place with a pin.

She had agonised over what to wear – her mother had sent suggestions such as Margaret Thatcher or Nancy Reagan – but she had finally decided to go with Andie from *Pretty in Pink*. She had sourced a redhaired wig in a costume shop near Sloane Square and had found a pink satin dress in a thrift shop. With her pale skin and her contacts inserted, she looked remarkably like the iconic character.

She stayed in the shadows, watching stars walk by. Such was the quality of their costumes, it took her a long time to figure out their true identities.

"Hey, Clio," came a voice from her right.

It was Ethan.

"Hi," she said, smiling.

"Has Fionn abandoned you already?"

"Almost straight away."

"Stella and I have a table over there. Join us."

"Okay." She followed him through the crowd towards the entrance to the marquee.

To the right of the tent were about ten bistro tables with ornate chairs. Stella, dressed as Cyndi Lauper, was sitting with Alex. He was dressed in jeans and a white T-shirt with "*Frankie Says Relax*" on the front. Ethan had opted to dress as Cameron Frye from *Ferris Bueller's Day Off*, complete with a Gordie Howe jersey. Stella had convinced him to shave his beard and he looked like a different person.

Vivienne was wearing a huge wig.

"Cool costume," said Alex. "Where's Ducky?"

"He stayed at home." She smiled.

"Who's Ducky?" asked Stella curiously.

"Andie's best friend in the movie." He grinned. "I'm a huge John Hughes fan."

"Really?" Ethan resumed his seat at the table.

Cliona took a seat next to Vivienne. "I like your hair," she said. "Who are you supposed to be?"

"Bonnie Tyler," she replied. "No one has guessed so far."

"I suppose it was a popular hairstyle in the eighties."

Stella stopped a passing waiter. "May we have more champagne?" she asked.

"Of course, madam. Coming up."

"Caspian looks furious about something," said Ethan. "He's had three whiskeys in quick succession."

"He must have had a fight with Yoko," said Alex. "She looks pretty angry too. Christ, it's always drama with those two." He glanced at Cliona. "Can you shed any light?"

Cliona shrugged. "I've no idea."

"Really? I thought you and Caspian were best friends." His face was impassive.

"No, we're not." She pursed her lips. "Not at all, in fact."

"Is that so?" His eyes connected with hers.

The waiter came back with a tray of champagne flutes.

"Thank you," said Stella. "Another glass of this and I'll be able to dance."

"The music is great," said Ethan, drumming his fingers on the table. "I love Bronski Beat."

Vivienne leaned over and kissed Alex. "Do you want to dance?"

Cliona looked away, feeling uncomfortable.

"Sure, why not?" He took her hand. "See you later, guys."

They walked off and disappeared into the marquee.

Madison stood frozen to the spot. She couldn't quite believe her eyes. Standing over by the grand piano in Bertie's drawing room was Cal Scott. Her first love. Looking gorgeous as fighter pilot Maverick from *Top Gun.* He had the white T-shirt, the brown leather bomber jacket and the aviator shades. When they were going out together, she had always told him that he had a look of a young Tom Cruise, only taller. She felt her heart pound.

Cal Scott. Lead singer of The Southsiders.

Cal Scott. The first man to break her heart.

She debated what to do. She could be mature and walk up and say hello. They hadn't spoken a word since she dumped him, despite their careers going from strength to strength. The Southsiders were the most successful boyband in the British Isles and were about to crack America.

Suddenly, he looked up. Taking off his shades, he looked as shocked as she was. Then he smiled and waved for her to come over. Holding her head high, she walked towards him, her long dress trailing behind her.

"Maddy!" He kissed her cheek. "Long time no see."

"Hi, Cal."

"Let me guess, you're Guinevere."

"No, I'm Buttercup from *The Princess Bride."*

"I'm not familiar."

"It doesn't matter."

They stared at each other.

"You haven't changed," he said softly.

She felt her breath quicken.

"I hear you're with that Cole guy now."

"Yeah," she said vaguely.

"Are you happy?"

"Of course."

He didn't look convinced. "I've heard the stories about him. The girls, the groupies."

"It's not true."

"Let's just say, I'd watch my back."

"Oh, I will." Her eyes glittered. "You taught me that."

"I taught you a lot of things as I recall." He moved closer. "Lots of nice things."

"Stop." She closed her eyes.

"We had something, Maddy. You know it."

He walked away, waving at other guests as he passed.

She felt like she couldn't breathe. Cal Scott. She had loved him so much.

She gave herself a talking to and walked in the direction of the garden. Then she turned and their eyes met. He winked and raised his glass to her. Like Orpheus, she cursed herself for looking back.

♫♫♫

Caspian drank his fifth whiskey and slammed the glass down on the bar. The DJ was playing "Karma Chameleon" and everyone was dancing. The wooden floor of the marquee moved with the revelry and he felt himself sway.

Ethan grabbed his arm. "Caspian, are you okay, mate?"

"Perfectly fine."

"You don't look it. Even with that mask, you can tell you're angry about something."

"How often do you and Stella have sex?" he asked directly. "On average."

Ethan held up his hands. "Christ, I didn't expect that."

"Tell me. Once? Twice a week? A day?"

"We have a good sex life. Why the hell are you asking me?"

"The last time Maddy and I made love was three weeks ago. Three weeks. Despite ample opportunity."

"So? You're busy."

"Not that busy."

"Caspian, she had a lot going on. So do you."

"She wants out."

"You don't know that."

"Yes, I do. She didn't come back for our gig because she hates me."

"You don't know that ..."

"Tonight this guy shouted about some Welsh girl who claims she hooked up with me after a gig. Maddy didn't really care. She accepted my side of the story without an argument. That would never have happened in the old days."

"Look, you need to talk to her." Ethan looked uncomfortable.

Caspian ordered another drink. "I would if I knew where she was."

Cliona gazed at the Matisse on the wall of Bertie's study. She had slipped into the quiet room when no one was looking. Books lined the shelves, some first editions, and a large desk stood by the window. A gold pen lay diagonally on a leather writing pad and there was a framed picture of Bertie and Obama on the desk.

Stella had stayed with her for a while, but then she and Ethan went dancing, leaving her alone. Wandering around the large garden, she had passed Aurora Sinclair, Raphael Baptiste, Emma Thompson, Rowan Atkinson and other well-known faces. Then, after her third glass of champagne, she found the door to the study and had sneaked inside.

She felt out of place. The only people she knew were the members of Doctor Eckleburg and Madison. She had made it her business to avoid Caspian so she didn't venture near the bar. He had stopped texting her and she was ambivalent about it. Her rational self knew it was the right thing, but part of her missed the attention.

The solitude of the study suited her. She ran her finger along the books and stopped at a worn edition of poetry by William Wordsworth. With a smile, she remembered her English teacher at school, repeating "The Daffodils" over and over. She scanned the rest of the shelf and saw volumes by Sylvia Plath, Robert Frost and Dylan Thomas.

Dad would love this library, she thought idly.

"Hey, Clio," came a voice from behind her. She jumped and turned around.

Alex was standing by the doorway.

"Hey!" she said in relief. "You gave me a fright there."

"Have you seen Vivienne around the place?"

She shook her head. "No, not at all."

They stared at each other.

"Are you having a good time?" she asked.

He shrugged. "I suppose. I mean, the music is a bit questionable in places but that was the eighties, I guess."

She giggled. "I know what you mean."

"Like now, for example." He walked to the window and opened it. Immediately the small room filled with sound from the marquee. It was "Listen To Your Heart" by Roxette.

"Oh no!" Cliona held up her hands in protest. "That is a classic, Alex."

"Really?" Alex put his hand behind his ear and listened.

Cliona closed her eyes. "It's a love song. I bet lots of couples are dancing."

He looked out the window. "Yep, you're right. I can see lots of swaying bodies." He turned back to her. "I can't dance at all."

"Really?"

"Not at all. Can you?"

She smiled. "Only from watching *Dirty Dancing*."

"I've never seen it."

"What? That's terrible."

"Oh, I know what it's about and all, but I've never actually sat down and watched it through." He moved forwards and grasped her wrist. "Will you teach me to dance?"

"Dance?" she squeaked.

"Yes, dance." He put his hand on her waist and pulled her closer so that her face was inches from his. His other hand clasped hers and he whispered, "So, can you teach me?"

She could feel her heart thudding in her ears. He was so close she could feel the heat emanating from his body.

She swallowed. "*Um*, you have a dance space and I have a dance space."

"A *what* space?"

She stood up straight. "You must be rigid and stand up straight."

"Right." He did as she asked.

"Now, we dance." She nudged his leg with her knee. "Backwards and forwards."

"Okay." He took the lead and started to move. He automatically looked down at his feet and she laughed. "Head up! Keep your eyes on me."

He laughed too. "Then there's a great chance that I'll stand on your foot."

"No, I'll probably stand on yours."

They started to move around the room clumsily at first. He swung her outwards and twirled her to the left and to the right. Then he pulled her back into his arms, but this time there was no dance space. He pressed his body against hers and stared into her eyes. They stopped moving and her face moved instinctively towards his. The song reached a crescendo outside as he bent his head and kissed her full on the mouth. She wrapped her arms around his neck and forgot about everything else. She had never been kissed like that before. It made the blood race through her veins.

His tongue explored her mouth and he ground against

her, making her stomach curl. Bending his head, he kissed her neck, then her earlobe and then her mouth again. She clung to him, unable to stand.

Suddenly Alex pulled back. She stumbled slightly but righted herself. He moved backwards and ran his fingers through his hair, a troubled look on his face.

"Are you okay?" she whispered. The song changed to a Bananarama track.

Alex strode over to the window and closed it firmly.

"I'm sorry, Cliona." He cleared his throat. "I shouldn't have done that."

Her chest heaved. "No, don't be sorry. I ..."

"No, it was wrong. I mean, I'm with Vivienne now. I'm sorry." His brown eyes met hers.

She walked towards him and touched his arm. "Please, don't apologise. I ..."

"I'm sorry," he repeated, removing her hand. "I've got to go."

"No, please ..."

The door slammed.

Cliona stayed in the study for half an hour, unsure of what to think. How did that happen? Alex was her friend. Her buddy. He taught her things like how to pick a courgette from a plant. He certainly didn't make her feel like that. She felt dizzy and exhilarated yet guilty as hell. What was it about her lately? Messing around with guys who were taken?

Straightening her pink dress, she took a deep breath. She had to leave. She couldn't face meeting him now. Not with Vivienne around the place.

As she sneaked past the bar, Caspian called out to her. "*Clio!*"

She ignored him and kept walking.

"*Cliona!*" he yelled again.

She stopped. "Yeah?" Her face looked guarded.

"Want to have a drink with me?" He gave her a lop-sided smile.

She shook her head. "I was just leaving. Sorry."

His expression changed and he looked shocked.

For the first time, she didn't even think about Caspian. Instead she couldn't get Alex out of her head. She could feel his lips on her skin and it thrilled her.

She walked out past the bouncers and met a security guard by the door.

"You're leaving?" he asked brusquely.

"Yes."

He held open the door. "Enjoy the rest of your night."

The door slammed.

There was one photographer outside, hoping to get a shot of someone famous. On reflex, he pointed his lens at her, but then lowered it again.

She pulled out her phone to call a taxi but, before she could dial, John appeared.

"Can I take you somewhere?" he asked.

"I want to go home," said Cliona, "but you can't just take off. What if Maddy needs you?"

"It's not far. Come on." He smiled. "There has to be some perks to your job."

"Thanks, John." She really meant it.

"No problem."

Chapter Thirty-six

Madison was on her way to find Caspian when she heard her name being called. She turned around to see Raphael Baptiste gesturing for her to join him. He held out his arms and kissed her on both cheeks. "Let me introduce you to my wife, Isabelle."

Madison stared. Isabelle had milky white skin and deep red hair, and didn't look much older than she was.

"Hello," said Madison.

"Good to meet you," said Isabelle warmly. "Raph was telling me all about you."

"Really?" Madison flushed with pleasure.

"Yeah, he said you're a great singer."

"Wow, that's lovely." She flushed with pleasure. His opinion meant everything.

A Duran Duran song was playing and the disco lights emitted bright colours from the marquee. Raphael held Isabelle's hand tightly and every now and then, he would stroke her wrist.

"Was Savannah invited?" asked Madison, looking around. "I was hoping to see her."

"Of course, but she would never come to a party like this," said Raphael. "She would hate the music and the costumes."

"Yes, I think you're right."

Bertie appeared with a huge globe glass full of gin and tonic. Aurora Sinclair was behind him, with a flute of champagne in her hand.

"Darlings!" said Bertie. "Are we having fun?"

"Awesome," said Isabelle, kissing his cheek. "I love the music."

"My parties are always, as you say, awesome." He put his arm around Aurora's shoulders. "Here is my Josephine, looking stunning as always."

Aurora laughed. "I'm not sure how stunning these leg-warmers are, Bertie."

"Who are you supposed to be?" asked Isabelle curiously.

"Susanna Hoffs."

"Who?" asked Raphael in confusion.

"The lead singer of The Bangles." She sang a few lines of "Manic Monday".

"Oh, right." He smiled. "I remember now."

Madison hung back, not sure of what to say. Aurora Sinclair was a rival. She was so pretty with her cloudy dark hair and brown eyes. People took her seriously; she was respected in the industry. She had never released songs like "Text Me Back" or collaborated with a rapper. Madison gazed at her enviously.

"Hello." Aurora held out her hand. "I love your song for the film. It's so catchy."

Madison shook it, disarmed by such friendliness. "Thanks a million," she said shyly. "Although I only sing it.

It was Susannah Morris who wrote it."

"But you give it your stamp. Your voice is so unique. It's a triumph." Aurora smiled.

Madison didn't know what to say. She was used to meeting other artists and competing with them. Aurora seemed genuinely nice.

"*Um*, thank you."

Bertie gasped. "Of course, you two should duet later. It would be sensational."

"Oh, I don't know about that ..." Madison blushed.

"Now, now. No time to be coy. I insist." Bertie beamed at them. "You would like Grace Kelly and Ava Gardner in that film *Mogambo* – blonde and brunette. It simply must happen!"

Across the room, Caspian watched Madison as she laughed at something Bertie said. Sometimes he felt like he didn't know her at all. The black scarf over his head and eyes was uncomfortable. It felt hot and claustrophobic and he wanted to tear it off.

She didn't love him anymore. A blind man could see it. In the early days of their relationship she had been jealous if he had even talked to a girl. Now, it was as if she didn't care. Even when that man had shouted about the Welsh girl, she didn't pursue it. There was no denying it – it was over.

Their relationship had never been plain sailing. More often than not, they fought over silly things. They were in constant competition with each other and this manifested when they appeared in public.

His mother had warned him about dating a superstar.

He had laughed it off. Now he wasn't so sure. Instead of yin and yang, they were yin and yin. They didn't complement each other as they were so similar. It's just sometimes he wished he had someone at home to welcome him after a concert or a tour. Someone to hug in bed at night. Someone to look after him and balance his moods. Instead, he felt isolated. He loved her but it was plain that she didn't need him.

Raphael held Isabelle's hand possessively. The marquee was crowded and the guests were so noisy. Bertie, being the host, was zipping here and there, meeting and greeting. The Cure was playing and the crowd stamped their feet.

Raphael scowled. There was no one of interest to him and he sipped his water with a bored expression.

"I must go and make a call," he said to Isabelle. "Will you be okay?"

She smiled. "Of course, baby. I'll go over and chat to Mia for a while."

Raphael kissed her lips. "Back in a second."

He walked through the crowd, pushing past a Simon Le Bon and one of The Three Amigos. There was a very convincing Boy George in front of the study door so he politely asked him to move aside. He had to admit that everyone had made a huge effort. Such was the influence of Bertie.

When he had finished his phone call, he went straight back to where he had left Isabelle, but there was no sign of her. He scanned the crowd for her frizzy wig, but that hairstyle was common. Then he spotted her over by the cheese platter. He smiled. She loved her cheese.

There was a man standing next to her – a tall man

dressed all in black. He wore a mask over his eyes and carried a sword. He was talking to Isabelle and he could sense that she was uncomfortable. He didn't know why, but he could tell that she wanted to get away.

He increased his pace and walked towards them, but he didn't make it in time. The man in black grabbed Isabelle by the waist and kissed her full on the lips. She tried to push him away, but he was too strong.

Raphael howled and ran towards him. "*Get the fuck off my wife!*" he yelled. "*Putain!*" He yanked the man away and, raising his fist, hit him square on the eye.

Caspian went out cold.

Ethan and Alex, alerted by the shouting, ran over.

"Christ! You've knocked him out," said Alex to Raphael.

Stella grabbed a glass of water from the drinks table and handed it to Ethan.

"Throw it on his face," she suggested.

"No," said Alex. "Let him come around in his own time."

Vivienne put her hand on Alex's shoulder. "Should we call the paramedics?"

Ethan shook his head. "He'll be fine. He's just plastered. We need to move him." He looked around. "Where the hell is Madison?"

A crowd had gathered in curiosity, looking at Caspian lying on the ground and Raphael's angry face.

Bertie ran up to them, his crown lopsided on his head. "What happened, my darlings?" he asked urgently. "Why the violence?"

"*He kissed my wife!*" roared Raphael. "He's lucky I didn't kill him."

Isabelle pushed Raphael back. “It’s fine, honey. He’s pretty drunk.”

“Don’t defend the indefensible.” Raphael’s eyes flashed. “Who is he anyway?” He bent down, pulled off the black cloth on his head and Caspian’s blonde hair tumbled out.

“Caspian Cole,” said Alex. “He’s with us.”

“*Who?*” asked Raphael rudely.

Bertie patted Raphael on the back. “Madison Ryan’s boyfriend. You know, the girl with the song.”

“Well, she needs to know what type he is.”

“Calm down, baby.” Isabelle took his hand. “I’m quite flattered actually. I mean, he was full on, but quite sweet.”

“Sweet?” Raphael stood up straight.

“It’s tough being pregnant. That guy restored my faith a little, I’ve got to say.”

“You’re too gracious.”

“He’s drunk. We all do stupid things when we are drunk. Let it go.”

“Well, if he goes near you again …”

“You’ll challenge him to a duel at dawn.” Her eyes twinkled.

“Don’t joke, Zsa Zsa.” He put his arm around her waist.

Bertie knelt down and checked Caspian’s pulse. “Vladimir?” he called. “We need your lovely muscles to move this man inside.”

“Yes, sir.” Vladimir grabbed Caspian by the arms and attempted to lift him.

“I’ll help,” said Ethan. “Alex, grab a leg.”

Together, they moved Caspian’s body into the house.

Suddenly there was movement in the crowd and Madison arrived, looking shocked.

"What the hell happened? Where are they taking Caspian?"

Raphael led Isabelle away and Bertie took Madison's arm. "Let's go into the library, my sweet. I asked Vladimir to put Caspian on the chaise longue."

"What happened?" she snapped, aware of all the eyes on her.

"Come, come." Bertie was insistent. "I'll explain all when we have some privacy."

Caspian woke up to see Madison's furious face over his.

"You absolute asshole," she seethed. "How could you?"

He rubbed his temple. "How could I what?"

"Hit on Raphael's wife? Are you insane?"

"What?" He genuinely couldn't remember.

"You kissed Isabelle Flynn. Right smack on the lips. Then Raphael knocked you out."

"I kissed who?"

Madison threw her arms up. "Jesus Christ, Caspian. How drunk are you?"

He sat up. "I'm not sure. I had a lot of whiskey."

"What possessed you to kiss another woman? I mean, do you do that often?" Her eyes flashed.

"No, no. I told you."

"Well, that guy shouting about a Bronwyn and now a public display. I'm starting to get paranoid."

"Would you care?"

She slapped his face. "Of course I'd care. You will not humiliate me, do you hear me?"

He rubbed his cheek. "Christ, Maddy. That hurt."

"You deserve it, you creep."

Bertie knocked on the door. "May I come in?" he asked.

"Yes," answered Madison brightly. "Now behave," she whispered loudly to Caspian. "Don't make this worse."

Bertie had a glass of water and some paracetamol. "I thought these might help," he said kindly. "Your head must be pounding."

Caspian accepted the tablets gratefully and took a huge gulp of water. "I'm sorry."

Bertie waved him away. "Happens to the best of us, my boy. Whiskey is dangerous. One should never consume too much of it."

"I should apologise ..."

"No, no. Not now. Best to leave things settle."

"We should leave," said Madison. "Caspian needs to sleep it off."

"If you must." Bertie looked relieved. "I'll call my driver."

"No need. John is right outside." Madison leaned up and kissed his cheek. "Thank you for having us."

"Anytime, my dear. I'll be in touch."

"Come on," she hissed at Caspian. "We're leaving."

Caspian stood up and wobbled slightly. He felt like hell. His sword was hanging off his belt at a strange angle and his headscarf had disappeared. They met Alex and Ethan in the hall.

"Are you okay, mate?" asked Ethan with a worried face. "You hit the ground with a right thwack."

"I'm fine." Caspian tried to smile. "We're heading off actually."

"Night." Alex nodded at him coolly. "Hope you feel better in the morning."

Madison, with Todd behind her, stalked off towards the front door. She could see the famous faces around her – everyone had seen the drama. She thanked God that there was no press. She could imagine the headlines.

Suddenly Raphael walked out of the study with a glass of water in his hand, just as Caspian was passing. They came face to face in the hallway, each as tall as each other. Raphael's lip curled and he made motions to move along, but Caspian held up his hand.

"Please."

Raphael stopped.

"I'm so sorry for what I did. I wasn't thinking straight."

Raphael raised his head haughtily.

"I'm sorry," Caspian repeated steadily.

Their eyes met. No one spoke for a few seconds.

Raphael looked away first. "*Bon*, I believe you."

"Thank you."

"Just stay away from her in the future."

"Of course."

Madison watched this exchange silently. Something niggled at her. She didn't know what, but something was annoying her. She just couldn't put her finger on it.

They walked past the security guards and waited at the door until John pulled up in the Mercedes. Todd stood like a human shield as Madison got into the car. A subdued Caspian followed. The door slammed.

The journey home was silent. Madison sat with her back to Caspian, fuming with rage. He had his eyes closed with his head leaning backwards on the head rest. His eye was turning a deep purple.

They pulled up outside Caspian's place in Knightsbridge.

Madison poked him awake.

"You're home," she said shortly.

"Are you coming in?" he asked. She turned her head away in response.

He exited the car and slammed the door.

"Drive," Madison ordered and the car sped away down the dark street.

Chapter Thirty-seven

Caspian called Madison the next morning. She ignored three of his calls but answered the fourth.

"Yeah?" Her tone was cold.

"We need to talk."

"There's nothing to say."

"There is, Maddy. We have to try and sort this."

"Sort out what? The fact that you kissed another woman? I mean, it's obvious that it's not the first time."

"Madison."

"No. I'm done with this."

She hung up the phone.

Caspian took a cab to Madison's flat. His injured eye had turned a dark blue so he wore large glasses. When the car pulled up outside Madison's gates, he used his fob to gain entry.

Then, he punched in the code and accessed the building. He met Todd in the foyer.

"Hey, Todd." He waved half-heartedly. "Is Madison in?"

Todd shook his head. "She's not here."

"What?"

"She asked me to relieve you of your keys."

"What?" He stared at him in disbelief. "But I need to talk to her. Jesus."

Todd crossed his arms. "No can do."

"Please."

"I'm not at liberty to do that, sir." He held out his hand. "The keys?"

Caspian deposited them in his hand.

"The fob?"

He gave him that too. "This is crazy. I don't get a chance to explain."

"I'll see you out, sir."

Caspian looked up sadly. "No need."

He strolled down the street and ignored the cars that beeped at him when he passed. He didn't care who saw him or who took his photo. He had never felt so miserable.

Crossing the road, he entered a small café. The girl behind the counter barely looked up as she took his order. He took a seat in the corner and added sugar to his americano.

He debated whether to call Madison but he knew there was no point. Instead, he dialled Cliona's number. She answered on the sixth ring.

"Hello?"

"Clio?"

"Yeah?" She sounded tired.

"Are you with Maddy?"

"No."

"Where is she?"

"I don't know. She left an hour ago and didn't say where she was going."

There was a pause.

"Clio, I need to talk to someone. Please come and meet me."

"No. I can't right now.

"Please."

"Sorry." She hung up the phone.

Cliona felt momentary guilt about Caspian but pushed it away. She had her own problems. She checked her phone every five minutes, waiting for a text from Alex, but none came. She kept replaying the night before in her head – how he turned up, danced with her and then left so abruptly.

She thought of how he had kissed her. Like she was the only girl on earth. No one had ever made her feel like that before. Alex had always been there in the background and now suddenly he was right in her line of vision.

How could she have been so stupid? It was like the fog had cleared and she could see the truth. All along he had been right in front of her nose and she had been too stupid to see it.

But he's with Vivienne now. He's taken.

She got up and grabbed her coat and bag. She paused to take off her glasses and replace them with contacts, but decided against it. Alex didn't care what she looked like. He never made her feel like she had to pretend. He had always been so kind to her, so sweet. She couldn't let it go on without sorting things out.

She had to face him and clear the air. He would tell her that it was a mistake and that he was drunk. At least then she'd know. What did he say to her before? All's fair in love and war.

♫ ♫ ♫

Alex and Ethan shared an apartment near London's docklands. It was in a trendy area by the river with a view of the city. Cliona pressed the intercom at the front door of the building. Then she pressed it again. Finally Ethan's voice came through the speaker.

"Yeah?"

"Ethan, it's me. Cliona."

"Hey, what's up?"

"Is Alex home?"

"No. He didn't come home last night. I suppose he's with Viv."

"Oh."

"Listen, do you want to come up?"

"No, it's okay. Thanks anyway."

She ran back to the tube station and debated what to do. She needed to talk to him face to face. Not over the phone. She had to read his expression and see if there was any hope. Something had happened and she couldn't ignore it. Her dad always told her that fortune favours the bold. But what if he rejected her? He may have seen that kiss as a giant mistake.

She was so deep in thought, she didn't notice a car pull up beside her. A window was rolled down and a familiar voice said, "Clio. Please talk to me. I really need you."

She looked up to see Caspian's handsome face staring out at her from a black cab.

"Caspian?" she said in disbelief.

"I was on my way to see the guys," he explained. "Then there you were, like an angel."

She tried not to feel flattered. "What's wrong?"

"What's right?" He sighed sadly. "Have you time to have a coffee somewhere?"

She paused.

"Please, Clio. I need advice."

"Oh?"

"On the Maddy situation."

She sighed. "Fine, just a quick one."

"Great, hop in." He beamed at her. "I know a great place near here."

They went to Urban Baristas in Wapping. It was a trendy coffee shop with a laid-back vibe and a large window looking out on the street. They ordered two coffees and tried to ignore the fingers pointing at Caspian.

One girl approached them for a selfie but he held up his hand. "Not today."

Such was the tone of his voice, she backed away and let them to it.

"I'm so glad you're here," he began, his brown eyes gazing searchingly at her. He reached out and took her hand in his.

"Why, Caspian?" Her eyes met his steadily as she removed her hand and placed it on her lap.

He sat back, a confused expression on his face. "Well, because you're my rock. The one I can rely on. You've always been there for me."

She laughed bitterly. "Yes, Clio the whipping boy. Clio the go-to person when you want to moan and complain. Clio the doormat."

"Hey, you're not any of those things."

"Yeah, right," she scoffed. "You played me for a fool."

"How?"

"You knew I fancied you. You knew how I felt and you used me."

He shifted uncomfortably in his seat. "That's not true."

"Yes, it is." She rounded on him angrily. "All those times you gave me false hope. What's worse is that I let it happen."

"I think you're sweet ..."

"Oh, stop it." She threw her teaspoon on the table with a clatter. "I've finally seen sense. You see, I'm over you. In fact, I have been for a long time but I didn't realise it."

"Oh?" He looked put out. "Who's the lucky guy?"

"No one," she lied. "Anyway, he's taken so it's not an issue."

"So he's not interested?"

"I don't know."

"Poor Clio." His face was filled with pity. "I hope it works out for you."

She bristled. "Don't feel sorry for me. He's far more honourable than you."

"What do you mean by that?"

"He is nice and kind and faithful." Their kiss flashed through her brain. "Well, most of the time."

"I'm faithful." Caspian looked affronted.

Her eyes met his and then they both laughed. "Okay, maybe that's a bit of a stretch," he admitted. The tension dissipated.

"Look, I'm not mad at you anymore," she said honestly. "You see, everything's changed. I'm not the person I used to be, hanging on every word you say and obsessing over that song."

"What song?"

"That song about the quiet girl coming out of her shell."

"What about it?" he asked, puzzled.

"You tell me – you wrote it."

"No, I didn't."

"What?"

"Alex did. I was impressed as he's never brought anything else to the table."

Cliona's eyes widened. The words were imprinted on her brain.

Come out of your shell, my love,
Come out and be free,
Take a chance on me, girl,
Give your heart to me.

"Oh my God." She stood up, knocking the chair backwards. "I have to go."

"What?"

"Sorry, I have to go."

"Clio! We still haven't sorted the Maddy thing."

But she was gone.

Madison sat in the back of her Mercedes and sighed. Cal had told her that he was in town. He had specifically said that he was at Claridge's. Was she insane? After all they'd been through?

John drummed his fingers on the steering wheel.

"What would you like to do?" he asked in his deep voice. "There's only so long we can park here."

She took out a pocket mirror and checked her reflection. Her blonde hair was tousled and her eyes smoky from the eyeliner she had applied.

"Call the hotel and ask them if I can use a private entrance."

"No problem."

She snapped her mirror shut and put it back in her bag. She had seen Cal walk into the hotel ten minutes before with his security. She knew that he was there. She undid another button of her shirt.

Cliona rang the buzzer incessantly and eventually Ethan answered the door. "This had better be important, Clio. You've woken me up twice and I need to sleep off my hangover."

"I'm sorry," she said breathlessly. "I need to find Alex."

"Ring him."

"No." She shook her head. "I want to see him face to face."

"He's probably at Viv's."

"Can you check?"

Ethan rubbed his temple. "Look, I don't understand what's happening here ..."

"Please, Ethan. Please call her." She looked at him pleadingly. "I really need to see him."

"Fine. Give me a second to get my phone."

He disappeared down the hallway.

She looked around the living room. It was sparsely decorated with three guitars on stands in the corner, a giant flat-screen TV and a large window looking out on the river. It was spotless – Stella liked to keep things clean – and there was a framed picture of a pig on the mantelpiece. She peered closer. The word "Bella" was engraved on the frame. She smiled.

Ethan walked back out of his bedroom, talking into his phone as he approached.

"Yeah, I'm looking for Alex."

Cliona held on to the bookshelf for support.

"He's not? Where is he?" Ethan frowned. "*Whoa, whoa!* Don't shout at me."

Cliona's heart started to pound.

"Okay, okay. I get it. Bye." He hung up the phone. "Jesus, that was awkward!"

"Awkward?" she breathed.

"Splitsville," he said, scratching his head. "Last night apparently. He broke it off."

"He did?"

"Yeah, she's pretty angry."

"Right."

"He's gone home to Kent, she says. He took off this morning." He rubbed his beard. "I mean, we had planned to rehearse tomorrow but I guess that's an impossibility."

"Kent?" She inhaled sharply and Ethan narrowed his eyes. Then the penny dropped. "Wait a second. Have you got anything to do with this?"

Cliona waved. "Thank you so much. I've got to go."

"Clio?"

She ran out the door.

John walked beside Madison as they made their way to the Mayfair Suite. She had her head down, a scarf around her famous hair and large glasses.

John knocked on the door. Then he knocked again.

"Thanks, John. I'll take it from here." Madison removed her glasses and shook out her hair.

"I'll just check this place out first."

"No need. He has security."

Cal's bodyguard opened the door and stepped outside. "Can I help you?" he asked coldly.

Madison pushed past him. "I'm Madison Ryan. I'm here to see Cal."

"Come back!" He turned liked lightning and grabbed her arm. "You can't just walk in there."

John grabbed him by the neck and pushed him up against the wall. "Don't touch her!"

Madison grinned. "At ease, John. It's okay."

Cal, alerted by the commotion, sauntered out of the living-room area. "Hey, Mads," he said with a smug smile. "I was expecting you."

Chapter Thirty-eight

Cliona took the three o'clock train from Victoria to Canterbury East Station. She ran along the platform and on exiting the building she hailed a cab.

Twenty minutes later, it pulled up outside Alex's home. There was a light on in the kitchen and smoke was coming from the chimney. She knocked on the door and waited.

Maia opened it and smiled.

"Well, hello!"

"Hi, Maia. Is Alex here?"

She shook her head. "He's gone to the pub with Dad."

Cliona's face fell.

"But come in. Mum, Daphne and I are making chutney."

The smell of ginger, cinnamon and apples floated out from the kitchen.

"Okay," said Cliona, following her inside.

Nancy's face broke into a huge smile. "Cliona? What a surprise!"

"Hi," she said shyly. "I hope I'm not imposing."

"Not in the slightest. Alex is gone for a pint with Jeff but should be back soon." Nancy pointed to a spare chair.

"Now, sit down and help chop some apples."

There was a spare wooden board and a sharp paring knife. Cliona sat and started to peel an apple, discarding the russet skin into a bowl in the centre of the table.

"We picked the last of the apples from the orchard," explained Nancy. "This chutney is wonderful with cheese at Christmas. You must take a pot home to your parents."

"Mum would love that." She chopped the flesh of the apple and tipped it into a pot. Daphne added spices, onions and vinegar.

"Is everything okay?" asked Nancy. "Alex arrived home this morning in a state, banging doors and scowling at everyone."

"Well, obviously, Mum. He just split with Viv," said Daphne.

"I'm glad," said Maia, sprinkling some cinnamon into the pot. "She was a strange one. She didn't like Bella for a start. She screamed when she saw her and ran away."

"Girls!" Nancy looked disapproving. "She was a nice girl."

"Oh, please!" Maia rolled her eyes. "You said it yourself – she would never fit in here."

"Maia!" Nancy looked embarrassed.

"Unlike you, Cliona," added Maia mischievously. "You'd fit in just fine."

Cliona blushed. "So, what time will they be back?" she asked shyly.

"In about an hour. Jeff left a tagine in the Aga which he'll need to take out." Nancy looked at her slyly. "Is everything okay?"

"Fine, fine." Cliona put down the knife. "Actually, where

is the pub exactly? I might just pop in and say hello."

"About half a mile down the road," said Maia helpfully. "It's called The Black Horse."

"If you don't mind ..." She got up.

"Not at all," said Nancy cheerfully. "I presume you'll be staying for tagine?"

Cliona bit her lip. "I hope so."

Minutes later she was half-running down the lane, her heart hammering in her chest. The sky looked grey and menacing and she felt the odd drop of cold rain on her cheeks. She just had to see him. She couldn't just sit around and wait for him to return home. His whole family would be there and what she had to say was private. She tried not to think about what could happen or possible scenarios. She was just going to say what was on her mind – without barriers – and deal with the consequences.

The country air was cold and her nose streamed. Slowing her pace, she pulled a tissue from her pocket and wiped her nose. She had no make-up on and her glasses were blurry from the spatters of rain, but she didn't care. Alex wouldn't care.

The weather worsened as she walked briskly along the road. A car passed and splashed her with a muddy puddle, soaking her jeans.

"*Damn!*" she shouted in annoyance.

Mercifully the pub came into view. Smoke trickled out of the chimney and there was a glow from the windows.

In the front porch she halted. She took off her glasses and rubbed them with another tissue, wiping away the raindrops. Squaring her shoulders, she took a deep breath and pushed open the door.

The pub was small with an oak bar and about seven high stools. There was an elderly man behind the counter, rubbing some glasses with a cloth. The fire burned merrily in the grate and low music played in the background. There was a woman with a buggy sitting in the corner eating a bowl of soup and an old lady drinking whiskey at the bar. There was no sign of Alex and his father.

She walked up to the barman and he smiled. "Can I help you, love?"

"I'm looking for Alex Ryder."

"I know Alex. He's Nancy's boy. Do you know that he's in a famous band?"

"Yes, that's him."

"You just missed him. He left a few minutes ago with his dad." He beamed at her.

Cliona felt herself deflate in dismay. She didn't pass them on the road. Where could they have gone?

"They were off to town to get some couscous or something daft like that," he went on. "Jeff is always cooking foreign things."

"Right."

"Would you like a drink?"

She shook her head. "I'm all right, thank you."

"Right you are then." He turned back to his glass polishing.

She walked out into the rain in dismay. The walk back to the farm seemed interminable. She was wet and cold, and suddenly she lacked the courage to say anything at all. Kicking a stone, she walked slowly along the route, her canvas shoes saturated from the grass that lined the dykes. The rain was pelting down now and the sky was dark and grey.

She felt her phone buzz in her pocket but it was too wet to take it out. Plus she knew it was probably Constance or Madison.

On and on she walked, getting more nervous by the second. Every car that passed made her heart jump as it could be Jeff's Land Rover. Each time it was the same – a nondescript car with a stranger behind the wheel.

As she turned down the lane to the farm, she heard someone calling her name. She stopped dead. Peering through her foggy glasses, she couldn't make out who it was until he was right in front of her.

"Clìona! Why are you out in this weather?" Alex took off his jacket and held it over both their heads. They huddled close together.

"I walked to the pub but the barman said you were gone to town with Jeff."

"No, I got Dad to drop me home first. Maia said you'd taken off to find me so I rang you. Why didn't you answer?"

"I didn't realise it was you." She shivered and he moved closer.

"I feel awful! I'm pretty sure we passed you on the road ..."

"I don't think so. I didn't see your dad's jeep ..."

"We took Mum's car."

"Oh." She stopped.

He let the jacket fall to his side and his red hair instantly turned darker from the rain.

"Why are you here?" he asked softly.

Her heart started to pound. This was the moment.

"I wanted to tell you something." She felt her cheeks redden.

"Oh?" he said softly.

"I wanted to tell you that I'm mad about you. I have been for ages but I didn't realise it."

His brown eyes widened slightly. "Really? What happened to Caspian?"

"That was silly. I just liked the idea of him. But you, you're different. You like me for me. You're interested in me and my life."

He stared at her as the rain coursed down his face.

"You're kind to me and make me laugh." She took off her glasses and put them in her pocket. "Even though you're a blur now, it doesn't matter." She paused for a moment. "You see, I love you for you and you love me for me." She closed her eyes. "I know that you do."

He took her face in his hands.

"So, can we start again?" she continued. "I'll even adopt Bella."

He laughed.

"Because I don't want anyone else."

"Me neither." He kissed her nose and her eyes and then her lips. "I fell for you the first time I met you. I thought you were adorable with your glasses and oversized T-shirts."

"Really?"

He smiled. "I asked Fionn if you were available and he read me the riot act and told me to stay well clear."

"Oh, he did?" She looked fierce.

"I tried to stay away but I couldn't get you out of my head." He leaned in and kissed her softly.

She pressed up against him, unaware of the rain pelting down.

"Come on," he said, taking her hand. "Let's get out of this weather."

He led her down the lane to the converted barn that was used for guests. Pushing open the door, he pulled her inside. Then he turned the lock on the door and faced her.

"You're soaked," he said, reaching out to squeeze some droplets from her hair.

"So are you," she said nervously.

He pushed her coat back off her shoulders and let it drop to the floor. Then he pulled her sodden T-shirt over her head.

"Your skin is so pale," he said in wonder, caressing her arms.

She reached out and yanked at his T-shirt. He held up his arms and she stood on her tiptoes in an effort to pull it off. He watched her in amusement.

"Let me help," he said eventually, removing the wet garment in one movement.

He lifted the strap of her bra, slowly taking it off her shoulder. Her chest heaved in anticipation. She felt like an amateur. Nerdy Gareth was the only guy she had ever been intimate with and that wasn't very often.

"Can I take it off?" he asked softly, his hands moving around to the clasp.

She nodded.

With one flick, he released her breasts and threw the bra to the side. He pulled her close so that all she could feel was his bare skin pressed against hers. Bending his head he kissed her deeply, his tongue exploring her mouth. She wrapped her arms around his neck and arched her back, luxuriating in the feel of his hard chest against her softness. He tugged at her jeans and she reciprocated until they were both naked. Taking her hand, he led her to the ladder of the mezzanine.

"Up you go," he said, breathing heavily.

She started to climb the steps and he kissed her leg as she ascended. When he reached her ankle, he bounded up the ladder after her and they rolled onto the soft bed.

She could feel her stomach flip as she waited in anticipation. He positioned himself and gently prised her legs apart. She felt a fullness as he slid inside her and began to move. Gasping in pleasure, she pulled him closer and closer. Nothing felt awkward or rehearsed. She felt consumed by him; pure joy coursed through her veins and she gloried in the solid weight on top of her.

"Why did we wait so long?" she said breathlessly into his ear.

"Because it had to be perfect."

Cal was sitting by the window with a cigarette in hand when Madison woke up. The pungent smell of tobacco made her retch and she waved the smoke away in disgust.

"*Yuk*, please don't do that."

He raised an eyebrow. "I'll do what I want, Maddy. This is my room."

"It's bad for your voice."

He looked bored. "Christ, you came here to fuck. Not to lecture me on my health. It's like the old days. Nagging all the time."

She pulled the blanket up around her chin. "No, it's not," she said quietly.

"Well, don't even start. I smoke, I do cocaine. I even take the odd tab of LSD. That's what stars do."

"I don't."

"Then you're a freak." He got up. "I have to meet the guys soon for a warm-up. It would be better if you were gone before I leave."

Her blue eyes stared up at him. "When will I see you again?"

He laughed. "What do you mean?"

"I mean, will we see each other later?"

"Poor Maddy." He stubbed his cigarette in a crystal ashtray and strode over to the bed. "Did you really think we'd be girlfriend and boyfriend again? Holding hands and canoodling?"

She scowled.

"I'm not into relationships," he went on. "Last night was fun but it was a once-off thing. I can't commit to anyone right now."

"I don't want to get married," she interrupted hotly.

"Sure, I get that. But you must understand that all I wanted was to screw your brains out. No strings. Then you turned up and we did just that."

"*Cal!*" She looked shocked.

"What? You feel used?" He laughed. "Oh, Maddy. You need to grow up."

She slapped his cheek hard. "You're a pig, Cal Scott. I hope I never see you again."

He slapped her back.

"*Ow!*" Her eyes stung.

"Don't give it if you can't take it." He glared at her. "Now get dressed and leave. I have to go out."

It was only after she had a long hot shower that Madison cried. She lay down on her bed and sobbed. What was it about her? Why did men treat her so badly?

The apartment was empty except for Todd. Cliona's phone was switched off and the rest of her staff were gone home. She had never felt so lonely in her life.

With a sniff, she sat up and crossed her legs. How she wished that she could ring her mother and talk about it. How she wished they were close. She envied Constance and Cliona so much. Sure, Clio complained when her mum texted her twenty times a day, but what they had was closeness. A bond.

She had royally ruined everything now. Going to Cal and letting him treat her like that. No one cared about her – not her dad, not Caspian. It was a joke.

Suddenly she knew what to do. A few days away would do the trick, away from all the drama.

She climbed under the covers and pulled them up to her chin. She knew exactly where to go.

Cliona sat up and stretched.

"Your dad's making tagine, isn't he?"

Alex kissed her ribcage. "Yes."

"I'm starving."

"Do you want to join them?"

She nodded. "Is that okay?"

He sat up and pulled her close. "Of course. I'd be proud to take you home to meet the parents."

"I've met them already."

"But not as my girlfriend."

She kissed him lovingly. "No, not as your girlfriend."

"The twins will be delighted," he went on. "They were always asking me about you."

"Really?" She flushed with pleasure.

"Yeah. They told me to up the ante and make a move."

"I didn't realise how I felt for so long. Then when you kissed me, it all made sense."

His expression darkened. "I shouldn't have done that. Not with Vivienne."

"I know. But I'm glad that you did." She turned around and cupped his face with her hands. "I'm in love with you, Alex. I think I have been for a very long time. I just didn't see it."

Chapter Thirty-nine

Caspian sat in his apartment in Kensington, brooding over Madison. He had called her over and over again but she hadn't picked up. He didn't blame her.

Why did he kiss that woman at the party? He couldn't remember why he even talked to her, let alone kissed her. It was a terrible thing to do – especially in front of Madison's peers and people she wanted to impress. Now he had to figure out a way to make things better. He just wished she knew where she was.

Her face filled his mind. They had something – he had grown used to having her around. Why did he cheat on her? He wasn't sure. Maybe it was because he wasn't sure of her. Or maybe she was too strong for him.

Did he want things to end? Not at all. He liked having her on his arm. She was pretty and funny and adored by millions. He liked her softer side; the times when they ate pizza and watched old movies wearing pyjamas. He knew a side to her that her fans didn't. Surely that counted for something?

Deep down he knew it was pointless. She had cut the

cord. What he had done was indefensible. Kissing that model and, of course, the rumours about that Welsh girl. Why would anyone want to be with him?

He toyed with going home for a few days. Banbury would be the perfect hideaway. Ever since he had installed cameras, gates and alarms, his childhood home was impermeable to outsiders. His mum would fuss over him like she always did and he could switch off completely, away from the public and the huge mess he had created.

The intercom buzzed once and then twice. He ignored it. He didn't want to face the world. The only person he wanted to see was Madison and she would never arrive unannounced.

However, it buzzed again, incessantly, until he got up and checked the CCTV screen. To his utter shock, his mother and father were standing in the foyer.

He gave them access immediately, surprised that they had travelled to London without calling him first. He opened the door of his apartment and waited for them to exit the elevator.

"Mum! Dad! This is a surprise. I was actually planning on coming home for a bit."

Prudence looked worried, her face pinched and drawn. George nodded at his son as he walked past him. Caspian closed the door.

"Why are you two in London?" he asked.

Prudence burst into tears, her shoulders hunched. George rubbed her back soothingly.

"We need to talk to you, son."

"Why? What's going on?"

"You'd better sit down."

♫ ♫ ♫

Madison gazed out the car window at the trees and fields. She had thrown some things in a bag and told John to take her back to Norfolk.

Savannah was power-washing a shed when the Mercedes pulled up. Such was the noise of the machine, she didn't notice their presence at first.

Madison tapped her on the shoulder and she jumped sky high.

"Madison!" she exclaimed. "Why are you here?"

"Can I stay for a while?"

"Stay?"

"Please."

Savannah paused. Madison prayed that she wouldn't send her away.

"Use the same room as last time. You'll have to put sheets on the bed." She switched on the power hose again and aimed it at the whitewashed wall.

Madison exhaled slowly.

"A man came to the house," said Prudence, after her tears had subsided. "He said he was a journalist. He had been everywhere, looking for information."

"On what?" asked Caspian.

"On you. On us. He was desperate to find something to print."

George looked sad, his eyes cast down.

"So, what happened?"

"He found out things. Private things. Things Daddy and I kept from you."

"What kind of things?"

Prudence started to cry again. "I never thought this day would come. I never thought we'd have to break your heart."

"What?" Caspian felt the room spin. "Break my heart? Are you sick, Mum? Dad?"

George shook his head. "No, son."

"Then what? *What?*"

Savannah cut a slice of sponge cake and carefully placed it on a pottery plate. She pushed it in front of Madison who was holding her teacup with both hands, her eyes dazed.

"Eat some of this," suggested Savannah. "You look thinner than I remember."

"I don't eat cream," said Madison automatically.

"It's buttercream. Now eat."

She picked up a fork and half-heartedly speared some cake.

Savannah watched her in amusement.

"I'm sensitive about my baking, you know."

Madison smiled. "Fine, I'll taste it." She chewed mechanically and swallowed. "See? *Yum.*"

"Why are you here?"

Madison put down the fork. "I don't know."

"You must have a reason to turn up out of the blue ..."

"Sorry about that. It's just impossible to contact you."

Savannah waved her away. "I don't mind in the slightest. I suppose I'm curious as to why."

Madison's blue eyes filled with tears. "I ... I ... I need to ..."

"Yes?" prompted Savannah gently.

"I need to sort out my life."

"In what way?"

"Caspian has been cheating on me."

"Are you surprised?"

Madison paused. "No, yes, I don't know. I mean, he's not the first to mess me around."

"Men are essentially simpletons when it comes to sex. They need it in a different way to us. For them it's purely physical and an essential outlet."

"Are you condoning his behaviour?" Madison asked, shocked.

"Not at all. However, humans are flawed and we have to try and understand one another."

Savannah poured more tea. "This Caspian. He has a high opinion of himself, no?"

Madison nodded. "Huge."

"As do you, I'd expect."

"Hey!"

"What I mean is that you don't give him what he needs. He wants to be adored and made feel like he's number one. You can't possibly give him that."

"So, he sleeps around to fill the void? Are you for real?"

"He needs to feel wanted," she concluded simply.

"That's no excuse. He should have come to me and worked it out."

"That would be admitting his insecurity."

Madison bit her lip. "So, what you're saying is that I should change who I am to please him and feed his ego."

"No, but try and understand him. Life throws things like this at you all the time. You have to look beyond your hurt and realise that maybe it was a cry for help. Maybe it was attention-seeking on his part."

Madison said nothing. Instead she viciously mashed the cake into smithereens.

"Look, Maddy. Your relationship hasn't a chance if you don't meet each other halfway. It's dysfunctional. One of you must take a back seat and let the other shine, or forget it."

"Well, I'm not taking a back seat."

"Then you have your answer."

Madison put her head on the oak table and groaned. "That's not all. I slept with my ex and it was the worst thing I could possibly have done."

"Which ex?"

"Cal. The one who cheated on me." She looked up. "My first love."

"Why did you do it?"

"I honestly don't know. To get back at Caspian maybe? To show Cal what he's missing?"

"Do you feel better?"

"No. I feel twenty million times worse."

"Let's have a limoncello. Times like this demand it."

Madison wiped her eyes with her sleeve. "I don't know. It's very sugary."

"We have a long evening ahead." Savannah took two small glasses from the cabinet. "Drink a few of these and you'll feel better."

Caspian stared at Prudence, desperately trying to process the words that came from her mouth.

You were adopted. We got you when you were a little baby. We were so blessed, blessed by God that you came into our lives.

He clutched his head. "I don't believe it."

George cleared his throat. "It's true."

"Why didn't you tell me?"

Prudence started to wring her handkerchief in her hands. "There was no need."

"Why?"

"There was no chance your real mother would come for you."

"My real mother?" He sat back, feeling faint.

Real mother.

"We felt that it was pointless. It was only her name on the birth certificate, you see. Then after the accident we ..."

"Accident?" He felt waves of revulsion.

Prudence nodded. "She was killed in a car crash when you were eight months old."

Caspian blanched.

"I'm so sorry, darling. I'm so sorry." She started to cry again. "We felt that it was the best to let things lie. There was no point upsetting you. I mean, she was gone and we didn't know who the father was ..."

He got up and started pacing the room. "Stop talking. Stop right now."

"Caspian," said George. "*Please*."

"So, I'm not your son. I've never been your son."

"*No!*" shouted Prudence, jumping to her feet. "You *are* our son. You've always been ours. Don't ever think any differently."

"But I'm not though." He faced them angrily. "Not at all in fact."

"Caspian!' George stood up sternly. "Calm down."

"How could you keep this from me?" Tears started to roll down his cheeks. "Why tell me now?"

"We were afraid someone else would find out and tell you," said Prudence helplessly. "We never thought we'd have to dig up the past."

"Where did I come from?" he whispered bleakly. "Where?"

"Ireland. It was all above board, I promise. Not like those awful stories you hear now about those wretched mothers and babies in homes."

"How? How did I end up with you?"

Prudence took a shaky breath. "We were living in Killarney back then. George was working for a bus company."

"Killarney? You told me we lived in Liverpool when I was a baby."

"We moved there afterwards."

"Afterwards?"

"After we got you. We were so delighted, Caspian. We never thought God would bless us with a child."

"Did you know my mother?"

Prudence glanced at George. "No. We never met."

"Why did she give me away?" He wiped the tears from his eyes. "Why?"

"She was only a child. Seventeen, I think it was. She wanted you to have a good life. She couldn't provide that."

"So she gave me up?"

Prudence nodded. "She was so brave. There isn't a day goes by that I don't think of her."

He picked up a cushion and clutched it to his chest.

"What about my father?"

George spoke first. "We don't know who it is. We never knew. His name wasn't on the birth certificate."

"What was her name?" A single tear rolled down his cheek.

Prudence looked at George and he nodded.

"Her name was Mary," she said sadly. "Mary Kennedy."

After a sleepless night, Prudence refused to leave Caspian alone, despite his insistence.

"I need some time to think," he said with conviction. "I need to be alone."

"No," she said worriedly. "I can't leave you now. This is too much to cope with on your own."

"Please, Mum." He put his face in his hands. "I need some time."

"No!"

Caspian banged the table in frustration. "I have been awake all night, going over and over everything. I need time alone to think."

George put his hand on his wife's shoulder. "Come on, Prue. He'll come to us when he's ready."

"No!" She held Caspian's hand like a vice. "I can't."

"Please, Mum." Caspian's brown eyes pleaded with her. "I need to process this."

She got up reluctantly and wiped her eyes with a white handkerchief. "Please don't shut me out," she said with a lump in her throat. "Don't push me away. I love you, darling."

Caspian said nothing. He just stared at the ground, his face ashen.

"Come on, love." George led her away.

When the door closed, Caspian went straight to his piano. Numbly, he played an arpeggio, his mind a blur.

All his life he had believed that he was someone else. The only son of George and Prue Cole. Sure, he didn't resemble them much, but lots of kids didn't look like their parents. No big deal.

Mary.

He screwed his eyes shut in pain.

His birth mother.

Why did she give him up?

His head fell on the keyboard and caused a discordant twang of notes. What the hell would he do? He couldn't just continue as normal and pretend it hadn't happened. But Mary was dead. Where would he even begin?

His body convulsed with heavy sobs as he sat alone in his huge apartment.

After half an hour, he pulled himself together. He picked up his phone and called Madison. It went straight to her messages. Then he called Cliona and the same thing happened. He didn't want to call his bandmates. Not about something like this.

His finger hovered over his call list as he pondered on what to do.

Finally, he pressed 'Mum' and she answered immediately.

"I need you, Mum. I need you here."

"I'm coming, my love. I'm only a few minutes away."

"You didn't go home?"

"No, of course not. We booked into a hotel."

Caspian sighed in relief. "See you soon."

Chapter Forty

Prudence insisted that Caspian come home to Banbury.

"We can work this out," she said insistently. "Come home and we can talk."

He agreed and they left immediately. He sat in the back of the car like he did when he was a child. Every now and then he noticed George squeeze Prudence's hand.

When they got to his childhood home, he went into the sitting room while Prudence made some tea. In a daze, he stared at the photos on the wall – his first day at school, his graduation, his first show. There was even a baby photo framed on the dresser. He was smiling with blonde curls and a rattle in his hand. He had to know. He had to know how he joined their family. Surely there was someone who could help.

Prudence put a tray with a teapot and cups on the coffee table. "Get some biscuits, George," she said.

Caspian sat down. "Tell me everything," he said bleakly.

Prudence poured a cup of tea and added milk. "I don't know a lot."

"Please."

George reappeared with a packet of Bourbons.

Prudence's eyes met Caspian's. "It all started when Nora, our neighbour, called over. She said this Sister Cecilia had rung her up for a chat and told her about a young girl in her school."

"Who was Sister Cecilia?"

"She was headmistress of a school in Cork."

"And?"

"Nora knew George and I were desperately looking to adopt. We couldn't have our own, you see. She thought this girl would be perfect."

"Mary," said Caspian bleakly.

Prudence nodded. "Mary." She sighed. "Cecilia had convinced her to consider adoption. That's when Nora suggested that we contact the agency." Prudence exhaled shakily. "We were told that Mary came from a modest background and she couldn't care for a baby. Her dad was out of work and her mother was dead. She had to make ends meet.

"Her dad?" Caspian looked up, a flame appearing in his dead eyes. "Is he alive?"

"I don't know," said Prudence honestly.

"I may have family in Ireland and you don't know?" He banged the armrest angrily. "Come on, I don't believe that."

"It's true! We sent updates to the agency and kept an open-door policy. We always said that we were open to contact."

"But she died."

"Yes, my darling. She did. Then the years passed and there was nothing. So, we moved on with our lives." Prudence started to cry. "It means that your original birth cert and records are stored in that agency. Once you were handed over, all that was filed away."

Caspian closed his eyes. "I don't believe this."

Prudence wiped her eyes with a handkerchief.

"And my father?" He looked up. "My real father? What about him?"

George winced.

"As I said, we were never told," said Prudence quietly.

"Someone must know."

She said nothing.

"Come on, why wasn't he in the picture? Is he alive?"

"All Cecilia said was that he didn't want anything to do with Mary and her situation. She didn't record his name on the birth cert so that's where the trail ends."

Caspian got up and started to pace the room. "Bullshit. There has to be someone who knows."

"I don't know ..."

"What about Cecilia? Is she still alive?"

Prudence closed her eyes. "Yes, I think so. Nora sends the odd letter and she's never mentioned she died."

"Then I've got to see her."

"No, Caspian. Please don't dig up all of this. You'll only get hurt."

"How could I be more hurt? *How?*"

"If you do track down your father he may not want to meet you."

"There has to be a way. There has to be a trail. I'm entitled to find out."

"The agency was Catholic run and based in Cork," said Prudence. "Cecilia was involved with them."

"What was it called?" Caspian pulled his phone out of his pocket. "I'll google it."

"I can't remember," said Prudence. "It was so long ago."

George nodded. "We tried to forget, Caspian."

"The agency were so helpful. They organised everything. We travelled to Cork when you were six weeks old. You were staying with a foster family at that point."

"A foster family?"

She nodded. "It took time to sort all the legalities so you were placed with them until we could officially bring you home." Her expression softened. "I remember the first time I saw you. We met at the agency and you were there, wrapped in a blue blanket." She hung her head. "We brought you home that day."

"Did you ever meet Mary?"

Prudence hung her head. "No. Your foster parents, Richard and Bernie, had you since you were three days old. They took you home from the hospital and kept you until you were handed over to us."

"So I was with her for three days." He shuddered. "I can't believe it."

"I'm sorry we didn't meet her now." Prudence looked up. "I always felt guilty about that. So we sent a considerable sum to Cecilia to give to her ..."

"What?"

"We sent some money ..."

"You bought me?" He clutched his hair. "She *sold* me?"

"We didn't buy you!' Prudence looked horrified. "Cecilia organised it and Mary agreed. I don't know, it seemed the right thing to do. To compensate for her loss."

"Fucking hell!" Caspian felt his world spin. "Who has information, Mum?"

"The agency. We only have your adoptive cert."

"Where can I find Cecilia?"

Prudence started to cry and George patted her back. "The last I heard she was in a retirement home in Cork. A special one for nuns. I don't have the address."

"Ring Nora."

"I can't, Caspian."

"Yes, you can. Otherwise I'll go to Liverpool now and ask her myself." He faced them. "I'm going to Ireland."

"Alone?" Prudence looked up in alarm.

"Yes." Caspian's face was set in a steely line. "Now, please find out the name of that agency. I have to make a few calls."

Madison forked up some buttery scrambled eggs and took a big bite of toast. "God, I have to stop eating."

Savannah smiled. "You need to put on a few pounds. You're far too skinny."

"I can't! You know that. The industry has strict rules."

"Screw the industry. I did."

They sat in silence for a while, comfortable with each other.

"I need to see Caspian."

"Oh?"

"Yes. I think the best way forward is to be friends. I need to forgive him and move on. That was the problem with Cal – I never had closure."

"Can you do that? Just be friends?"

Madison nodded. "I think so. I mean, the sex is great but we barely have time to meet. Why tie myself down with a guy who doesn't respect me? I'd like to stay friends as we'll inevitably meet at ceremonies and parties."

"If you're sure." Savannah started to clear the breakfast plates.

"I am. I can do this. I can be the bigger person. I need to see him and tell him how I feel."

Savannah scraped the leftover food into the compost bin. "I think that's best."

Madison refilled her mug with tea. It was time to go back. It was time to move on.

It took two days to find all the information. Prudence had unearthed all the documents linked to the adoption and discovered the name of the agency: St. Theresa's. Caspian googled it and found that it had closed in 2002.

"*What will I do now?*" he yelled in frustration.

Prudence put on her glasses. "The Southern Health Board, which is now called the HSE, were given all the files when the agency closed. You'll have to apply for information. If they don't have the files, then it says that you'll have to apply to the Adoption Authority in Ireland."

"How long will that take?"

She took off her glasses and rubbed her eyes. "I don't know, darling. I really don't."

"I need to go to Ireland."

"Please don't do anything rash. Let me talk to Nora."

"Don't tell her why you're asking. I don't want Cecilia to have any warning."

"She's going to be curious, Caspian. I mean, it will be out of the blue."

"*No!*" he shouted. "Don't give her time to cover anything up. I'm just going to arrive and surprise her."

"That's awful! She's an old lady."

"I don't care." His eyes narrowed.

George drove Caspian home to London and they pulled up outside his building. Rain fell on the windscreen in rivulets, pushed to the left and right by the incessant wipers. The grey sky matched Caspian's mood.

"Are you sure we can't go with you, son?" he asked gruffly. "Prue is so upset at the thought of you being alone."

"No, Dad. I'll take it from here."

"You have Cecilia's address?"

"In my pocket."

They embraced briefly.

"Give us a ring and let us know." George's eyes were shining with tears. "Please."

Caspian patted his shoulder. "Of course."

He got out of the car.

Up in his bedroom, he threw some jeans, socks, boxers and a few sweatshirts into a bag. He unplugged his phone charger and threw that in too. The cleaner had been so the apartment was spotless. His toothbrush was standing in a gold container on the sink, next to his toothpaste. He placed them in a plastic bag, along with some shaving foam, aftershave and deodorant, and sealed it. Now all he had to do was organise a flight.

There were five missed calls from Tommy on his phone but he ignored them. He couldn't care less about Doctor Eckleburg now.

The front door slammed and he jumped. No one had a key except him and Madison. He walked out into the living area to find her standing by the sofa.

"Hey," she said guardedly. She looked beautiful in a Burberry Mac, skinny jeans and black high-heeled boots. Her blonde hair was loose and slightly wavy.

"Why are you here?" He couldn't cope with a fight now. He hoped she wasn't her usual belligerent self.

"I came to talk," she said softly.

"Talk?" he repeated.

"About us." She flicked her blonde hair.

"I can't right now, Mads." He rubbed his temple. "I'll call you when I get back."

"Get back?" she said in alarm. "From where?"

"Ireland."

"Why?" Her blue eyes were puzzled.

"I can't talk about it now. Please, save whatever you want to say until I get back."

He disappeared into his room. Confused, she followed him.

"What's going on, Caspian?" she demanded. "You look terrible."

He ignored her and grabbed his jacket.

"Caspian!" She stood in the doorway, blocking his exit. "What's the matter?"

"I said I didn't want to talk about it."

"I came here to make up with you. To offer you friendship." She pummelled his chest. "Don't shut me out."

He grabbed her wrists. "Stop hitting me," he said wearily. "I can't deal with it."

"With what?" She stroked his hair. "What's the matter?"

The smell of her perfume was so familiar. He buried his face in her neck. She held him close, caressing his head. "Talk to me, baby. What's going on?"

He exhaled slowly and it came out as a shuddering breath. "I'm adopted."

She jumped. "*What?*"

"I'm adopted," he repeated. "Mum and Dad told me. I was born in Ireland and sold to them."

"*Sold?* What?"

"Sold."

"My God!" She couldn't believe it. "You had no idea about this?"

"None."

"Why did they tell you?" Madison looked genuinely horrified. "Why now?"

"Some journalist was poking around and asking questions. Mum panicked. I don't know."

Madison took his hand and led him to the couch. "Sit down," she said gently.

He obeyed and put his head in his hands. "My real mother is dead. She was killed in a car crash."

"Oh, Caspian." She rubbed his back.

"My father's identity is a mystery. His name wasn't recorded on the birth cert." He looked up. "That's why I have to go to Ireland. I have to find Sister Cecilia – the nun who knew my mother and arranged it all – and find out the truth."

"Alone?" she said startled.

"I tried calling you. You didn't answer."

"I was in Norfolk," she said blandly. "Sorry about that."

"I thought you hated me."

"I don't hate you," she said carefully. "I just don't really like you right now. I think we should stay friends."

Caspian smiled sadly. "I guess I deserve that."

"Well, no. You deserve a lot worse, but you've enough to deal with right now."

His handsome face looked drawn and pale. "Anyway, I was just on my way out." He stood up. "Thanks for calling. I suppose I don't need to say that this is a secret."

"Of course." She stood up too so that they were facing each other. "The thing is, I have a few days free."

"That's nice," he said absentmindedly, putting his jacket over his arm.

"So I could come with you."

He stopped dead. "Come with me?"

"Yes."

"But surely you're too busy. You're always too busy."

"Well, I did have a photo shoot with *Vogue* but that can wait."

Caspian frowned. "This is strange, Maddy. Why would you come with me?"

"Because that's what friends do. They look out for each other."

"You're frightening me." He held up his hands. "Can the real Madison Ryan please stand up?"

She held her head up haughtily. "Cut that right out. I've turned over a new leaf. I'm going to think of others from now on. First, you. Then my dad. I need to sort that out."

"So, you're serious? You'll come to Cork?" He didn't dare believe it.

She nodded. "Being a Dublin girl, that's a big ask, but I'll do it." She grinned. "We don't really venture outside the Pale."

"The what?"

"Nothing. Historical reference. Basically, the area

around County Dublin."

His face changed. "God, Maddy, maybe this is a bad idea."

"Why? Because of the friends thing?"

"No, because you're so recognisable. I mean, I don't want fans running after us. I can manage going incognito with a hat and glasses, but you? You're impossible to hide."

"I have wigs ..."

"Seriously."

"Are you saying that I'm more famous than you?" She smiled playfully.

He raised his head haughtily. "Maybe, but for all the wrong reasons. I'm famous for my art, for my talent. I always knew I was going to be great, ever since I was little."

Madison shook her head, bemused as she always was when he made such speeches. God, he really was arrogant! But maybe it wasn't arrogance? More a deep belief in his god-given gift.

"Have you booked a flight?" she asked.

He shook his head. "I was just going to get a taxi and take the next available one."

"Oh, no," she said firmly. "I'll just call John to sort it out. We'll book a private jet."

"A jet? No, Maddy. Not after that Greta Thunberg kid sailed to New York."

"*I can't fly economy!*" she yelled.

He groaned. "You see, this is what I don't need. All this drama."

"Fine, fine. I'll ask John to sort it. Let's go back to my place."

"John? Where's Clio? I thought that was her job."

"Good question. Her phone is switched off and I've left thousands of messages."

Caspian said nothing. He had been unable to contact her too, but had presumed she was avoiding him. He felt slightly better.

"She's dead to me now," went on Madison fiercely. "I had to make my own dental appointment this morning and everything."

Caspian took her hand in his. "Poor Maddy," he mocked, leading her to the door.

"I'm not sure about holding hands anymore," she said seriously. "That's outside of the Friendzone."

He shrugged. "Humour me today. I'm so glad you're with me, Mads. Honestly. Thank you."

Chapter Forty-one

An hour later, Madison was on her iPad, googling adoption in Ireland. She was sitting on her couch, her long legs crossed underneath her. Caspian was watching television with a faraway look on his face.

"Gosh, some of the stories on here would make you want to cry," she said, swiping with her finger. "Thank God you weren't born in the fifties."

"Yeah."

She held the screen closer to read an article. "It says here that if all else fails, you can hire a private investigator."

"Really?"

"Yeah. Maybe you should. Then they could find your real father."

He shook his head. "I can't face that right now, Maddy. I need to see that nun and find out what she knows."

"It's an option," she said, exiting the article. "They would have to sign a non-disclosure and all that. I mean, you're not some nobody from nowhere."

The door of the apartment slammed and Cliona appeared. She was wearing her glasses and her long brown hair fell around her face. She took off her jacket and hung it on the rack.

"Clio!" Madison narrowed her eyes. "Where the hell have you been? I should fire you."

"With Alex." She glowed with pleasure.

Caspian sat up straight. "Really?"

She nodded. "He's just gone home to get some stuff."

"Some stuff?" Madison looked suspicious. "For what?"

Cliona took a deep breath. "Can I speak to you alone?" she said to Madison.

Caspian got up. "Sure, I'll just watch TV in the bedroom."

Cliona smiled gratefully at him as he walked away.

"What do you need to talk to me about?" Madison put her iPad carefully on the couch.

Cliona sat on the chair that Caspian had vacated. "Well, Alex thinks I should stop burying my head in the sand and follow my dreams."

"What?" Madison sat up straight.

"I have to quit, Mads. I have to start working with film and pursuing my real passion in life."

"Quit?" Her voice came out as a squeak. "Are you for real?"

"Yes!" said Cliona happily. "I've never felt more real in my life."

Madison got up and started pacing. "You can't just up and leave, Clio. I can't survive without you."

"Yes, you can."

"I mean, John has been trying to get airspace all morning for a jet and he still hasn't succeeded. You never had any problems organising things."

"Air space? Why? Where are you going?"

"To Ireland." Madison stopped. "To Cork."

"Cork?"

"Yeah, Caspian and I are heading to Ireland for a break." She looked away. "We're working things out," she lied.

"Really?" Cliona jumped up and hugged her. "That's so great, Mads. I'm happy for you."

"Yes, well. We're never going to get there at this rate."

Cliona frowned. "I'll sort it. I may not be able to get a jet so would you fly commercial?"

"Christ, no."

"The Cambridges did it the other day. Everyone loved them for it. I mean, you're famous and all, but you're not heir to the throne."

Madison threw up her hands. "Look, fine. See what you can get."

"Where are you planning to stay?"

"Just pick the best hotel and ask for complete discretion."

Cliona bit her lip as she googled. Suddenly she stopped. "I have it! Why don't I text Colin? He lives in Cork. He's bound to know the best place to stay."

"Who the hell is Colin?" Madison asked, puzzled.

Cliona clapped her hands together. "He used to live near us in Dublin. His mum is great pals with mine. He adopted a baby, remember?"

"No."

"He was at that New Year's Eve party. Curly hair, great dress sense?"

"Oh yeah, him," Madison said blandly.

"Will I ask him?"

"Gosh, I don't know. What if he leaks our whereabouts to the press?"

"Oh, Colin is used to famous people. He works in fashion. Give me a second."

She texted a message like lightning and Madison watched her with mixed emotions. She wanted Cliona to be happy but she really didn't want to lose her.

"So, where are you planning on finding a job?" she asked airily. "You've little or no experience really."

"I've got to start somewhere. Would two weeks' notice be okay? It's just Alex is going to pull strings and get me on set for their next music video." She looked up. "Also, is there any chance you'd ask your dad for any tips?"

Madison made a face. "No way."

Cliona sighed. "Thanks anyway." Her phone pinged. "Ah, that's Colin." She read the text. "He says that the apartment across the hall from him is free as Luca and Lydia are in New York."

"Who?"

"Doesn't matter." She smiled. "It's perfect. Discreet and in a nice part of town. You can come and go as you please.

"Really?"

"The privacy of his place would be better than a hotel. He's a great cook too by all accounts. Diana is always telling Mum about it."

Madison called Caspian back into the room. "Clio thinks that we should stay with Colin, a guy who used to live down the road from us in Dublin."

"He lives in Cork now," added Cliona.

"Sure, sure. I don't mind."

"And, she wants to fly commercial."

"Well, I'm all for that."

"*And,* she's quitting."

Caspian smiled at Cliona. "You are? I'm delighted."

"Thanks." Cliona beamed at him.

"Well, I'm not," said Madison huffily. "It's just so inconvenient."

Cliona got them on the six o'clock flight from Gatwick.

"I can't believe we can't hire a jet," grumbled Madison as the Mercedes sped along the motorway.

"Please." He closed his eyes. "Just don't go on about it."

"You're making this friend thing really hard," she said coldly. "I'm here, trying my best and you're being mean to me."

"I'm not." He sighed. "I'm just all over the place. Please, just be there for me. Without talking. Please."

Madison turned away and focused on the grey sky. English weather was so depressing. She made a note to book a break in the Maldives soon. She could do with some sun.

"Isn't it crazy about Alex and Clio? I didn't see that one coming."

"Yeah."

"Imagine Cliona with a boyfriend. The only guy I ever saw her with was Nerdy Gareth when she was in college."

"Leave her alone. She's sweet."

"I know, I know. It's just I see her as a teenager. All sweet and innocent."

Caspian gazed at the blurry cars as they raced past in the opposite direction. His birth mother was a teenager when she fell pregnant with him. What kind of bastard got her in trouble and then abandoned her? What kind of monster would do that? His face hardened.

♫ ♫ ♫

They boarded the plane wearing their hoods up and large glasses. Todd stood sentinel by their sides as they took their seats. He then plonked down beside Caspian. Such was his bulk, Caspian had to move to his right and Madison moaned.

"A girl needs room, you know."

"It's not my fault," hissed Caspian.

John sat on the third seat of the opposite row, blocking the view from his left. No one noticed their presence until a young girl went to the bathroom and spotted Caspian on her way back to her seat. Her eyes widened and she was about to say something, when he put his finger to his lips and said "*Shhh*". She nodded, blushing, and walked on.

"That's why I love the Irish," murmured Madison. "They leave the likes of us alone."

"How do you know she's Irish?"

"I just know."

She checked Twitter on her phone and saw a picture of them walking through security with the headline: **Patching Things Up?**

"Oh God," she said with a moan. "They papped us at Gatwick."

"Really?"

"Yep. Just before we went through security. *Damn.* I thought I was unrecognisable in this hoodie."

"It doesn't matter. They can't possibly know where we're going."

"Oh, they know. They know everything. They can get information for a nominal sum."

"Why do they even care?" he asked wearily.

She took his hand in hers. "Don't think about it. Just forget about the press. You've too much on your plate."

Caspian put his head back and closed his eyes. His body felt numb – it was like a defence mechanism against the enormity of the situation. If he couldn't feel anything, then he couldn't get hurt. If he shut down his emotions, he could face anything.

The plane landed in Cork an hour later. The air hostess opened the door and beckoned to them to disembark first so as to avoid the crowds. They ventured out into the cold air and descended the steps. A man in a high-viz jacket waved them on and they walked towards the terminal building.

Todd walked in front of Madison as they sped down the corridor until they got to Passport Control. A man in uniform checked their passports and raised an eyebrow. He checked the photos and then looked at them again, as if to make sure. Finally, he handed them back and said, "Welcome to Cork".

Madison smiled coldly and walked on. Caspian held his passport in his hand, feeling like a fraud. The name recorded on it was a fake name – a name chosen by Prudence and George. Would he ever know his real name? Did Mary even choose one?

He walked out the gates and found Madison with her hood up and dark glasses on.

"Come on, " she whispered urgently. "John is outside."

A girl pointed at them and nudged her friend. They held up their phones immediately to get a shot. Caspian pulled his hat down over his ears and they followed Todd out through the main doors of the terminal. Cameras flashed as they scurried away.

Colin's flat was situated in the centre of Cork city. It was in a chic area by the university alongside a river lined with willow trees. Cliona had texted the address and Colin's phone number, so Madison called him to open the main door of the building. He was waiting in the foyer when they walked in.

Todd asked him to raise his arms immediately and he checked him for weapons.

"*Oooh*, this is exciting!" said Colin in delight, his hands in the air.

"Just doing my job, sir." Todd blushed slightly and stood back.

"Welcome!' said Colin with a smile. He leaned in and air-kissed both Madison and Caspian. "Just hop in the lift and we'll head upstairs. I've the fire lighting and dinner in the oven."

"Thank you for having us," said Caspian politely as the doors of the lift closed. "We won't be here for long."

"Oh, it's no bother," said Colin warmly. "Luca and Lydia's place is perfect for you."

"Is there space for Todd, my bodyguard?" asked Madison. "My driver can book into a hotel, but I'd like Todd with me constantly."

"Sure."

Madison and Caspian walked out into a dimly lit hallway and waited while Colin opened a heavy brown door.

"Welcome to Chez Moi!" he said, waving them inside.

A pungent smell of oregano hit their nostrils as they walked into the apartment.

Val, Colin's husband, was sitting on the couch watching football. The baby, Orlando, was bouncing in his Jumperoo, clapping his hands and laughing. He was a chubby little thing with blonde hair that was starting to curl.

"Hello!" said Val with a small wave. "Welcome to Cork."

Caspian clasped Madison's hand tightly. She could feel the tension coming off him and squeezed his fingers.

"So, I made cannelloni for dinner," said Colin, taking two wine glasses down from a shelf. "Spinach and ricotta. I wasn't sure if you ate meat so I went for a safe option." He poured two generous glasses of red. "Take a seat in there and I'll be right in. I just need to perfect my béchamel."

Caspian sat on the couch next to Val and gestured at the screen. "Do you support Man United?"

"Always." Val nodded solemnly. "Until my dying day."

"I'm a Liverpool fan."

"Can you sit over there?" Val shifted to the right in mock disgust and then smiled.

Madison knelt down and tickled Orlando. "Look at you jumping around," she said softly.

Caspian watched her as she stroked the baby's cheek and made silly noises. She was different. She had changed. She had softened somehow. He couldn't quite believe that she had agreed to come with him. He was so glad he hadn't travelled alone.

Colin, wearing an apron that said *I Kiss Better Than I Cook*, placed a bowl of crisps on the coffee table. "Help yourselves," he said, placing napkins nearby.

Val roared at the screen. "*That was definitely off-side!*"

Colin rolled his eyes. "If I've said it once, I've said it a million times. Football is the bane of my life." He walked into the kitchen. "Dinner is almost ready, guys."

Madison was surprised to find that she was hungry. She had a large helping of cannelloni and two glasses of red wine. Caspian, who was used to her finicky eating habits, was astonished.

"What about your strict diet?" he whispered as she mopped up the sauce with some bread.

"I'm taking a few hours off."

He had barely touched his meal. His head was spinning. Being so close to the truth made his stomach curl. Cecilia's address burned a hole in his pocket and he couldn't wait for the next morning when he could take a taxi out there right away.

"So, what brings you to Cork?" asked Colin.

Madison rubbed Caspian's leg comfortingly under the table.

"We have some people to visit. Old friends," she said smoothly.

"There are loads of comments on Twitter about it," went on Colin, sprinkling some pepper on his food. "Is this a reconciliation trip?"

Madison plastered a smile on her face. "Maybe."

"Anyway, moving on." Val nudged Colin pointedly to drop it.

Colin made an '*oh*' sound and turned to Caspian.

"So, I love your new song. I'm singing it all the time at karaoke night down the pub."

"That's nice,' said Caspian distractedly.

"And of course, 'Possess Me' is already a classic."

"Thanks," said Madison automatically.

"When's the première of the film? I must cover the style aspect for my column."

"You're a journalist?" she asked in surprise.

"Of course." Colin looked puzzled. "Surely you've heard of me? I'm Ireland's leading fashion guru."

Val snorted. "You are, yeah."

"*I am!*" protested Colin hotly. "I have over ten thousand followers on Instagram and I can make or break a new designer."

"Ten thousand?" said Madison. "Really?"

"Yes. I only follow two hundred and three people. I'm proud of my skinny ratio." Colin looked at her. "How many have you?"

"Eighteen million or something," said Madison nonchalantly.

"Of course you do." Colin gulped. "I knew that."

Caspian pushed his plate away. "I think I'll go and lie down." He stood up apologetically. "I'm not feeling well."

"Oh my God! I hope it wasn't my cannelloni!" Colin looked appalled.

"No, no. I'm just feeling a bit off." Caspian attempted to smile. "I just need to sleep."

Madison pushed her plate to the side and stood up too. "I'll go with him."

"Of course," said Colin, dropping his fork. "I'll show you to your room across the hall."

He walked over to the hall table and picked up a set of keys with a dolphin keyring.

Todd was standing outside the door when they opened it.

"All okay, ma'am?" he asked.

"We're heading to bed," she informed him. "We're staying in the apartment across the hall."

"I'll just check the premises first, ma'am," he said, relieving Colin of the keys.

"Is he this thorough all the time?" asked Colin in fascination, watching him disappear through the door.

"Yep."

They waited patiently until Todd returned. "All's clear."

Colin walked in and dropped the keys on the kitchen counter.

"Look, they store the coffee in here," he said, opening a cupboard. "Towels are on the bed and that TV over there has every channel known to man."

He led them into a guest bedroom which had a double bed, an en-suite bathroom and a pile of boxes stacked in the corner.

"Luca and Lydia are not the tidiest people in the world," said Colin. "What I would give to organise this place but I know it would be futile as they would destroy it in three minutes."

He then showed Todd a second bedroom with a four-poster single bed, stencils of Disney princesses on the walls and a white dressing table strewn with jewellery and cosmetics.

"This is their daughter Sienna's room. It's either this or the sofa, Todd."

Todd nodded. "I'll probably sleep on the sofa, sir."

"I totally get that." Colin ushered him out. "I love pink and all, but this is too much."

♫ ♫ ♫

Caspian took off his hoodie and sat on the bed. "It looks like we'll have to share."

Madison bit her lip. "I can sleep on Colin's sofa?"

"No!" He stood up. "Please stay with me. I don't want to be alone."

He looked so lost, she didn't argue.

"Fine. But no funny business. We're friends now and that's all."

Caspian shrugged. "To be honest, it's the last thing on my mind."

In the middle of the night, he woke suddenly. Sitting up straight, he felt like he couldn't breathe. He had been dreaming about Mary. At least, he thought it was her. She was running away from him and he was calling her, but she couldn't hear.

He wiped his brow and inhaled deeply. His heart was racing and he felt waves of anxiety wash over him. Madison shifted in the bed beside him. Her blonde hair fanned over her pillow and her chest heaved as she slept.

He placed his arm around her waist and lay his head on her shoulder. The warmth from her body comforted him. She felt real in a world where nothing was definite anymore.

Chapter Forty-two

The next morning, Colin left a bag of croissants outside the main door with a handwritten note.

Have a great day! Visit the English Market if you can. Don't forget your keys. Col x

Madison dressed carefully. She scraped her hair back into a ponytail and put on a large black hooded sweatshirt. Grabbing her habitual big sunglasses, she then zipped up black boots over skinny black jeans.

"You look like a ninja," said Caspian, placing a beanie hat over his blonde hair. He too had a large jacket and glasses.

"Is it too much black?" she asked in concern. "I mean, chances are I'll be photographed, despite my disguise."

"You look fine."

John was waiting outside. He opened the door of the Mercedes and they got in. The blacked-out windows gave them temporary reprieve so they took off the hoods and glasses.

"So, this nun has no idea we're coming?"

Caspian shook his head. "Mum made Nora swear not to warn her."

"Do you think she'll know much?"

"She organised the whole thing, so yes." His face was grim as the car crossed a bridge. "She's the key to finding my father."

St Aloysius Care Home was situated near Montenotte on the north side of the city. It was home to fifteen retired nuns and had a great view of Cork City with its numerous spires and meandering river. A receptionist with a friendly face smiled at them as they approached the desk. Caspian took off his glasses and his hat. Her eyes widened slightly, but she said nothing. Madison stood in the background with her back turned. Todd had been told to wait outside – Caspian had insisted, as a religious care home was a minimal threat. Madison didn't argue. She could tell he was stressed and she had promised not to create a circus.

"I'm here to see Sister Cecilia, please," said Caspian politely.

"Is she expecting you?"

"No."

"May I have your name?"

He paused for a moment. "Caspian Cole."

She raised an eyebrow but again kept her composure. "I'll just call the nurse," she said professionally. "Please take a seat and I'll call you."

"Thank you."

He walked over to Madison and they sat on the hard two-seater sofa in the lobby. A large plant shielded them slightly and she linked arms with him.

"It's going to be fine," she whispered.

He didn't reply. Instead, a muscle flickered in his cheek.

A nurse dressed in blue scrubs appeared. "Hello," she said with a smile. "My name is Kathleen. I hear you want to see Cecilia."

Caspian stood up. "Yes."

"She's a bit flustered as she wasn't expecting you."

"I'm sorry about that."

"May I ask what it is in relation to? I don't want anything to upset her."

Caspian inhaled sharply. "I'm afraid it's a private matter." He looked at the receptionist and then back to the nurse. "I would appreciate complete discretion from all of you regarding this visit."

"We won't tell a soul," said the nurse. "However, my duty of care is to my patient and when I said your name she went pale."

"I just need some information from her," he said quietly. "It won't take long."

"Give me a few minutes." The nurse disappeared down the corridor.

The receptionist pretended to type something on her computer, but she kept glancing furtively at Caspian. Madison, her face and hair completely concealed, kept her head down.

Finally, the nurse reappeared and waved at them to come forward. "She'll see you now."

Caspian walked towards her and Madison followed.

"Just you," the nurse said to Caspian.

"Sorry, Maddy." He ran his fingers through his hair. "Do you mind?"

The receptionist's eyes widened at the sound of 'Maddy' but again she said nothing.

Madison shrugged. "I'll wait in the car. Call me if you need me." She kissed his cheek and scurried outside to where Todd was standing. The car door slammed.

Caspian followed the nurse down a long corridor, through a common room and into a small conservatory. An old woman was sitting in a wheelchair by a giant fern, her legs covered with a patchwork blanket. She had white hair and a wizened face. As Caspian approached, she looked up and her wise old eyes narrowed.

"You're Prue's boy, am I right?"

He nodded. "I need to talk to you."

She sighed. "Then you'd better sit down."

Caspian sat on a wicker chair. "I'm here to find out about my mother. My real mother."

"Mary," she stated matter-of-factly.

"Yes."

"You have a look of her. Around the mouth. Of course, the blonde hair too."

His face tightened. "I wouldn't know. I have no idea what she looked like."

"Mary? She was a pretty little thing as I recall. Bright too. I had high hopes for her in the Leaving."

"The Leaving?"

"The Leaving Cert final exams. The results decide a university place."

"What happened? Why did she give me up?"

Cecilia gestured to her wheelchair. "Will you push me? We should walk."

Caspian stood up and grasped the handles. He manoeuvred the chair past the plants and down the corridor.

"Where are you two off to?" asked Kathleen the nurse with her hands on her hips.

"For some fresh air." Cecilia waved her away.

"It's cold outside ..."

"It's fine."

Caspian kept walking until they reached double doors. They opened automatically and they ventured out into a beautiful garden with a vegetable patch, trees and a manicured lawn.

It was indeed cold; Caspian moved faster.

They reached a pond and Cecilia asked him to stop.

She smoothed the blanket on her knees. "Mary didn't have many options," she began.

"Why?"

"Her father Noel was out of work and her mother died of cancer when she was small. She needed guidance."

"Is Noel still alive?"

"No." She sighed. "I'm sorry to say this, but he died a long time ago."

"What? How?"

"After Mary died I kept an eye on him. He started drinking heavily and there were some incidents. I helped organise Meals on Wheels and urged him to come to Mass on Sundays, but he became more and more isolated."

"What happened then?"

"There were reports of odd behaviour. Then he wasn't seen for about a week. We found him by Mary's grave, frozen to the bone, singing old songs and crying." She looked up. "Then he went missing again. Eventually they found him in the river after a four-day search."

"The river," Caspian echoed in horror.

"Yes, we're not sure of he fell in or not. I hope for his soul's sake he did fall." She made a Sign of the Cross.

"How awful!" Caspian went white.

"They cleared out the house and now there's a Polish family living there, I believe."

He stared aghast at the still water in the pond. It was dark green with sludge and looked stagnant. He couldn't quite process what she was saying. His grandfather. The river.

"Take me back, young man. I'm starting to get cold."

Caspian started to wheel her back towards the main building. Kathleen the nurse was watching them from a large bay window.

"I need to find my real father," said Caspian quietly.

"She never told me a name. All I knew was that he told her to terminate the pregnancy."

"He what?" He stopped dead.

"I'm sorry."

He walked around the wheelchair to face her. "So why didn't she just do that? It would have been a lot simpler."

"Abortion was illegal in Ireland back then and I thank God for that."

"Is my real father alive?"

"I don't know."

"You must know something." He kicked a stone in frustration.

"I don't. She never said anything." She looked up. "I swear to you."

"Are my foster parents still alive?"

"Yes. As far as I know." Cecilia pulled her blanket tightly around her knees. "Richard and Bernie were great. They took in countless kids over the years. However, they don't know anything. They weren't privy to details and names."

"There has to be someone."

"Well, you'll have to apply to the HSE. That's the Health Board here. They must have the original cert. St Theresa's handed over all their files when they closed. Maybe she named the father on that but I doubt it."

"Please help me, Cecilia." He knelt down so that he as at her eye level. "Please. There has to be something else."

The old lady paused, thinking. "Well, her best friend was called Viola Collins. She lives in Bishopstown now."

"Where?" His eyes lit up.

"It's not far from here. I can ring someone and get the address." Cecilia made a Sign of the Cross again. "God bless you but that's all I can do. I'm sorry, but I can't help you any further."

Madison was talking to Ross when he got into the car half an hour later.

"No, Ross. I can't do it. I won't be back in time. No, no. I'm fine. We just took a small break. Yes, yes, to work on things. Yes. I'll call you when I'm back in London. Get Angelica to postpone *Vogue*. She knows Anna Wintour. Right, see you soon. Bye."

She threw her phone to one side. "What happened?"

He put his head in his hands. "I have to visit someone."

She took his hand in hers. "Are we going there now?"

"Yes."

"Who?"

"Her best friend. Viola."

Chapter Forty-three

"*Pauline Harte! You get down here right now and tidy up this mess!*"

Viola stood at the bottom the stairs, shouting at her middle daughter.

"*Pauline! I know you can hear me! Move it!*"

She swept back into the kitchen and wrinkled her nose at the debris on the table. How could she keep on top of housework and work full-time at the school? She loved her children but they were bone lazy. As for her husband? He was a lost cause too.

She had just turned forty-two but she felt a lot older. Two kids, close in age, made the last few years a blur. Now the eldest, a boy called Rob, was about to start his final exams at school. He was a quiet boy who liked GAA and science. He hoped to attend the local university and study chemistry so he was working hard to get enough points for entry. Pauline, her sixteen-year-old daughter, was proving difficult to manage. Things were so much easier in her day – they didn't have phones and Snapchat and fake tan. Pauline was the worst for staining the shower with orange streaks prior to a night out. Three weeks before, she had caught her with a bottle of vodka stashed in her bag and all hell had broken loose.

A disgruntled Pauline appeared and started to stack the plates and cups.

"This is not a hotel, young lady. If you have breakfast, you clean up afterwards."

"Rob never cleans up after himself," complained Pauline with a scowl. "I suppose it's because he's your favourite."

"He is in his eye!"

"He is so! He gets away with murder."

"Well, he can fold the clothes later when they're dry."

"Fold? Are you joking me? He couldn't fold to save his life." She emptied mugs of cold tea into the sink. "You promised me money to buy those jeans."

"Money? How much?"

"Eighty euros."

"For jeans?"

"Yeah! I told you ages ago."

"Well, you'll have to earn it. I'm not made of money."

"This is so unfair. You said I could and now I can't."

"I said you can if you earn it." Viola threw her eyes to heaven. "I have to go out and I expect this place to be tidy when I get back, okay?" She turned around to put her phone in her bag. "I'm sick of living in squalor. You have an hour to sort out this place or else."

"Fine." Pauline stuck out her tongue at her mother's back as she left the kitchen.

Viola got to the front door and took her scarf off the hook. Winding it around her neck, she slipped on her black jacket and opened the door. Walking out into the winter sunshine, she bashed straight into a tall man in a beanie hat.

"Oh, I'm sorry!" she said automatically.

"Not at all," he said in a British accent.

There was a girl behind him, all dressed in black.

"Can I help you?" she asked.

"I'm looking for Viola Collins."

She blinked. "Viola Collins?"

"Yes." He took off his hat and his blonde hair tumbled out. "I'm here to talk about Mary. Mary Kennedy."

She stepped backwards. "Who?"

"May we go inside? I need to talk to you."

Pauline was sitting at the table, texting her best friend when she heard the front door slam.

"*Shit*," she said, dropping the phone, jumping up and shoving some plates into the dishwasher. She heard the front room door open and close and some muffled voices.

Curious, she ventured out into the hall and put her ear against the door. There was man speaking but she couldn't make out what he was saying.

Suddenly the door opened and she fell backwards.

"Pauline!" It was her mother. "Can you make a pot of tea? There's three of us."

She was about to suggest that Rob do it when she saw her mother's face. She looked deathly pale and on the verge of tears.

"Okay."

The door closed again.

She filled the kettle and switched it on. Then she placed three mugs on a tray along with some milk and sugar. Opening the biscuit tin, she saw a few Jaffa cakes and some Rich Tea which she scattered on a plate.

When the tea was ready, she carried the tray to the front room and kicked the door gently.

"Mam? Let me in."

The door opened and Viola took the tray from her hands. "Thanks," she said, pushing the door closed again.

Pauline huffed in annoyance. She wanted to see who was in the room. Why all the secrecy?

She met a sleepy-looking Rob coming down the stairs.

"Mam wants you to sort out the washing,' she said bossily. "And don't make your usual mess in the kitchen. I've been cleaning it all morning."

Rob gave her the finger and walked past.

"*Rob!*" she shrieked. "You're dead if you don't. Mam said."

Viola poured some tea with a shaking hand. "Milk? Sugar?"

Caspian didn't even answer. Madison, who had removed her hat and glasses, shook her head. "Just black for me, thanks."

"You're Madison Ryan, aren't you?" Viola looked up. "My Pauline has a poster of you on her wall."

"Yes." She smiled. "*Aw*, that's sweet."

"And you." She turned to Caspian. "You're a singer in a band. I can't remember the name but I've seen you on the telly."

"Yes. My name is Caspian Cole."

Viola didn't react. Instead she stared at him. "Why are you here? I mean, this is a normal Saturday morning. I don't understand. Why are you asking about Mary?"

Caspian sat down on an armchair. "Mary was my mother. My birth mother."

Viola's eyes widened.

"I only just found out. I'm trying to find my real father."

"You're Mary's boy?" she whispered.

He nodded. "I appreciate that this is a shock. Believe me, it's a huge shock for me too."

Viola stared at him dumbfounded.

"I visited Sister Cecilia."

"Cecilia?" she echoed.

"She gave me your address."

Viola bent her head and put her face in her hands. "I'm sorry, I can't believe that you're here and you're saying this. When Mary died, I pushed all of this out of my head."

Madison leaned forward beseechingly. "We need your help, Viola. You're the key. No one knows anything about Caspian's real father."

"Oh my God."

"Please." Caspian looked wretched. "Please tell me anything you know that might help."

"I don't know a lot." She felt breathless. Different memories flashed through her brain. Mary filling a vodka and coke. The tall Frenchman with the long hair and dark eyes. The smoky nightclub. Mary's face over hers the next morning.

"You were her best friend! She must have told you."

"I ..."

Caspian banged his fist on the table. "*Jesus!* This is my life, Viola. You've got to tell me."

"Please, I need to think ..."

"Did she write his name on the birth cert? Do you know?"

Viola shook her head. "She didn't. I was there when we registered the birth." Her eyes filled with tears. "We had to go to the registrar's office about a week after you were born. We couldn't do it at the hospital, you see. Being unmarried is complicated."

"You went with her? Where was he? Where was my father?"

"He wasn't on the scene." She started to cry. "Mary was devastated."

"She was?"

"Of course she was." Viola looked fierce. "Everything she did, she did for you. You must understand that."

"Did she give me a name?" Caspian looked deathly pale. "Did she choose a name for me that day?"

Viola started to shake. "Yes, yes, she did."

"What was it?"

"She called you Colm." She wiped the tears from her cheek. "After her grandad."

Caspian felt like getting sick. It was as if Viola's words had bounced off his mind and hadn't sunk in. He felt numb and removed from it all. It reminded him of an Emily Dickinson poem he'd read in school. How after great pain, the body goes into shut-down mode.

Now he got it. Now he understood.

"Do you have a photo of her?"

"Somewhere." Viola got up and went to a row of photo albums on the bookshelf. "Most of these are of the kids but I had one from my schooldays." She opened a blue one. "I'm sure it's this one." She riffled through a few pages. "There." She pulled out a photo from the see-through sleeve. "That's Mary."

Caspian took the photo from her outstretched hand and gazed at it. It was of a young girl smiling, her blonde hair blowing in the breeze. She was wearing a T-shirt and jeans, and looked young and carefree.

"That was taken on the day we got our exam results."

He didn't respond.

"She was thrilled because she got an 'A' in music."

Madison looked over Caspian's shoulder. "She was so pretty!" she exclaimed.

"Yes, she was. Imagine, she was only sixteen there. She always looked older."

Suddenly the door burst open and Pauline stumbled in. "Gosh, sorry! I was just wondering if you wanted more …" The words died on her lips. "*You!*" She pointed at Madison in shock. "*And you!*" She gazed at Caspian. Then her expression changed from disbelief to delight. "*Oh my God!*"

"Pauline!' Viola pushed her out the door. "Out! Now!"

"No, Mam. Let me in. I love Doctor Eckleburg. *Mam!*"

Viola closed the door and turned the key. Then she rested her head against it.

"Viola," Caspian began.

"Please." A solitary tear rolled down her cheek. "Please, give me a moment."

"I need to know, Viola. I need to know who I am."

"I understand."

"Did you know my father? Does he live around here?"

Viola didn't answer.

Madison walked over to her and grasped her arm. "I know this is a shock. I know it's difficult to think about Mary, but we need to know everything."

"I just need some time …"

"Of course." Madison gave Caspian a meaningful look. "Come on, Caspian. Let's go. We can come back tomorrow."

Caspian wiped his face with his sleeve. "Look, I'm sorry

for just turning up like this."

Viola turned around, her expression haunted.

Madison took Caspian's arm. "We'd love to talk to you again. When you're ready."

"Yes, of course." Viola was reeling.

Madison put on her hat and glasses. "Please keep this quiet. As you can imagine, the press hound us and this is very sensitive."

"Of course."

"Do you have a pen and a piece of paper?"

"Sure, give me a minute." Viola went out into the hall and ripped a page from the phonebook.

"*Pauline? Do you have a pen?*" she shouted.

Pauline burst out of the kitchen. "Give me a second." She opened her schoolbag and pulled out a bright-pink pencil case. "Here," she said to her mother. "Can I come in now?"

"No." Viola went back into the sitting room and closed the door.

"Let me give you my bodyguard's number," said Madison. "In case you remember anything."

She scribbled it down on the scrap of paper.

"Okay." Viola's eyes darted from Caspian to Madison. "I hope you understand. I need to think about this. I need some time."

"We understand." Madison pulled up her hood. "Thank you."

Chapter Forty-four

Pauline stared at her mother. "Why the hell were Madison Ryan and Caspian Cole in my house? *And why didn't you let me take a selfie?*"

Viola filled a glass of water and drank it thirstily.

"Mam? You have to tell me."

"I can't. Now, go upstairs. I need some time alone."

"Mam! This is the most exciting thing to happen ever. You have to tell me why they were here!"

"Pauline,' she said wearily. "Not now. Please go upstairs."

"*Fine!*" She stalked off and banged the door.

Viola took out her phone and googled 'Raphael Baptiste'. Hundreds of pictures appeared, some recent and some from years ago when he was flying high in Hollywood.

She focused in on a young Raphael holding his Oscar in the air. It was like a brown-haired Caspian.

She dropped her phone on the counter, ran out into the hall and up the stairs. Grabbing the pole for the attic, she hooked the latch and pulled open the trapdoor. The spring groaned as it unfolded and the ladder made its slow descent.

Pauline watched her suspiciously from the doorway of her bedroom.

"What are you doing now?" she asked.

"Going up to the attic."

"Well, I can see that." She rolled her eyes. "But why?"

Viola didn't answer. Instead she climbed the ladder and disappeared through the entrance.

She switched on the light and headed straight for the boxes stacked on the right-hand side. She pushed Christmas decorations out of the way, along with the barbecue and a tent. Deeper and deeper she went, until she was lying flat on her belly, under the rafters of the house. She grabbed a box marked 'Hen Night' and a plastic container filled with old photo negatives. Finally, she found what she was looking for. A small brown box, sealed with masking tape.

She yanked it out and sat up straight.

Pauline's head popped up through the trapdoor.

"Mam! You're all dust. Why did you crawl under there?"

Viola didn't answer. Instead, she picked up the brown box and made her way to the ladder once more.

"Stop asking questions," she said in a shaky voice. "Just help me carry this down."

Viola's husband came home for lunch. A builder by trade, he was working locally and fancied a sandwich made from last night's leftover beef. He found his wife sobbing in the kitchen, hunched over the sink.

"What's the matter, Vi?" he said immediately, rushing over to her.

"Oh, Brian. It's terrible. Just terrible."

"What's terrible?"

"Remember I told you about Mary? My friend?"

"The one who died?"

Viola nodded. "She had a baby. She gave it up."

"What do you mean?" He rubbed his temple.

"She gave him up for adoption."

"So?"

"That baby called to the house today. He came to find out about his mother."

"Vi, you look awful. Sit down." Brian steered his wife to a seat. "Why did he call here?"

"To find out about his real father. I know, you see. I'm the only one who does." She started to cry again.

Brian hugged her, horrified. "Don't be upset, sweetheart. It's okay."

Viola rubbed her eyes. "It brings up so many memories."

"Of course it does." He kissed her forehead. "So, who was the real father?"

"You'll never believe it."

"Try me."

"You must keep it top secret. It cannot leave these four walls."

Brian's face was serious. "I won't tell a soul."

"Jesus, that's a bit mad alright, isn't it?" Brian whistled.

"I know." Viola blew her nose with some kitchen paper. "I mean, we didn't know at the time that he would become so famous. Then she was killed and that was that. I mean, there was no choice but to leave sleeping dogs lie."

"He has no idea?"

"None."

"How are you going to tell him, Vi? No offense, but he may not believe you. Have you proof?"

"Nothing. Only the fact that he's the image of him."

"Christ."

"The poor fella is all up in a heap. I mean, he's desperate to know."

"And you're positive it was this Baptiste who did the job?"

"Positive. He stuck out like a sore thumb. She was drawn to him straight away with those looks and that accent. He took her back to his hotel room and that was that."

"You'll have to tell this Caspian."

"I know." Her face was grim. "But how?"

Caspian refused food and went straight to bed.

Madison stayed with him for a while, scrolling through Instagram and checking her emails. Bethany had called saying that it was all over the papers about their reconciliation trip to Cork. Old photos had surfaced of Caspian and groupies with headlines asking if she could ever trust him again?

Madison emailed back and told her not to comment on anything. It was all speculation and her private business. Ross called again, asking if she was coming back to London. She told him it would be a few days. He then asked her if it was true that she and Caspian had reconciled. Jax was thrilled at the prospect and so was he. She didn't reply.

She went for a shower and emerged in a towel.

"I need to talk to Viola again," Caspian said with his

eyes closed. "It's torture. I know that she knows."

"She'll call, baby. Just give her a chance." Madison rubbed her hair dry with a towel.

"I'd like to visit Mary's grave."

"Of course." She wound the towel into a turban and applied some moisturiser.

"Viola would show me where it is."

"I'm sure she would. Now, keep those eyes closed. I need to get dressed."

"Maddy, I've seen you naked countless times."

"Yes, but were friends now. It's inappropriate."

"Fine." He turned over and put a pillow over his head.

Viola texted late that night, suggesting that they call the next day around noon.

"She'll send her kids to the cinema," said Madison, reading the text.

Caspian sat up straight. "Do you think she'll tell me the truth?"

"Well, seems like she must have something to say."

He brought his knees up to his chin. "I have a strange feeling about this. I feel like my real father is alive somewhere and knowing his name will change my life forever."

"Well, it's definitely going to change your life," she said gently. "If he's alive, that is."

Caspian's face dropped. "Can I just have some time alone?" he asked, lying back and pulling the duvet over his body.

"Sure. I'll just pop across to Colin's."

"Don't say anything about this."

"I'm not even going to answer that." She shook her hair,

working out all the knots with her fingers. "I miss Mona. I miss being looked after. I mean, I can't style my hair by myself."

"See you later," said Caspian pointedly.

As soon as she closed the door, he sat up and picked up his phone. There were five missed calls from Prudence and three from Tommy. There was a voicemail from Fionn, asking about rehearsal and texts from Jax about Madison and their possible reconciliation.

He called his mother straight away.

"Caspian!" She sounded tearful. "I've been so worried."

"Everything's fine, Mum."

"Where are you?"

"Staying at a friend's place in Cork."

"Are you okay? I wish I could be there with you."

"I'm fine," he lied.

"Did Cecilia shed any light on things?"

"Not really."

"Oh." She sounded relieved. "When will you be home? Dad and I are beside ourselves."

"In a few days."

"Come and see us, darling. I'll cook something nice."

"I will."

"I love you."

"I love you, too."

"Come in," Viola said.

Caspian walked in and Madison followed. Todd stood outside, concealed by a large rowan tree in the garden.

"Brian, my husband, has taken the kids to Mahon Point Cinema. They'll be back around five."

"I appreciate that." Caspian took off his hat.

"I made some fruit cake and I've a pot of tea brewing."

"Lovely." Madison smiled at her.

"We might as well go into the kitchen."

They walked into the kitchen and took a seat at the table. There wasn't a speck of dirt to be seen and the floor gleamed from being newly mopped.

On the table there was a teapot, a bowl of sugar, a jug of milk, a plate of fruit cake, three mugs, and a brown box.

Caspian twisted his beanie hat around and around.

Viola poured three cups of tea and pushed the plate of cake towards them. "Help yourselves."

"Can you tell me more about Mary?" said Caspian, discarding his hat to the side.

Viola took a deep breath. "She was my best friend." She cupped her mug with her hands. "She was bright and funny, and she loved music."

Caspian's face tightened. "I always wondered about that. My parents didn't play an instrument yet I found it so easy."

"Oh, Mary didn't play an instrument. She couldn't afford lessons. But she could sing, my God she could sing. She'd often perform in the pub with Noel on a Sunday evening."

"What kind of songs?" asked Madison curiously.

"Oh, traditional ones. She was amazing at the *Sean Nós* as we call it – the Old Style Irish singing. However, she could sing all sorts – folk, pop, country. Her favourite was 'Willie MacBride'."

Caspian looked up. "I'm not familiar."

"It's a song about a young soldier in the First World War

who died when he was nineteen." She looked up. "The same age as Mary when she passed." She shuddered. "In this box, I have an old video tape of her singing it." She smiled sadly. "She won *Scór na nÓg* that year. The school made a copy of her performance for Noel. He was so proud of her."

"What's *Scór na nÓg*? I don't remember that in Dublin," asked Madison curiously.

"It was a talent competition for young people back in the day," explained Viola.

She opened the box. "When Noel died, the County Council came to clear out the house. I went over and gathered some things of Mary's. I seemed to be the only one who cared."

"How do you mean?" asked Caspian.

"Oh, Noel has a brother in Australia and I'm pretty sure Annette, Mary's mother, had a sister but I'm not sure. No one turned up at the funeral. I remember Mary taking about a rift. I'm not sure."

She took out a worn copy of *Pride and Prejudice,* a mix tape, random photos of Mary and Viola, a poster of the *Definitely Maybe* album cover, a mood ring, a video tape and a tatty teddy bear.

Caspian stared wordlessly. "Oasis?" he said, picking up the poster. "Was she a fan?"

Viola laughed. "A super fan. She adored the Gallagher brothers. Her favourite song was 'Live Forever'. She sang it constantly."

"And this?" He held up the book.

"She wanted to find a man like Mr Darcy. She was a real romantic."

He riffled through the photos, drinking in her face and

trying to imagine what she was doing when that moment was caught forever on film.

"That's not all." Viola reached into the box and retrieved a little box. "I found this when they were clearing out her bedroom."

Caspian took it from her hand and opened the lid. Inside was a blue name tag and a lock of blonde hair, taped onto a piece of paper.

"*Baby Kennedy, 23/5/96, Erinville Hospital.*"

A tear rolled down his cheek. "She kept it."

Viola nodded.

"My hair?"

"You had a shock of blonde hair when you were born."

Madison rubbed his shoulder. "Oh, Caspian. I'm so sorry."

"Can I see the video?" he asked, wiping his tears with his sleeve.

"Sure. We have an old VCR in the sitting room. I just need to plug it in."

The VCR was on a shelf above the Sky box and a small DVD player. Viola found the lead at the back and plugged it in at the wall. Switching on the television, she pressed the AV button and inserted the tape in the machine. They could hear a sound of winding tape and then a fuzzy screen appeared.

Caspian sat on the couch, clutching Madison's hand.

A blurry picture appeared which slowly came into focus. It was of a noisy crowd of children and a stage.

"That's the old GAA hall," said Viola. "It was packed with parents and kids. It was like *The X Factor* back in my day."

A woman walked onto the stage and asked the crowd to quieten down.

"Now," she said in her Cork accent, "we have a young

girl called Mary Kennedy singing 'Willie MacBride'. She will be accompanied by Denise Walsh on guitar."

The crowd roared in approval and a young black-haired girl came on stage and took a seat on a chair. She put her guitar on her knees and strummed to check if it was in tune. Then a blonde girl followed.

"Mary," said Caspian softly.

She bounded onto the stage and took the microphone from the lady who had introduced her.

Her blonde hair was tied in a ponytail and Caspian guessed that she was around fourteen years old. She was wearing a black top, jeans and boots. On her finger was the same mood ring he had seen in the brown box.

"This song is for my dad, Noel," she said in a soft voice.

The crowd cheered.

Denise played the intro, picking the strings gently with her finger. Then Mary started to sing.

Caspian watched, mesmerised as she told the tale of a young soldier called Willie MacBride who died in France during World War One. She closed her eyes as she sang the chorus, her lilting voice soaring over the melody of the guitar.

Madison felt shivers go down her spine.

Caspian never took his eyes off the screen. He stared at her in fascination. Then the song ended and Mary smiled. Taking a small bow, she did a pirouette and walked off stage, blowing kisses at the crowd.

"She was amazing, wasn't she?" Viola wiped a tear away. "She never stopped singing. I swear, I threatened to gag her a thousand times."

"May I keep that tape?" asked Caspian, stunned.

"Of course."

Caspian took a deep shuddering breath. "Thank you for showing me this. It's all so overwhelming."

"Yes, it is." Viola's expression was warm. "Mary was a beautiful person, Caspian. You are lucky to have had her as a mother."

"I didn't," he said bitterly.

"Oh, but you did." She got up and walked over to him. "You see, she loved you and always had you in here." She touched his chest. "She kept you in her heart."

He grasped her hand. "Tell me about my father, Viola. Was he married? *Please. I have to know.*"

She paused. "It's not easy."

"I don't care. Please tell me."

"I'm not sure if you'll believe me." She twisted her hands.

"How do you mean?" asked Caspian.

"Your father isn't just some Joe Soap from down the road." She looked up. "Your father is famous."

"What?" said Madison in surprise.

"This is why I'm addled. She met him when he was in Cork for an exhibition. They only spent one night together. Then he told her to have an abortion. I mean, we never heard from him after that."

"But if he was famous you must have known where he was!" said Caspian.

"Well, he wasn't famous at the time. But his grandad was a photographer or something and he came to Cork to open an exhibition at the Crawford."

"The what?"

"The art gallery here in Cork." Her expression softened. "You know, you look like him. I swear to God, you are the spit of him. *Jesus Christ.*"

Madison sat up. "Who is this guy? A singer?"

Viola shook her head. "No, he makes films. I used to call him the Ninja Turtle."

"*Who? Tell me who he is!*" Caspian almost shouted.

"Raphael Baptiste." She exhaled slowly. "I'll never forget that name. We rang him in France and everything, but he told her to get rid of the baby." She looked up. "To get rid of you."

Caspian was thunderstruck. "I'm sorry, what did you say?"

"I know, it's mad, isn't it? I mean, this is bizarre." She threw up her hands. "It's like when Paula Yates found out her real dad was that famous radio presenter Hughie Green."

Madison's mouth was open. "Raphael?" she said, astounded. She stared at Caspian and it all made sense. It was true. She was sure of it. He was a blonde version and just as arrogant. For months something had annoyed her and she couldn't put her finger on it. Now she understood. All that time, Caspian had reminded her of Raphael.

She gazed at him. "Caspian, this is incredible. I mean, it's destiny or something. Oh my God."

But Caspian wasn't listening. He stood up as though he'd been electrocuted and held up his hands. "*This is bullshit!*" he roared. "*You're messing with me. You're joking and you think this is funny. Who's my real dad then? A drug addict from the wrong side of the tracks? A married man? A priest? Who are you protecting?*" His face contorted in rage. "*Is this some kind of sick joke? Is it? Is it?*"

Madison sprang up. "She's not joking. She's not." She tried to hug him. "I believe her, baby. Seriously, as mad as it seems, it's true."

He shoved her aside. "How do you know? Just back off."

Viola stood up. "I've never been more serious. Yes, it seems unlikely but it's true. The fact that you're famous is strange, but maybe it's genetic. Maybe you were destined to be."

Caspian was stunned. He had always known he would be great. He had believed it since he was a small child. He had always accepted it as his destiny.

"Does Raphael know about Caspian?" asked Madison, pulling him down on the sofa next to her.

Viola shook her head. "He never knew she had the baby. Cecilia advised her to keep it quiet as it would complicate the adoption. He thinks she went through with the abortion."

Caspian stood up. "I'm sorry, but I think I'm going to be sick. May I use your toilet?"

Viola stood up in a panic. "Of course, it's out here. Follow me."

They left straight away afterwards. Caspian walked straight to the car, forgetting to wear his hat. His blonde hair gleamed as he got into the car. There was a flash, but Madison put it down to the winter sun reflecting off the car window.

She apologised to Viola as she left.

"Don't even think about it," Viola said kindly. "The poor man is in shock." She grabbed Madison's arm. "You have my number, don't you?"

"Yes, from when you texted last night."

"Give me a ring when he's calmer."

"I will."

Chapter Forty-five

"I can't go back to the apartment," said Caspian as the car sped along the road. "I can't meet anyone else right now."

"I know."

"I'd love a drink."

"You just got sick."

He glared at her.

"Fine! Well, we can't go to a bar. That's asking for trouble." She tapped John's shoulder. "Find an off-licence on the Sat Nav and take us there."

"No problem."

Caspian's knuckles were clenched and his body was rigid. His mind couldn't process anything.

Raphael. How could this be? How could fate be so cruel? He groaned. Not only had they already met, but he had tried it on with his wife. His father's wife.

John pulled up outside O'Donovan's Off-Licence and stopped the car.

"Can you get us a small bottle of whiskey?" said Madison. "Hurry."

He nodded and exited the car.

There was silence as they waited. Todd shifted in his seat and Madison stroked Caspian's lifeless hand. Then John returned.

"Just drive," she ordered. "It doesn't matter where."

"Of course." The car pulled out onto the busy road once more as Madison opened the bottle.

"Here," she said, handing it to Caspian. "Take a swig of this."

He accepted it gladly and gulped down a sizable amount. Then he coughed and almost threw up.

"Jesus, slow down." She patted his back.

"Do you think it's true?" he said suddenly, wiping his lip. "I'm sorry but it seems so far-fetched. It's just Viola seems so nice and normal. I don't see why she would lie."

Madison took a sip of whiskey. "You do look like him."

"So, you believe her."

"Yes, I do actually. She has no reason to lie."

"Don't you think it's crazy?"

"Yes, but life is crazy. Things like this happen all the time. Remember that story on Facebook that I showed you about the identical twins who were separated at birth?"

"No."

"They found each other by chance through a mutual friend. One lived in China and the other in Chicago. It was pure coincidence they saw each other's profile pictures and sought each other out. I mean, they didn't even know they had a twin. I read these kind of stories on Uberfacts all the time."

"Should I tell him?" He took another swig of whiskey. "I've no proof. He'll never believe it."

"Do you want to tell him?" she asked gently. "I mean, he need never know if that's what you want."

Caspian stared out the window.

"Still, look on the bright side. You'll be heir to millions if your singing career doesn't work out."

"Why wouldn't it work out?" he asked in surprise.

"I'm joking."

"I don't want anything from him," he said viciously. "Nothing."

"Caspian!"

"He abandoned Mary. He left her alone to sort out his mess."

"To be fair, he didn't know she kept the baby."

"Even still, he should have looked after her. All he did was tell her to get rid of a problem."

"Look, we don't know that for sure."

He gulped down some more whiskey and coughed. "Yes, we do. If he had been supportive, she would never have given me up."

Madison stroked his arm. "You don't know that. It was a one-night stand, Caspian. It was unlikely he would have done the decent thing. Don't be so harsh."

He glared at her. "Don't defend him, Maddy."

"I'm not. It's just he didn't have a chance. She did all this without his knowledge."

"She had no choice."

"We need to draw up an NDA as soon as possible ..."

"Leave it, Maddy." Caspian shook his head.

"We need a Non-Disclosure Agreement in a case like this! What if she sells your story to the tabloids?"

"She won't."

Madison sat back and said nothing. She could see that he was on the verge of tears so she didn't push it. She tried to imagine how she would feel if she found out something so life-changing. In her case, it would explain a lot of things – her cold relationship with her parents; the fact that she had nothing in common with them.

"We've reached the road to Dublin," said John. "Will I keep driving?"

Madison shook her head. "Take us back to the apartment," she said. "We need some time to think."

Caspian went straight to bed and pulled the duvet up over his head. "*Leave me alone*," he said forcefully.

Madison didn't argue. "I'll just pop over to Colin."

He didn't respond.

Todd opened the door for her and shielded her as she crossed the hallway. Then he knocked on the door.

Colin opened it up, his brown curls bouncing. "Hi, Todd!" he said with a big smile. "It's feeding time at the zoo, hence the food-stained T-shirt."

"Miss Madison would like to join you," Todd said.

Colin waved her in. "Todd?"

Todd shook his head and Colin shut the door.

"I'm just giving Orlando his dinner. Grab a chair."

Madison wrinkled her nose at the green concoction in the bowl. "What the hell is that?"

"Avocado mixed with cream cheese."

"Poor Orlando."

Britney the dog rubbed against her legs and barked.

"Yes, girl, I'll make you dinner now." Colin looked flustered. "She gets jealous when I feed Orlando first. I'm flat out, Madison. I mean, it's like having twins." He handed Orlando the plastic spoon and he started banging it on the tray of his highchair and laughing.

"So, did you two have fun today?"

Madison reddened. "We drove around a lot."

"Really?"

"It's safer, you see. When we go out in public, we're recognised."

Colin took some free-range chicken fillets out of the fridge. "So, where did you drive?"

"I'm not sure."

She watched him squirt some oil in a frying pan.

"So, will I cater for you tonight? I'm doing jambalaya."

"No, Caspian is still feeling a bit off."

Colin tried to mask his disappointment. "He'd want to get that sorted. He must have some gastro or something."

She shifted in her chair. "*Um*, Colin? Could I have a cup of herbal tea?"

She prayed that he would stop asking questions.

"Of course. I have camomile, nettle but I'm all out of ginger."

The next morning, Caspian rang Viola and asked if she would take him to see Mary's grave.

Madison opted not to go.

"I hate cemeteries," she said apologetically. "Cemeteries and clowns are my absolute nightmares. Do you mind?"

"It's fine." Caspian put his hat on once more. "Can I borrow John?"

"I suppose." Madison sighed. "Although, Colin did mention a trip to a spa." She bit her lip. "But I don't need to go at all."

Caspian rolled his eyes. "Look, I'm sure Viola could

drive if I ask her."

"But you wouldn't have blacked-out windows!" Madison looked shocked.

"It's fine," said Caspian. "No one will recognise me. What's the address here?"

"Todd, go and ask Colin for his address."

"Right away, ma'am."

Viola arrived in a battered old jeep. It had two seats and was filled with empty coffee cups, papers and loose nails.

"My husband took my car so we have to travel in this banger," she said apologetically.

"It's fine." Caspian put on his seatbelt. "I'm sorry for the way I acted yesterday."

"Don't even think about it."

"I got a huge shock."

"I know."

They pulled out onto the main road and were stopped at traffic lights almost straight away.

"They buried Mary near her mother," said Viola.

Caspian couldn't bear to think about it. Instead, he just watched life pass him by. Women waiting to cross the road with buggies and shopping bags. People getting off at a bus stop and others getting on. Lights changing from red to green and back to orange almost immediately. Car horns blaring and teenagers loitering around street corners.

Viola indicated right and he saw a sign for St Michael's Cemetery. His stomach flipped over and he felt the bile rise in his throat.

The jeep came to a halt. Viola switched off the engine and there was silence.

"What happened the night she died?"

Viola took a deep breath and grasped the steering wheel. "We were supposed to go to a nightclub in Kinsale. A friend said he'd get his dad's car and drive us down there. It's about half an hour from the city."

"Us?"

"Well, I was supposed to go but I was asked out on a date at the last minute. This guy called Martin."

"So Mary went on her own."

Viola nodded. "She was drinking a lot. She had been for months. She was grieving, you see. Trying to forget. The car lost control on a bad bend. She was killed instantly. The driver and the others survived."

"Was he over the limit?"

"No. It was speed, they said. Noel didn't believe the guards when they told him." She looked up with tearfilled eyes. "He was devastated."

"How old was she?"

"She had just turned nineteen."

He opened the door of the jeep. "Will you show me her grave?"

Viola nodded. "It's just down the right side."

The winter air was cold as they headed down a small pebbly path. They passed grave after grave, all inscribed with names and dates of all walks of life. Viola slowed down as they approached a simple white headstone. Caspian walked up to it and knelt down. It read:

Here lies Mary Kennedy
Born 1978
Died 1997
Rest in Peace

Caspian traced Mary's name with his finger. He was openly crying now and he took off his hat as a mark of respect. The wind blew his long blonde hair from his face.

Viola stood back and let him mourn. She hadn't been to the grave in years. She had visited a lot when she was younger. Then the kids came along and she was busy with work.

It had certainly fallen into disrepair. The tombstone was stained and there were weeds all over the place.

She put her hand on his shoulder and let him sob. She couldn't even imagine how he was feeling. To have his whole world turned upside down and to have never had the chance to know his family.

Caspian stood up and wiped his eyes. "We need to get someone down here to tidy this place up," he said shakily. "I'll sort that out."

Viola nodded. "That would be nice."

"Where are her parents buried?"

"Just over here." Viola led him to an overgrown grave with a black tombstone. Again, he traced the names with his finger: Annette and Noel Kennedy.

"Annette was a lovely lady," said Viola softly. "She had blonde hair like Mary, like you. I remember her fairy cakes when we were little. She'd ice them and put Smarties on top."

"And Noel?"

"Noel was a kind man," said Viola carefully. "He loved Mary and was good to her."

"But?"

"But nothing."

"Go on, you were going to say something."

Viola bit her lip. "Noel didn't like to face reality. He tended to bury his head in the sand. Mary had a lot to cope with at a young age."

Caspian winced.

"But she adored him and he adored her. They were happy, despite their troubles."

"Can you take me to where she lived? Her house?"

"I can show you the outside but that's all. There's a new family living there now. Social housing is hard to come by in Ireland so it was snapped up right away."

"That's fine." He put on his hat again. "Just take me there."

They walked off in the direction of the car and didn't notice the man squatting behind a giant tombstone in the distance.

Caspian got back to the apartment building two hours later.

Todd nodded at him. "Miss Madison is in here," he said, opening the door of Colin's apartment.

Madison didn't see him at first. She was laughing, rolling out pizza dough in irregular shapes. She had flour on her cheek.

"Savannah let me help her all the time when I stayed at her place," she informed Colin. "I learned how to make kale pizza."

"What's she like?" asked Colin curiously. "Word on the street is that she's a bit of a dragon."

"She's lovely," said Madison firmly.

Caspian cleared his throat. "Hi."

Madison looked up. "Hey! How did it go?"

Caspian forced a smile. "Fine. I'm just going to take a shower."

"Grand. Hope your tummy is better. I make the best pizza. Like a real Italian." Colin winked at him.

"I'll pop over in a minute." Madison gave Caspian a searching look.

"Okay."

He passed Todd again as he opened the door of the other apartment. Throwing his jacket on the couch, he went straight to the bedroom and flopped down on the bed. Viola had driven him to the street where Mary and Noel had lived. Their house, if you could even call it that, was a tiny affair with one window. He tried to imagine the inside but failed. Even though Viola had assured him that Mary had been happy there, he cursed fate for denying him the chance to buy her a bigger place. To spoil her and give her nice things. If she were alive now, he could make her life so much better. She wouldn't have had to work nights or weekends and she certainly wouldn't have been stuck for money. How he wished he could have helped her and taken the pain away!

Madison appeared in the doorway and rushed over to him. "How was it?" she asked. "Sorry I took so long. I didn't want to make Colin suspicious."

"Shit."

"Can I do anything?"

"No."

"Will you join us for dinner?"

"No."

"Caspian! You've got to eat."

He turned away. "Leave me alone. We should fly home tomorrow. Can you ask Clio to sort it out?"

Madison sighed. "Okay. Do you mind if I go to Colin's for pizza? Having made it and all."

"It's fine." He plumped his pillow.

"See you later."

"Bye."

Colin had made a pepperoni, a beetroot and cheddar, a Hawaiian and a prosciutto-and-rocket pizza. Val whistled when he saw them. "Who are we feeding exactly? Orlando can't eat pizza yet and Britney doesn't like Italian food."

"As if I'd give Britney carbs anyway, Val. I mean, really." Colin rolled his eyes. "Caspian doesn't want any and there's poor old Todd outside. He looks like a man who'd eat two of these."

"Fair enough."

"Wine?" Colin held up a bottle of red.

"I'll have a beer." Val saluted Madison and walked over to the fridge.

Madison smiled and sipped her wine. The smell from the oven was delicious and she felt her stomach rumble. She had texted Cliona to sort out flights and she was gratified to learn that she had secured airspace for a jet the next morning. Caspian didn't look well enough to be seen in public. She wondered should she book an appointment with a therapist in London. He would need it.

"We're heading back to London tomorrow."

"Oh?"

"Work." She smiled. "Thanks for your hospitality."

"Gosh, that's no problem. I'm sorry Caspian was so sick though. It can't have been very romantic."

"Oh, he's fine," she said airily.

"Can Todd join us? The poor man must be exhausted from standing outside the door."

"Why not?"

Chapter Forty-six

Cliona's alarm clock send a trilling sound through her bedroom. Groggily, she sat up and stopped it.

"Go back to sleep," murmured Alex, pulling her back under the duvet.

"I can't," she said, wiggling away. "Madison is due back in an hour and I have a list of things to do."

"Just half an hour more. I like having you close."

She put on her glasses. "I can't. Look, I know I'm quitting, but I have to maintain my impeccable standard until the last day."

He rested his head on the crook of his arm. "You're too honourable."

"Ross postponed the *Vogue* shoot so she needs a million things done before that. Plus, there's that concert coming up."

"Fine, fine." He rolled over. "But when you move in with me, alarm clocks are banned."

John dropped Caspian to his apartment first.

"Will you be okay?" Madison asked Caspian.

He shrugged. "I need some sleep."

She kissed his cheek. "I'll call you later."

"Fine." He got out of the car.

"*Caspian!*" she called. "You should meet the boys and rehearse. Try and get back to normal."

He didn't reply. He just walked away towards the entrance to his building.

"*Caspian, I'm worried about you!*" she called from the backseat. "You need to talk to someone."

The door closed and he disappeared from view.

Madison called Prudence right away.

"He's at home," she said. "I don't think he should be alone."

"I have my bag packed. Thanks for the call."

Madison went straight back to work. After a gruelling photo shoot, she was back in the studio recording a new track for a Christmas Charity album. She called Caspian constantly, but his answers became more and more monosyllabic. Prudence, despite being told to go back to Banbury, insisted on staying with him and it comforted Madison to know that he was being looked after.

She didn't know how to play things. They weren't a couple, yet she felt responsible for him. They had a history and she was one of the few who knew the truth.

Her daily phone conversations with Prudence told her that he had not revealed any information about Raphael to his parents. It was as if he'd gone into a trance. He refused to meet the band for rehearsals and didn't explain why. Cliona kept relating tales of how angry Alex was and how selfish Caspian was being, especially as their upcoming American tour was fast approaching.

Ross called, asking why Caspian had gone AWOL, complaining that both Jax and Tommy were constantly on the phone. He urged her to tell Caspian to make contact with people. It wasn't a joke – lots of people's careers depended on him.

"We're not officially a couple anymore," was her answer to everyone.

"*So why the hell did you go on a minibreak?*" Jax yelled.

After a week, Prudence went home. Caspian had insisted so she rang Madison and pleaded with her to keep an eye on him.

"He's like a ghost," she said on the phone. "Please call over as much as you can. I'll be back myself in a few days. I just don't want to crowd him."

That evening, Madison asked John to drop her over for a quick visit. Todd walked ahead of her and she used her keys to open the apartment door. What greeted her was the sound of deafening music and a dark room with the curtains closed.

"*Hello?*" she yelled over the din. It was the *Definitely Maybe* album by Oasis – she recognised Liam Gallagher's nasal twang. "*Hello?*" she yelled again.

Suddenly she saw someone huddled in the corner, rocking to and fro.

"Caspian?" She rushed over. "Caspian? What's the matter? Please talk to me. Caspian?"

He looked up, his eyes red from crying.

"Maddy," he said hoarsely. "Oh, Maddy!"

She knelt down and hugged him close to her chest as the opening bars of "Live Forever" began to play.

"This was her favourite song," he said, his voice muffled.

He felt lifeless in her arms and she soothed him as best she could. Suddenly his head moved upwards and he kissed her. Madison, caught by surprise, didn't stop him.

Todd discreetly went outside the door.

He had never kissed her like that – never once in their whole time together. She clung to his neck and didn't protest. He needed it. He needed to feel close to someone – she got that.

Then he stopped and buried his face in her neck. "Don't leave me," he whispered hoarsely. "I need you, Maddy. Please don't leave."

"I won't, " she said, kissing his forehead. "*Shhh*. I'm here. It's going to be okay."

She packed a bag of spare clothes and brought him back to her apartment.

Cliona gaped at them when they arrived. Caspian looked terrible – his face was drawn and haggard.

Madison put her finger to her lips. "Caspian's going to stay over for a few days. I'll just take him into my room. Can you change the sheets in the guest room?"

"I can't keep up with you two," said Cliona later, when Caspian had gone to bed. "One minute you're on, the next you're off."

"It's complicated." Madison felt weary.

"Maddy, I know you better than anyone. What's really going on?"

Madison felt an urge to tell her. She felt exhausted from

guarding the secret for so long. Cliona would understand. Cliona would know what was best.

"He … I …" She paused. "He's … oh, look. It doesn't matter."

"Right." Cliona looked puzzled. "Anyway, my last day is coming up. Have you found a replacement yet?"

"I'm working on it." In truth, she hadn't even started.

"Mum's birthday party is next weekend. I'm taking Alex home to meet them as my boyfriend. Imagine that!"

"That's nice."

A week later Bethany called to go through publicity shots with Madison, earmarking ones she wanted to publish. Caspian hadn't surfaced yet, preferring to stay in a dark room.

"So, *Empire* magazine want to do a piece on your new look. I can organise that for the New Year." Bethany tilted her laptop towards Madison. "What do you think of this shot?"

"That's fine." Madison, who was reading an article on Angelina Jolie, glanced at the photo on the screen. "I like my hair up actually." She popped a grape in her mouth.

Bethany's phone buzzed and she picked it up.

"*Fucking hell!*" Bethany gasped and Madison looked up.

"Are you talking to me?"

"It's an email from my source in the press."

Madison rubbed her eyes. "What does it say?"

Bethany scanned the content. "It says here that Caspian was adopted. It says that he's in Cork looking for his birth mother. It says that she's dead." Her eyes widened. "It says that Caspian was sold by the nuns!"

"Well, that's not true," said Madison.

"What's not true?"

"The nun bit."

"Wait, it gets worse. It says that Raphael Baptiste is his father and that it's going to press in the next few days." Bethany looked genuinely shocked. "This is Fake News, right? I mean, it's ludicrous."

Madison bit her lip. "I can't really talk about it."

Bethany sat up straight and became business-like immediately. "Madison, you've got to tell me! This has implications for you, with the movie coming up and everything. As far as the world knows, you and Caspian are an item."

"How did they find out?" wondered Madison aloud.

"Who?" she said abruptly. "The press? They know everything. You were followed obviously."

"But who told them about the adoption?"

"They have moles everywhere, Madison. You know that."

Madison stood up. "I need to tell Caspian."

"I'm going to ring Tommy and see what we can do. Maybe we can get a privacy order ..." She disappeared into the next room.

Madison got up and met Todd in the doorway. "Todd," she said, looking him straight in the eye, "I have to ask – did you speak to anyone about why Caspian and I went to Ireland?"

He shook his head. "I did not, ma'am."

"Of course you didn't. Sorry."

"*Tommy says to tell Caspian to turn on his phone!*" shouted Bethany down the hall.

Madison walked into her bedroom. Caspian was huddled under the duvet, his eyes wide open and staring into space.

"Caspian?" she whispered. "Caspian, something has happened."

He continued to stare.

"Caspian, the story is out. I don't know how, but Bethany just got a tip-off."

His eyes focused on her face. "What did you say?"

"Bethany got an email with the whole story. You, Mary, Raphael …"

He sat up and rubbed his eyes. "You must be mistaken. That's impossible."

"Tommy wants to speak with you." She handed him his phone and he switched it on. Within seconds, message after message came through. Missed calls, texts, and voicemails. Just as he was about to read one from his mother, his phone rang. He answered it automatically.

"Caspian! Thank Christ! I've been calling and calling." It was Tommy. "Why don't you answer your fucking phone?"

"What's wrong?" he said carefully.

"The shit has hit the fan, my son. Bigtime. Some journo is about to publish a piece about you and your birth mother. Your bloody birth mother. Why wasn't I told about this?"

"I just found out myself." He felt nauseated.

"This will go global, mate. Fucking global. We've got to get a gagging order."

"A what?" His voice was barely audible.

"We've got to apply for a privacy injunction. That can

take a few days. We've got to stall them."

"I can't deal with this now."

"Caspian, for fuck's sake. My job is to make these things go away. You made a right pig's ear of this, sunshine. You were followed since the moment you left London, thanks to your girlfriend."

"Shit."

"Yes, it is shit. I mean, Baptiste isn't just some nobody from down the road. He's powerful. This is public interest. I don't know if we'll be able to suppress it."

"It doesn't matter."

"Caspian! They're sitting on this story for twenty-four hours tops. We don't have much time."

Caspian hung up the phone. "I need to ring Mum," he said to Madison. "I need to warn her."

Madison rubbed his back. "What did Tommy say? Bethany wants to know what to do."

"Say nothing. It's none of her business. It's nobody's business."

She bit her lip. "All of this has implications, you know. I have to be careful."

"Why? It might damage your new career?"

"What do you mean?"

"Oh, you want to be a movie star. Now you're afraid to piss off Baptiste, am I right?"

"No! It's just with the première coming up and all."

"Just go away, Maddy. I need to figure out who sold me out."

"I'm not going away." Her eyes flashed. "I'm sleeping in the guest room for you. I'm here to support you and that's what I'm going to do."

"You just draw attention. I knew this would happen."

"I didn't tell if that's what you're insinuating."

"Don't be fatuous."

"Nor did Todd. He's devoted to me."

"Then who? Who's the leak? Cecilia?" His haunted eyes met hers. "*Viola?*"

"I don't know, Casp. You should've made her sign a non-disclosure. I told you!"

"Call her. Call her now."

"Fine. Jesus." She stalked out into the kitchen and he followed.

Bethany stared at Caspian in horror. "You look awful!" she blurted out.

"Mads, get rid of her, please." He took the phone from Todd's hand and dialled.

Bethany grabbed her coat and walked out. "Call me," she said to Madison. "Keep me in the loop."

"Hello? Hello? Viola? Yes, it's Caspian. Did you talk to the press? Well, someone did. You're the only one who knows. I don't care. It has to be you. They know everything. Absolutely everything. It's going to be published. Do you realise the implications of this? For me? For Baptiste? I didn't want him to find out. Whatever, don't ever call me again." He threw the phone onto the table.

It rang again almost immediately. "Don't answer it," he ordered.

"You can't ignore her!" Madison picked up the phone and accepted the call.

"Tell Caspian that he is wrong," said a shaken Viola. "I would never try and make money from my friend's misfortune. I can't believe he'd accuse me of it."

"*Hang up the fucking phone! It's probably bugged!*" he roared.

"Sorry, Viola. Sorry." Madison hung up.

"What are we going to do now?"

"*I don't know!*" he shouted. "*I need some air!*"

"Don't go out. You'll be followed." She opened the curtain and gasped. "Look, there's a group of photographers outside already."

He kicked a chair. "She cashed in on this, Mads. I can't believe it."

"Don't go outside. They'll eat you alive."

But Caspian had left.

"Todd! Get him back in here. I need to call Jax."

Todd nodded and followed Caspian out into the hall.

"Miss Madison needs you,' he said, grabbing Caspian's arm and forcibly hauling him back into the apartment.

"Shut the door, Todd," ordered Madison. "I need to figure out what to do."

Viola stared at her husband. "I presume it wasn't you."

He made a face. "What do you think?" He turned down the television.

"Then who?"

Pauline passed by and grabbed some Celebrations from the tin. "*Yum*, I love the Mars ones," she said happily. "Can you change the channel, Dad?"

Viola stared at her daughter. "Are those new jeans?" she asked with a sinking heart.

Pauline blushed. "These things? God, no. They're ancient."

"Pauline ..."

"They are! I got them in Penney's ages ago."

Viola knew she was lying. She could see it on her face.

"Pauline, this is serious. You have to tell me the truth."

"About what?"

"Did you speak to anyone about our visitors?"

"What visitors?"

"*Stop this playacting!*" roared Brian. "*Answer your mother!*"

Pauline shifted uncomfortably on the seat. "Well, this man walked me home from the shop last week. He said he was Caspian Cole's PR manager. He told me that he wanted to assess damage limitation or something? I didn't really understand."

"What?" Viola felt weak.

"He said that sensitive information about Caspian was about to be leaked and he wanted to know exactly what people knew so he could prevent it."

"But you didn't know anything, right?"

Pauline blushed. "Well, I heard you and Dad talking in the kitchen. I saw your search history on your phone." She looked sheepish. "You're right. He's the image of that director fella."

"Please tell me you didn't say any of this."

"Why?" Pauline looked worried. "That guy was so nice and he was trying to help."

"No, he wasn't."

"I just told him about Mary and that French guy. I said he came over for some exhibition. I didn't know the year but he said he'd figure that out. That's all. Then he gave me one hundred euros and told me that he'd take care of it." She looked at her parents. "I thought I was helping, Mam. I promise."

"*You accepted cash off a stranger?*" Brian banged his fist on the coffee table. "*Have you lost your mind?*"

"I needed the jeans and Mam wouldn't give me the money."

Viola got up and walked into the kitchen, leaving the raised voices behind. She would have to call Caspian back and tell him that it was all her fault.

"You need to find Raphael. He needs to know."

Madison stroked Caspian's hair as he sat immobile on the couch.

"No."

"The press know everything, Caspian. My guess is they're preparing the story as we speak. Tommy can't possibly prevent it now. Even if he gets an injunction, it will only contain it here. The law only applies to England and Wales. I guarantee it will be on Twitter within minutes."

"I don't want to see him. He's not even in my train of thought."

"Listen, like it or not, he's a part of you. You have to face this. Talk to him and walk away. At least spare him reading about it in a newspaper."

"No. Tommy will stop this. The papers won't risk being sued. They don't have proof."

"Caspian!"

"No, Maddy. Let it go."

Tommy called over that night. "It's a fucking nightmare," he said furiously. "They're crawling all over it. My man on the inside said they've checked records at that gallery and it verifies Baptiste's whereabouts that summer."

"That's not enough."

"It's pretty circumstantial, mate. Not to mind the fact that you're the image of him."

Madison drummed her fingers on the table. "Can we stop it breaking?"

Tommy shook his head. "I don't think so. If it's uploaded online on a server outside of Britain, it's unstoppable. It's too big not to publish. I mean, they'll risk being sued – it's not libel if it's true."

"But it's an invasion of privacy," protested Madison. "It's a sensitive matter."

"So? That's what the press do. Bring personal stories of the rich and famous to the masses under the guise of public interest."

Caspian shrugged. "Then let's face the storm. Karma is a bitch. Baptiste will have to face his past and maybe that's a good thing."

Madison shook her head. "You're not thinking straight. You don't want this story getting out. It's traumatic enough without millions of people getting involved. Can you imagine the headlines? The comments? The tweets? The discussions on daytime TV?"

Tommy started to pace the room. "We'll have to release a statement asking for consideration at this troubled time." Suddenly he brightened. "You know, this could work to our advantage. I mean, publicity is publicity after all. I wonder if we could angle the story to coincide with the American tour. Have you any songs that we could market to reflect this revelation? Remember how Justin Timberlake released a song about cheating after he and Britney split? It went down in history." He clapped his hands together.

"The fans would eat it up."

Caspian stared at him in horror.

Madison stood up. "We'd like you to leave, Tommy. We'll be in touch."

"Hear me out ..."

"*Get out.*" She raised her chin. "*Now.*"

Chapter Forty-seven

It took two days for the story to break. It gave Caspian time to warn his parents and his friends. First, he rang Prudence and George and asked them to come to his apartment. There, he told them the full story with Madison by his side.

Prudence's eyes widened when he revealed Raphael's involvement. "I always knew you were special," she said, amazed. "So talented and such charisma."

"I just want you to know that nothing has changed." He hugged them both. "You're my parents and that's it. I don't want anything from anyone else."

Caspian called a band meeting and explained why he had been so distant of late. He related the story in a monotonous voice, only breaking slightly when he described his mother. Ethan got up straightaway and hugged him. Fionn followed suit and finally, Alex.

"I'm so sorry," said Ethan with a white face. "That's heart-breaking, mate."

"Are you going to tell Raphael?" asked Fionn. "I mean,

the poor guy has no idea."

Madison grasped Caspian's hand in comfort.

"No," said Caspian definitely. "I don't want to meet him or even try and have a relationship with him. He left Mary alone – he expected her to deal with everything on her own. My allegiance is to her memory, not to him."

"Christ, I think it's a bit harsh to let him read about it," said Alex. "Come on, Caspian. That's not right."

"I'm not engaging with this story and I'm asking all of you to do the same." He looked up. "If you're asked, which you will be, say you have no comment. If you're followed, no comment. Tommy wants to release a statement but I'm not doing that."

Fionn looked at Ethan with a worried expression.

"Doctor Eckleburg is about music and should only be about music. Not me or my past or Raphael Baptiste. That's the end of it."

"Baptiste will probably sue," said Alex sensibly. "I would."

"That's his prerogative." Caspian regarded them all steadily. "Now, we should practise. How about tomorrow at mine?"

"Tomorrow?" echoed Fionn in disbelief.

"Life goes on." Caspian stood up. "Now, if you'll excuse me, I need to lie down."

Madison showed them to the door.

"He's got PTSD or something," said Fionn in an undertone. "This is crazy, Maddy. He can't just get on with things."

"I know," she said, her brow furrowed. "He won't listen. Tomorrow the world is going to wake up to this and all hell will break loose. He can't hide from it."

"Who sold him out?" asked Alex.

"It doesn't matter." She sighed. "It's awful for me too. I mean, I have to walk the red carpet with Raphael in the new year."

Ethan gave her a hug. "You've been great, Maddy. Thanks for looking after him. It can't be easy."

"He needed me," she said simply.

"So, are you two an item again?" asked Fionn.

She shook her head. "Just friends."

"Right." Fionn looked dubious. "We'll call you tomorrow."

"Sure." She pulled at Alex's sleeve. "Tell Clio that if she has time to write down all my quirks it would be a great help for her replacement."

"Seriously?"

"Yes," she said in surprise. "She owes me for calling my dad. He's going to let her go on location with him after Christmas."

"Bye, Maddy," said Alex, laughing.

Raphael and Isabelle spent the day in Paris with Agathe, Raphael's mother. She had organised a lunch to celebrate her birthday and had insisted that the whole family attend. After some coffee and petits fours, Raphael kissed his mother's cheek and he and Isabelle headed back home to Amiens. Two hours later, the car drove down the tree-lined road towards the main gates of their house.

Suddenly the car came to a halt.

"*Putain!*" shouted Raphael, who had fallen forward. He held up his arm automatically to shield Isabelle.

"*Monsieur, il y a un problème,*" said the driver, pointing to the crowd of reporters and photographers outside the gate.

Isabelle rubbed the condensation from the window. "*Whoa!* What's this about?"

"*Allez!*" said Raphael with a steely expression. "Keep going!"

The driver pressed the accelerator and the car started to wade through the crowd. Cameras flashed and there was lots of shouting and elbows on the window panes.

"*N'arrêtez pas, Pascal!*" Raphael shouted.

The car kept moving slowly and the shouts got louder.

"*Papa ... Caspian ...*" was what they heard.

"What's happening?" asked a frightened Isabelle. "Raph, I'm scared." She rubbed her belly protectively.

"I don't know," he said wildly. "I have no idea."

The large gates opened and the car went through. One journalist got through too and ran alongside the car. "*Have you any comment?*" he shouted through the window.

"*Stop!*" Raphael ordered Pascal. He opened the door, got out and grabbed the man. "*Get the fuck off my property!*" he roared. Then he dragged him by the lapel of his jacket to the gate. He opened the pedestrian entrance and threw the man out and onto the ground.

"Do that again, and I'll have you arrested."

"Come on, Raph! You must have some comment," said one balding man with a Dictaphone.

"Comment on what?" Raphael asked angrily.

"Your child."

"What do you mean?" His face went magenta. Surely the clinic was confidential ...

"Your son, matey!"

"Fuck off!" Raphael stalked off and got into the car.

"Are you okay, honey?" asked a concerned Isabelle. "I

thought you'd kill that photographer."

"I'm fine." He tapped Pascal's shoulder. "Drive."

The housekeeper was waiting for them in the hallway.

"Monsieur Baptiste," she said, "you have a visitor."

"What?" He strode into the sitting room and came to a halt. "Bertie?"

"Hello, Raph."

"I thought you were in New York."

"No, I was in London. I flew in this morning."

"But why?"

"You'd better sit down."

Isabelle walked in. "Bertie!" she said in delight. It's so good to see you."

They embraced.

"Is it possible that you look even more delightful?" he said, kissing her pale cheek.

"Bertie!" said Raphael sharply. "Why are you here?"

Isabelle sat down on a chaise longue.

"Have you seen the news today?"

"No, I never watch television. You know that."

"Have you checked your phone?"

"No, we limit cell-phone use around the baby."

"Yeah, he never lets me use my phone," said Isabelle with a pained look. "I just read books now which is amazing as I was a big Instagram girl in my day."

"I thought that might be the case," said Bertie. "That's why I flew over here."

"What? Why?" Raphael ran his fingers through his hair in confusion.

"Well, old chap. There's a defamatory story circulating about you. It broke this morning."

"Defamatory? In what way?"

"Apparently you abandoned a young girl who was pregnant with your baby."

Raphael went rigid. "What did you say?"

Isabelle's hand flew to her mouth. "What?"

"Oh, there's all this poppycock about adoption and abortion, but the most ridiculous part is they're naming that singer as your son."

"Singer?"

"The one that got drunk at my party. Remember? He kissed Isabelle."

Raphael raised himself up to his full height. "*What?*"

"That blonde guy?" Isabelle's eyes widened.

"Exactly. They'd print anything these days. The gall of them. Gutter journalism."

"Which paper? Where?"

Bertie looked sympathetic. "It's all over the place, Raph. It's trending on Twitter. I don't think anyone will believe it."

"Believe what exactly?"

"Here." Bertie handed him a newspaper with the headline: **ABANDONNÉ!**

Raphael threw the paper away in disgust. "Where did this come from? That singer? Is he trying to cash in on my fame?"

"Well, he's famous enough in his own right," said Bertie fairly. "You should read it. It gets more outrageous by the second. That you met this girl in Ireland when you opened an exhibition and spent the night with her in a hotel."

Raphael's head shot up. "*What?*"

"Then you left for France and she gave the child up for adoption."

Raphael picked up the paper again with a shaking hand. "Where did you read this?"

"A couple of paragraphs down." Bertie laughed. "I mean, what is the world coming to? They talk about 'a source'. That means it's untrue. I mean, why they even bothered printing it is beyond me."

Raphael scanned the article, his face pale.

Isabelle watched him closely.

"Are you okay, honey?" she asked. "You look awful."

Raphael didn't respond. Instead he kept reading, a muscle moving in his cheek. When he had finished, he looked up.

"This is rubbish. Forget it."

Isabelle got up, grabbed his arm and forced him to look at her. "What is it? Raph? Talk to me."

"My only concern is you and our baby," he said vehemently. "You don't need stress like this. Leave this to me."

"Hey, now. I'm not some dumb Yankee." Isabelle's legendary temper started to surface. "Tell me what the hell is going on!"

"There's nothing going on."

Bertie led Isabelle back to her chair. "Sit down, my sweet. Don't be upset." He turned to Raphael. "You look like death, old boy. Don't give this a second thought. Stories like this are easy to quash. It's libel."

"I'm not sure ..."

"Of course it is."

"I don't want this now, not with the baby coming."

"I have the number of the best lawyer in London. Let me sort this for you. You should sue and put the money

from the damages in a trust fund for the new addition."
Bertie clapped him on the back. "Chin up. A lot worse could happen. Now, let's have some lunch. I'm peckish after my journey."

When they had finished, Isabelle went to lie down.

Bertie sipped his espresso and regarded his friend.

"Cheer up! You've weathered worse over the years."

Raphael shook his head. "No, no. You don't understand. Bertie, I did meet a girl. I did sleep with a girl. A long time ago."

Bertie laughed. "I'm sure there were many."

"*No!* In Cork. When I opened that exhibition. She told me she was pregnant. I told her to terminate it."

"What?"

"There was a girl." He rubbed his eyes. "She was called Mary."

"My Lord." Bertie picked up the paper. "Are you saying that this could be true?"

"I don't know." Raphael's expression darkened. "No."

Bertie stared at the picture of Caspian and then looked at Raphael.

"Did you know she kept the baby?"

He shook his head. "No."

"Then this Caspian could be yours."

"No! Are you crazy? It would be too much of a coincidence. It's not possible."

"I don't know, Raph. Look at Oedipus and Laius? That was destiny at its most tragic. Fate brought them together, as unlikely as it seemed."

"Forget it. It's false."

Bertie looked at Caspian's picture again. "He does look like you."

"Not really. He's tall and his hair is similar to mine. Someone decided to link us to sell newspapers. That's all. Now, keep this quiet. Isabelle must be kept away from all of this."

Bertie put the paper on the coffee table. "You know that's impossible. You must tell her."

"No."

"It happened long before she met you. She needs to know."

Raphael crumbled a biscuit in his big hand.

"I also think you should prepare a statement," continued Bertie.

"What? Are you joking?"

"No, I'm not. It will be expected. Remember when you went into rehab that time? We did it then."

"I've nothing to say."

"Staying silent will only exacerbate things. You have the première coming up."

"I'm saying nothing because I know nothing. All they have are rumours. There's no proof. Don't talk to anyone, Bertie. I don't want this to leave this four walls."

"What do you take me for?"

"Now, get me that lawyer's number. I'm going to make them wish they'd never been born."

Chapter Forty-eight

Caspian asked the band to meet him at his apartment. Hordes of photographers followed the car as John drove off down the street. Todd went with him for protection at Madison's insistence. When they reached his apartment ten minutes later, they were greeted by even more of the media together with fans.

"*Caspian! We love you, Caspian!*" screamed one girl with a banner.

"*Caspian, have you any comment?*" A journalist pushed forward.

"*Caspian, have you spoken to your new dad?*" asked another.

"*Caspian, is it true your mother sold you?*" asked a small man with a hat.

Caspian stopped and howled. Grabbing the man by the neck, he shoved him violently backwards. "*Shut the fuck up! Shut up!*"

Todd pulled Caspian back. "Don't do that, sir."

"*Let me go!*" he shouted. "*He deserves it!*"

Todd calmly yanked him away and, using his massive

bulk, he pushed through to the doors of the building. Once inside, he released Caspian.

"No violence, sir. That was the brief."

"From whom?"

"Miss Madison, sir."

Caspian jabbed the button for the elevator. "*If I want to kill someone, I will! Just back off!*"

Todd let him rant and accompanied him into the elevator.

The apartment was sparkling clean and someone had ignited the fake log fire.

Caspian went straight to his piano. It felt like he hadn't played in years. Lovingly, he trailed his fingers along the keys, playing C and then G. All the emotion of the past few weeks was pent up inside him and he felt like he was going to burst. Sitting on the stool, he broke into Beethoven before switching to Chopin. Closing his eyes, he played and played, the thunderous sound of the music echoing through the apartment.

He didn't notice the rest of Doctor Eckleburg arriving. He didn't stop until the very last note had been played.

Fionn cleared his throat to announce their presence.

"How are you holding up?" he asked.

Caspian opened his eyes. "I think we should start with 'Charisma'. It gets the crowd on side."

"Sorry, what?" Alex looked confused.

"On the tour. We need to plan our set list. I also have a new song for you to listen to. It's in its infancy but I think it has potential."

"Caspian, we can't go on like nothing has happened, mate." Ethan stepped forward. "You've got to talk about this."

"No, I don't actually." His eyes glittered. "All I want is to get on with my life."

Caspian refused to go back to Madison's that night. He had tons of lyrics and notes floating around in his head and he needed to work. It felt nice to connect with his piano again. Lost in his music, there was no sense of reality. Mary's image filled his mind and he felt inspired. He would write an album for her – he would immortalise her forever in his work.

Madison predictably got angry.

"This is no time for you to be alone!"

"I'm fine."

"Caspian, I'm coming over."

"Don't."

"I am."

"Maddy! I need to write. You can't stop talking and you distract me. I'll see you in the morning."

"What about Todd?"

"I'm sending him home."

"*Caspian!*" she yelled, but he hung up the phone.

Madison called Prudence and George and they drove down from Banbury straight away.

Caspian groaned when he saw them on the monitor. "Christ."

Prudence burst into the apartment and hugged him close.

"I've been following the story all day, sweetheart. It's dreadful all the things they're saying."

"I don't want to talk about it."

"Caspian!"

"I'm working, Mum. Please. I need to be alone."

She started to cry. "I feel like you're going to do something silly. I'm worried."

"I won't."

"Has that Baptiste man been in touch?"

"I don't know and I don't care."

"Caspian! This isn't going to disappear. You'll have to face it."

"No," he said simply. "You see, there's no need at all for me to face it. He has never been a father to me so I don't need him now. I'm only interested in Mary – in honouring her memory."

"Caspian," said George, "I think you should meet him."

"Why? So he can show me how to play football and teach me to shave? It's too late, Dad. That ship has sailed. We don't need each other."

"Will you come and have dinner with us?"

"No."

"Caspian, you need company at a time like this."

"I just want to write, Mum. Honestly. That's when I'm happiest. When I'm playing my piano."

"I'll ring you later then."

He ushered them out the door. "You do that. As far as I'm concerned, nothing has changed. You're my parents. That's all I need."

Prudence rang Madison from the car. "We've booked into a hotel down the road. I have to be close by."

"Great. He's being really weird, isn't he?"

"Oh, I googled all of this. It's a typical reaction. He wants to continue as normal and block it out. Of course, it will all come out eventually and I plan to be right there when it does."

"How do you feel about it?"

Prudence paused for a moment. "You know, it's a relief. I've guarded this secret for so long and now it's out in the open."

"He loves you so much."

"I know." She smiled sadly. "He'll always be mine."

"Raph?" Isabelle shook him awake. "*Raph, wake up!*"

He opened his eyes.

"I think you should see this." She held up her laptop. It was an article about Bertie's party and how Raphael had punched Caspian.

He sat up straight. "How did you come across that trash?"

"Mom called and told me to go online. So, I did."

"*Putain!*"

"It's fine. Google sends me an alert when my name is mentioned anyway." Her green eyes were warm. "He's your son, isn't he?"

Raphael shook his head. "No. It's preposterous."

"I think he might be. You know, he looks like you."

"This is my child," he said, holding her bump. "This is my legacy. I'm not interested in some tabloid lies."

"Raph," she said gently. "Did you meet a girl in Ireland that time?"

He glowered at her.

"Did you sleep with her?"

His brown eyes met hers and she knew the answer.

"Then you've got to face this. It's too coincidental."

"No." He sat up and turned his strong back to her.

"What if it's true? What if this guy is your son and you deny him. I mean, he's a half-brother to my baby in here."

"Please, Zsa Zsa. Don't."

"You know what you've got to do." She got up and wrapped her robe around her.

Cliona offered to stay on until the Caspian affair settled. Madison hugged her fiercely.

"You've no idea what this means to me," she said.

"Well, my first job was assisting on Doctor Eckleburg's new music video but that's been postponed now."

"I'm so busy, Clio. Those few days in Cork have set me back so much. Ross is on my back to get into the studio, I have rehearsals for that show in the O2 and that *Vogue* shoot has been rescheduled."

"I'll sort things." Cliona took out her phone. "I'll just liaise with Bethany."

Madison exhaled slowly. Cliona's presence was calming and reassuring. She felt like she had been carrying everything for so long. Caspian had refused to leave his apartment so she had organised a timetable for people to call and check up on him. Each member of the band, Prudence and George, Jax and even Tommy had a slot. All the reports were the same. Caspian didn't want to talk about anything but his music. Madison herself called as often as she could, but there was so much to do and so little time. She also wanted to distance herself slightly, as she didn't want to give him the wrong impression. They were friends now. Nothing more.

About a week after the story broke, she dropped in on her way back from the gym. Caspian was sound asleep on the sofa, his blonde hair greasy and unkempt. He had stubble too and she was pretty sure he was wearing the same clothes she had seen him in a few days before.

He looked peaceful as he slept. His chest moved up and down rhythmically and his long legs were strewn casually over the edge of the couch.

There were empty pizza boxes everywhere along with beer cans and ashtrays filled with joint butts. Walking over to the piano, she saw sheets and sheets of music with notes crossed out in pencil. Judging by the amount of sheets, she guessed there were at least a dozen songs in the pipeline. Bending down, she picked up one entitled 'I Wish'. There were lyrics scribbled along the edges of the paper and most were indecipherable. One line stood out and she felt her eyes fill with tears.

"*I wish I could tell you how I feel,*

Will it be when in front of God I kneel?"

"Oh, Caspian," she whispered. "I'm so sorry."

Someone tapped her on the shoulder and she jumped.

"What are you doing?" He rubbed his eyes and stretched.

"Nothing." She put the sheet back on the piano. "Just checking to see that you're okay."

"I'm fine."

"You need a shower."

"Really?" He sauntered over to the kitchen.

"Yes! A beards doesn't suit you. This place smells. When did you last brush your teeth?"

"Stop nagging, Mads. You're not my girlfriend anymore."

"I still care about you."

"Really?"

She ran up to him and started hitting his chest. "*Snap out of it, Caspian! I can't deal with this. I've had enough, okay? I'm exhausted from worrying about you and organising everything. You have to sort this out!*"

He grabbed her wrists and held her at arm's length. "Stop, Maddy."

"No!" She was openly crying now. "This hasn't been easy for me too. I can't cope with it anymore. I come here, after a long gruelling workout, to find you living like a hobo and ruining your good looks."

He smiled slightly at this.

"You have to get up and face the world. You have to, Caspian."

He released her. "So, if I shave and brush my teeth, you'll lay off me?"

She nodded.

"Fine. Will you wait until I'm ready? I want to show you some songs." He pulled his T-shirt over his head, revealing his brown muscular chest. Then he pulled off his jeans and threw them on the ground, followed by his boxers.

"Caspian!" She averted her eyes. He watched her in amusement and walked into the bathroom and seconds later she heard the shower.

Cliona and Alex were watching *The Wind that Shakes the Barley* when Madison got back home.

"Why are you watching that?" she asked, throwing her phone on the counter.

"Alex needs some history lessons about our home country." She kissed his nose. "Of course, there's Cillian Murphy too."

"Enough said."

"How was the gym?"

"Hard. Boris is a demon." She filled a glass with pomegranate juice.

"Did you see Caspian?" asked Alex.

She nodded. "He was in better form. I made him take a shower and then he showed me his new songs."

"He's obsessed with the tour," said Alex. "I've never seen such enthusiasm."

"It takes his mind off things," concluded Cliona.

"I'm going to bed." Madison waved and walked down the corridor. It was only when she was in the solitude of her bedroom that she cried. Falling onto her bed, she sobbed her heart out.

She wasn't lying when she said she was exhausted. Both physically and emotionally. She had hit a wall and she wasn't sure how much more of it she could cope with.

Three days later, the great gates of Raphael's mansion opened and a Bentley drove in. An elegant woman in a fur coat sat in the back, her haughty face lined with age. Her driver opened the door and helped her out of the car. She looked at the old stone walls of her family home and felt a momentary pang of regret. Her husband had died ten years before and that was when she couldn't bear to live there any longer. Every room, every painting, every step reminded her of him.

So she had signed it over to her son and moved to a smaller house near Paris. However, the smell of the pine and the familiarity made her nostalgic.

She climbed the steps and nodded at Coralie the housekeeper as she walked past. She could hear Isabelle's American accent coming from the conservatory. Her son's choice of bride had been a surprise. He had always had a penchant for models, but she never expected someone so brash. Isabelle was a nice girl but she tended to be loud.

She took off her gloves and walked straight into the garden room.

Raphael started when he saw her. "*Maman!*"

"Hello to you both." She always spoke English when Isabelle was present as she knew the young girl had a dubious grasp of her native tongue.

"Hi, Agathe," said Isabelle, beaming at her. "What brings you out here?"

"We have something to discuss." She handed her coat to Coralie who left the room.

Then she sat on the armchair and crossed her legs elegantly.

"What is this I read about you and this boy?"

"It's nothing." Raphael typed something into his Mac. "I'm going to sue."

"Sue? Why?"

"It's defamatory."

"I'm not sure you will win, *mon petit*. He is undoubtedly yours."

"*Maman?*" He snapped his laptop shut.

"He is a Baptiste. I am sure of it."

Raphael stared at her. "How can you say that?"

"I know it. I looked at photos and clips online. He reminds me of Louis, your grandfather." She smiled. "He was a talented pianist. When that boy closes his eyes and sings, I can see Papi like it was yesterday."

Isabelle stood up and took Raphael's arm. "Are you okay?"

He kept staring at his mother. "How can you be so calm, *Maman?*"

"I always knew you had skeletons in your wardrobe."

"Closet," interjected Isabelle smiling, but Agathe ignored her.

"It was inevitable that something like this would emerge."

"I don't want this," said Raphael bleakly. "I don't need to form a relationship with this boy. Our baby is all I need."

"Has he tried to contact you?"

"No. there's been nothing."

Agathe raised her head. "You will acknowledge this child."

"No."

"If you don't, I will." She stood up. "You have a responsibility, Raphael. His mother is dead. He needs you now."

"But I don't want him."

"Raphael!" Isabelle looked shocked. "How could you?"

"I'm not interested," he repeated obstinately.

Agathe smiled. "You've always been stubborn but I know better. This boy will bring you happiness. Just give it a chance." She stood up. "Now, that is all."

"Will you stay for lunch?" asked Isabelle hurriedly.

"*Non*. I must get back." She walked over to Raphael. "He is a Baptiste, *mon petit*. Bring him into the fold."

♫ ♫ ♫

Raphael stalked out into the garden and into the fields. Isabelle knew better than to follow him.

He walked and walked until he reached a large oak tree by the border of his land. He used to sit in its boughs as a child, swinging from the branches and building forts.

He tried to picture Mary. In truth, he could barely remember her. He could recall the phone call – her friend had done the majority of the talking – but that was all. It was so long ago and so much had happened since.

Would he change things if he had the chance? Not at all. Telling her to terminate the pregnancy was the sensible thing to do. She had agreed and he had believed her.

A cold wind whipped past him as he sat in deep contemplation. His mother was right – he had to meet this boy. Then he would know once and for all the right course of action to take.

Chapter Forty-nine

The crowd of reporters stationed outside Caspian's building started to dwindle. Other stories took precedence and soon there was only a couple of photographers waiting for him to appear. Then there was no one. Only the odd paparazzo, hoping to catch him on the move.

Ten days after the world read about his past, Caspian decided it was time to venture outside. He needed to breathe in some fresh air and feel the sun on his face. Winter in London afforded little sunshine, but on that Thursday morning, the sky was clear, the temperature was close to freezing and the sun's rays illuminated the park near his house.

He pulled a woollen hat down over his ears and buttoned up his duffel coat. A short walk and maybe a coffee from his favourite barista would do the trick. He had moped around long enough.

Life, in its inexhaustible fashion, went on. Despite his heartache and sense of displacement, he was learning to adjust. In those dark moments, when he didn't know night from day, he had realised that he was luckier than most.

He had Prudence and George who adored him. He had an amazing band and great friends. He now had Viola as a link to Mary. He had her memory, locked safely in his heart. She would be forever young in this image. She would never age.

His phone buzzed and looking down at the screen, he saw Maddy's name. He smiled. She was like clockwork. Every day at eleven, she would text to see if he was okay and if he needed anything. Part of him suspected that it might be Cliona at the other end of the phone, instructed by Madison, but he didn't mind. At least she cared.

He texted back saying that he was fine. He didn't mention his planned walk around the park. She wouldn't approve.

Madison. His expression softened. Never in a million years did he think she'd look after him like she did. When he was in the doldrums of pain, she'd been there, rubbing his back and putting up with his moods.

He no longer had any doubt – she was the one and now he had to get her back.

He walked to the door and was just about to unlock it when the intercom buzzed. He looked up at the four screens and saw a man in black jacket with a grey scarf. He had his head bent down low so he couldn't see his face.

The intercom buzzed again. Caspian debated what to do. This man didn't look like a journalist. He pressed the button.

"Yes?"

The man looked up at the camera and Caspian gasped.

"Can I come up?" Raphael stared at him from the screen.

Caspian didn't answer. Instead, he granted access and waited for the knock on the front door.

Three minutes later, it came. Two loud knocks that reverberated through the apartment.

Caspian opened the door and came face to face with Raphael. Their eyes, which were at exactly the same height, met and Caspian pulled off his hat.

"May I come in?" Raphael asked in perfect English.

Caspian nodded.

Raphael walked into the living room area and took off his scarf. Then he removed his coat.

"How were you not followed here?" asked a bemused Caspian. "The press are all over this story."

"One can be discreet if one wants to be." He regarded him haughtily. "We need to talk."

"Oh?"

"This story: the story of Mary and you and the adoption. Is it true?"

Caspian nodded.

"How do you know?"

"Viola."

Raphael recognised the name. Viola was the friend. The girl who rang him that time. The girl Mary shared her Coke with in the nightclub. The girl who told him that he should fly over and sort things out.

"She is sure?"

"Yes." Caspian didn't move.

"What will we do?"

No one spoke for about thirty seconds. The men eyed each other warily, afraid to take the next step.

"Nothing," said Caspian eventually. "We don't need to

do anything. This is clearly an inconvenience for you and I have no interest in forming a relationship."

"*Ah, bon?*"

"George Cole is the only father I'll ever need." He gestured to the door. "So, if you don't mind."

"I do mind. In fact, I mind very much." Raphael glared at him. "I left my pregnant wife to travel here to see you and you tell me to leave?"

"Yes." Caspian glared back. "I'm surprised you're concerned for your wife. I didn't think pregnancy was your thing."

"You're angry."

"Of course. You abandoned Mary."

"I offered to send money. I didn't realise that abortion was so complicated in Ireland."

"Money?"

"What did you think I would do? Marry her? I was at university in Paris. It would've been impossible. We were too young."

"She was all alone. She had to go through everything on her own."

"I regret not offering more, okay? Does that satisfy you? I should've been there."

"What? To make sure she went through with the abortion? No offense, but I'm glad you stayed away."

"Caspian –"

"None of this matters anymore. She's dead. There's no need for you to turn up here looking for some kind of absolution."

"I didn't come for that!"

"So why are you here? To ask for a DNA test? To

ascertain if I'm after your millions? Well, you need not worry. I don't want anything from you. Your new baby can have it all."

"That is not why I came."

"Then why?"

"I came to wish you happiness in life. I came to tell you that my door is open if you want to meet sometime." Raphael looked at him steadily. "I'm as shocked as you are but I'm willing to try and move forward."

"So, you'll come to my concerts and wipe my brow when I'm ill?"

"Don't be ridiculous."

"Then what?"

"Perhaps you could visit us in Amiens sometime. Perhaps we could eat dinner together and talk about our lives. We might find we are similar."

Caspian looked mutinous.

Raphael held out his hand. "I want us to be allies, not enemies. Life is so short – we need to seize the opportunity now."

Caspian trembled. He stared at Raphael's outstretched hand and debated what to do. Did he want to know this man? What would Mary have wanted?

He grasped his hand and shook it formally. "Okay, let's keep the lines of communication open."

"Good." Raphael was relieved.

"I have a big tour coming up so I don't have much free time, but ..."

"I have commitments too. We'll take things as they come."

"Good luck with your baby."

"Thank you. Good luck with your tour." He picked up his jacket. "*À bientôt.*"

Caspian walked him to the door.

"Are you and Madison still together?" he asked suddenly, just as he was on the threshold.

Caspian shook his head. "She dumped me."

"Then get her back." He wrapped his scarf around his neck. "And stay away from my wife." He winked and Caspian reddened.

"I'm terribly sorry about that."

"Evidently we Baptiste men have similar taste." He saluted him and walked down the corridor.

Caspian closed the door and rested his head against it.

Later that night, Madison was in bed when Todd knocked on her door.

"Miss Madison! Are you awake?"

"What is it?" she asked in a panic. "What's wrong?"

"Calm down, ma'am. I just wanted to tell you that Caspian is here."

"What?" She threw away the magazine she was reading.

"Will I send him away, ma'am?"

"No, no. I'll be right out." She grabbed her robe, checked her reflection quickly in the mirror and then followed Todd out into the kitchen.

Caspian was standing by the front door, his hat in his hand.

"What's wrong?" she asked in concern.

"Nothing, I just wanted to see you."

She pulled he robe tightly around her and eyed him suspiciously. "Have you been drinking?"

"No."

"Drugs?"

"No." He laughed. "Maddy!" He moved forwards and grasped her arm. "I love you. I love you so much I can't breathe. I need you."

"Caspian ..."

"Let me sleep with you. Let me hold you."

Todd shifted uncomfortably. "Ma'am?"

Madison stared into Caspian's eyes.

"Please, Maddy. I'm sorry. I'm sorry for everything I did."

"Stop!"

"I didn't realise how much I had to lose. Please forgive me."

She gazed at him. He looked so genuine. Cal's image floated through her head and she felt momentary guilt. Was she any better? She had broken her vows, albeit not as often as him, but she had. They were damaged but not broken. Maybe they could work it out. Maybe.

Her expression softened. "Todd, give us a minute."

"Yes, ma'am." Todd disappeared down the hall.

"We're too similar. We'll always compete with each other."

He wrapped his arms around her waist. "We won't. We can make it work." He kissed her neck and she shivered.

"But we'll be separated all the time. You have tours, I have tours ..."

He nibbled on her ear. "We'll make it work," he said again. Then he kissed her mouth, tilting her head backwards and pressing her body against his. "Stay with me," he whispered hoarsely, coming up for air. "I love you, Maddy."

She closed her eyes and felt herself relax, luxuriating in the closeness.

"I love you," he repeated.

"I love you too," she said softly and, taking his hand, she led him to her bedroom and closed the door.

Chapter Fifty

Two months later ...

"Tiffany's? Really?" Caspian groaned. "This will cost me a fortune."

Madison punched him playfully on the arm. "Only the best for me. Now, come on. John can drop us to the door."

They were in New York for the opening night of Doctor Eckleburg's American Tour. Madison had taken a month's break and had flown out with the band, taking a back seat to her famous boyfriend. The world had rejoiced at their renewed love and their album sales soared. Ross had called, asking them to record a duet like Shawn Mendes and Camila Cabello, and she hadn't ruled it out. She felt intoxicated with love and was beaming at everyone she knew. The past was pushed aside and it was like a new relationship with a new set of rules.

Cliona had been replaced by a brilliant young man called Romeo who was just out of Art School. He was quick and super-efficient, and Madison adored him. Even though she missed her chats with Cliona, she was happy for her friend who was following her dreams. It also helped that Romeo was so good at his job.

Cliona had gone on to assist the director of Doctor Eckleburg's latest music video and was booked on a flight to South America in February to start work on Kevin Ryan's latest project about the Galapagos. She and Alex were blissfully happy and, when they were all in London, they went out as a foursome.

Raphael and Isabelle had welcomed little Anouk Elaine Baptiste three weeks before. They sent photos to Caspian and an invitation to visit.

The Mercedes moved down Fifth Avenue towards Central Park. The pavements were uncharacteristically quiet, the long street stretching down as far as the Plaza and the entrance to the park. John indicated right as they approached Tiffany's and parked close to the iconic building. Todd got out and opened the door. John had arranged a private showing for the famous couple and the staff were on high alert.

"Ma'am, sir," he said, shielding them as they walked in.

The manager greeted them warmly and led them into a back room where rows of jewellery were laid out. The diamond rings sparkled under the lights and Madison squealed in delight. "This is a dream come true! I've always wanted a massive solitaire."

Caspian watched her as she moved from glass case to glass case. Jewellery didn't interest him, but he knew how much this ring meant to Madison. She had been talking about it since he proposed on New Year's Eve. She tried on ring after ring until she found a two-carat princess-cut solitaire. She slipped it onto her finger and screamed.

"*This is it!* I know it. This is the one." She stretched out her hand so as to view it properly and did a little jig of joy.

Caspian took out his card. "Then get it."

"You have to propose again," she insisted. "For luck. Go down on one knee and put it on my finger."

He sighed and did as he was told.

"Madison Ryan, will you marry me?" He looked up at her expectantly.

"*Yes!*" she yelled and the staff clapped. "*Yes, yes, yes!*"

He whirled her around and they kissed each other deeply.

"It's official," she said, beaming. "I mean, I know we've been engaged since New Year, but now it feels real."

Later that evening, they headed south to Greenwich Village. Aurora Sinclair lived there with her photographer boyfriend James. When she heard that Doctor Eckleburg were kicking off their American tour in New York, she had invited them to dinner.

They had met at various parties recently as the première of *Josephine* was fast approaching. Madison found she really liked the young actress and that they had a lot in common. When she ceased to see Aurora as a threat, she found that she was a loyal and interesting friend.

Aurora herself opened the door of her apartment and held open her arms.

"I'm so thrilled you could make it!"

"Thanks for having us."

"James is cooking I'm afraid, so be prepared." She took their coats. "Did I hear correctly that there are wedding bells on the horizon?"

Madison held up her left hand.

"Oh my goodness!' Aurora gasped. "That's gorgeous!"

"I know!" said Madison gleefully.

James popped his head out from the kitchen. "Don't mind me. I'm grappling with a pot of rice. I don't want it to end up as mush."

Aurora ushered them into the living room. "I'm so glad you had time to come over. We love seeing people from home."

"You've a lovely apartment," said Madison, noticing the huge photo prints framed on the wall. "Did James take those pictures?"

"Yes," said Aurora proudly. "He's very talented. Now, can I get you a drink?"

"Wine is fine."

"Coming up." Aurora busied herself with preparing drinks.

Caspian and Madison sat on the couch. Soft music played in the background and the lights of the city sparkled through the big window by the fireplace.

"We should move to the table and sample James' attempt at Thai cuisine," said Aurora when she returned.

James put a large pot of curry on the table. "This is the best yet, Borealis," he said, using his pet name for Aurora. "I think those lime leaves made all the difference."

"He had me traipsing around New York looking for Nam Pla and fancy lime leaves this morning."

"Taste it and you'll see it was worth it."

They all sat down. James piled rice on plates and handed them around.

"So, the first concert is tomorrow evening," said James. "I'm looking forward to it."

"I'll sort out backstage passes for you," said Caspian. "You'll be on the list."

"It'll be wonderful," said Aurora. "I simply adore your new work."

When James was washing up, Aurora refilled the wine glasses.

"Have you seen Raphael lately?" she asked Caspian directly. "I hope you don't mind my asking."

Caspian shrugged. "No, it's fine. We met at Christmas."

"Oh?"

"Maddy and I flew to France for two days."

"Did you have a good time?" Aurora's dark eyes were filled with compassion.

Caspian shrugged again. "It was okay. Isabelle was really nice. Her parents were over from America so that made it easier, you know, when there's a crowd."

"And Raphael?"

"He found it awkward, as did I." Caspian sat up straight. "Too much time has passed for us to be close. I can't see us ringing each other up every day for a chat."

Aurora nodded but said nothing.

"I mean, he made a big effort and his mother came for lunch. I played piano for her and she loved it." He looked up. "I'll go to Paris to see the baby after the tour. I promised that I would."

"I presume he's not here for your concert," said Aurora practically.

Caspian shook his head. "Not with the baby."

Madison held up her phone. "Just look at her! She's so small and cute. I can't wait to meet her."

Aurora put her hand on her heart. "She's like a little doll. So like Raphael."

Caspian squeezed Madison's hand. "Maddy and I made a deal. We'd both make an effort with our fathers and make peace with the past."

Madison rolled her eyes. "I tried my best, but Dad and I were arguing within an hour. Still, he bonded with you." She kissed Caspian's cheek. "I think he's always wanted a son."

"I'm so glad you worked things out," said Aurora. "Raphael is difficult, but so wonderful."

"It's early days," said Caspian guardedly.

"I know, but it's so important to make the effort. You know, I was adopted too. When I first met my father – my real father – it felt so strange. I wasn't sure where to begin. A whole lifetime had passed and I felt that we would never catch up." Her beautiful eyes looked sad. "I felt like a changeling: like I didn't belong. That I had been lied to all my life."

Caspian nodded. "I get that."

"I never knew my mother either. I was so angry."

Caspian nodded.

"But then I realised that I was so lucky. I had been given a second chance." She smiled and raised her glass. "To new beginnings!"

Caspian kissed Madison. "To new beginnings!"

Backstage at Madison Square Garden was buzzing the next day. Make-up artists, celebrities, musicians, bodyguards, roadies and family were wandering around, chatting and laughing.

Caspian sat in his dressing room, warming up his voice.

Tommy was tweeting about the concert and Bethany was waiting to upload a picture of the engagement ring to Instagram. She wanted to time it for an hour before the band played so as to maximise the PR opportunity.

Madison and Cliona sat in the VIP lounge with Viola, whom Caspian had flown in for the concert. Her husband had been invited too, but Viola had come alone. Caspian didn't explain why but he said it was imperative she be there. She was his link to Mary; she was the one who knew her best. He organised a room at The Four Seasons for her and made sure she had the best of everything. Viola, who had never experienced luxury like it, rang home constantly, bragging about her giant marble bathroom and the lobster she had ordered on room service.

"Don't lose the run of yourself, Mam," said a disgruntled Pauline who was green with envy.

Alex, Ethan and Fionn were all drinking bottles of beer and discussing the set list. Jeff and Nancy were there along with the twins. They had flown to Dublin for New Year's Eve for the annual party at Sorrento Terrace. Constance had purchased two more futons to accommodate them all and both families had hit it off immediately.

Constance and Aonghus had also flown over for the gig and had spent two days visiting museums and landmarks. Constance was particularly impressed with the bus tour they had taken earlier that day.

"The 9/11 memorial is so moving," said Constance, with her hand on her chest. "So serene and peaceful with all that water flowing down."

"We passed Herman Melville's house," added Aonghus. "I never knew that baldy little singer was his relative.

That's why he called himself Moby."

The support act, a young grunge band from Ohio, finished their set to rapturous applause. There was a brief interlude where Bethany uploaded the picture of the ring.

"This will break the internet," she said in satisfaction. "I bet it will beat Jennifer Aniston's *Friends* reunion selfie."

Madison smiled. "We should take a bet on how many 'likes' we'll get."

Cliona shoved her gently. "You're so vain, Mads."

Viola hugged Caspian. "Best of luck," she said warmly. "I haven't been to a concert in twenty years. The last gig I saw was David Gray in Connolly's of Leap. Thank you for bringing me here."

He kissed her cheek. "I'm delighted that you're here."

Then it was Doctor Eckleburg's turn to play. Caspian jumped up and stretched his arms. He walked over to Madison, kissed her thoroughly and then walked out onto the stage. The crowd roared. Then the four members of Doctor Eckleburg were standing on the big stage, staring out at the crowd. The laser lights beamed up and created a kaleidoscopic effect on the ceiling. The air smelt of beer, smoke and sweat.

Fionn took at a seat at the drum kit and flexed his arms. Ethan tuned his guitar slightly and Alex did the same. Caspian sat at the piano and played some scales. When he was ready, he pressed his lips against the microphone and said, "*Hello, New York!*"

They screamed and stamped their feet in response.

"Here's 'Charisma'!" He played the intro, closed his eyes and started to sing.

After almost two hours of a performance, Caspian took the microphone and tried to quieten the crowd.

"This will be our last song of the night," he said to shouts of protest. "It's a song about someone who lost their life too young. Someone who never got a chance."

More screams.

Caspian looked out to the wings of the stage. There he could see Viola and Madison, standing side by side.

"This is 'Willie MacBride'."

He picked up a guitar and hoisted it over his shoulder. Checking the strings, he nodded at Ethan. They had practised it over and over until it was just right. The rest of the band knew what it meant to him and all stood up straight in a show of respect.

Caspian began to pluck the melody of the well-known song and started to sing. A huge screen at the back of the stage showed his face. His voice broke slightly when he sang the line about Willie being only nineteen, but regained his composure immediately. In his mind he pictured Mary performing on that video tape, her blonde hair swinging from side to side. Every word he sang felt like hers. He projected his voice out onto the audience as though he were reaching up to heaven.

When it came to the chorus, Fionn began to play, rapping the military drums in ceremonious style, his head held high in reverence. Ethan harmonised with his guitar and Alex joined in with his bass guitar.

The crowd swayed and some sang along, hundreds of people moving in unison.

At the beginning of the second verse, a spotlight shone on stage left and a violinist appeared. Lifting the bow, she began to play in harmony with the band. Her slender arm moved up and down, as she drew across the strings. The mellow timbre of her sound brought even more pathos to the song, giving it depth and emotion. Her face filled the screen as she played and the crowd clapped in response.

In the wings of the stage, Viola was openly crying. The song was synonymous with Mary. It brought her back to her childhood and to a time when there had been so much hope and potential. To the time before her best friend was cruelly snatched from her, never to return. Now her lost son was paying homage to her memory. She felt her heart brim with emotion and the tears coursed down her cheeks.

The crowd, unused to this style of music from Doctor Eckleburg, lit lighters and swayed to the song. Hundreds of cameras flashed and thousands of photos and videos were uploaded onto the internet. What followed was a huge surge in downloads for the song, as Doctor Eckleburg's fans added it to their collection.

When the song ended, there was silence. Caspian bowed his head and inhaled deeply. He could hear the rhythmic beating of his heart as he waited for the crowd to respond. That few seconds of peace before the screams and roars gave him chance to compose himself. In those few moments, he silently told Mary that he loved her and she would live forever within him. Then he held out his hand and called for Madison to join him on stage. She squared her shoulders, flicked back her blonde hair and walked out to meet him.

There was thunderous applause and shrieks. There was a tsunami of camera flashes and shouts of joy.

"I just want the world to know that I love this woman."

Thousands of voices roared in response.

Caspian bent his head and kissed Madison. The big screen was filled with their heads and the crowd went wild. He kissed her nose and her eyelids and then her lips once more. Then he turned back to the audience.

"*The Beatles once said that all you need is love!*" he shouted into the microphone. "*They were right. I love you, New York!*"

The lights dimmed and the stage went black.

Bethany was waiting for them offstage. "Four million 'likes' in two hours. Not bad," she said, holding up her iPhone in satisfaction.

Madison laughed. "All you need is likes," she quipped as she took Caspian's hand, and they walked to the VIP lounge where the champagne was already flowing.

THE END

Also by Poolbeg.com

Echoes of Grace

CARAGH BELL

Even in death, love survives

Grace Molloy was the darling of the theatre scene. Young and dazzling, she gave it all up to marry the playwright Henry Sinclair, thirty years her senior. Then, one stormy night, she died giving birth to her daughter, Aurora.

Left with no memory of her mother, Aurora is raised by Henry and her nanny, Maggie, in a huge old house on the Cornish coastline. All the little girl has of Grace is a portrait – a painting of a woman in a white dress, her beautiful face frozen in time.

Aurora grows up, resembling Grace in looks and talent. She pursues her dream of being on the stage and soon achieves great success in the world of theatre, like her mother before her. Then a secret unfolds – a secret that could threaten all that she holds dear . . .

Echoes of Grace is the story of a young woman who, having overcome a painful past, must now embrace it to find her real self.

ISBN 978-178199-804-5

Also by Poolbeg.com

Gabrielle

CARAGH BELL

'All she needed was one person to take notice – one person who could catapult her into the big time'

Gabriella Álvarez dreams of being the next Coco Chanel. Born in the Bronx of Puerto Rican descent, she lives with her mother and beloved grandmother, Lita, who recognises the young girl's talent and teaches her to sew.

When Gabriella gains a coveted scholarship to the famous Parson's School of Design on Fifth Avenue, she is thrilled. There she meets the beautiful, aspiring model Isabelle Flynn and together they vow to make it to the top.

Then superstar fashion designer Oberon crosses her path and she sees her chance. If only he'd notice her. If only he wasn't so out of reach . . .

This is a story of a young girl's determination to achieve the American Dream. Life throws obstacles in her path, but she never gives up, intent on achieving her heart's desire.

This is Caragh Bell's fifth novel, following on from the bestselling *Echoes of Grace*.

ISBN 978-178199-762-8

If you enjoyed this book
why not visit our website

poolbeg.com

and get another book delivered straight
to your home or a friend's home.

All books are despatched within [illegible] hours

Free postage in the UK & Ireland only

Why not join our mailing list at
www.poolbeg.com and get some
fantastic offers, competitions, author interviews,
new releases and much more?